ANNA

KARENINA

by Leo Tolstoy

Translated by Constance Garnett

pac ps
Pacific Publishing Studio

Published in the United States by Madison Park, an imprint of Pacific Publishing Studio.

www.PacPS.com

ISBN-13: 978-1461195191

ISBN-10: 1461195195

CHAPTER ONE

HAPPY FAMILIES ARE all alike; every unhappy family is unhappy in its own way.

Everything was in confusion in the Oblonskys' house. The wife had discovered that the husband was carrying on an intrigue with a French girl, who had been a governess in their family, and she had announced to her husband that she could not go on living in the same house with him. This position of affairs had now lasted three days, and not only the husband and wife themselves, but all the members of their family and household, were painfully conscious of it. Every person in the house felt that there was no sense in their living together, and that the stray people brought together by chance in any inn had more in common with one another than they, the members of the family and household of the Oblonskys. The wife did not leave her own room, the husband had not been at home for three days. The children ran wild all over the house; the English governess quarreled with the housekeeper, and wrote to a friend asking her to look out for a new situation for her; the man-cook had walked off the day before just at dinner time; the kitchen-maid, and the coachman had given warning.

Three days after the quarrel, Prince Stepan Arkadyevitch Oblonsky—Stiva, as he was called in the fashionable world— woke up at his usual hour, that is, at eight o'clock in the morning, not in his wife's bedroom, but on the leather-covered sofa in his study. He turned over his stout, well-cared-for person on the springy sofa, as though he would sink into a long sleep again; he vigorously embraced the pillow on the other side and buried his face in it; but all at once he jumped up, sat up on the sofa, and opened his eyes.

"Yes, yes, how was it now?" he thought, going over his dream. "Now, how was it? To be sure! Alabin was giving a dinner at Darmstadt; no, not Darmstadt, but something American. Yes, but then, Darmstadt was in America. Yes, Alabin was giving a dinner on glass tables, and the tables sang, *Il mio tesoro*—not *Il mio tesoro* though, but something better, and there were some sort of little decanters on the table, and they were women, too," he remembered.

Stepan Arkadyevitch's eyes twinkled gaily, and he pondered with a smile. "Yes, it was nice, very nice. There was a great deal more that was delightful, only there's no putting it into words, or even expressing it in one's thoughts awake." And noticing a gleam of light peeping in beside one of the serge curtains, he cheerfully dropped his feet over the edge of the sofa, and felt about with them for his slippers, a present on his last birthday, worked for him by his wife on gold-colored morocco. And, as he had done every day for the last nine years, he stretched out his hand, without getting up, towards the place where his dressing-gown always hung in his bedroom. And thereupon he suddenly remembered that he was not sleeping in his wife's room, but in his study, and why: the smile vanished from his face, he knitted his brows.

"Ah, ah, ah! Oo!..." he muttered, recalling everything that had happened. And again every detail of his quarrel with his wife was present to his imagination, all the hopelessness of his position, and worst of all, his own fault.

"Yes, she won't forgive me, and she can't forgive me. And the most awful thing about it is that it's all my fault—all my fault, though I'm not to blame. That's the point of the whole situation," he reflected. "Oh, oh, oh!" he kept repeating in despair, as he remembered the acutely painful sensations caused him by this quarrel.

Most unpleasant of all was the first minute when, on coming, happy and good-humored, from the theater, with a huge pear in his hand for his wife, he had not found his wife in the drawing-room, to his surprise had not found her in the study either, and saw her at last in her bedroom with the unlucky letter that revealed everything in her hand.

She, his Dolly, forever fussing and worrying over household details, and limited in her ideas, as he considered, was sitting perfectly still with the letter in her hand, looking at him with an expression of horror, despair, and indignation.

"What's this? this?" she asked, pointing to the letter.

And at this recollection, Stepan Arkadyevitch, as is so often the case, was not so much annoyed at the fact itself as at the way in which he had met his wife's words.

There happened to him at that instant what does happen to people when they are unexpectedly caught in something very disgraceful. He did not succeed in adapting his face to the position in which he was placed towards his wife by the discovery of his fault. Instead of being hurt, denying, defending himself, begging forgiveness, instead of remaining indifferent even—anything would have been better than what he did do—his face utterly involuntarily (reflex spinal action, reflected Stepan Arkadyevitch, who was fond of physiology)—utterly involuntarily assumed its habitual, good-humored, and therefore idiotic smile.

This idiotic smile he could not forgive himself. Catching sight of that smile, Dolly shuddered as though at physical pain, broke out with her characteristic heat into a flood of cruel words, and rushed out of the room. Since then she had refused to see her husband.

"It's that idiotic smile that's to blame for it all," thought Stepan Arkadyevitch.

"But what's to be done? What's to be done?" he said to himself in despair, and found no answer.

Stepan Arkadyevitch was a truthful man in his relations with himself. He was incapable of deceiving himself and persuading himself that he repented of his conduct. He could not at this date repent of the fact that he, a handsome, susceptible man of thirty-four, was not in love with his wife, the mother of five living and two dead children, and only a year younger than himself. All he repented of was that he had not succeeded better in hiding it from his wife. But he felt all the difficulty of his position and was sorry for his wife, his children, and himself. Possibly he might have managed to conceal his sins better from his wife if he had anticipated that the knowledge of them would have had such an effect on her. He had never clearly thought out the subject, but he had vaguely conceived that his wife must long ago have suspected him of being unfaithful to her, and shut her eyes to the fact. He had even supposed that she, a worn-out woman no longer young or good-looking, and in no way remarkable or interesting, merely a good mother, ought from a sense of fairness to take an indulgent view. It had turned out quite the other way.

"Oh, it's awful! oh dear, oh dear! awful!" Stepan Arkadyevitch kept repeating to himself, and he could think of nothing to be done. "And how well things were going up till now! how well we got on! She was contented and happy in her children; I never interfered with her in anything; I let her manage the children and the house just as she liked. It's true it's bad *her* having been a governess in our house. That's bad! There's something common, vulgar, in flirting with one's governess. But what a governess!" (He vividly recalled the roguish black eyes of Mlle. Roland and her smile.) "But after all, while she was in the house, I kept myself in hand. And the worst of it all is that she's already...it seems as if ill-luck would have it so! Oh, oh! But what, what is to be done?"

There was no solution, but that universal solution which life gives to all questions, even the most complex and insoluble. That answer is: one must live in the needs of the day—that is, forget oneself. To forget himself in sleep was impossible now, at least till nighttime; he could not go back now to the music sung by the decanter-women; so he must forget himself in the dream of daily life.

"Then we shall see," Stepan Arkadyevitch said to himself, and getting up he put on a gray dressing-gown lined with blue silk, tied the tassels in a knot, and, drawing a deep breath of air into his broad, bare chest, he walked to the window with his usual confident step, turning out his feet that carried his full frame so easily. He pulled up the blind and rang the bell loudly. It was at once answered by the appearance of an old friend, his valet, Matvey, carrying his clothes, his boots, and a telegram. Matvey was followed by the barber with all the necessaries for shaving.

"Are there any papers from the office?" asked Stepan Arkadyevitch, taking the telegram and seating himself at the looking-glass.

"On the table," replied Matvey, glancing with inquiring sympathy at his master; and, after a short pause, he added with a sly smile, "They've sent from the carriage-jobbers."

Stepan Arkadyevitch made no reply, he merely glanced at Matvey in the looking-glass. In the glance, in which their eyes met in the looking-glass, it was clear that they understood one another. Stepan Arkadyevitch's eyes asked: "Why do you tell me that? don't you know?"

Matvey put his hands in his jacket pockets, thrust out one leg, and gazed silently, good-humoredly, with a faint smile, at his master.

"I told them to come on Sunday, and till then not to trouble you or themselves for nothing," he said. He had obviously prepared the sentence beforehand.

Stepan Arkadyevitch saw Matvey wanted to make a joke and attract attention to himself. Tearing open the telegram, he read it through, guessing at the words, misspelt as they always are in telegrams, and his face brightened.

"Matvey, my sister Anna Arkadyevna will be here tomorrow," he said, checking for a minute the sleek, plump hand of the barber, cutting a pink path through his long, curly whiskers.

"Thank God!" said Matvey, showing by this response that he, like his master, realized the significance of this arrival—that is, that Anna Arkadyevna, the sister he was so fond of, might bring about a reconciliation between husband and wife.

"Alone, or with her husband?" inquired Matvey.

Stepan Arkadyevitch could not answer, as the barber was at work on his upper lip, and he raised one finger. Matvey nodded at the looking-glass.

"Alone. Is the room to be got ready upstairs?"

"Inform Darya Alexandrovna: where she orders."

"Darya Alexandrovna?" Matvey repeated, as though in doubt.

"Yes, inform her. Here, take the telegram; give it to her, and then do what she tells you."

"You want to try it on," Matvey understood, but he only said, "Yes sir."

Stepan Arkadyevitch was already washed and combed and ready to be dressed, when Matvey, stepping deliberately in his creaky boots, came back into the room with the telegram in his hand. The barber had gone.

"Darya Alexandrovna told me to inform you that she is going away. Let him do—that is you—do as he likes," he said, laughing only with his eyes, and putting his hands in his pockets, he watched his master with his head on one side. Stepan Arkadyevitch was silent a minute. Then a good-humored and rather pitiful smile showed itself on his handsome face.

"Eh, Matvey?" he said, shaking his head.

"It's all right, sir; she will come round," said Matvey.

"Come round?"

"Yes, sir."

"Do you think so? Who's there?" asked Stepan Arkadyevitch, hearing the rustle of a woman's dress at the door.

"It's I," said a firm, pleasant, woman's voice, and the stern, pockmarked face of Matrona Philimonovna, the nurse, was thrust in at the doorway.

"Well, what is it, Matrona?" queried Stepan Arkadyevitch, going up to her at the door.

Although Stepan Arkadyevitch was completely in the wrong as regards his wife, and was conscious of this himself, almost every one in the house (even the nurse, Darya Alexandrovna's chief ally) was on his side.

"Well, what now?" he asked disconsolately.

"Go to her, sir; own your fault again. Maybe God will aid you. She is suffering so, it's sad to hee her; and besides, everything in the house is topsy-turvy. You must have pity, sir, on the children. Beg her forgiveness, sir. There's no help for it! One must take the consequences..."

"But she won't see me."

"You do your part. God is merciful; pray to God, sir, pray to God."

"Come, that'll do, you can go," said Stepan Arkadyevitch, blushing suddenly. "Well now, do dress me." He turned to Matvey and threw off his dressing-gown decisively.

Matvey was already holding up the shirt like a horse's collar, and, blowing off some invisible speck, he slipped it with obvious pleasure over the well-groomed body of his master.

When he was dressed, Stepan Arkadyevitch sprinkled some scent on himself, pulled down his shirt-cuffs, distributed into his pockets his cigarettes, pocketbook, matches, and watch with its double chain and seals, and shaking out his handkerchief, feeling himself clean, fragrant, healthy, and physically at ease, in spite of his unhappiness, he walked with a slight swing on each leg into the dining-room, where coffee was already waiting for him, and beside the coffee, letters and papers from the office.

He read the letters. One was very unpleasant, from a merchant who was buying a forest on his wife's property. To sell this forest was absolutely essential; but at present, until he was reconciled with his wife, the subject could not be discussed. The most unpleasant thing of all was that his pecuniary interests should in this way enter into the question of his reconciliation with his wife. And the idea that he might be led on by his interests, that he might seek a reconciliation with his wife on account of the sale of the forest—that idea hurt him.

When he had finished his letters, Stepan Arkadyevitch moved the office-papers close to him, rapidly looked through two pieces of business, made a few notes with a big pencil, and pushing away the papers, turned to his coffee. As he sipped his coffee, he opened a still damp morning paper, and began reading it.

Stepan Arkadyevitch took in and read a liberal paper, not an extreme one, but one advocating the views held by the majority. And in spite of the fact that science, art, and politics had no special interest for him, he firmly held those views on all these subjects which were held by the majority and by his paper, and he only changed them when the majority changed them—or, more strictly speaking, he did not change them, but they imperceptibly changed of themselves within him.

Stepan Arkadyevitch had not chosen his political opinions or his views; these political opinions and views had come to him of themselves, just as he did not choose the shapes of his hat and coat, but simply took those that were being worn. And for him, living in a certain society—owing to the need, ordinarily developed at years of discretion, for some degree of mental activity—to have views was just as indispensable as to have a hat. If there was a reason for his preferring liberal to conservative views, which were held also by many of his circle, it arose not from his considering liberalism more rational, but from its being in closer accordance with his manner of life. The liberal party said that in Russia everything is wrong, and certainly Stepan Arkadyevitch had many debts and was decidedly short of money. The liberal party said that marriage is an institution quite out of date, and that it needs reconstruction; and family life certainly afforded Stepan Arkadyevitch little gratification, and forced him into lying and hypocrisy, which was so repulsive to his nature. The liberal party said, or rather allowed it to be understood, that religion is only a curb to keep in check the barbarous classes of the people; and Stepan Arkadyevitch could not get through even a short service without his legs aching from standing up, and could never make out what was the object of all the terrible and high-flown language about another world when life might be so very amusing in this world. And with all this, Stepan Arkadyevitch, who liked a joke, was fond of puzzling a plain man by saying that if he prided himself on his origin, he ought not to stop at Rurik and disown the first founder of his family—the monkey. And so Liberalism had become a habit of Stepan Arkadyevitch's, and he liked his newspaper, as he did his cigar after dinner, for the slight fog it diffused in his brain. He read the leading article, in which it was maintained that it was quite senseless in our day to raise an outcry that radicalism was threatening to swallow up all conservative elements, and that the government ought to take measures to crush the revolutionary hydra; that, on the contrary, "in our opinion the danger lies not in that fantastic revolutionary hydra, but in the obstinacy of traditionalism clogging progress," etc., etc. He read another article, too, a financial one, which alluded to Bentham and Mill, and dropped some innuendoes reflecting on the ministry. With his characteristic quickwittedness he caught the drift of each innuendo, divined whence it came, at whom and on what ground it was aimed, and that afforded him, as it always did, a certain satisfaction. But today that satisfaction was embittered by Matrona Philimonovna's advice and the unsatisfactory state of the household. He read, too, that Count Beist was rumored to have left for Wiesbaden, and that one need have no more gray hair, and of the sale of a light carriage, and of a young person seeking a situation; but these items of information did not give him, as usual, a quiet, ironical gratification. Having finished the paper, a second cup of coffee and a roll and butter, he got up, shaking the crumbs of the roll off his waistcoat; and, squaring his broad chest, he smiled joyously: not because there was anything particularly agreeable in his mind—the joyous smile was evoked by a good digestion.

But this joyous smile at once recalled everything to him, and he grew thoughtful.

Two childish voices (Stepan Arkadyevitch recognized the voices of Grisha, his youngest boy, and Tanya, his eldest girl) were heard outside the door. They were carrying something, and dropped it.

"I told you not to sit passengers on the roof," said the little girl in English; "there, pick them up!"

"Everything's in confusion," thought Stepan Arkadyevitch; "there are the children running about by themselves." And going to the door, he called them. They threw down the box, that represented a train, and came in to their father.

The little girl, her father's favorite, ran up boldly, embraced him, and hung laughingly on his neck, enjoying as she always did the smell of scent that came from his whiskers. At last the little girl kissed his face, which was flushed from his stooping posture and beaming with tenderness, loosed her hands, and was about to run away again; but her father held her back.

"How is mamma?" he asked, passing his hand over his daughter's smooth, soft little neck. "Good morning," he said, smiling to the boy, who had come up to greet him. He was conscious that he loved the boy less, and always tried to be fair; but the boy felt it, and did not respond with a smile to his father's chilly smile.

"Mamma? She is up," answered the girl.

Stepan Arkadyevitch sighed. "That means that she's not slept again all night," he thought. "Well, is she cheerful?"

The little girl knew that there was a quarrel between her father and mother, and that her mother could not be cheerful, and that her father must be aware of this, and that he was pretending when he asked about it so lightly. And she blushed for her father. He at once perceived it, and blushed too.

"I don't know," she said. "She did not say we must do our lessons, but she said we were to go for a walk with Miss Hoole to grandmamma's."

"Well, go, Tanya, my darling. Oh, wait a minute, though," he said, still holding her and stroking her soft little hand.

He took off the mantelpiece, where he had put it yesterday, a little box of sweets, and gave her two, picking out her favorites, a chocolate and a fondant.

"For Grisha?" said the little girl, pointing to the chocolate.

"Yes, yes." And still stroking her little shoulder, he kissed her on the roots of her hair and neck, and let her go.

"The carriage is ready," said Matvey; "but there's some one to see you with a petition."

"Been here long?" asked Stepan Arkadyevitch.

"Half an hour."

"How many times have I told you to tell me at once?"

"One must let you drink your coffee in peace, at least," said Matvey, in the affectionately gruff tone with which it was impossible to be angry.

"Well, show the person up at once," said Oblonsky, frowning with vexation.

The petitioner, the widow of a staff captain Kalinin, came with a request impossible and unreasonable; but Stepan Arkadyevitch, as he generally did, made her sit down, heard her to the end attentively without interrupting her, and gave her detailed advice as to how and to whom to apply, and even wrote her, in his large, sprawling, good and legible hand, a confident and fluent little note to a personage who might be of use to her. Having got rid of the staff captain's widow, Stepan Arkadyevitch took his hat and stopped to recollect whether he had forgotten anything. It appeared that he had forgotten nothing except what he wanted to forget—his wife.

"Ah, yes!" He bowed his head, and his handsome face assumed a harassed expression. "To go, or not to go!" he said to himself; and an inner voice told him he must not go, that nothing could come of it but falsity; that to amend, to set right their relations was impossible, because it was impossible to make her attractive again and able to inspire love, or to make him an old man, not susceptible to love. Except deceit and lying nothing could come of it now; and deceit and lying were opposed to his nature.

"It must be some time, though: it can't go on like this," he said, trying to give himself courage. He squared his chest, took out a cigarette, took two whiffs at it, flung it into a mother-of-pearl ashtray, and with rapid steps walked through the drawing room, and opened the other door into his wife's bedroom.

Darya Alexandrovna, in a dressing jacket, and with her now scanty, once luxuriant and beautiful hair fastened up with hairpins on the nape of her neck, with a sunken, thin face and large, startled eyes, which looked prominent from the thinness of her face, was standing among a litter of all sorts of things scattered all over the room, before an open bureau, from which she was taking something. Hearing her husband's steps, she stopped, looking towards the door, and trying assiduously to give her features a severe and contemptuous expression. She felt she was afraid of him, and afraid of the coming interview. She was just attempting to do what she had attempted to do ten times already in these last three days—to sort out the children's things and her own, so as to take them to her mother's—and again she could not bring herself to do this; but now again, as each time before, she kept saying to herself, "that things cannot go on like this, that she must take some step" to punish him, put him to shame, avenge on him some little part at least of the suffering he had caused her. She still continued to tell herself that she should leave him, but she was conscious that this was impossible; it was impossible because she could not get out of the habit of regarding him as her husband and loving him. Besides this, she realized that if even here in her own house she could hardly manage to look after her five children properly, they would be still worse off where she was going with them all. As it was, even in the course of these three days, the youngest was unwell from being given unwholesome soup, and the others had almost gone without their dinner the day before. She was conscious that it was impossible to go away; but, cheating herself, she went on all the same sorting out her things and pretending she was going.

Seeing her husband, she dropped her hands into the drawer of the bureau as though looking for something, and only looked round at him when he had come quite up to her. But her face, to which she tried to give a severe and resolute expression, betrayed bewilderment and suffering.

"Dolly!" he said in a subdued and timid voice. He bent his head towards his shoulder and tried to look pitiful and humble, but for all that he was radiant with freshness and health. In a rapid glance she scanned his figure that beamed with health and freshness. "Yes, he is happy and content!" she thought; "while I.... And that disgusting good nature, which every one likes him for and praises—I hate that good nature of his," she thought. Her mouth stiffened, the muscles of the cheek contracted on the right side of her pale, nervous face.

"What do you want?" she said in a rapid, deep, unnatural voice.

"Dolly!" he repeated, with a quiver in his voice. "Anna is coming today."

"Well, what is that to me? I can't see her!" she cried.

"But you must, really, Dolly..."

"Go away, go away, go away!" she shrieked, not looking at him, as though this shriek were called up by physical pain.

Stepan Arkadyevitch could be calm when he thought of his wife, he could hope that she would *come round*, as Matvey expressed it, and could quietly go on reading his paper and drinking his coffee; but when he saw her tortured, suffering face, heard the tone of her voice, submissive to fate and full of despair, there was a catch in his breath and a lump in his throat, and his eyes began to shine with tears.

"My God! what have I done? Dolly! For God's sake!.... You know...." He could not go on; there was a sob in his throat.

She shut the bureau with a slam, and glanced at him.

"Dolly, what can I say?.... One thing: forgive...Remember, cannot nine years of my life atone for an instant...."

She dropped her eyes and listened, expecting what he would say, as it were beseeching him in some way or other to make her believe differently.

"—instant of passion?" he said, and would have gone on, but at that word, as at a pang of physical pain, her lips stiffened again, and again the muscles of her right cheek worked.

"Go away, go out of the room!" she shrieked still more shrilly, "and don't talk to me of your passion and your loathsomeness."

She tried to go out, but tottered, and clung to the back of a chair to support herself. His face relaxed, his lips swelled, his eyes were swimming with tears.

"Dolly!" he said, sobbing now; "for mercy's sake, think of the children; they are not to blame! I am to blame, and punish me, make me expiate my fault. Anything I can do, I am ready to do anything! I am to blame, no words can express how much I am to blame! But, Dolly, forgive me!"

She sat down. He listened to her hard, heavy breathing, and he was unutterably sorry for her. She tried several times to begin to speak, but could not. He waited.

"You remember the children, Stiva, to play with them; but I remember them, and know that this means their ruin," she said—obviously one of the phrases she had more than once repeated to herself in the course of the last few days.

She had called him "Stiva," and he glanced at her with gratitude, and moved to take her hand, but she drew back from him with aversion.

"I think of the children, and for that reason I would do anything in the world to save them, but I don't myself know how to save them. By taking them away from their father, or by leaving them with a vicious father—yes, a vicious father.... Tell me, after what...has happened, can we live together? Is that possible? Tell me, eh, is it possible?" she repeated, raising her voice, "after my husband, the father of my children, enters into a love affair with his own children's governess?"

"But what could I do? what could I do?" he kept saying in a pitiful voice, not knowing what he was saying, as his head sank lower and lower.

"You are loathsome to me, repulsive!" she shrieked, getting more and more heated. "Your tears mean nothing! You have never loved me; you have neither heart nor honorable feeling! You are hateful to me, disgusting, a stranger—yes, a complete stranger!" With pain and wrath she uttered the word so terrible to herself—*stranger*.

He looked at her, and the fury expressed in her face alarmed and amazed him. He did not understand how his pity for her exasperated her. She saw in him sympathy for her, but not love. "No, she hates me. She will not forgive me," he thought.

"It is awful! awful!" he said.

At that moment in the next room a child began to cry; probably it had fallen down. Darya Alexandrovna listened, and her face suddenly softened.

She seemed to be pulling herself together for a few seconds, as though she did not know where she was, and what she was doing, and getting up rapidly, she moved towards the door.

"Well, she loves my child," he thought, noticing the change of her face at the child's cry, "my child: how can she hate me?"

"Dolly, one word more," he said, following her.

"If you come near me, I will call in the servants, the children! They may all know you are a scoundrel! I am going away at once, and you may live here with your mistress!"

And she went out, slamming the door.

Stepan Arkadyevitch sighed, wiped his face, and with a subdued tread walked out of the room. "Matvey says she will come round; but how? I don't see the least chance of it. Ah, oh, how horrible it is! And how vulgarly she shouted," he said to himself, remembering her shriek and the words—"scoundrel" and "mistress." "And very likely the maids were listening! Horribly vulgar! horrible!" Stepan Arkadyevitch stood a few seconds alone, wiped his face, squared his chest, and walked out of the room.

It was Friday, and in the dining room the German watchmaker was winding up the clock. Stepan Arkadyevitch remembered his joke about this punctual, bald watchmaker, "that the German was wound up for a whole lifetime himself, to wind up watches," and he smiled. Stepan Arkadyevitch was fond of a joke: "And maybe she will come round! That's a good expression, '*come round*,'" he thought. "I must repeat that."

"Matvey!" he shouted. "Arrange everything with Darya in the sitting room for Anna Arkadyevna," he said to Matvey when he came in.

"Yes, sir."

Stepan Arkadyevitch put on his fur coat and went out onto the steps.

"You won't dine at home?" said Matvey, seeing him off.

"That's as it happens. But here's for the housekeeping," he said, taking ten roubles from his pocketbook. "That'll be enough."

"Enough or not enough, we must make it do," said Matvey, slamming the carriage door and stepping back onto the steps.

Darya Alexandrovna meanwhile having pacified the child, and knowing from the sound of the carriage that he had gone off, went back again to her bedroom. It was her solitary refuge from the household cares which crowded upon her directly she went out from it. Even now, in the short time she had been in the nursery, the English governess and Matrona Philimonovna had succeeded in putting several questions to her, which did not admit of delay, and which only she could answer: "What were the children to put on for their walk? Should they have any milk? Should not a new cook be sent for?"

"Ah, let me alone, let me alone!" she said, and going back to her bedroom she sat down in the same place as she had sat when talking to her husband, clasping tightly her thin hands with the rings that slipped down on her bony fingers, and fell to going over in her memory all the conversation. "He has gone! But has he broken it off with her?" she thought. "Can it be he sees her? Why didn't I ask him! No, no, reconciliation is impossible. Even if we remain in the same house, we are strangers—strangers forever!" She repeated again with special significance the word so dreadful to her. "And how I loved him! my God, how I loved him!.... How I loved him! And now don't I love him? Don't I love him more than before? The most horrible thing is," she began, but did not finish her thought, because Matrona Philimonovna put her head in at the door.

"Let us send for my brother," she said; "he can get a dinner anyway, or we shall have the children getting nothing to eat till six again, like yesterday."

"Very well, I will come directly and see about it. But did you send for some new milk?"

And Darya Alexandrovna plunged into the duties of the day, and drowned her grief in them for a time.

Stepan Arkadyevitch had learned easily at school, thanks to his excellent abilities, but he had been idle and mischievous, and therefore was one of the lowest in his class. But in spite of his habitually dissipated mode of life, his inferior grade in the service, and his comparative youth, he occupied the honorable and lucrative position of president of one of the government boards at Moscow. This post he had received through his sister Anna's husband, Alexey Alexandrovitch Karenin, who held one of the most important positions in the ministry to whose department the Moscow office belonged. But if Karenin had not got his brother- in-law this berth, then through a hundred other personages— brothers, sisters, cousins, uncles, and aunts—Stiva Oblonsky would have received this post, or some other similar one, together with the salary of six thousand absolutely needful for him, as his affairs, in spite of his wife's considerable property, were in an embarrassed condition.

Half Moscow and Petersburg were friends and relations of Stepan Arkadyevitch. He was born in the midst of those who had been and are the powerful ones of this world. One-third of the men in the government, the older men, had been friends of his father's, and had known him in petticoats; another third were his intimate chums, and the remainder were friendly acquaintances. Consequently the distributors of earthly blessings in the shape of places, rents, shares, and such, were all his friends, and could not overlook one of their own set; and Oblonsky had no need to make any special exertion to get a lucrative post. He had only not to refuse things, not to show jealousy, not to be quarrelsome or take offense, all of which from his characteristic good nature he never did. It would have struck him as absurd if he had been told that he would not get a position with the salary he required, especially as he expected nothing out of the way; he only wanted what the men of his own age and standing did get, and he was no worse qualified for performing duties of the kind than any other man.

Stepan Arkadyevitch was not merely liked by all who knew him for his good humor, but for his bright disposition, and his unquestionable honesty. In him, in his handsome, radiant figure, his sparkling eyes, black hair and eyebrows, and the white and red of his face, there was something which produced a physical effect of kindliness and good humor on the people who met him. "Aha! Stiva! Oblonsky! Here he is!" was almost always said with a smile of delight on meeting him. Even though it happened at times that after a conversation with him it seemed that nothing particularly delightful had happened, the next day, and the next, every one was just as delighted at meeting him again.

After filling for three years the post of president of one of the government boards at Moscow, Stepan Arkadyevitch had won the respect, as well as the liking, of his fellow-officials, subordinates, and superiors, and all who had had business with him. The principal qualities in Stepan Arkadyevitch which had gained him this universal respect in the service consisted, in the first place, of his extreme indulgence for others, founded on a consciousness of his own shortcomings; secondly, of his perfect liberalism—not the liberalism he read of in the papers, but the liberalism that was in his blood, in virtue of which he treated all men perfectly equally and exactly the same, whatever their fortune or calling might be; and thirdly—the most important point—his complete indifference to the business in which he was engaged, in consequence of which he was never carried away, and never made mistakes.

On reaching the offices of the board, Stepan Arkadyevitch, escorted by a deferential porter with a portfolio, went into his little private room, put on his uniform, and went into the boardroom. The clerks and copyists all rose, greeting him with good-humored deference. Stepan Arkadyevitch moved quickly, as ever, to his place, shook hands with his colleagues, and sat down. He made a joke or two, and talked just as much as was consistent with due decorum, and began work. No one knew better than Stepan Arkadyevitch how to hit on the exact line between freedom, simplicity, and official stiffness necessary for the agreeable conduct of business. A secretary, with the good-humored deference common to every one in

Stepan Arkadyevitch's office, came up with papers, and began to speak in the familiar and easy tone which had been introduced by Stepan Arkadyevitch.

"We have succeeded in getting the information from the government department of Penza. Here, would you care?...."

"You've got them at last?" said Stepan Arkadyevitch, laying his finger on the paper. "Now, gentlemen...."

And the sitting of the board began.

"If they knew," he thought, bending his head with a significant air as he listened to the report, "what a guilty little boy their president was half an hour ago." And his eyes were laughing during the reading of the report. Till two o'clock the sitting would go on without a break, and at two o'clock there would be an interval and luncheon.

It was not yet two, when the large glass doors of the boardroom suddenly opened and someone came in.

All the officials sitting on the further side under the portrait of the Tsar and the eagle, delighted at any distraction, looked round at the door; but the doorkeeper standing at the door at once drove out the intruder, and closed the glass door after him.

When the case had been read through, Stepan Arkadyevitch got up and stretched, and by way of tribute to the liberalism of the times took out a cigarette in the boardroom and went into his private room. Two of the members of the board, the old veteran in the service, Nikitin, and the *Kammerjunker Grinevitch*, went in with him.

"We shall have time to finish after lunch," said Stepan Arkadyevitch.

"To be sure we shall!" said Nikitin.

"A pretty sharp fellow this Fomin must be," said Grinevitch of one of the persons taking part in the case they were examining.

Stepan Arkadyevitch frowned at Grinevitch's words, giving him thereby to understand that it was improper to pass judgment prematurely, and made him no reply.

"Who was that came in?" he asked the doorkeeper.

"Someone, your excellency, crept in without permission directly my back was turned. He was asking for you. I told him: when the members come out, then..."

"Where is he?"

"Maybe he's gone into the passage, but here he comes anyway. That is he," said the doorkeeper, pointing to a strongly built, broad-shouldered man with a curly beard, who, without taking off his sheepskin cap, was running lightly and rapidly up the worn steps of the stone staircase. One of the members going down—a lean official with a portfolio—stood out of his way and looked disapprovingly at the legs of the stranger, then glanced inquiringly at Oblonsky.

Stepan Arkadyevitch was standing at the top of the stairs. His good-naturedly beaming face above the embroidered collar of his uniform beamed more than ever when he recognized the man coming up.

"Why, it's actually you, Levin, at last!" he said with a friendly mocking smile, scanning Levin as he approached. "How is it you have deigned to look me up in this den?" said Stepan Arkadyevitch, and not content with shaking hands, he kissed his friend. "Have you been here long?"

"I have just come, and very much wanted to see you," said Levin, looking shyly and at the same time angrily and uneasily around.

"Well, let's go into my room," said Stepan Arkadyevitch, who knew his friend's sensitive and irritable shyness, and, taking his arm, he drew him along, as though guiding him through dangers.

Stepan Arkadyevitch was on familiar terms with almost all his acquaintances, and called almost all of them by their Christian names: old men of sixty, boys of twenty, actors, ministers, merchants, and adjutant-generals, so that many of his intimate chums were to be found at the extreme ends of the social ladder, and would have been very much surprised to learn that they had, through the medium of Oblonsky, something in common. He was the familiar friend of everyone with whom he took a glass of champagne, and he took a glass of champagne with everyone, and when in consequence he met any of his disreputable chums, as he used in joke to call many of his friends, in the presence of his subordinates, he well knew how, with his characteristic tact, to diminish the disagreeable impression made on them. Levin was not a disreputable chum, but Oblonsky, with his ready tact, felt that Levin fancied he might not care to show his intimacy with him before his subordinates, and so he made haste to take him off into his room.

Levin was almost of the same age as Oblonsky; their intimacy did not rest merely on champagne. Levin had been the friend and companion of his early youth. They were fond of one another in spite of the difference of their characters and tastes, as friends are fond of one another who have been together in early youth. But in spite of this, each of them—as is often the way with men who have selected careers of different kinds—though in discussion he would even justify the other's career, in his heart despised it. It seemed to each of them that the life he led himself was the only real life, and the life led by his friend was a mere phantasm. Oblonsky could not restrain a slight mocking smile at the sight of Levin. How often he had seen him come up to Moscow from the country where he was doing something, but what precisely Stepan Arkadyevitch could never quite make out, and indeed he took no interest in the matter. Levin arrived in Moscow always excited and in a hurry, rather ill at ease and irritated by his own want of ease, and for the most part with a perfectly new, unexpected view of things. Stepan Arkadyevitch laughed at this, and liked it. In the same way Levin in his heart despised the town mode of life of his friend, and his official duties, which he laughed at, and regarded as trifling. But the difference was that Oblonsky, as he was doing the same as every one did, laughed complacently and good-humoredly, while Levin laughed without complacency and sometimes angrily.

"We have long been expecting you," said Stepan Arkadyevitch, going into his room and letting Levin's hand go as though to show that here all danger was over. "I am very, very glad to see you," he went on. "Well, how are you? Eh? When did you come?"

Levin was silent, looking at the unknown faces of Oblonsky's two companions, and especially at the hand of the elegant Grinevitch, which had such long white fingers, such long yellow filbert-shaped nails, and such huge shining studs on the shirt-cuff, that apparently they absorbed all his attention, and allowed him no freedom of thought. Oblonsky noticed this at once, and smiled.

"Ah, to be sure, let me introduce you," he said. "My colleagues: Philip Ivanitch Nikitin, Mihail Stanislavitch Grinevitch"—and turning to Levin—"a district councilor, a modern district councilman, a gymnast who lifts thirteen stone with one hand, a cattle-breeder and sportsman, and my friend, Konstantin Dmitrievitch Levin, the brother of Sergey Ivanovitch Koznishev."

"Delighted," said the veteran.

"I have the honor of knowing your brother, Sergey Ivanovitch," said Grinevitch, holding out his slender hand with its long nails.

Levin frowned, shook hands coldly, and at once turned to Oblonsky. Though he had a great respect for his half-brother, an author well known to all Russia, he could not endure it when people treated him not as Konstantin Levin, but as the brother of the celebrated Koznishev.

"No, I am no longer a district councilor. I have quarreled with them all, and don't go to the meetings any more," he said, turning to Oblonsky.

"You've been quick about it!" said Oblonsky with a smile. "But how? why?"

"It's a long story. I will tell you some time," said Levin, but he began telling him at once. "Well, to put it shortly, I was convinced that nothing was really done by the district councils, or ever could be," he began, as though some one had just insulted him. "On one side it's a plaything; they play at being a parliament, and I'm neither young enough nor old enough to find amusement in playthings; and on the other side" (he stammered) "it's a means for the coterie of the district to make money. Formerly they had wardships, courts of justice, now they have the district council—not in the form of bribes, but in the form of unearned salary," he said, as hotly as though someone of those present had opposed his opinion.

"Aha! You're in a new phase again, I see—a conservative," said Stepan Arkadyevitch. "However, we can go into that later."

"Yes, later. But I wanted to see you," said Levin, looking with hatred at Grinevitch's hand.

Stepan Arkadyevitch gave a scarcely perceptible smile.

"How was it you used to say you would never wear European dress again?" he said, scanning his new suit, obviously cut by a French tailor. "Ah! I see: a new phase."

Levin suddenly blushed, not as grown men blush, slightly, without being themselves aware of it, but as boys blush, feeling that they are ridiculous through their shyness, and consequently ashamed of it and blushing still more, almost to the point of tears. And it was so strange to see this sensible, manly face in such a childish plight, that Oblonsky left off looking at him.

"Oh, where shall we meet? You know I want very much to talk to you," said Levin.

Oblonsky seemed to ponder.

"I'll tell you what: let's go to Gurin's to lunch, and there we can talk. I am free till three."

"No," answered Levin, after an instant's thought, "I have got to go on somewhere else."

"All right, then, let's dine together."

"Dine together? But I have nothing very particular, only a few words to say, and a question I want to ask you, and we can have a talk afterwards."

"Well, say the few words, then, at once, and we'll gossip after dinner."

"Well, it's this," said Levin; "but it's of no importance, though."

His face all at once took an expression of anger from the effort he was making to surmount his shyness.

"What are the Shtcherbatskys doing? Everything as it used to be?" he said.

Stepan Arkadyevitch, who had long known that Levin was in love with his sister-in-law, Kitty, gave a hardly perceptible smile, and his eyes sparkled merrily.

"You said a few words, but I can't answer in a few words, because.... Excuse me a minute..."

A secretary came in, with respectful familiarity and the modest consciousness, characteristic of every secretary, of superiority to his chief in the knowledge of their business; he went up to Oblonsky with some papers, and began, under pretense of asking a question, to explain some objection. Stepan Arkadyevitch, without hearing him out, laid his hand genially on the secretary's sleeve.

"No, you do as I told you," he said, softening his words with a smile, and with a brief explanation of his view of the matter he turned away from the papers, and said: "So do it that way, if you please, Zahar Nikititch."

The secretary retired in confusion. During the consultation with the secretary Levin had completely recovered from his embarrassment. He was standing with his elbows on the back of a chair, and on his face was a look of ironical attention.

"I don't understand it, I don't understand it," he said.

"What don't you understand?" said Oblonsky, smiling as brightly as ever, and picking up a cigarette. He expected some queer outburst from Levin.

"I don't understand what you are doing," said Levin, shrugging his shoulders. "How can you do it seriously?"

"Why not?"

"Why, because there's nothing in it."

"You think so, but we're overwhelmed with work."

"On paper. But, there, you've a gift for it," added Levin.

"That's to say, you think there's a lack of something in me?"

"Perhaps so," said Levin. "But all the same I admire your grandeur, and am proud that I've a friend in such a great person. You've not answered my question, though," he went on, with a desperate effort looking Oblonsky straight in the face.

"Oh, that's all very well. You wait a bit, and you'll come to this yourself. It's very nice for you to have over six thousand acres in the Karazinsky district, and such muscles, and the freshness of a girl of twelve; still you'll be one of us one day. Yes, as to your question, there is no change, but it's a pity you've been away so long."

"Oh, why so?" Levin queried, panic-stricken.

"Oh, nothing," responded Oblonsky. "We'll talk it over. But what's brought you up to town?"

"Oh, we'll talk about that, too, later on," said Levin, reddening again up to his ears.

"All right. I see," said Stepan Arkadyevitch. "I should ask you to come to us, you know, but my wife's not quite the thing. But I tell you what; if you want to see them, they're sure now to be at the Zoological Gardens from four to five. Kitty skates. You drive along there, and I'll come and fetch you, and we'll go and dine somewhere together."

"Capital. So good-bye till then."

"Now mind, you'll forget, I know you, or rush off home to the country!" Stepan Arkadyevitch called out laughing.

"No, truly!"

And Levin went out of the room, only when he was in the doorway remembering that he had forgotten to take leave of Oblonsky's colleagues.

"That gentleman must be a man of great energy," said Grinevitch, when Levin had gone away.

"Yes, my dear boy," said Stepan Arkadyevitch, nodding his head, "he's a lucky fellow! Over six thousand acres in the Karazinsky district; everything before him; and what youth and vigor! Not like some of us."

"You have a great deal to complain of, haven't you, Stepan Arkadyevitch?"

"Ah, yes, I'm in a poor way, a bad way," said Stepan Arkadyevitch with a heavy sigh.

When Oblonsky asked Levin what had brought him to town, Levin blushed, and was furious with himself for blushing, because he could not answer, "I have come to make your sister-in-law an offer," though that was precisely what he had come for.

The families of the Levins and the Shtcherbatskys were old, noble Moscow families, and had always been on intimate and friendly terms. This intimacy had grown still closer during Levin's student days. He had both prepared for the university with the young Prince Shtcherbatsky, the brother of Kitty and Dolly, and had entered at the same time with him. In those days Levin used often to be in the Shtcherbatskys' house, and he was in love with the Shtcherbatsky household. Strange as it may appear, it was with the household, the family, that Konstantin Levin was in love, especially with the feminine half of the household. Levin did not remember his own mother, and his only sister was older than he was, so that it was in the Shtcherbatskys' house that he saw for the first time that inner life of an old, noble, cultivated, and honorable family of which he had been deprived by the death of his father and mother. All the members of that family, especially the feminine half, were pictured by him, as it were, wrapped about with a mysterious poetical veil, and he not only perceived no defects whatever in them, but under the poetical veil that shrouded them he assumed the existence of the loftiest sentiments and every possible perfection. Why it was the three young ladies had one day to speak French, and the next English; why it was that at certain hours they played by turns on the piano, the sounds of which were audible in their brother's room above, where the students used to work; why they were visited by those professors of French literature, of music, of drawing, of dancing; why at certain hours all the three young ladies, with Mademoiselle Linon, drove in the coach to the Tversky boulevard, dressed in their satin cloaks, Dolly in a long one, Natalia in a half-long one, and Kitty in one so short that her shapely legs in tightly-drawn red stockings were visible to all beholders; why it was they had to walk about the Tversky boulevard escorted by a footman with a gold cockade in his hat—all this and much more that was done in their mysterious world he did not understand, but he was sure that everything that was done there was very good, and he was in love precisely with the mystery of the proceedings.

In his student days he had all but been in love with the eldest, Dolly, but she was soon married to Oblonsky. Then he began being in love with the second. He felt, as it were, that he had to be in love with one of the sisters, only he could not quite make out which. But Natalia, too, had hardly made her appearance in the world when she married the diplomat Lvov. Kitty was still a child when Levin left the university. Young Shtcherbatsky went into the navy, was drowned in the Baltic, and Levin's relations with the Shtcherbatskys, in spite of his friendship with Oblonsky, became less intimate. But when early in the winter of this year Levin came to Moscow, after a year in the country, and saw the Shtcherbatskys, he realized which of the three sisters he was indeed destined to love.

One would have thought that nothing could be simpler than for him, a man of good family, rather rich than poor, and thirty-two years old, to make the young Princess Shtcherbatskaya an offer of marriage; in all likelihood he would at once have been looked upon as a good match. But Levin was in love, and so it seemed to him that Kitty was so perfect in every respect that she was a creature far above everything earthly; and that he was a creature so low and so earthly that it could not even be conceived that other people and she herself could regard him as worthy of her.

After spending two months in Moscow in a state of enchantment, seeing Kitty almost every day in society, into which he went so as to meet her, he abruptly decided that it could not be, and went back to the country.

Levin's conviction that it could not be was founded on the idea that in the eyes of her family he was a disadvantageous and worthless match for the charming Kitty, and that Kitty herself could not love him. In her family's eyes he had no ordinary, definite career and position in society, while his contemporaries by this time, when he was thirty-two, were already, one a colonel, and another a professor, another director of a bank and railways, or president of a board like Oblonsky. But he (he knew very well how he must appear to others) was a country gentleman, occupied in breeding cattle, shooting game, and building barns; in other words, a fellow of no ability, who had not turned out well, and who was doing just what, according to the ideas of the world, is done by people fit for nothing else.

The mysterious, enchanting Kitty herself could not love such an ugly person as he conceived himself to be, and, above all, such an ordinary, in no way striking person. Moreover, his attitude to Kitty in the past—the attitude of a grown-up person to a child, arising from his friendship with her brother—seemed to him yet another obstacle to love. An ugly, good-natured man, as he considered himself, might, he supposed, be liked as a friend; but to be loved with such a love as that with which he loved Kitty, one would need to be a handsome and, still more, a distinguished man.

He had heard that women often did care for ugly and ordinary men, but he did not believe it, for he judged by himself, and he could not himself have loved any but beautiful, mysterious, and exceptional women.

But after spending two months alone in the country, he was convinced that this was not one of those passions of which he had had experience in his early youth; that this feeling gave him not an instant's rest; that he could not live without deciding the question, would she or would she not be his wife, and that his despair had arisen only from his own imaginings, that he had no sort of proof that he would be rejected. And he had now come to Moscow with a firm determination to make an offer, and get married if he were accepted. Or...he could not conceive what would become of him if he were rejected.

On arriving in Moscow by a morning train, Levin had put up at the house of his elder half-brother, Koznishev. After changing his clothes he went down to his brother's study, intending to talk to him at once about the object of his visit, and to ask his advice; but his brother was not alone. With him there was a well-known professor of philosophy, who had come from Harkov expressly to clear up a difference that had arisen between them on a very important philosophical question. The professor was carrying on a hot crusade against materialists. Sergey Koznishev had been following this crusade with interest, and after reading the professor's last article, he had written him a letter stating his objections. He accused the professor of making too great concessions to the materialists. And the professor had promptly appeared to argue the matter out. The point in discussion was the question then in vogue: Is there a line to be drawn between psychological and physiological phenomena in man? and if so, where?

Sergey Ivanovitch met his brother with the smile of chilly friendliness he always had for everyone, and introducing him to the professor, went on with the conversation.

A little man in spectacles, with a narrow forehead, tore himself from the discussion for an instant to greet Levin, and then went on talking without paying any further attention to him. Levin sat down to wait till the professor should go, but he soon began to get interested in the subject under discussion.

Levin had come across the magazine articles about which they were disputing, and had read them, interested in them as a development of the first principles of science, familiar to him as a natural science student at the university. But he had never connected these scientific deductions as to the origin of man as an animal, as to reflex action, biology, and sociology, with those questions as to the meaning of life and death to himself, which had of late been more and more often in his mind.

As he listened to his brother's argument with the professor, he noticed that they connected these scientific questions with those spiritual problems, that at times they almost touched on the latter; but every time they were close upon what seemed to him the chief point, they promptly beat a hasty retreat, and plunged again into a sea of subtle distinctions, reservations, quotations, allusions, and appeals to authorities, and it was with difficulty that he understood what they were talking about.

"I cannot admit it," said Sergey Ivanovitch, with his habitual clearness, precision of expression, and elegance of phrase. "I cannot in any case agree with Keiss that my whole conception of the external world has been derived from perceptions. The most fundamental idea, the idea of existence, has not been received by me through sensation; indeed, there is no special sense-organ for the transmission of such an idea."

"Yes, but they—Wurt, and Knaust, and Pripasov—would answer that your consciousness of existence is derived from the conjunction of all your sensations, that that consciousness of existence is the result of your sensations. Wurt, indeed, says plainly that, assuming there are no sensations, it follows that there is no idea of existence."

"I maintain the contrary," began Sergey Ivanovitch.

But here it seemed to Levin that just as they were close upon the real point of the matter, they were again retreating, and he made up his mind to put a question to the professor.

"According to that, if my senses are annihilated, if my body is dead, I can have no existence of any sort?" he queried.

The professor, in annoyance, and, as it were, mental suffering at the interruption, looked round at the strange inquirer, more like a bargeman than a philosopher, and turned his eyes upon Sergey Ivanovitch, as though to ask: What's one to say to him? But Sergey Ivanovitch, who had been talking with far less heat and one-sidedness than the professor, and who had sufficient breadth of mind to answer the professor, and at the same time to comprehend the simple and natural point of view from which the question was put, smiled and said:

"That question we have no right to answer as yet."

"We have not the requisite data," chimed in the professor, and he went back to his argument. "No," he said; "I would point out the fact that if, as Pripasov directly asserts, perception is based on sensation, then we are bound to distinguish sharply between these two conceptions."

Levin listened no more, and simply waited for the professor to go.

When the professor had gone, Sergey Ivanovitch turned to his brother.

"Delighted that you've come. For some time, is it? How's your farming getting on?"

Levin knew that his elder brother took little interest in farming, and only put the question in deference to him, and so he only told him about the sale of his wheat and money matters.

Levin had meant to tell his brother of his determination to get married, and to ask his advice; he had indeed firmly resolved to do so. But after seeing his brother, listening to his conversation with the professor, hearing afterwards the unconsciously patronizing tone in which his brother questioned him about agricultural matters (their mother's property had not been divided, and Levin took charge of both their shares), Levin felt that he could not for some reason begin to talk to him of his intention of marrying. He felt that his brother would not look at it as he would have wished him to.

"Well, how is your district council doing?" asked Sergey Ivanovitch, who was greatly interested in these local boards and attached great importance to them.

"I really don't know."

"What! Why, surely you're a member of the board?"

"No, I'm not a member now; I've resigned," answered Levin, "and I no longer attend the meetings."

"What a pity!" commented Sergey Ivanovitch, frowning.

Levin in self-defense began to describe what took place in the meetings in his district.

"That's how it always is!" Sergey Ivanovitch interrupted him. "We Russians are always like that. Perhaps it's our strong point, really, the faculty of seeing our own shortcomings; but we overdo it, we comfort ourselves with irony which we always have on the tip of our tongues. All I say is, give such rights as our local self-government to any other European people—why, the Germans or the English would have worked their way to freedom from them, while we simply turn them into ridicule."

"But how can it be helped?" said Levin penitently. "It was my last effort. And I did try with all my soul. I can't. I'm no good at it."

"It's not that you're no good at it," said Sergey Ivanovitch; "it is that you don't look at it as you should."

"Perhaps not," Levin answered dejectedly.

"Oh! do you know brother Nikolay's turned up again?"

This brother Nikolay was the elder brother of Konstantin Levin, and half-brother of Sergey Ivanovitch; a man utterly ruined, who had dissipated the greater part of his fortune, was living in the strangest and lowest company, and had quarreled with his brothers.

"What did you say?" Levin cried with horror. "How do you know?"

"Prokofy saw him in the street."

"Here in Moscow? Where is he? Do you know?" Levin got up from his chair, as though on the point of starting off at once.

"I am sorry I told you," said Sergey Ivanovitch, shaking his head at his younger brother's excitement. "I sent to find out where he is living, and sent him his IOU to Trubin, which I paid. This is the answer he sent me."

And Sergey Ivanovitch took a note from under a paper-weight and handed it to his brother.

Levin read in the queer, familiar handwriting: "I humbly beg you to leave me in peace. That's the only favor I ask of my gracious brothers.—Nikolay Levin."

Levin read it, and without raising his head stood with the note in his hands opposite Sergey Ivanovitch.

There was a struggle in his heart between the desire to forget his unhappy brother for the time, and the consciousness that it would be base to do so.

"He obviously wants to offend me," pursued Sergey Ivanovitch; "but he cannot offend me, and I should have wished with all my heart to assist him, but I know it's impossible to do that."

"Yes, yes," repeated Levin. "I understand and appreciate your attitude to him; but I shall go and see him."

"If you want to, do; but I shouldn't advise it," said Sergey Ivanovitch. "As regards myself, I have no fear of your doing so; he will not make you quarrel with me; but for your own sake, I should say you would do better not to go. You can't do him any good; still, do as you please."

"Very likely I can't do any good, but I feel—especially at such a moment—but that's another thing—I feel I could not be at peace."

"Well, that I don't understand," said Sergey Ivanovitch. "One thing I do understand," he added; "it's a lesson in humility. I have come to look very differently and more charitably on what is called infamous since brother Nikolay has become what he is...you know what he did..."

"Oh, it's awful, awful!" repeated Levin.

After obtaining his brother's address from Sergey Ivanovitch's footman, Levin was on the point of setting off at once to see him, but on second thought he decided to put off his visit till the evening. The first thing to do to set his heart at rest was to accomplish what he had come to Moscow for. From his brother's Levin went to Oblonsky's office, and on getting news of the Shtcherbatskys from him, he drove to the place where he had been told he might find Kitty.

At four o'clock, conscious of his throbbing heart, Levin stepped out of a hired sledge at the Zoological Gardens, and turned along the path to the frozen mounds and the skating ground, knowing that he would certainly find her there, as he had seen the Shtcherbatskys' carriage at the entrance.

It was a bright, frosty day. Rows of carriages, sledges, drivers, and policemen were standing in the approach. Crowds of well-dressed people, with hats bright in the sun, swarmed about the entrance and along the well-swept little paths between the little houses adorned with carving in the Russian style. The old curly birches of the gardens, all their twigs laden with snow, looked as though freshly decked in sacred vestments.

He walked along the path towards the skating-ground, and kept saying to himself—"You mustn't be excited, you must be calm. What's the matter with you? What do you want? Be quiet, stupid," he conjured his heart. And the more he tried to compose himself, the more breathless he found himself. An acquaintance met him and called him by his name, but Levin did not even recognize him. He went towards the mounds, whence came the clank of the chains of sledges as they slipped down or were dragged up, the rumble of the sliding sledges, and the sounds of merry voices. He walked on a few steps, and the skating-ground lay open before his eyes, and at once, amidst all the skaters, he knew her.

He knew she was there by the rapture and the terror that seized on his heart. She was standing talking to a lady at the opposite end of the ground. There was apparently nothing striking either in her dress or her attitude. But for Levin she was as easy to find in that crowd as a rose among nettles. Everything was made bright by her. She was the smile that shed light on all round her. "Is it possible I can go over there on the ice, go up to her?" he thought. The place where she stood seemed to him a holy shrine, unapproachable, and there was one moment when he was almost retreating, so overwhelmed was he with terror. He had to make an effort to master himself, and to remind himself that people of all sorts were moving about her, and that he too might come there to skate. He walked down, for a long while avoiding looking at her as at the sun, but seeing her, as one does the sun, without looking.

On that day of the week and at that time of day people of one set, all acquainted with one another, used to meet on the ice. There were crack skaters there, showing off their skill, and learners clinging to chairs with timid, awkward movements, boys, and elderly people skating with hygienic motives. They seemed to Levin an elect band of blissful beings because they were here, near her. All the skaters, it seemed, with perfect self-possession, skated towards her, skated by her, even spoke to her, and were happy, quite apart from her, enjoying the capital ice and the fine weather.

Nikolay Shtcherbatsky, Kitty's cousin, in a short jacket and tight trousers, was sitting on a garden seat with his skates on. Seeing Levin, he shouted to him:

"Ah, the first skater in Russia! Been here long? First-rate ice—do put your skates on."

"I haven't got my skates," Levin answered, marveling at this boldness and ease in her presence, and not for one second losing sight of her, though he did not look at her. He felt as though the sun were coming near him. She was in a corner, and turning out her slender feet in their high boots with obvious timidity, she skated towards him. A boy in Russian dress, desperately waving his arms and bowed down to the ground, overtook her. She skated a little uncertainly; taking her hands out of the little muff that hung on a cord, she held them ready for emergency, and looking towards Levin, whom she had recognized, she smiled at him, and at her own fears. When she had got round the turn, she gave herself a push off with one foot, and skated straight up to Shtcherbatsky. Clutching at his arm, she nodded smiling to Levin. She was more splendid than he had imagined her.

When he thought of her, he could call up a vivid picture of her to himself, especially the charm of that little fair head, so freely set on the shapely girlish shoulders, and so full of childish brightness and good humor. The childishness of her expression, together with the delicate beauty of her figure, made up her special charm, and that he fully realized. But what always struck him in her as something unlooked for, was the expression of her eyes, soft, serene, and truthful, and above all, her smile, which always transported Levin to an enchanted world, where he felt himself softened and tender, as he remembered himself in some days of his early childhood.

"Have you been here long?" she said, giving him her hand. "Thank you," she added, as he picked up the handkerchief that had fallen out of her muff.

"I? I've not long...yesterday...I mean today...I arrived," answered Levin, in his emotion not at once understanding her question. "I was meaning to come and see you," he said; and then, recollecting with what intention he was trying to see her, he was promptly overcome with confusion and blushed.

"I didn't know you could skate, and skate so well."

She looked at him earnestly, as though wishing to make out the cause of his confusion.

"Your praise is worth having. The tradition is kept up here that you are the best of skaters," she said, with her little black-gloved hand brushing a grain of hoarfrost off her muff.

"Yes, I used once to skate with passion; I wanted to reach perfection."

"You do everything with passion, I think," she said smiling. "I should so like to see how you skate. Put on skates, and let us skate together."

"Skate together! Can that be possible?" thought Levin, gazing at her.

"I'll put them on directly," he said.

And he went off to get skates.

"It's a long while since we've seen you here, sir," said the attendant, supporting his foot, and screwing on the heel of the skate. "Except you, there's none of the gentlemen first-rate skaters. Will that be all right?" said he, tightening the strap.

"Oh, yes, yes; make haste, please," answered Levin, with difficulty restraining the smile of rapture which would overspread his face. "Yes," he thought, "this now is life, this is happiness! *Together,* she said; *let us skate together!* Speak to her now? But that's just why I'm afraid to speak—because I'm happy now, happy in hope, anyway.... And then?.... But I must! I must! I must! Away with weakness!"

Levin rose to his feet, took off his overcoat, and scurrying over the rough ice round the hut, came out on the smooth ice and skated without effort, as it were, by simple exercise of will, increasing and slackening speed and turning his course. He approached with timidity, but again her smile reassured him.

She gave him her hand, and they set off side by side, going faster and faster, and the more rapidly they moved the more tightly she grasped his hand.

"With you I should soon learn; I somehow feel confidence in you," she said to him.

"And I have confidence in myself when you are leaning on me," he said, but was at once panic-stricken at what he had said, and blushed. And indeed, no sooner had he uttered these words, when all at once, like the sun going behind a cloud, her face lost all its friendliness, and Levin detected the familiar change in her expression that denoted the working of thought; a crease showed on her smooth brow.

"Is there anything troubling you?—though I've no right to ask such a question," he added hurriedly.

"Oh, why so?.... No, I have nothing to trouble me," she responded coldly; and she added immediately: "You haven't seen Mlle. Linon, have you?"

"Not yet."

"Go and speak to her, she likes you so much."

"What's wrong? I have offended her. Lord help me!" thought Levin, and he flew towards the old Frenchwoman with the gray ringlets, who was sitting on a bench. Smiling and showing her false teeth, she greeted him as an old friend.

"Yes, you see we're growing up," she said to him, glancing towards Kitty, "and growing old. *Tiny bear* has grown big now!" pursued the Frenchwoman, laughing, and she reminded him of his joke about the three young ladies whom he had compared to the three bears in the English nursery tale. "Do you remember that's what you used to call them?"

He remembered absolutely nothing, but she had been laughing at the joke for ten years now, and was fond of it.

"Now, go and skate, go and skate. Our Kitty has learned to skate nicely, hasn't she?"

When Levin darted up to Kitty her face was no longer stern; her eyes looked at him with the same sincerity and friendliness, but Levin fancied that in her friendliness there was a certain note of deliberate composure. And he felt depressed. After talking a little of her old governess and her peculiarities, she questioned him about his life.

"Surely you must be dull in the country in the winter, aren't you?" she said.

"No, I'm not dull, I am very busy," he said, feeling that she was holding him in check by her composed tone, which he would not have the force to break through, just as it had been at the beginning of the winter.

"Are you going to stay in town long?" Kitty questioned him.

"I don't know," he answered, not thinking of what he was saying. The thought that if he were held in check by her tone of quiet friendliness he would end by going back again without deciding anything came into his mind, and he resolved to make a struggle against it.

"How is it you don't know?"

"I don't know. It depends upon you," he said, and was immediately horror-stricken at his own words.

Whether it was that she had heard his words, or that she did not want to hear them, she made a sort of stumble, twice struck out, and hurriedly skated away from him. She skated up to Mlle. Linon, said something to her, and went towards the pavilion where the ladies took off their skates.

"My God! what have I done! Merciful God! help me, guide me," said Levin, praying inwardly, and at the same time, feeling a need of violent exercise, he skated about describing inner and outer circles.

At that moment one of the young men, the best of the skaters of the day, came out of the coffee-house in his skates, with a cigarette in his mouth. Taking a run, he dashed down the steps in his skates, crashing and bounding up and down. He flew down, and without even changing the position of his hands, skated away over the ice.

"Ah, that's a new trick!" said Levin, and he promptly ran up to the top to do this new trick.

"Don't break your neck! it needs practice!" Nikolay Shtcherbatsky shouted after him.

Levin went to the steps, took a run from above as best he could, and dashed down, preserving his balance in this unwonted movement with his hands. On the last step he stumbled, but barely touching the ice with his hand, with a violent effort recovered himself, and skated off, laughing.

"How splendid, how nice he is!" Kitty was thinking at that time, as she came out of the pavilion with Mlle. Linon, and looked towards him with a smile of quiet affection, as though he were a favorite brother. "And can it be my fault, can I have done anything wrong? They talk of flirtation. I know it's not he that I love; but still I am happy with him, and he's so jolly. Only, why did he say that?..." she mused.

Catching sight of Kitty going away, and her mother meeting her at the steps, Levin, flushed from his rapid exercise, stood still and pondered a minute. He took off his skates, and overtook the mother and daughter at the entrance of the gardens.

"Delighted to see you," said Princess Shtcherbatskaya. "On Thursdays we are home, as always."

"Today, then?"

"We shall be pleased to see you," the princess said stiffly.

This stiffness hurt Kitty, and she could not resist the desire to smooth over her mother's coldness. She turned her head, and with a smile said:

"Good-bye till this evening."

At that moment Stepan Arkadyevitch, his hat cocked on one side, with beaming face and eyes, strode into the garden like a conquering hero. But as he approached his mother-in-law, he responded in a mournful and crestfallen tone to her inquiries about Dolly's health. After a little subdued and dejected conversation with his mother-in-law, he threw out his chest again, and put his arm in Levin's.

"Well, shall we set off?" he asked. "I've been thinking about you all this time, and I'm very, very glad you've come," he said, looking him in the face with a significant air.

"Yes, come along," answered Levin in ecstasy, hearing unceasingly the sound of that voice saying, "Good-bye till this evening," and seeing the smile with which it was said.

"To the England or the Hermitage?"

"I don't mind which."

"All right, then, the England," said Stepan Arkadyevitch, selecting that restaurant because he owed more there than at the Hermitage, and consequently considered it mean to avoid it. "Have you got a sledge? That's first-rate, for I sent my carriage home."

The friends hardly spoke all the way. Levin was wondering what that change in Kitty's expression had meant, and alternately assuring himself that there was hope, and falling into despair, seeing clearly that his hopes were insane, and yet all the while he felt himself quite another man, utterly unlike what he had been before her smile and those words, "Good-bye till this evening."

Stepan Arkadyevitch was absorbed during the drive in composing the menu of the dinner.

"You like turbot, don't you?" he said to Levin as they were arriving.

"Eh?" responded Levin. "Turbot? Yes, I'm *awfully* fond of turbot."

CHAPTER TWO

THE YOUNG PRINCESS Kitty Shtcherbatskaya was eighteen. It was the first winter that she had been out in the world. Her success in society had been greater than that of either of her elder sisters, and greater even than her mother had anticipated. To say nothing of the young men who danced at the Moscow balls being almost all in love with Kitty, two serious suitors had already this first winter made their appearance: Levin, and immediately after his departure, Count Vronsky.

Levin's appearance at the beginning of the winter, his frequent visits, and evident love for Kitty, had led to the first serious conversations between Kitty's parents as to her future, and to disputes between them. The prince was on Levin's side; he said he wished for nothing better for Kitty. The princess for her part, going round the question in the manner peculiar to women, maintained that Kitty was too young, that Levin had done nothing to prove that he had serious intentions, that Kitty felt no great attraction to him, and other side issues; but she did not state the principal point, which was that she looked for a better match for her daughter, and that Levin was not to her liking, and she did not understand him. When Levin had abruptly departed, the princess was delighted, and said to her husband triumphantly: "You see I was right." When Vronsky appeared on the scene, she was still more delighted, confirmed in her opinion that Kitty was to make not simply a good, but a brilliant match.

In the mother's eyes there could be no comparison between Vronsky and Levin. She disliked in Levin his strange and uncompromising opinions and his shyness in society, founded, as she supposed, on his pride and his queer sort of life, as she considered it, absorbed in cattle and peasants. She did not very much like it that he, who was in love with her daughter, had kept coming to the house for six weeks, as though he were waiting for something, inspecting, as though he were afraid he might be doing them too great an honor by making an offer, and did not realize that a man, who continually visits at a house where there is a young unmarried girl, is bound to make his intentions clear. And suddenly, without doing so, he disappeared. "It's as well he's not attractive enough for Kitty to have fallen in love with him," thought the mother.

Vronsky satisfied all the mother's desires. Very wealthy, clever, of aristocratic family, on the highroad to a brilliant career in the army and at court, and a fascinating man. Nothing better could be wished for.

Vronsky openly flirted with Kitty at balls, danced with her, and came continually to the house, consequently there could be no doubt of the seriousness of his intentions. But, in spite of that, the mother had spent the whole of that winter in a state of terrible anxiety and agitation.

Princess Shtcherbatskaya had herself been married thirty years ago, her aunt arranging the match. Her husband, about whom everything was well known before hand, had come, looked at his future bride, and been looked at. The match-making aunt had ascertained and communicated their mutual impression. That impression had been favorable. Afterwards, on a day fixed beforehand, the expected offer was made to her parents, and accepted. All had passed very simply and easily. So it seemed, at least, to the princess. But over her own daughters she had felt how far from simple and easy is the business, apparently so commonplace, of marrying off one's daughters. The panics that had been lived through, the thoughts that had been brooded over, the money that had been wasted, and the disputes with her husband over marrying the two elder girls, Darya and Natalia! Now, since the youngest had come out, she was going through the same terrors, the same doubts, and still more violent quarrels with her husband than she had over the elder girls. The old prince, like all fathers indeed, was exceedingly punctilious on the score of the honor and reputation of his daughters. He was irrationally jealous over his daughters, especially over Kitty, who was his favorite. At every turn he had scenes with the princess for compromising her daughter. The princess had grown accustomed to this already with her other daughters, but now she felt that there was more ground for the prince's touchiness. She saw that of late years much was changed in the manners of society, that a mother's duties had become still more difficult. She saw that girls of Kitty's age formed some sort of clubs, went to some sort of lectures, mixed freely in men's society; drove about the streets alone, many of them did not curtsey, and, what was the most important thing, all the girls were firmly convinced that to choose their husbands was their own affair, and not their parents'. "Marriages aren't made nowadays as they used to be," was thought and said by all these young girls, and even by their elders. But how marriages were made now, the princess could not learn from any one. The French fashion—of the parents arranging their children's future—was not accepted; it was condemned. The English fashion of the complete independence of girls was also not accepted, and not possible in Russian society. The Russian fashion of match-making by the offices of intermediate persons was for some reason considered unseemly; it was ridiculed by every one, and by the princess herself. But how girls were to be married, and how parents were to marry them, no one knew. Everyone with whom the princess had chanced to discuss the matter said the same thing: "Mercy on us, it's high time in our day to cast off all that old-fashioned business. It's the young people have to marry; and not their parents; and so we ought to leave the young people to arrange it as they choose." It was very easy for anyone to say that who had no daughters, but the princess realized that in the process of getting to know each other, her daughter might fall in love, and fall in love with someone who did not care to marry her or who was quite unfit to be her husband. And, however much it was instilled into the princess that in our times young people ought to arrange their lives for themselves, she was unable to believe it, just as she would have been unable to believe that, at any time whatever, the most suitable playthings for children five years old ought to be loaded pistols. And so the princess was more uneasy over Kitty than she had been over her elder sisters.

Now she was afraid that Vronsky might confine himself to simply flirting with her daughter. She saw that her daughter was in love with him, but tried to comfort herself with the thought that he was an honorable man, and would not do this. But at the same time she knew how easy it is, with the freedom of manners of today, to turn a girl's head, and how lightly men generally regard such a crime. The week before, Kitty had told her mother of a conversation she had with Vronsky during a mazurka. This conversation had partly reassured the princess; but perfectly at ease she could not be. Vronsky had told Kitty that both he and his brother were so used to obeying their mother that they never made up their minds to any important undertaking without consulting her. "And just now, I am impatiently awaiting my mother's arrival from Petersburg, as peculiarly fortunate," he told her.

Kitty had repeated this without attaching any significance to the words. But her mother saw them in a different light. She knew that the old lady was expected from day to day, that she would be pleased at her son's choice, and she felt it strange that he should not make his offer through fear of vexing his mother. However, she was so anxious for the marriage itself, and still more for relief from her fears, that she believed it was so. Bitter as it was for the princess to see the unhappiness of her eldest daughter, Dolly, on the point of leaving her husband, her anxiety over the decision of her youngest daughter's fate engrossed all her feelings. Today, with Levin's reappearance, a fresh source of anxiety arose. She was afraid that her daughter, who had at one time, as she fancied, a feeling for Levin, might, from extreme sense of honor, refuse Vronsky, and that Levin's arrival might generally complicate and delay the affair so near being concluded.

"Why, has he been here long?" the princess asked about Levin, as they returned home.

"He came today, mamma."

"There's one thing I want to say..." began the princess, and from her serious and alert face, Kitty guessed what it would be.

"Mamma," she said, flushing hotly and turning quickly to her, "please, please don't say anything about that. I know, I know all about it."

She wished for what her mother wished for, but the motives of her mother's wishes wounded her.

"I only want to say that to raise hopes..."

"Mamma, darling, for goodness' sake, don't talk about it. It's so horrible to talk about it."

"I won't," said her mother, seeing the tears in her daughter's eyes; "but one thing, my love; you promised me you would have no secrets from me. You won't?"

"Never, mamma, none," answered Kitty, flushing a little, and looking her mother straight in the face, "but there's no use in my telling you anything, and I...I...if I wanted to, I don't know what to say or how...I don't know..."

"No, she could not tell an untruth with those eyes," thought the mother, smiling at her agitation and happiness. The princess smiled that what was taking place just now in her soul seemed to the poor child so immense and so important.

After dinner, and till the beginning of the evening, Kitty was feeling a sensation akin to the sensation of a young man before a battle. Her heart throbbed violently, and her thoughts would not rest on anything.

She felt that this evening, when they would both meet for the first time, would be a turning point in her life. And she was continually picturing them to herself, at one moment each separately, and then both together. When she mused on the past, she dwelt with pleasure, with tenderness, on the memories of her relations with Levin. The memories of childhood and of Levin's friendship with her dead brother gave a special poetic charm to her relations with him. His love for her, of which she felt certain, was flattering and delightful to her; and it was pleasant for her to think of Levin. In her memories of Vronsky there always entered a certain element of awkwardness, though he was in the highest degree well-bred and at ease, as though there were some false note—not in Vronsky, he was very simple and nice, but in herself, while with Levin she felt perfectly simple and clear. But, on the other hand, directly she thought of the future with Vronsky, there arose before her a perspective of brilliant happiness; with Levin the future seemed misty.

When she went upstairs to dress, and looked into the looking-glass, she noticed with joy that it was one of her good days, and that she was in complete possession of all her forces,— she needed this so for what lay before her: she was conscious of external composure and free grace in her movements.

At half-past seven she had only just gone down into the drawing room, when the footman announced, "Konstantin Dmitrievitch Levin." The princess was still in her room, and the prince had not come in. "So it is to be," thought Kitty, and all the blood seemed to rush to her heart. She was horrified at her paleness, as she glanced into the looking-glass. At that moment she knew beyond doubt that he had come early on purpose to find her alone and to make her an offer. And only then for the first time the whole thing presented itself in a new, different aspect; only then she realized that the question did not affect her only— with whom she would be happy, and whom she loved—but that she would have that moment to wound a man whom she liked. And to wound him cruelly. What for? Because he, dear fellow, loved her, was in love with her. But there was no help for it, so it must be, so it would have to be.

"My God! shall I myself really have to say it to him?" she thought. "Can I tell him I don't love him? That will be a lie. What am I to say to him? That I love someone else? No, that's impossible. I'm going away, I'm going away."

She had reached the door, when she heard his step. "No! it's not honest. What have I to be afraid of? I have done nothing wrong. What is to be, will be! I'll tell the truth. And with him one can't be ill at ease. Here he is," she said to herself, seeing his powerful, shy figure, with his shining eyes fixed on her. She looked straight into his face, as though imploring him to spare her, and gave her hand.

"It's not time yet; I think I'm too early," he said glancing round the empty drawing room. When he saw that his expectations were realized, that there was nothing to prevent him from speaking, his face became gloomy.

"Oh, no," said Kitty, and sat down at the table.

"But this was just what I wanted, to find you alone," he began, not sitting down, and not looking at her, so as not to lose courage.

"Mamma will be down directly. She was very much tired.... Yesterday..."

She talked on, not knowing what her lips were uttering, and not taking her supplicating and caressing eyes off him.

He glanced at her; she blushed, and ceased speaking.

"I told you I did not know whether I should be here long...that it depended on you..."

She dropped her head lower and lower, not knowing herself what answer she should make to what was coming.

"That it depended on you," he repeated. "I meant to say...I meant to say...I came for this...to be my wife!" he brought out, not knowing what he was saying; but feeling that the most terrible thing was said, he stopped short and looked at her...

She was breathing heavily, not looking at him. She was feeling ecstasy. Her soul was flooded with happiness. She had never anticipated that the utterance of love would produce such a powerful effect on her. But it lasted only an instant. She remembered Vronsky. She lifted her clear, truthful eyes, and seeing his desperate face, she answered hastily:

"That cannot be...forgive me."

A moment ago, and how close she had been to him, of what importance in his life! And how aloof and remote from him she had become now!

"It was bound to be so," he said, not looking at her.

He bowed, and was meaning to retreat.

At the end of the evening Kitty told her mother of her conversation with Levin, and in spite of all the pity she felt for Levin, she was glad at the thought that she had received an *offer*. She had no doubt that she had acted rightly. But after she had gone to bed, for a long while she could not sleep. One impression pursued her relentlessly. It was Levin's face, with his scowling brows, and his kind eyes looking out in dark dejection below them, as he stood listening to her father, and glancing at her and at Vronsky. And she felt so sorry for him that tears came into her eyes. But immediately she thought of the man for whom she had given him up. She vividly recalled his manly, resolute face, his noble self-possession, and the good nature conspicuous in everything towards everyone. She remembered the love for her of the man she loved, and once more all was gladness in her soul, and she lay on the pillow, smiling with happiness. "I'm sorry, I'm sorry; but what could I do? It's not my fault," she said to herself; but an inner voice told her something else. Whether she felt remorse at having won Levin's love, or at having refused him, she did not know. But her happiness was poisoned by doubts. "Lord, have pity on us; Lord, have pity on us; Lord, have pity on us!" she repeated to herself, till she fell asleep.

Meanwhile there took place below, in the prince's little library, one of the scenes so often repeated between the parents on account of their favorite daughter.

"What? I'll tell you what!" shouted the prince, waving his arms, and at once wrapping his squirrel-lined dressing-gown round him again. "That you've no pride, no dignity; that you're disgracing, ruining your daughter by this vulgar, stupid match-making!"

"But, really, for mercy's sake, prince, what have I done?" said the princess, almost crying.

She, pleased and happy after her conversation with her daughter, had gone to the prince to say good-night as usual, and though she had no intention of telling him of Levin's offer and Kitty's refusal, still she hinted to her husband that she fancied things were practically settled with Vronsky, and that he would declare himself so soon as his mother arrived. And thereupon, at those words, the prince had all at once flown into a passion, and began to use unseemly language.

"What have you done? I'll tell you what. First of all, you're trying to catch an eligible gentleman, and all Moscow will be talking of it, and with good reason. If you have evening parties, invite everyone, don't pick out the possible suitors. Invite all the young bucks. Engage a piano player, and let them dance, and not as you do things nowadays, hunting up good matches. It makes me sick, sick to see it, and you've gone on till you've turned the poor wench's head. Levin's a thousand times the better man. As for this little Petersburg swell, they're turned out by machinery, all on one pattern, and all precious rubbish. But if he were a prince of the blood, my daughter need not run after anyone."

"But what have I done?"

"Why, you've..." The prince was crying wrathfully.

"I know if one were to listen to you," interrupted the princess, "we should never marry our daughter. If it's to be so, we'd better go into the country."

"Well, and we had better."

"But do wait a minute. Do I try and catch them? I don't try to catch them in the least. A young man, and a very nice one, has fallen in love with her, and she, I fancy..."

"Oh, yes, you fancy! And how if she really is in love, and he's no more thinking of marriage than I am!... Oh, that I should live to see it! Ah! spiritualism! Ah! Nice! Ah! the ball!" And the prince, imagining that he was mimicking his wife, made a mincing curtsey at each word. "And this is how we're preparing wretchedness for Kitty; and she's really got the notion into her head..."

"But what makes you suppose so?"

"I don't suppose; I know. We have eyes for such things, though women-folk haven't. I see a man who has serious intentions, that's Levin: and I see a peacock, like this feather-head, who's only amusing himself."

"Oh, well, when once you get an idea into your head!..."

"Well, you'll remember my words, but too late, just as with Dolly."

"Well, well, we won't talk of it," the princess stopped him, recollecting her unlucky Dolly.

"By all means, and good night!"

And signing each other with the cross, the husband and wife parted with a kiss, feeling that they each remained of their own opinion.

The princess had at first been quite certain that that evening had settled Kitty's future, and that there could be no doubt of Vronsky's intentions, but her husband's words had disturbed her. And returning to her own room, in terror before the unknown future, she, too, like Kitty, repeated several times in her heart, "Lord, have pity; Lord, have pity; Lord, have pity."

Next day at eleven o'clock in the morning Vronsky drove to the station of the Petersburg railway to meet his mother, and the first person he came across on the great flight of steps was Oblonsky, who was expecting his sister by the same train.

"Ah! your excellency!" cried Oblonsky, "whom are you meeting?"

"My mother," Vronsky responded, smiling, as everyone did who met Oblonsky. He shook hands with him, and together they ascended the steps. "She is to be here from Petersburg today."

"I was looking out for you till two o'clock last night. Where did you go after the Shtcherbatskys'?"

"Home," answered Vronsky. "I must own I felt so well content yesterday after the Shtcherbatskys' that I didn't care to go anywhere."

"I know a gallant steed by tokens sure. And by his eyes I know a youth in love,"

declaimed Stepan Arkadyevitch, just as he had done before to Levin.

Vronsky smiled with a look that seemed to say that he did not deny it, but he promptly changed the subject.

"And whom are you meeting?" he asked.

"I? I've come to meet a pretty woman," said Oblonsky.

"You don't say so!"

"*Honi soit qui mal y pense!* My sister Anna."

"Ah! that's Madame Karenina," said Vronsky.

"You know her, no doubt?"

"I think I do. Or perhaps not...I really am not sure," Vronsky answered heedlessly, with a vague recollection of something stiff and tedious evoked by the name Karenina.

"But Alexey Alexandrovitch, my celebrated brother-in-law, you surely must know. All the world knows him."

"I know him by reputation and by sight. I know that he's clever, learned, religious somewhat.... But you know that's not...*not in my line,*" said Vronsky in English.

"Yes, he's a very remarkable man; rather a conservative, but a splendid man," observed Stepan Arkadyevitch, "a splendid man."

"Oh, well, so much the better for him," said Vronsky smiling. "Oh, you've come," he said, addressing a tall old footman of his mother's, standing at the door; "come here."

Besides the charm Oblonsky had in general for everyone, Vronsky had felt of late specially drawn to him by the fact that in his imagination he was associated with Kitty.

"Well, what do you say? Shall we give a supper on Sunday for the *diva?*" he said to him with a smile, taking his arm.

"Of course. I'm collecting subscriptions. Oh, did you make the acquaintance of my friend Levin?" asked Stepan Arkadyevitch.

"Yes; but he left rather early."

"He's a capital fellow," pursued Oblonsky. "Isn't he?"

"I don't know why it is," responded Vronsky, "in all Moscow people—present company of course excepted," he put in jestingly, "there's something uncompromising. They are all on the defensive, lose their tempers, as though they all want to make one feel something..."

"Yes, that's true, it is so," said Stepan Arkadyevitch, laughing good-humoredly.

"Will the train soon be in?" Vronsky asked a railway official.

"The train's signaled," answered the man.

The approach of the train was more and more evident by the preparatory bustle in the station, the rush of porters, the movement of policemen and attendants, and people meeting the train. Through the frosty vapor could be seen workmen in short sheepskins and soft felt boots crossing the rails of the curving line. The hiss of the boiler could be heard on the distant rails, and the rumble of something heavy.

"No," said Stepan Arkadyevitch, who felt a great inclination to tell Vronsky of Levin's intentions in regard to Kitty. "No, you've not got a true impression of Levin. He's a very nervous man, and is sometimes out of humor, it's true, but then he is often very nice. He's such a true, honest nature, and a heart of gold. But yesterday there were special reasons," pursued Stepan Arkadyevitch, with a meaning smile, totally oblivious of the genuine sympathy he had felt the day before for his friend, and feeling the same sympathy now, only for Vronsky. "Yes, there were reasons why he could not help being either particularly happy or particularly unhappy."

Vronsky stood still and asked directly: "How so? Do you mean he made your *belle-soeur* an offer yesterday?"

"Maybe," said Stepan Arkadyevitch. "I fancied something of the sort yesterday. Yes, if he went away early, and was out of humor too, it must mean it.... He's been so long in love, and I'm very sorry for him."

"So that's it! I should imagine, though, she might reckon on a better match," said Vronsky, drawing himself up and walking about again, "though I don't know him, of course," he added. "Yes, that is a hateful position! That's why most fellows prefer to have to do with Klaras. If you don't succeed with them it only proves that you've not enough cash, but in this case one's dignity's at stake. But here's the train."

The engine had already whistled in the distance. A few instants later the platform was quivering, and with puffs of steam hanging low in the air from the frost, the engine rolled up, with the lever of the middle wheel rhythmically moving up and down, and the stooping figure of the engine-driver covered with frost. Behind the tender, setting the platform more and more slowly swaying, came the luggage van with a dog whining in it. At last the passenger carriages rolled in, oscillating before coming to a standstill.

A smart guard jumped out, giving a whistle, and after him one by one the impatient passengers began to get down: an officer of the guards, holding himself erect, and looking severely about him; a nimble little merchant with a satchel, smiling gaily; a peasant with a sack over his shoulder.

Vronsky, standing beside Oblonsky, watched the carriages and the passengers, totally oblivious of his mother. What he had just heard about Kitty excited and delighted him. Unconsciously he arched his chest, and his eyes flashed. He felt himself a conqueror.

"Countess Vronskaya is in that compartment," said the smart guard, going up to Vronsky.

The guard's words roused him, and forced him to think of his mother and his approaching meeting with her. He did not in his heart respect his mother, and without acknowledging it to himself, he did not love her, though in accordance with the ideas of the set in which he lived, and with his own education, he could not have conceived of any behavior to his mother not in the highest degree respectful and obedient, and the more externally obedient and respectful his behavior, the less in his heart he respected and loved her.

CHAPTER THREE

THE HIGHEST PETERSBURG society is essentially one: in it everyone knows everyone else, everyone even visits everyone else. But this great set has its subdivisions. Anna Arkadyevna Karenina had friends and close ties in three different circles of this highest society. One circle was her husband's government official set, consisting of his colleagues and subordinates, brought together in the most various and capricious manner, and belonging to different social strata. Anna found it difficult now to recall the feeling of almost awe-stricken reverence which she had at first entertained for these persons. Now she knew all of them as people know one another in a country town; she knew their habits and weaknesses, and where the shoe pinched each one of them. She knew their relations with one another and with the head authorities, knew who was for whom, and how each one maintained his position, and where they agreed and disagreed. But the circle of political, masculine interests had never interested her, in spite of countess Lidia Ivanovna's influence, and she avoided it.

Another little set with which Anna was in close relations was the one by means of which Alexey Alexandrovitch had made his career. The center of this circle was the Countess Lidia Ivanovna. It was a set made up of elderly, ugly, benevolent, and godly women, and clever, learned, and ambitious men. One of the clever people belonging to the set had called it "the conscience of Petersburg society." Alexey Alexandrovitch had the highest esteem for this circle, and Anna with her special gift for getting on with everyone, had in the early days of her life in Petersburg made friends in this circle also. Now, since her return from Moscow, she had come to feel this set insufferable. It seemed to her that both she and all of them were insincere, and she felt so bored and ill at ease in that world that she went to see the Countess Lidia Ivanovna as little as possible.

The third circle with which Anna had ties was preeminently the fashionable world—the world of balls, of dinners, of sumptuous dresses, the world that hung on to the court with one hand, so as to avoid sinking to the level of the demi-monde. For the demi-monde the members of that fashionable world believed that they despised, though their tastes were not merely similar, but in fact identical. Her connection with this circle was kept up through Princess Betsy Tverskaya, her cousin's wife, who had an income of a hundred and twenty thousand roubles, and who had taken a great fancy to Anna ever since she first came out, showed her much attention, and drew her into her set, making fun of Countess Lidia Ivanovna's coterie.

"When I'm old and ugly I'll be the same," Betsy used to say; "but for a pretty young woman like you it's early days for that house of charity."

Anna had at first avoided as far as she could Princess Tverskaya's world, because it necessitated an expenditure beyond her means, and besides in her heart she preferred the first circle. But since her visit to Moscow she had done quite the contrary. She avoided her serious-minded friends, and went out into the fashionable world. There she met Vronsky, and experienced an agitating joy at those meetings. She met Vronsky specially often at Betsy's for Betsy was a Vronsky by birth and his cousin. Vronsky was everywhere where he had any chance of meeting Anna, and speaking to her, when he could, of his love. She gave him no encouragement, but every time she met him there surged up in her heart that same feeling of quickened life that had come upon her that day in the railway carriage when she saw him for the first time. She was conscious herself that her delight sparkled in her eyes and curved her lips into a smile, and she could not quench the expression of this delight.

At first Anna sincerely believed that she was displeased with him for daring to pursue her. Soon after her return from Moscow, on arriving at a soiree where she had expected to meet him, and not finding him there, she realized distinctly from the rush of disappointment that she had been deceiving herself, and that this pursuit was not merely not distasteful to her, but that it made the whole interest of her life.

A celebrated singer was singing for the second time, and all the fashionable world was in the theater. Vronsky, seeing his cousin from his stall in the front row, did not wait till the entr'acte, but went to her box.

"Why didn't you come to dinner?" she said to him. "I marvel at the second sight of lovers," she added with a smile, so that no one but he could hear; "*she wasn't there*. But come after the opera."

Vronsky looked inquiringly at her. She nodded. He thanked her by a smile, and sat down beside her.

"But how I remember your jeers!" continued Princess Betsy, who took a peculiar pleasure in following up this passion to a successful issue. "What's become of all that? You're caught, my dear boy."

"That's my one desire, to be caught," answered Vronsky, with his serene, good-humored smile. "If I complain of anything it's only that I'm not caught enough, to tell the truth. I begin to lose hope."

"Why, whatever hope can you have?" said Betsy, offended on behalf of her friend. "*Enendons nous....*" But in her eyes there were gleams of light that betrayed that she understood perfectly and precisely as he did what hope he might have.

"None whatever," said Vronsky, laughing and showing his even rows of teeth. "Excuse me," he added, taking an opera glass out of her hand, and proceeding to scrutinize, over her bare shoulder, the row of boxes facing them. "I'm afraid I'm becoming ridiculous."

He was very well aware that he ran no risk of being ridiculous in the eyes of Betsy or any other fashionable people. He was very well aware that in their eyes the position of an unsuccessful lover of a girl, or of any woman free to marry, might be ridiculous. But the position of a man pursuing a married woman, and, regardless of everything, staking his life on drawing her into adultery, has something fine and grand about it, and can never be ridiculous; and so it was with a proud and gay smile under his mustaches that he lowered the opera glass and looked at his cousin.

"But why was it you didn't come to dinner?" she said, admiring him.

"I must tell you about that. I was busily employed, and doing what, do you suppose? I'll give you a hundred guesses, a thousand...you'd never guess. I've been reconciling a husband with a man who'd insulted his wife. Yes, really!"

"Well, did you succeed?"

"Almost."

"You really must tell me about it," she said, getting up. "Come to me in the next *entr'acte*."

"I can't; I'm going to the French theater."

"From Nilsson?" Betsy queried in horror, though she could not herself have distinguished Nilsson's voice from any chorus girl's.

"Can't help it. I've an appointment there, all to do with my mission of peace."

"'Blessed are the peacemakers; theirs is the kingdom of heaven,'" said Betsy, vaguely recollecting she had heard some similar saying from someone. "Very well, then, sit down, and tell me what it's all about."

And she sat down again.

Princess Betsy drove home from the theater, without waiting for the end of the last act. She had only just time to go into her dressing room, sprinkle her long, pale face with powder, rub it, set her dress to rights, and order tea in the big drawing room, when one after another carriages drove up to her huge house in Bolshaia Morskaia. Her guests stepped out at the wide entrance, and the stout porter, who used to read the newspapers in the mornings behind the glass door, to the edification of the passers-by, noiselessly opened the immense door, letting the visitors pass by him into the house.

Almost at the same instant the hostess, with freshly arranged coiffure and freshened face, walked in at one door and her guests at the other door of the drawing room, a large room with dark walls, downy rugs, and a brightly lighted table, gleaming with the light of candles, white cloth, silver samovar, and transparent china tea things.

The hostess sat down at the table and took off her gloves. Chairs were set with the aid of footmen, moving almost imperceptibly about the room; the party settled itself, divided into two groups: one round the samovar near the hostess, the other at the opposite end of the drawing room, round the handsome wife of an ambassador, in black velvet, with sharply defined black eyebrows. In both groups conversation wavered, as it always does, for the first few minutes, broken up by meetings, greetings, offers of tea, and as it were, feeling about for something to rest upon.

"She's exceptionally good as an actress; one can see she's studied Kaulbach," said a diplomatic attache in the group round the ambassador's wife. "Did you notice how she fell down?..."

"Oh, please, don't let us talk about Nilsson! No one can possibly say anything new about her," said a fat, red-faced, flaxen-headed lady, without eyebrows and chignon, wearing an old silk dress. This was Princess Myakaya, noted for her simplicity and the roughness of her manners, and nicknamed *enfant terrible*. Princess Myakaya, sitting in the middle between the two groups, and listening to both, took part in the conversation first of one and then of the other. "Three people have used that very phrase about Kaulbach to me today already, just as though they had made a compact about it. And I can't see why they liked that remark so."

The conversation was cut short by this observation, and a new subject had to be thought of again.

"Do tell me something amusing but not spiteful," said the ambassador's wife, a great proficient in the art of that elegant conversation called by the English, *small talk*. She addressed the attache, who was at a loss now what to begin upon.

"They say that that's a difficult task, that nothing's amusing that isn't spiteful," he began with a smile. "But I'll try. Get me a subject. It all lies in the subject. If a subject's given me, it's easy to spin something round it. I often think that the celebrated talkers of the last century would have found it difficult to talk cleverly now. Everything clever is so stale..."

"That has been said long ago," the ambassador's wife interrupted him, laughing.

The conversation began amiably, but just because it was too amiable, it came to a stop again. They had to have recourse to the sure, never-failing topic—gossip.

"Don't you think there's something Louis Quinze about Tushkevitch?" he said, glancing towards a handsome, fair-haired young man, standing at the table.

"Oh, yes! He's in the same style as the drawing room and that's why it is he's so often here."

This conversation was maintained, since it rested on allusions to what could not be talked of in that room—that is to say, of the relations of Tushkevitch with their hostess.

Round the samovar and the hostess the conversation had been meanwhile vacillating in just the same way between three inevitable topics: the latest piece of public news, the theater, and scandal. It, too, came finally to rest on the last topic, that is, ill-natured gossip.

"Have you heard the Maltishtcheva woman—the mother, not the daughter—has ordered a costume in *diable rose* color?"

"Nonsense! No, that's too lovely!"

"I wonder that with her sense—for she's not a fool, you know— that she doesn't see how funny she is."

Everyone had something to say in censure or ridicule of the luckless Madame Maltishtcheva, and the conversation crackled merrily, like a burning faggot-stack.

The husband of Princess Betsy, a good-natured fat man, an ardent collector of engravings, hearing that his wife had visitors, came into the drawing room before going to his club. Stepping noiselessly over the thick rugs, he went up to Princess Myakaya.

"How did you like Nilsson?" he asked.

"Oh, how can you steal upon anyone like that! How you startled me!" she responded. "Please don't talk to me about the opera; you know nothing about music. I'd better meet you on your own ground, and talk about your majolica and engravings. Come now, what treasure have you been buying lately at the old curiosity shops?"

"Would you like me to show you? But you don't understand such things."

"Oh, do show me! I've been learning about them at those—what's their names?...the bankers...they've some splendid engravings. They showed them to us."

"Why, have you been at the Schützburgs?" asked the hostess from the samovar.

"Yes, *ma chere*. They asked my husband and me to dinner, and told us the sauce at that dinner cost a hundred pounds," Princess Myakaya said, speaking loudly, and conscious everyone was listening; "and very nasty sauce it was, some green mess. We had to ask them, and I made them sauce for eighteen pence, and everybody was very much pleased with it. I can't run to hundred-pound sauces."

"She's unique!" said the lady of the house.

"Marvelous!" said someone.

The sensation produced by Princess Myakaya's speeches was always unique, and the secret of the sensation she produced lay in the fact that though she spoke not always appropriately, as now, she said simple things with some sense in them. In the society in which she lived such plain statements produced the effect of the wittiest epigram. Princess Myakaya could never see why it had that effect, but she knew it had, and took advantage of it.

As everyone had been listening while Princess Myakaya spoke, and so the conversation around the ambassador's wife had dropped, Princess Betsy tried to bring the whole party together, and turned to the ambassador's wife.

"Will you really not have tea? You should come over here by us."

"No, we're very happy here," the ambassador's wife responded with a smile, and she went on with the conversation that had been begun.

"It was a very agreeable conversation. They were criticizing the Karenins, husband and wife.

"Anna is quite changed since her stay in Moscow. There's something strange about her," said her friend.

"The great change is that she brought back with her the shadow of Alexey Vronsky," said the ambassador's wife.

"Well, what of it? There's a fable of Grimm's about a man without a shadow, a man who's lost his shadow. And that's his punishment for something. I never could understand how it was a punishment. But a woman must dislike being without a shadow."

"Yes, but women with a shadow usually come to a bad end," said Anna's friend.

"Bad luck to your tongue!" said Princess Myakaya suddenly. "Madame Karenina's a splendid woman. I don't like her husband, but I like her very much."

"Why don't you like her husband? He's such a remarkable man," said the ambassador's wife. "My husband says there are few statesmen like him in Europe."

"And my husband tells me just the same, but I don't believe it," said Princess Myakaya. "If our husbands didn't talk to us, we should see the facts as they are. Alexey Alexandrovitch, to my thinking, is simply a fool. I say it in a whisper...but doesn't it really make everything clear? Before, when I was told to consider him clever, I kept looking for his ability, and thought myself a fool for not seeing it; but directly I said, *he's a fool*, though only in a whisper, everything's explained, isn't it?"

"How spiteful you are today!"

"Not a bit. I'd no other way out of it. One of the two had to be a fool. And, well, you know one can't say that of oneself."

"'No one is satisfied with his fortune, and everyone is satisfied with his wit.'" The attaché repeated the French saying.

"That's just it, just it," Princess Myakaya turned to him. "But the point is that I won't abandon Anna to your mercies. She's so nice, so charming. How can she help it if they're all in love with her, and follow her about like shadows?"

"Oh, I had no idea of blaming her for it," Anna's friend said in self-defense.

"If no one follows us about like a shadow, that's no proof that we've any right to blame her."

And having duly disposed of Anna's friend, the Princess Myakaya got up, and together with the ambassador's wife, joined the group at the table, where the conversation was dealing with the king of Prussia.

"What wicked gossip were you talking over there?" asked Betsy.

"About the Karenins. The princess gave us a sketch of Alexey Alexandrovitch," said the ambassador's wife with a smile, as she sat down at the table.

"Pity we didn't hear it!" said Princess Betsy, glancing towards the door. "Ah, here you are at last!" she said, turning with a smile to Vronsky, as he came in.

Vronsky was not merely acquainted with all the persons whom he was meeting here; he saw them all every day; and so he came in with the quiet manner with which one enters a room full of people from whom one has only just parted.

"Where do I come from?" he said, in answer to a question from the ambassador's wife. "Well, there's no help for it, I must confess. From the *opera bouffé*. I do believe I've seen it a hundred times, and always with fresh enjoyment. It's exquisite! I know it's disgraceful, but I go to sleep at the opera, and I sit out the *opera bouffé* to the last minute, and enjoy it. This evening..."

He mentioned a French actress, and was going to tell something about her; but the ambassador's wife, with playful horror, cut him short.

"Please don't tell us about that horror."

"All right, I won't especially as everyone knows those horrors."

"And we should all go to see them if it were accepted as the correct thing, like the opera," chimed in Princess Myakaya.

Steps were heard at the door, and Princess Betsy, knowing it was Madame Karenina, glanced at Vronsky. He was looking towards the door, and his face wore a strange new expression. Joyfully, intently, and at the same time timidly, he gazed at the approaching figure, and slowly he rose to his feet. Anna walked into the drawing room. Holding herself extremely erect, as always, looking straight before her, and moving with her swift, resolute, and light step, that distinguished her from all other society women, she crossed the short space to her hostess, shook hands with her, smiled, and with the same smile looked around at Vronsky. Vronsky bowed low and pushed a chair up for her.

She acknowledged this only by a slight nod, flushed a little, and frowned. But immediately, while rapidly greeting her acquaintances, and shaking the hands proffered to her, she addressed Princess Betsy:

"I have been at Countess Lidia's, and meant to have come here earlier, but I stayed on. Sir John was there. He's very interesting."

"Oh, that's this missionary?"

"Yes; he told us about the life in India, most interesting things."

The conversation, interrupted by her coming in, flickered up again like the light of a lamp being blown out.

"Sir John! Yes, Sir John; I've seen him. He speaks well. The Vlassieva girl's quite in love with him."

"And is it true the younger Vlassieva girl's to marry Topov?"

"Yes, they say it's quite a settled thing."

"I wonder at the parents! They say it's a marriage for love."

"For love? What antediluvian notions you have! Can one talk of love in these days?" said the ambassador's wife.

"What's to be done? It's a foolish old fashion that's kept up still," said Vronsky.

"So much the worse for those who keep up the fashion. The only happy marriages I know are marriages of prudence."

"Yes, but then how often the happiness of these prudent marriages flies away like dust just because that passion turns up that they have refused to recognize," said Vronsky.

"But by marriages of prudence we mean those in which both parties have sown their wild oats already. That's like scarlatina—one has to go through it and get it over."

"Then they ought to find out how to vaccinate for love, like smallpox."

"I was in love in my young days with a deacon," said the Princess Myakaya. "I don't know that it did me any good."

"No; I imagine, joking apart, that to know love, one must make mistakes and then correct them," said Princess Betsy.

"Even after marriage?" said the ambassador's wife playfully.

"'It's never too late to mend.'" The attaché repeated the English proverb.

"Just so," Betsy agreed; "one must make mistakes and correct them. What do you think about it?" she turned to Anna, who, with a faintly perceptible resolute smile on her lips, was listening in silence to the conversation.

"I think," said Anna, playing with the glove she had taken off, "I think...of so many men, so many minds, certainly so many hearts, so many kinds of love."

Vronsky was gazing at Anna, and with a fainting heart waiting for what she would say. He sighed as after a danger escaped when she uttered these words.

Anna suddenly turned to him.

"Oh, I have had a letter from Moscow. They write me that Kitty Shtcherbatskaya's very ill."

"Really?" said Vronsky, knitting his brows.

Anna looked sternly at him.

"That doesn't interest you?"

"On the contrary, it does, very much. What was it exactly they told you, if I may know?" he questioned.

Anna got up and went to Betsy.

"Give me a cup of tea," she said, standing at her table.

While Betsy was pouring out the tea, Vronsky went up to Anna.

"What is it they write to you?" he repeated.

"I often think men have no understanding of what's not honorable though they're always talking of it," said Anna, without answering him. "I've wanted to tell you so a long while," she added, and moving a few steps away, she sat down at a table in a corner covered with albums.

"I don't quite understand the meaning of your words," he said, handing her the cup.

She glanced towards the sofa beside her, and he instantly sat down.

"Yes, I have been wanting to tell you," she said, not looking at him. "You behaved wrongly, very wrongly."

"Do you suppose I don't know that I've acted wrongly? But who was the cause of my doing so?"

"What do you say that to me for?" she said, glancing severely at him.

"You know what for," he answered boldly and joyfully, meeting her glance and not dropping his eyes.

Not he, but she, was confused.

"That only shows you have no heart," she said. But her eyes said that she knew he had a heart, and that was why she was afraid of him.

"What you spoke of just now was a mistake, and not love."

"Remember that I have forbidden you to utter that word, that hateful word," said Anna, with a shudder. But at once she felt that by that very word "forbidden" she had shown that she acknowledged certain rights over him, and by that very fact was encouraging him to speak of love. "I have long meant to tell you this," she went on, looking resolutely into his eyes, and hot all over from the burning flush on her cheeks. "I've come on purpose this evening, knowing I should meet you. I have come to tell you that this must end. I have never blushed before anyone, and you force me to feel to blame for something."

He looked at her and was struck by a new spiritual beauty in her face.

"What do you wish of me?" he said simply and seriously.

"I want you to go to Moscow and ask for Kitty's forgiveness," she said.

"You don't wish that?" he said.

He saw she was saying what she forced herself to say, not what she wanted to say.

"If you love me, as you say," she whispered, "do so that I may be at peace."

His face grew radiant.

"Don't you know that you're all my life to me? But I know no peace, and I can't give it to you; all myself—and love...yes. I can't think of you and myself apart. You and I are one to me. And I see no chance before us of peace for me or for you. I see a chance of despair, of wretchedness...or I see a chance of bliss, what bliss!... Can it be there's no chance of it?" he murmured with his lips; but she heard.

She strained every effort of her mind to say what ought to be said. But instead of that she let her eyes rest on him, full of love, and made no answer.

"It's come!" he thought in ecstasy. "When I was beginning to despair, and it seemed there would be no end—it's come! She loves me! She owns it!"

"Then do this for me: never say such things to me, and let us be friends," she said in words; but her eyes spoke quite differently.

"Friends we shall never be, you know that yourself. Whether we shall be the happiest or the wretchedest of people—that's in your hands."

She would have said something, but he interrupted her.

"I ask one thing only: I ask for the right to hope, to suffer as I do. But if even that cannot be, command me to disappear, and I disappear. You shall not see me if my presence is distasteful to you."

"I don't want to drive you away."

"Only don't change anything, leave everything as it is," he said in a shaky voice. "Here's your husband."

At that instant Alexey Alexandrovitch did in fact walk into the room with his calm, awkward gait.

Glancing at his wife and Vronsky, he went up to the lady of the house, and sitting down for a cup of tea, began talking in his deliberate, always audible voice, in his habitual tone of banter, ridiculing someone.

"Your Rambouillet is in full conclave," he said, looking round at all the party; "the graces and the muses."

But Princess Betsy could not endure that tone of his— "sneering," as she called it, using the English word, and like a skillful hostess she at once brought him into a serious conversation on the subject of universal conscription. Alexey Alexandrovitch was immediately interested in the subject, and began seriously defending the new imperial decree against Princess Betsy, who had attacked it.

Vronsky and Anna still sat at the little table.

"This is getting indecorous," whispered one lady, with an expressive glance at Madame Karenina, Vronsky, and her husband.

"What did I tell you?" said Anna's friend.

But not only those ladies, almost everyone in the room, even the Princess Myakaya and Betsy herself, looked several times in the direction of the two who had withdrawn from the general circle, as though that were a disturbing fact. Alexey Alexandrovitch was the only person who did not once look in that direction, and was not diverted from the interesting discussion he had entered upon.

Noticing the disagreeable impression that was being made on everyone, Princess Betsy slipped someone else into her place to listen to Alexey Alexandrovitch, and went up to Anna.

"I'm always amazed at the clearness and precision of your husband's language," she said. "The most transcendental ideas seem to be within my grasp when he's speaking."

"Oh, yes!" said Anna, radiant with a smile of happiness, and not understanding a word of what Betsy had said. She crossed over to the big table and took part in the general conversation.

Alexey Alexandrovitch, after staying half an hour, went up to his wife and suggested that they should go home together. But she answered, not looking at him, that she was staying to supper. Alexey Alexandrovitch made his bows and withdrew.

The fat old Tatar, Madame Karenina's coachman, was with difficulty holding one of her pair of grays, chilled with the cold and rearing at the entrance. A footman stood opening the carriage door. The hall porter stood holding open the great door of the house. Anna Arkadyevna, with her quick little hand, was unfastening the lace of her sleeve, caught in the hook of her fur cloak, and with bent head listening to the words Vronsky murmured as he escorted her down.

"You've said nothing, of course, and I ask nothing," he was saying; "but you know that friendship's not what I want: that there's only one happiness in life for me, that word that you dislike so...yes, love!..."

"Love," she repeated slowly, in an inner voice, and suddenly, at the very instant she unhooked the lace, she added, "Why I don't like the word is that it means too much to me, far more than you can understand," and she glanced into his face. "*Au revoir!*"

She gave him her hand, and with her rapid, springy step she passed by the porter and vanished into the carriage.

Her glance, the touch of her hand, set him aflame. He kissed the palm of his hand where she had touched it, and went home, happy in the sense that he had got nearer to the attainment of his aims that evening than during the last two months.

In the early days after his return from Moscow, whenever Levin shuddered and grew red, remembering the disgrace of his rejection, he said to himself: "This was just how I used to shudder and blush, thinking myself utterly lost, when I was plucked in physics and did not get my remove; and how I thought myself utterly ruined after I had mismanaged that affair of my sister's that was entrusted to me. And yet, now that years have passed, I recall it and wonder that it could distress me so much. It will be the same thing too with this trouble. Time will go by and I shall not mind about this either."

But three months had passed and he had not left off minding about it; and it was as painful for him to think of it as it had been those first days. He could not be at peace because after dreaming so long of family life, and feeling himself so ripe for it, he was still not married, and was further than ever from marriage. He was painfully conscious himself, as were all about him, that at his years it is not well for man to be alone. He remembered how before starting for Moscow he had once said to his cowman Nikolay, a simple-hearted peasant, whom he liked talking to: "Well, Nikolay! I mean to get married," and how Nikolay had promptly answered, as of a matter on which there could be no possible doubt: "And high time too,

Konstantin Demitrievitch." But marriage had now become further off than ever. The place was taken, and whenever he tried to imagine any of the girls he knew in that place, he felt that it was utterly impossible. Moreover, the recollection of the rejection and the part he had played in the affair tortured him with shame. However often he told himself that he was in no wise to blame in it, that recollection, like other humiliating reminiscences of a similar kind, made him twinge and blush. There had been in his past, as in every man's, actions, recognized by him as bad, for which his conscience ought to have tormented him; but the memory of these evil actions was far from causing him so much suffering as those trivial but humiliating reminiscences. These wounds never healed. And with these memories was now ranged his rejection and the pitiful position in which he must have appeared to others that evening. But time and work did their part. Bitter memories were more and more covered up by the incidents—paltry in his eyes, but really important—of his country life. Every week he thought less often of Kitty. He was impatiently looking forward to the news that she was married, or just going to be married, hoping that such news would, like having a tooth out, completely cure him.

Meanwhile spring came on, beautiful and kindly, without the delays and treacheries of spring,—one of those rare springs in which plants, beasts, and man rejoice alike. This lovely spring roused Levin still more, and strengthened him in his resolution of renouncing all his past and building up his lonely life firmly and independently. Though many of the plans with which he had returned to the country had not been carried out, still his most important resolution—that of purity—had been kept by him. He was free from that shame, which had usually harassed him after a fall; and he could look everyone straight in the face. In February he had received a letter from Marya Nikolaevna telling him that his brother Nikolay's health was getting worse, but that he would not take advice, and in consequence of this letter Levin went to Moscow to his brother's and succeeded in persuading him to see a doctor and to go to a watering-place abroad. He succeeded so well in persuading his brother, and in lending him money for the journey without irritating him, that he was satisfied with himself in that matter. In addition to his farming, which called for special attention in spring, and in addition to reading, Levin had begun that winter a work on agriculture, the plan of which turned on taking into account the character of the laborer on the land as one of the unalterable data of the question, like the climate and the soil, and consequently deducing all the principles of scientific culture, not simply from the data of soil and climate, but from the data of soil, climate, and a certain unalterable character of the laborer. Thus, in spite of his solitude, or in consequence of his solitude, his life was exceedingly full. Only rarely he suffered from an unsatisfied desire to communicate his stray ideas to someone besides Agafea Mihalovna. With her indeed he not infrequently fell into discussion upon physics, the theory of agriculture, and especially philosophy; philosophy was Agafea Mihalovna's favorite subject.

Spring was slow in unfolding. For the last few weeks it had been steadily fine frosty weather. In the daytime it thawed in the sun, but at night there were even seven degrees of frost. There was such a frozen surface on the snow that they drove the wagons anywhere off the roads. Easter came in the snow. Then all of a sudden, on Easter Monday, a warm wind sprang up, storm clouds swooped down, and for three days and three nights the warm, driving rain fell in streams. On Thursday the wind dropped, and a thick gray fog brooded over the land as though hiding the mysteries of the transformations that were being wrought in nature. Behind the fog there was the flowing of water, the cracking and floating of ice, the swift rush of turbid, foaming torrents; and on the following Monday, in the evening, the fog parted, the storm clouds split up into little curling crests of cloud, the sky cleared, and the real spring had come. In the morning the sun rose brilliant and quickly wore away the thin layer of ice that covered the water, and all the warm air was quivering with the steam that rose up from the quickened earth. The old grass looked greener, and the young grass thrust up its tiny blades; the buds of the guelder-rose and of the currant and the sticky birch-buds were swollen with sap, and an exploring bee was humming about the golden blossoms that studded the willow. Larks trilled unseen above the velvety green fields and the ice-covered stubble-land; peewits wailed over the low lands and marshes flooded by the pools; cranes and wild geese flew high across the sky uttering their spring calls. The cattle, bald in patches where the new hair had not grown yet, lowed in the pastures; the bowlegged lambs frisked round their bleating mothers. Nimble children ran about the drying paths, covered with the prints of bare feet. There was a merry chatter of peasant women over their linen at the pond, and the ring of axes in the yard, where the peasants were repairing ploughs and harrows. The real spring had come.

Levin put on his big boots, and, for the first time, a cloth jacket, instead of his fur cloak, and went out to look after his farm, stepping over streams of water that flashed in the sunshine and dazzled his eyes, and treading one minute on ice and the next into sticky mud.

Spring is the time of plans and projects. And, as he came out into the farmyard, Levin, like a tree in spring that knows not what form will be taken by the young shoots and twigs imprisoned in its swelling buds, hardly knew what undertakings he was going to begin upon now in the farm work that was so dear to him. But he felt that he was full of the most splendid plans and projects. First of all he went to the cattle. The cows had been let out into their paddock, and their smooth sides were already shining with their new, sleek, spring coats; they basked in the sunshine and lowed to go to the meadow. Levin gazed admiringly at the cows he knew so intimately to the minutest detail of their condition, and gave orders for them to be driven out into the meadow, and the calves to be let into the paddock. The herdsman ran gaily to get ready for the meadow. The cowherd girls, picking up their petticoats, ran splashing through the mud with bare legs, still white, not yet brown from the sun, waving brush wood in their hands, chasing the calves that frolicked in the mirth of spring.

After admiring the young ones of that year, who were particularly fine—the early calves were the size of a peasant's cow, and Pava's daughter, at three months old, was as big as a yearling— Levin gave orders for a trough to be brought out and for them to be fed in the paddock. But it appeared that as the paddock had not been used during the winter, the hurdles made in the autumn for it were broken. He sent for the carpenter, who, according to his orders, ought to have been at work at the thrashing machine. But it appeared that the carpenter was repairing the harrows, which ought to have been repaired before Lent. This was very annoying to Levin. It was annoying to come upon that everlasting slovenliness in the farm work against which he had been striving with all his might for so many years. The hurdles, as he ascertained, being not wanted in winter, had been carried to the cart-horses' stable; and there broken, as they were of light construction, only meant for feeding calves. Moreover, it was apparent also that the harrows and all the agricultural implements, which he had directed to be looked over and repaired in the winter, for which very purpose he had hired three carpenters, had not been put into repair, and the harrows were being repaired when they ought to have been harrowing the field. Levin sent for his bailiff, but immediately went off himself to look for him. The bailiff, beaming all over, like everyone that day, in a sheepskin bordered with astrachan, came out of the barn, twisting a bit of straw in his hands.

"Why isn't the carpenter at the thrashing machine?"

"Oh, I meant to tell you yesterday, the harrows want repairing. Here it's time they got to work in the fields."

"But what were they doing in the winter, then?"

"But what did you want the carpenter for?"

"Where are the hurdles for the calves' paddock?"

"I ordered them to be got ready. What would you have with those peasants!" said the bailiff, with a wave of his hand.

"It's not those peasants but this bailiff!" said Levin, getting angry. "Why, what do I keep you for?" he cried. But, bethinking himself that this would not help matters, he stopped short in the middle of a sentence, and merely sighed. "Well, what do you say? Can sowing begin?" he asked, after a pause.

"Behind Turkin tomorrow or the next day they might begin."

"And the clover?"

"I've sent Vassily and Mishka; they're sowing. Only I don't know if they'll manage to get through; it's so slushy."

"How many acres?"

"About fifteen."

"Why not sow all?" cried Levin.

That they were only sowing the clover on fifteen acres, not on all the forty-five, was still more annoying to him. Clover, as he knew, both from books and from his own experience, never did well except when it was sown as early as possible, almost in the snow. And yet Levin could never get this done.

"There's no one to send. What would you have with such a set of peasants? Three haven't turned up. And there's Semyon..."

"Well, you should have taken some men from the thatching."

"And so I have, as it is."

"Where are the peasants, then?"

"Five are making compôte" (which meant compost), "four are shifting the oats for fear of a touch of mildew, Konstantin Dmitrievitch."

Levin knew very well that "a touch of mildew" meant that his English seed oats were already ruined. Again they had not done as he had ordered.

"Why, but I told you during Lent to put in pipes," he cried.

"Don't put yourself out; we shall get it all done in time."

Levin waved his hand angrily, went into the granary to glance at the oats, and then to the stable. The oats were not yet spoiled. But the peasants were carrying the oats in spades when they might simply let them slide down into the lower granary; and arranging for this to be done, and taking two workmen from there for sowing clover, Levin got over his vexation with the bailiff. Indeed, it was such a lovely day that one could not be angry.

"Ignat!" he called to the coachman, who, with his sleeves tucked up, was washing the carriage wheels, "saddle me..."

"Which, sir?"

"Well, let it be Kolpik."

"Yes, sir."

While they were saddling his horse, Levin again called up the bailiff, who was hanging about in sight, to make it up with him, and began talking to him about the spring operations before them, and his plans for the farm.

The wagons were to begin carting manure earlier, so as to get all done before the early mowing. And the ploughing of the further land to go on without a break so as to let it ripen lying fallow. And the mowing to be all done by hired labor, not on half-profits. The bailiff listened attentively, and obviously made an effort to approve of his employer's projects. But still he had that look Levin knew so well that always irritated him, a look of hopelessness and despondency. That look said: "That's all very well, but as God wills."

Nothing mortified Levin so much as that tone. But it was the tone common to all the bailiffs he had ever had. They had all taken up that attitude to his plans, and so now he was not angered by it, but mortified, and felt all the more roused to struggle against this, as it seemed, elemental force continually ranged against him, for which he could find no other expression than "as God wills."

"If we can manage it, Konstantin Dmitrievitch," said the bailiff.

"Why ever shouldn't you manage it?"

"We positively must have another fifteen laborers. And they don't turn up. There were some here today asking seventy roubles for the summer."

Levin was silent. Again he was brought face to face with that opposing force. He knew that however much they tried, they could not hire more than forty—thirty-seven perhaps or thirty-eight— laborers for a reasonable sum. Some forty had been taken on, and there were no more. But still he could not help struggling against it.

"Send to Sury, to Tchefirovka; if they don't come we must look for them."

"Oh, I'll send, to be sure," said Vassily Fedorovitch despondently. "But there are the horses, too, they're not good for much."

"We'll get some more. I know, of course," Levin added laughing, "you always want to do with as little and as poor quality as possible; but this year I'm not going to let you have things your own way. I'll see to everything myself."

"Why, I don't think you take much rest as it is. It cheers us up to work under the master's eye..."

"So they're sowing clover behind the Birch Dale? I'll go and have a look at them," he said, getting on to the little bay cob, Kolpik, who was led up by the coachman.

"You can't get across the streams, Konstantin Dmitrievitch," the coachman shouted.

"All right, I'll go by the forest."

And Levin rode through the slush of the farmyard to the gate and out into the open country, his good little horse, after his long inactivity, stepping out gallantly, snorting over the pools, and asking, as it were, for guidance. If Levin had felt happy before in the cattle pens and farmyard, he felt happier yet in the open country. Swaying rhythmically with the ambling paces of his good little cob, drinking in the warm yet fresh scent of the snow and the air, as he rode through his forest over the crumbling, wasted snow, still left in parts, and covered with dissolving tracks, he rejoiced over every tree, with the moss reviving on its bark and the buds swelling on its shoots. When he came out of the forest, in the immense plain before him, his grass fields stretched in an unbroken carpet of green, without one bare place or swamp, only spotted here and there in the hollows with patches of melting snow. He was not put out of temper even by the sight of the peasants' horses and colts trampling down his young grass (he told a peasant he met to drive them out), nor by the sarcastic and stupid reply of the peasant Ipat, whom he met on the way, and asked, "Well, Ipat, shall we soon be sowing?" "We must get the ploughing done first, Konstantin Dmitrievitch," answered Ipat. The further he rode, the happier he became, and plans for the land rose to his mind each better than the last; to plant all his fields with hedges along the southern borders, so that the snow should not lie under them; to divide them up into six fields of arable and three of pasture and hay; to build a cattle yard at the further end of the estate, and to dig a pond and to construct movable pens for the cattle as a means of manuring the land. And then eight hundred acres of wheat, three hundred of potatoes, and four hundred of clover, and not one acre exhausted.

Absorbed in such dreams, carefully keeping his horse by the hedges, so as not to trample his young crops, he rode up to the laborers who had been sent to sow clover. A cart with the seed in it was standing, not at the edge, but in the middle of the crop, and the winter corn had been torn up by the wheels and trampled by the horse. Both the laborers were sitting in the hedge, probably smoking a pipe together. The earth in the cart, with which the seed was mixed, was not crushed to powder, but crusted together or adhering in clods. Seeing the master, the laborer, Vassily, went towards the cart, while Mishka set to work sowing. This was not as it should be, but with the laborers Levin seldom lost his temper. When Vassily came up, Levin told him to lead the horse to the hedge.

"It's all right, sir, it'll spring up again," responded Vassily.

"Please don't argue," said Levin, "but do as you're told."

"Yes, sir," answered Vassily, and he took the horse's head. "What a sowing, Konstantin Dmitrievitch," he said, hesitating; "first rate. Only it's a work to get about! You drag a ton of earth on your shoes."

"Why is it you have earth that's not sifted?" said Levin.

"Well, we crumble it up," answered Vassily, taking up some seed and rolling the earth in his palms.

Vassily was not to blame for their having filled up his cart with unsifted earth, but still it was annoying.

Levin had more than once already tried a way he knew for stifling his anger, and turning all that seemed dark right again, and he tried that way now. He watched how Mishka strode along, swinging the huge clods of earth that clung to each foot; and getting off his horse, he took the sieve from Vassily and started sowing himself.

"Where did you stop?"

Vassily pointed to the mark with his foot, and Levin went forward as best he could, scattering the seed on the land. Walking was as difficult as on a bog, and by the time Levin had ended the row he was in a great heat, and he stopped and gave up the sieve to Vassily.

"Well, master, when summer's here, mind you don't scold me for these rows," said Vassily.

"Eh?" said Levin cheerily, already feeling the effect of his method.

"Why, you'll see in the summer time. It'll look different. Look you where I sowed last spring. How I did work at it! I do my best, Konstantin Dmitrievitch, d'ye see, as I would for my own father. I don't like bad work myself, nor would I let another man do it. What's good for the master's good for us too. To look out yonder now," said Vassily, pointing, "it does one's heart good."

"It's a lovely spring, Vassily."

"Why, it's a spring such as the old men don't remember the like of. I was up home; an old man up there has sown wheat too, about an acre of it. He was saying you wouldn't know it from rye."

"Have you been sowing wheat long?"

"Why, sir, it was you taught us the year before last. You gave me two measures. We sold about eight bushels and sowed a rood."

"Well, mind you crumble up the clods," said Levin, going towards his horse, "and keep an eye on Mishka. And if there's a good crop you shall have half a rouble for every acre."

"Humbly thankful. We are very well content, sir, as it is."

Levin got on his horse and rode towards the field where was last year's clover, and the one which was ploughed ready for the spring corn.

The crop of clover coming up in the stubble was magnificent. It had survived everything, and stood up vividly green through the broken stalks of last year's wheat. The horse sank in up to the pasterns, and he drew each hoof with a sucking sound out of the half-thawed ground. Over the ploughland riding was utterly impossible; the horse could only keep a foothold where there was ice, and in the thawing furrows he sank deep in at each step. The ploughland was in splendid condition; in a couple of days it would be fit for harrowing and sowing. Everything was capital, everything was cheering. Levin rode back across the streams, hoping the water would have gone down. And he did in fact get across, and startled two ducks. "There must be snipe too," he thought, and just as he reached the turning homewards he met the forest keeper, who confirmed his theory about the snipe.

Levin went home at a trot, so as to have time to eat his dinner and get his gun ready for the evening.

As he rode up to the house in the happiest frame of mind, Levin heard the bell ring at the side of the principal entrance of the house.

"Yes, that's someone from the railway station," he thought, "just the time to be here from the Moscow train...Who could it be? What if it's brother Nikolay? He did say: 'Maybe I'll go to the waters, or maybe I'll come down to you.'" He felt dismayed and vexed for the first minute, that his brother Nikolay's presence should come to disturb his happy mood of spring. But he felt ashamed of the feeling, and at once he opened, as it were, the arms of his soul, and with a softened feeling of joy and expectation, now he hoped with all his heart that it was his brother. He pricked up his horse, and riding out from behind the acacias he saw a hired three-horse sledge from the railway station, and a gentleman in a fur coat. It was not his brother. "Oh, if it were only some nice person one could talk to a little!" he thought.

"Ah," cried Levin joyfully, flinging up both his hands. "Here's a delightful visitor! Ah, how glad I am to see you!" he shouted, recognizing Stepan Arkadyevitch.

"I shall find out for certain whether she's married, or when she's going to be married," he thought. And on that delicious spring day he felt that the thought of her did not hurt him at all.

"Well, you didn't expect me, eh?" said Stepan Arkadyevitch, getting out of the sledge, splashed with mud on the bridge of his nose, on his cheek, and on his eyebrows, but radiant with health and good spirits. "I've come to see you in the first place," he said, embracing and kissing him, "to have some stand-shooting second, and to sell the forest at Ergushovo third."

"Delightful! What a spring we're having! How ever did you get along in a sledge?"

"In a cart it would have been worse still, Konstantin Dmitrievitch," answered the driver, who knew him.

"Well, I'm very, very glad to see you," said Levin, with a genuine smile of childlike delight.

Levin led his friend to the room set apart for visitors, where Stepan Arkadyevitch's things were carried also—a bag, a gun in a case, a satchel for cigars. Leaving him there to wash and change his clothes, Levin went off to the counting house to speak about the ploughing and clover. Agafea Mihalovna, always very anxious for the credit of the house, met him in the hall with inquiries about dinner.

"Do just as you like, only let it be as soon as possible," he said, and went to the bailiff.

When he came back, Stepan Arkadyevitch, washed and combed, came out of his room with a beaming smile, and they went upstairs together.

"Well, I am glad I managed to get away to you! Now I shall understand what the mysterious business is that you are always absorbed in here. No, really, I envy you. What a house, how nice it all is! So bright, so cheerful!" said Stepan Arkadyevitch, forgetting that it was not always spring and fine weather like that day. "And your nurse is simply charming! A pretty maid in an apron might be even more agreeable, perhaps; but for your severe monastic style it does very well."

Stepan Arkadyevitch told him many interesting pieces of news; especially interesting to Levin was the news that his brother, Sergey Ivanovitch, was intending to pay him a visit in the summer.

Not one word did Stepan Arkadyevitch say in reference to Kitty and the Shtcherbatskys; he merely gave him greetings from his wife. Levin was grateful to him for his delicacy and was very glad of his visitor. As always happened with him during his solitude, a mass of ideas and feelings had been accumulating within him, which he could not communicate to those about him. And now he poured out upon Stepan Arkadyevitch his poetic joy in the spring, and his failures and plans for the land, and his thoughts and criticisms on the books he had been reading, and the idea of his own book, the basis of which really was, though he was unaware of it himself, a criticism of all the old books on agriculture. Stepan Arkadyevitch, always charming, understanding everything at the slightest reference, was particularly charming on this visit, and Levin noticed in him a special tenderness, as it were, and a new tone of respect that flattered him.

The efforts of Agafea Mihalovna and the cook, that the dinner should be particularly good, only ended in the two famished friends attacking the preliminary course, eating a great deal of bread and butter, salt goose and salted mushrooms, and in Levin's finally ordering the soup to be served without the accompaniment of little pies, with which the cook had particularly meant to impress their visitor. But though Stepan Arkadyevitch was accustomed to very different dinners, he thought everything excellent: the herb brandy, and the bread, and the butter, and above all the salt goose and the mushrooms, and the nettle soup, and the chicken in white sauce, and the white Crimean wine— everything was superb and delicious.

"Splendid, splendid!" he said, lighting a fat cigar after the roast. "I feel as if, coming to you, I had landed on a peaceful shore after the noise and jolting of a steamer. And so you maintain that the laborer himself is an element to be studied and to regulate the choice of methods in agriculture. Of course, I'm an ignorant outsider; but I should fancy theory and its application will have its influence on the laborer too."

"Yes, but wait a bit. I'm not talking of political economy, I'm talking of the science of agriculture. It ought to be like the natural sciences, and to observe given phenomena and the laborer in his economic, ethnographical..."

At that instant Agafea Mihalovna came in with jam.

"Oh, Agafea Mihalovna," said Stepan Arkadyevitch, kissing the tips of his plump fingers, "what salt goose, what herb brandy!...What do you think, isn't it time to start, Kostya?" he added.

Levin looked out of the window at the sun sinking behind the bare tree-tops of the forest.

"Yes, it's time," he said. "Kouzma, get ready the trap," and he ran downstairs.

Stepan Arkadyevitch, going down, carefully took the canvas cover off his varnished gun case with his own hands, and opening it, began to get ready his expensive new-fashioned gun. Kouzma, who already scented a big tip, never left Stepan Arkadyevitch's side, and put on him both his stockings and boots, a task which Stepan Arkadyevitch readily left him.

"Kostya, give orders that if the merchant Ryabinin comes...I told him to come today, he's to be brought in and to wait for me..."

"Why, do you mean to say you're selling the forest to Ryabinin?"

"Yes. Do you know him?"

"To be sure I do. I have had to do business with him, 'positively and conclusively.'"

Stepan Arkadyevitch laughed. "Positively and conclusively" were the merchant's favorite words.

"Yes, it's wonderfully funny the way he talks. She knows where her master's going!" he added, patting Laska, who hung about Levin, whining and licking his hands, his boots, and his gun.

The trap was already at the steps when they went out.

"I told them to bring the trap round; or would you rather walk?"

"No, we'd better drive," said Stepan Arkadyevitch, getting into the trap. He sat down, tucked the tiger-skin rug round him, and lighted a cigar. "How is it you don't smoke? A cigar is a sort of thing, not exactly a pleasure, but the crown and outward sign of pleasure. Come, this is life! How splendid it is! This is how I should like to live!"

"Why, who prevents you?" said Levin, smiling.

"No, you're a lucky man! You've got everything you like. You like horses—and you have them; dogs—you have them; shooting— you have it; farming—you have it."

"Perhaps because I rejoice in what I have, and don't fret for what I haven't," said Levin, thinking of Kitty.

Stepan Arkadyevitch comprehended, looked at him, but said nothing.

Levin was grateful to Oblonsky for noticing, with his never-failing tact, that he dreaded conversation about the Shtcherbatskys, and so saying nothing about them. But now Levin was longing to find out what was tormenting him so, yet he had not the courage to begin.

"Come, tell me how things are going with you," said Levin, bethinking himself that it was not nice of him to think only of himself.

Stepan Arkadyevitch's eyes sparkled merrily.

"You don't admit, I know, that one can be fond of new rolls when one has had one's rations of bread—to your mind it's a crime; but I don't count life as life without love," he said, taking Levin's question his own way. "What am I to do? I'm made that way. And really, one does so little harm to anyone, and gives oneself so much pleasure..."

"What! is there something new, then?" queried Levin.

"Yes, my boy, there is! There, do you see, you know the type of Ossian's women.... Women, such as one sees in dreams.... Well, these women are sometimes to be met in reality...and these women are terrible. Woman, don't you know, is such a subject that however much you study it, it's always perfectly new."

"Well, then, it would be better not to study it."

"No. Some mathematician has said that enjoyment lies in the search for truth, not in the finding it."

Levin listened in silence, and in spite of all the efforts he made, he could not in the least enter into the feelings of his friend and understand his sentiments and the charm of studying such women.

On the way home Levin asked all details of Kitty's illness and the Shtcherbatskys' plans, and though he would have been ashamed to admit it, he was pleased at what he heard. He was pleased that there was still hope, and still more pleased that she should be suffering who had made him suffer so much. But when Stepan Arkadyevitch began to speak of the causes of Kitty's illness, and mentioned Vronsky's name, Levin cut him short.

"I have no right whatever to know family matters, and, to tell the truth, no interest in them either."

Stepan Arkadyevitch smiled hardly perceptibly, catching the instantaneous change he knew so well in Levin's face, which had become as gloomy as it had been bright a minute before.

"Have you quite settled about the forest with Ryabinin?" asked Levin.

"Yes, it's settled. The price is magnificent; thirty-eight thousand. Eight straight away, and the rest in six years. I've been bothering about it for ever so long. No one would give more."

"Then you've as good as given away your forest for nothing," said Levin gloomily.

"How do you mean for nothing?" said Stepan Arkadyevitch with a good-humored smile, knowing that nothing would be right in Levin's eyes now.

"Because the forest is worth at least a hundred and fifty roubles the acre," answered Levin.

"Oh, these farmers!" said Stepan Arkadyevitch playfully. "Your tone of contempt for us poor townsfolk!... But when it comes to business, we do it better than anyone. I assure you I have reckoned it all out," he said, "and the forest is fetching a very good price—so much so that I'm afraid of this fellow's crying off, in fact. You know it's not 'timber,'" said Stepan Arkadyevitch, hoping by this distinction to convince Levin completely of the unfairness of his doubts. "And it won't run to more than twenty-five yards of fagots per acre, and he's giving me at the rate of seventy roubles the acre."

Levin smiled contemptuously. "I know," he thought, "that fashion not only in him, but in all city people, who, after being twice in ten years in the country, pick up two or three phrases and use them in season and out of season, firmly persuaded that they know all about it. 'Timber, run to so many yards the acre.' He says those words without understanding them himself."

"I wouldn't attempt to teach you what you write about in your office," said he, "and if need arose, I should come to you to ask about it. But you're so positive you know all the lore of the forest. It's difficult. Have you counted the trees?"

"How count the trees?" said Stepan Arkadyevitch, laughing, still trying to draw his friend out of his ill-temper. "Count the sands of the sea, number the stars. Some higher power might do it."

"Oh, well, the higher power of Ryabinin can. Not a single merchant ever buys a forest without counting the trees, unless they get it given them for nothing, as you're doing now. I know your forest. I go there every year shooting, and your forest's worth a hundred and fifty roubles an acre paid down, while he's giving you sixty by installments. So that in fact you're making him a present of thirty thousand."

"Come, don't let your imagination run away with you," said Stepan Arkadyevitch piteously. "Why was it none would give it, then?"

"Why, because he has an understanding with the merchants; he's bought them off. I've had to do with all of them; I know them. They're not merchants, you know: they're speculators. He wouldn't look at a bargain that gave him ten, fifteen per cent profit, but holds back to buy a rouble's worth for twenty kopecks."

"Well, enough of it! You're out of temper."

"Not the least," said Levin gloomily, as they drove up to the house.

At the steps there stood a trap tightly covered with iron and leather, with a sleek horse tightly harnessed with broad collar-straps. In the trap sat the chubby, tightly belted clerk who served Ryabinin as coachman. Ryabinin himself was already in the house, and met the friends in the hall. Ryabinin was a tall, thinnish, middle-aged man, with mustache and a projecting clean-shaven chin, and prominent muddy-looking eyes. He was dressed in a long-skirted blue coat, with buttons below the waist at the back, and wore high boots wri

nkled over the ankles and straight over the calf, with big galoshes drawn over them. He rubbed his face with his handkerchief, and wrapping round him his coat, which sat extremely well as it was, he greeted them with a smile, holding out his hand to Stepan Arkadyevitch, as though he wanted to catch something.

"So here you are," said Stepan Arkadyevitch, giving him his hand. "That's capital."

"I did not venture to disregard your excellency's commands, though the road was extremely bad. I positively walked the whole way, but I am here at my time. Konstantin Dmitrievitch, my respects"; he turned to Levin, trying to seize his hand too. But Levin, scowling, made as though he did not notice his hand, and took out the snipe. "Your honors have been diverting yourselves with the chase? What kind of bird may it be, pray?" added Ryabinin, looking contemptuously at the snipe: "a great delicacy, I suppose." And he shook his head disapprovingly, as though he had grave doubts whether this game were worth the candle.

"Would you like to go into my study?" Levin said in French to Stepan Arkadyevitch, scowling morosely. "Go into my study; you can talk there."

"Quite so, where you please," said Ryabinin with contemptuous dignity, as though wishing to make it felt that others might be in difficulties as to how to behave, but that he could never be in any difficulty about anything.

On entering the study Ryabinin looked about, as his habit was, as though seeking the holy picture, but when he had found it, he did not cross himself. He scanned the bookcases and bookshelves, and with the same dubious air with which he had regarded the snipe, he smiled contemptuously and shook his head disapprovingly, as though by no means willing to allow that this game were worth the candle.

"Well, have you brought the money?" asked Oblonsky. "Sit down."

"Oh, don't trouble about the money. I've come to see you to talk it over."

"What is there to talk over? But do sit down."

"I don't mind if I do," said Ryabinin, sitting down and leaning his elbows on the back of his chair in a position of the intensest discomfort to himself. "You must knock it down a bit, prince. It would be too bad. The money is ready conclusively to the last farthing. As to paying the money down, there'll be no hitch there."

Levin, who had meanwhile been putting his gun away in the cupboard, was just going out of the door, but catching the merchant's words, he stopped.

"Why, you've got the forest for nothing as it is," he said. "He came to me too late, or I'd have fixed the price for him."

Ryabinin got up, and in silence, with a smile, he looked Levin down and up.

"Very close about money is Konstantin Dmitrievitch," he said with a smile, turning to Stepan Arkadyevitch; "there's positively no dealing with him. I was bargaining for some wheat of him, and a pretty price I offered too."

"Why should I give you my goods for nothing? I didn't pick it up on the ground, nor steal it either."

"Mercy on us! nowadays there's no chance at all of stealing. With the open courts and everything done in style, nowadays there's no question of stealing. We are just talking things over like gentlemen. His excellency's asking too much for the forest. I can't make both ends meet over it. I must ask for a little concession."

"But is the thing settled between you or not? If it's settled, it's useless haggling; but if it's not," said Levin, "I'll buy the forest."

The smile vanished at once from Ryabinin's face. A hawklike, greedy, cruel expression was left upon it. With rapid, bony fingers he unbuttoned his coat, revealing a shirt, bronze waistcoat buttons, and a watch chain, and quickly pulled out a fat old pocketbook.

"Here you are, the forest is mine," he said, crossing himself quickly, and holding out his hand. "Take the money; it's my forest. That's Ryabinin's way of doing business; he doesn't haggle over every half-penny," he added, scowling and waving the pocketbook.

"I wouldn't be in a hurry if I were you," said Levin.

"Come, really," said Oblonsky in surprise. "I've given my word, you know."

Levin went out of the room, slamming the door. Ryabinin looked towards the door and shook his head with a smile.

"It's all youthfulness—positively nothing but boyishness. Why, I'm buying it, upon my honor, simply, believe me, for the glory of it, that Ryabinin, and no one else, should have bought the copse of Oblonsky. And as to the profits, why, I must make what God gives. In God's name. If you would kindly sign the title-deed..."

Within an hour the merchant, stroking his big overcoat neatly down, and hooking up his jacket, with the agreement in his pocket, seated himself in his tightly covered trap, and drove homewards.

"Ugh, these gentlefolks!" he said to the clerk. "They—they're a nice lot!"

"That's so," responded the clerk, handing him the reins and buttoning the leather apron. "But I can congratulate you on the purchase, Mihail Ignatitch?"

"Well, well..."

Although all Vronsky's inner life was absorbed in his passion, his external life unalterably and inevitably followed along the old accustomed lines of his social and regimental ties and interests. The interests of his regiment took an important place in Vronsky's life, both because he was fond of the regiment, and because the regiment was fond of him. They were not only fond of Vronsky in his regiment, they respected him too, and were proud of him; proud that this man, with his immense wealth, his brilliant education and abilities, and the path open before him to every kind of success, distinction, and ambition, had disregarded all that, and of all the interests of life had the interests of his regiment and his comrades nearest to his heart. Vronsky was aware of his comrades' view of him, and in addition to his liking for the life, he felt bound to keep up that reputation.

It need not be said that he did not speak of his love to any of his comrades, nor did he betray his secret even in the wildest drinking bouts (though indeed he was never so drunk as to lose all control of himself). And he shut up any of his thoughtless comrades who attempted to allude to his connection. But in spite of that, his love was known to all the town; everyone guessed with more or less confidence at his relations with Madame Karenina. The majority of the younger men envied him for just what was the most irksome factor in his love—the exalted position of Karenin, and the consequent publicity of their connection in society.

The greater number of the young women, who envied Anna and had long been weary of hearing her called *virtuous*, rejoiced at the fulfillment of their predictions, and were only waiting for a decisive turn in public opinion to fall upon her with all the weight of their scorn. They were already making ready their handfuls of mud to fling at her when the right moment arrived. The greater number of the middle-aged people and certain great personages were displeased at the prospect of the impending scandal in society.

Vronsky's mother, on hearing of his connection, was at first pleased at it, because nothing to her mind gave such a finishing touch to a brilliant young man as a *liaison* in the highest society; she was pleased, too, that Madame Karenina, who had so taken her fancy, and had talked so much of her son, was, after all, just like all other pretty and well-bred women,—at least according to the Countess Vronskaya's ideas. But she had heard of late that her son had refused a position offered him of great importance to his career, simply in order to remain in the regiment, where he could be constantly seeing Madame Karenina. She learned that great personages were displeased with him on this account, and she changed her opinion. She was vexed, too, that from all she could learn of this connection it was not that brilliant, graceful, worldly *liaison* which she would have welcomed, but a sort of Wertherish, desperate passion, so she was told, which might well lead him into imprudence. She had not seen him since his abrupt departure from Moscow, and she sent her elder son to bid him come to see her.

This elder son, too, was displeased with his younger brother. He did not distinguish what sort of love his might be, big or little, passionate or passionless, lasting or passing (he kept a ballet girl himself, though he was the father of a family, so he was lenient in these matters), but he knew that this love affair was viewed with displeasure by those whom it was necessary to please, and therefore he did not approve of his brother's conduct.

Besides the service and society, Vronsky had another great interest—horses; he was passionately fond of horses.

That year races and a steeplechase had been arranged for the officers. Vronsky had put his name down, bought a thoroughbred English mare, and in spite of his love affair, he was looking forward to the races with intense, though reserved, excitement...

These two passions did not interfere with one another. On the contrary, he needed occupation and distraction quite apart from his love, so as to recruit and rest himself from the violent emotions that agitated him.

CHAPTER FOUR

PRINCESS SHTCHERBATSKAYA CONSIDERED that it was out of the question for the wedding to take place before Lent, just five weeks off, since not half the trousseau could possibly be ready by that time. But she could not but agree with Levin that to fix it for after Lent would be putting it off too late, as an old aunt of Prince Shtcherbatsky's was seriously ill and might die, and then the mourning would delay the wedding still longer. And therefore, deciding to divide the trousseau into two parts—a larger and smaller trousseau—the princess consented to have the wedding before Lent. She determined that she would get the smaller part of the trousseau all ready now, and the larger part should be made later, and she was much vexed with Levin because he was incapable of giving her a serious answer to the question whether he agreed to this arrangement or not. The arrangement was the more suitable as, immediately after the wedding, the young people were to go to the country, where the more important part of the trousseau would not be wanted.

Levin still continued in the same delirious condition in which it seemed to him that he and his happiness constituted the chief and sole aim of all existence, and that he need not now think or care about anything, that everything was being done and would be done for him by others. He had not even plans and aims for the future, he left its arrangement to others, knowing that everything would be delightful. His brother Sergey Ivanovitch, Stepan Arkadyevitch, and the princess guided him in doing what he had to do. All he did was to agree entirely with everything suggested to him. His brother raised money for him, the princess advised him to leave Moscow after the wedding. Stepan Arkadyevitch advised him to go abroad. He agreed to everything. "Do what you choose, if it amuses you. I'm happy, and my happiness can be no greater and no less for anything you do," he thought. When he told Kitty of Stepan Arkadyevitch's advice that they should go abroad, he was much surprised that she did not agree to this, and had some definite requirements of her own in regard to their future. She knew Levin had work he loved in the country. She did not, as he saw, understand this work, she did not even care to understand it. But that did not prevent her from regarding it as a matter of great importance. And then she knew their home would be in the country, and she wanted to go, not abroad where she was not going to live, but to the place where their home would be. This definitely expressed purpose astonished Levin. But since he did not care either way, he immediately asked Stepan Arkadyevitch, as though it were his duty, to go down to the country and to arrange everything there to the best of his ability with the taste of which he had so much.

"But I say," Stepan Arkadyevitch said to him one day after he had come back from the country, where he had got everything ready for the young people's arrival, "have you a certificate of having been at confession?"

"No. But what of it?"

"You can't be married without it."

"*Aïe, aïe, aïe!*" cried Levin. "Why, I believe it's nine years since I've taken the sacrament! I never thought of it."

"You're a pretty fellow!" said Stepan Arkadyevitch laughing, "and you call me a Nihilist! But this won't do, you know. You must take the sacrament."

"When? There are four days left now."

Stepan Arkadyevitch arranged this also, and Levin had to go to confession. To Levin, as to any unbeliever who respects the beliefs of others, it was exceedingly disagreeable to be present at and take part in church ceremonies. At this moment, in his present softened state of feeling, sensitive to everything, this inevitable act of hypocrisy was not merely painful to Levin, it seemed to him utterly impossible. Now, in the heyday of his highest glory, his fullest flower, he would have to be a liar or a scoffer. He felt incapable of being either. But though he repeatedly plied Stepan Arkadyevitch with questions as to the possibility of obtaining a certificate without actually communicating, Stepan Arkadyevitch maintained that it was out of the question.

"Besides, what is it to you—two days? And he's an awfully nice clever old fellow. He'll pull the tooth out for you so gently, you won't notice it."

Standing at the first litany, Levin attempted to revive in himself his youthful recollections of the intense religious emotion he had passed through between the ages of sixteen and seventeen.

But he was at once convinced that it was utterly impossible to him. He attempted to look at it all as an empty custom, having no sort of meaning, like the custom of paying calls. But he felt that he could not do that either. Levin found himself, like the majority of his contemporaries, in the vaguest position in regard to religion. Believe he could not, and at the same time he had no firm conviction that it was all wrong. And consequently, not being able to believe in the significance of what he was doing nor to regard it with indifference as an empty formality, during the whole period of preparing for the sacrament he was conscious of a feeling of discomfort and shame at doing what he did not himself understand, and what, as an inner voice told him, was therefore false and wrong.

During the service he would first listen to the prayers, trying to attach some meaning to them not discordant with his own views; then feeling that he could not understand and must condemn them, he tried not to listen to them, but to attend to the thoughts, observations, and memories which floated through his brain with extreme vividness during this idle time of standing in church.

He had stood through the litany, the evening service and the midnight service, and the next day he got up earlier than usual, and without having tea went at eight o'clock in the morning to the church for the morning service and the confession.

There was no one in the church but a beggar soldier, two old women, and the church officials. A young deacon, whose long back showed in two distinct halves through his thin undercassock, met him, and at once going to a little table at the wall read the exhortation. During the reading, especially at the frequent and rapid repetition of the same words, "Lord, have mercy on us!" which resounded with an echo, Levin felt that thought was shut and sealed up, and that it must not be touched or stirred now or confusion would be the result; and so standing behind the deacon he went on thinking of his own affairs, neither listening nor examining what was said. "It's wonderful what expression there is in her hand," he thought, remembering how they had been sitting the day before at a corner table. They had nothing to talk about, as was almost always the case at this time, and laying her hand on the table she kept opening and shutting it, and laughed herself as she watched her action. He remembered how he had kissed it and then had examined the lines on the pink palm. "Have mercy on us again!" thought Levin, crossing himself, bowing, and looking at the supple spring of the deacon's back bowing before him. "She took my hand then and examined the lines 'You've got a splendid hand,' she said." And he looked at his own hand and the short hand of the deacon. "Yes, now it will soon be over," he thought. "No, it seems to be beginning again," he thought, listening to the prayers. "No, it's just ending: there he is bowing down to the ground. That's always at the end."

The deacon's hand in a plush cuff accepted a three-rouble note unobtrusively, and the deacon said he would put it down in the register, and his new boots creaking jauntily over the flagstones of the empty church, he went to the altar. A moment later he peeped out thence and beckoned to Levin. Thought, till then locked up, began to stir in Levin's head, but he made haste to drive it away. "It will come right somehow," he thought, and went towards the altar-rails. He went up the steps, and turning to the right saw the priest. The priest, a little old man with a scanty grizzled beard and weary, good-natured eyes, was standing at the altar-rails, turning over the pages of a missal. With a slight bow to Levin he began immediately reading prayers in the official voice. When he had finished them he bowed down to the ground and turned, facing Levin.

"Christ is present here unseen, receiving your confession," he said, pointing to the crucifix. "Do you believe in all the doctrines of the Holy Apostolic Church?" the priest went on, turning his eyes away from Levin's face and folding his hands under his stole.

"I have doubted, I doubt everything," said Levin in a voice that jarred on himself, and he ceased speaking.

Leo Tolstoy   43

The priest waited a few seconds to see if he would not say more, and closing his eyes he said quickly, with a broad, Vladimirsky accent:

"Doubt is natural to the weakness of mankind, but we must pray that God in His mercy will strengthen us. What are your special sins?" he added, without the slightest interval, as though anxious not to waste time.

"My chief sin is doubt. I have doubts of everything, and for the most part I am in doubt."

"Doubt is natural to the weakness of mankind," the priest repeated the same words. "What do you doubt about principally?"

"I doubt of everything. I sometimes even have doubts of the existence of God," Levin could not help saying, and he was horrified at the impropriety of what he was saying. But Levin's words did not, it seemed, make much impression on the priest.

"What sort of doubt can there be of the existence of God?" he said hurriedly, with a just perceptible smile.

Levin did not speak.

"What doubt can you have of the Creator when you behold His creation?" the priest went on in the rapid customary jargon. "Who has decked the heavenly firmament with its lights? Who has clothed the earth in its beauty? How explain it without the Creator?" he said, looking inquiringly at Levin.

Levin felt that it would be improper to enter upon a metaphysical discussion with the priest, and so he said in reply merely what was a direct answer to the question.

"I don't know," he said.

"You don't know! Then how can you doubt that God created all?" the priest said, with good-humored perplexity.

"I don't understand it at all," said Levin, blushing, and feeling that his words were stupid, and that they could not be anything but stupid in such a position.

"Pray to God and beseech Him. Even the holy fathers had doubts, and prayed to God to strengthen their faith. The devil has great power, and we must resist him. Pray to God, beseech Him. Pray to God," he repeated hurriedly.

The priest paused for some time, as though meditating.

"You're about, I hear, to marry the daughter of my parishioner and son in the spirit, Prince Shtcherbatsky?" he resumed, with a smile. "An excellent young lady."

"Yes," answered Levin, blushing for the priest. "What does he want to ask me about this at confession for?" he thought.

And, as though answering his thought, the priest said to him:

"You are about to enter into holy matrimony, and God may bless you with offspring. Well, what sort of bringing-up can you give your babes if you do not overcome the temptation of the devil, enticing you to infidelity?" he said, with gentle reproachfulness. "If you love your child as a good father, you will not desire only wealth, luxury, honor for your infant; you will be anxious for his salvation, his spiritual enlightenment with the light of truth. Eh? What answer will you make him when the innocent babe asks you: 'Papa! who made all that enchants me in this world—the earth, the waters, the sun, the flowers, the grass?' Can you say to him: 'I don't know'? You cannot but know, since the Lord God in His infinite mercy has revealed it to us. Or your child will ask you: 'What awaits me in the life beyond the tomb?' What will you say to him when you know nothing? How will you answer him? Will you leave him to the allurements of the world and the devil? That's not right," he said, and he stopped, putting his head on one side and looking at Levin with his kindly, gentle eyes.

Levin made no answer this time, not because he did not want to enter upon a discussion with the priest, but because, so far, no one had ever asked him such questions, and when his babes did ask him those questions, it would be time enough to think about answering them.

"You are entering upon a time of life," pursued the priest, "when you must choose your path and keep to it. Pray to God that He may in His mercy aid you and have mercy on you!" he concluded. "Our Lord and God, Jesus Christ, in the abundance and riches of His lovingkindness, forgives this child..." and, finishing the prayer of absolution, the priest blessed him and dismissed him.

On getting home that day, Levin had a delightful sense of relief at the awkward position being over and having been got through without his having to tell a lie. Apart from this, there remained a vague memory that what the kind, nice old fellow had said had not been at all so stupid as he had fancied at first, and that there was something in it that must be cleared up.

"Of course, not now," thought Levin, "but some day later on." Levin felt more than ever now that there was something not clear and not clean in his soul, and that, in regard to religion, he was in the same position which he perceived so clearly and disliked in others, and for which he blamed his friend Sviazhsky.

Levin spent that evening with his betrothed at Dolly's, and was in very high spirits. To explain to Stepan Arkadyevitch the state of excitement in which he found himself, he said that he was happy like a dog being trained to jump through a hoop, who, having at last caught the idea, and done what was required of him, whines and wags its tail, and jumps up to the table and the windows in its delight.

On the day of the wedding, according to the Russian custom (the princess and Darya Alexandrovna insisted on strictly keeping all the customs), Levin did not see his betrothed, and dined at his hotel with three bachelor friends, casually brought together at his rooms. These were Sergey Ivanovitch, Katavasov, a university friend, now professor of natural science, whom Levin had met in the street and insisted on taking home with him, and Tchirikov, his best man, a Moscow conciliation-board judge, Levin's companion in his bear-hunts. The dinner was a very merry one: Sergey Ivanovitch was in his happiest mood, and was much amused by Katavasov's originality. Katavasov, feeling his originality was appreciated and understood, made the most of it. Tchirikov always gave a lively and good-humored support to conversation of any sort.

"See, now," said Katavasov, drawling his words from a habit acquired in the lecture-room, "what a capable fellow was our friend Konstantin Dmitrievitch. I'm not speaking of present company, for he's absent. At the time he left the university he was fond of science, took an interest in humanity; now one-half of his abilities is devoted to deceiving himself, and the other to justifying the deceit."

"A more determined enemy of matrimony than you I never saw," said Sergey Ivanovitch.

"Oh, no, I'm not an enemy of matrimony. I'm in favor of division of labor. People who can do nothing else ought to rear people while the rest work for their happiness and enlightenment. That's how I look at it. To muddle up two trades is the error of the amateur; I'm not one of their number."

"How happy I shall be when I hear that you're in love!" said Levin. "Please invite me to the wedding."

"I'm in love now."

"Yes, with a cuttlefish! You know," Levin turned to his brother, "Mihail Semyonovitch is writing a work on the digestive organs of the..."

"Now, make a muddle of it! It doesn't matter what about. And the fact is, I certainly do love cuttlefish."

"But that's no hindrance to your loving your wife."

"The cuttlefish is no hindrance. The wife is the hindrance."

"Why so?"

"Oh, you'll see! You care about farming, hunting,—well, you'd better look out!"

"Arhip was here today; he said there were a lot of elks in Prudno, and two bears," said Tchirikov.

"Well, you must go and get them without me."

"Ah, that's the truth," said Sergey Ivanovitch. "And you may say good-bye to bear-hunting for the future—your wife won't allow it!"

Levin smiled. The picture of his wife not letting him go was so pleasant that he was ready to renounce the delights of looking upon bears forever.

"Still, it's a pity they should get those two bears without you. Do you remember last time at Hapilovo? That was a delightful hunt!" said Tchirikov.

Levin had not the heart to disillusion him of the notion that there could be something delightful apart from her, and so said nothing.

"There's some sense in this custom of saying good-bye to bachelor life," said Sergey Ivanovitch. "However happy you may be, you must regret your freedom."

"And confess there is a feeling that you want to jump out of the window, like Gogol's bridegroom?"

"Of course there is, but it isn't confessed," said Katavasov, and he broke into loud laughter.

"Oh, well, the window's open. Let's start off this instant to Tver! There's a big she-bear; one can go right up to the lair. Seriously, let's go by the five o'clock! And here let them do what they like," said Tchirikov, smiling.

"Well, now, on my honor," said Levin, smiling, "I can't find in my heart that feeling of regret for my freedom."

"Yes, there's such a chaos in your heart just now that you can't find anything there," said Katavasov. "Wait a bit, when you set it to rights a little, you'll find it!"

"No; if so, I should have felt a little, apart from my feeling" (he could not say love before them) "and happiness, a certain regret at losing my freedom.... On the contrary, I am glad at the very loss of my freedom."

"Awful! It's a hopeless case!" said Katavasov. "Well, let's drink to his recovery, or wish that a hundredth part of his dreams may be realized—and that would be happiness such as never has been seen on earth!"

Soon after dinner the guests went away to be in time to be dressed for the wedding.

When he was left alone, and recalled the conversation of these bachelor friends, Levin asked himself: had he in his heart that regret for his freedom of which they had spoken? He smiled at the question. "Freedom! What is freedom for? Happiness is only in loving and wishing her wishes, thinking her thoughts, that is to say, not freedom at all—that's happiness!"

"But do I know her ideas, her wishes, her feelings?" some voice suddenly whispered to him. The smile died away from his face, and he grew thoughtful. And suddenly a strange feeling came upon him. There came over him a dread and doubt—doubt of everything.

"What if she does not love me? What if she's marrying me simply to be married? What if she doesn't see herself what she's doing?" he asked himself. "She may come to her senses, and only when she is being married realize that she does not and cannot love me." And strange, most evil thoughts of her began to come to him. He was jealous of Vronsky, as he had been a year ago, as though the evening he had seen her with Vronsky had been yesterday. He suspected she had not told him everything.

He jumped up quickly. "No, this can't go on!" he said to himself in despair. "I'll go to her; I'll ask her; I'll say for the last time: we are free, and hadn't we better stay so? Anything's better than endless misery, disgrace, unfaithfulness!" With despair in his heart and bitter anger against all men, against himself, against her, he went out of the hotel and drove to her house.

He found her in one of the back rooms. She was sitting on a chest and making some arrangements with her maid, sorting over heaps of dresses of different colors, spread on the backs of chairs and on the floor.

"Ah!" she cried, seeing him, and beaming with delight. "Kostya! Konstantin Dmitrievitch!" (These latter days she used these names almost alternately.) "I didn't expect you! I'm going through my wardrobe to see what's for whom..."

"Oh! that's very nice!" he said gloomily, looking at the maid.

"You can go, Dunyasha, I'll call you presently," said Kitty. "Kostya, what's the matter?" she asked, definitely adopting this familiar name as soon as the maid had gone out. She noticed his strange face, agitated and gloomy, and a panic came over her.

"Kitty! I'm in torture. I can't suffer alone," he said with despair in his voice, standing before her and looking imploringly into her eyes. He saw already from her loving, truthful face, that nothing could come of what he had meant to say, but yet he wanted her to reassure him herself. "I've come to say that there's still time. This can all be stopped and set right."

"What? I don't understand. What is the matter?"

"What I have said a thousand times over, and can't help thinking ...that I'm not worthy of you. You couldn't consent to marry me. Think a little. You've made a mistake. Think it over thoroughly. You can't love me.... If...better say so," he said, not looking at her. "I shall be wretched. Let people say what they like; anything's better than misery.... Far better now while there's still time...."

"I don't understand," she answered, panic-stricken; "you mean you want to give it up...don't want it?"

"Yes, if you don't love me."

"You're out of your mind!" she cried, turning crimson with vexation. But his face was so piteous, that she restrained her vexation, and flinging some clothes off an arm-chair, she sat down beside him. "What are you thinking? tell me all."

"I am thinking you can't love me. What can you love me for?"

"My God! what can I do?..." she said, and burst into tears.

"Oh! what have I done?" he cried, and kneeling before her, he fell to kissing her hands.

When the princess came into the room five minutes later, she found them completely reconciled. Kitty had not simply assured him that she loved him, but had gone so far—in answer to his question, what she loved him for—as to explain what for. She told him that she loved him because she understood him completely, because she knew what he would like, and because everything he liked was good. And this seemed to him perfectly clear. When the princess came to them, they were sitting side by side on the chest, sorting the dresses and disputing over Kitty's wanting to give Dunyasha the brown dress she had been wearing when Levin proposed to her, while he insisted that that dress must never be given away, but Dunyasha must have the blue one.

"How is it you don't see? She's a brunette, and it won't suit her.... I've worked it all out."

Hearing why he had come, the princess was half humorously, half seriously angry with him, and sent him home to dress and not to hinder Kitty's hair-dressing, as Charles the hair-dresser was just coming.

"As it is, she's been eating nothing lately and is losing her looks, and then you must come and upset her with your nonsense," she said to him. "Get along with you, my dear!"

Levin, guilty and shamefaced, but pacified, went back to his hotel. His brother, Darya Alexandrovna, and Stepan Arkadyevitch, all in full dress, were waiting for him to bless him with the holy picture. There was no time to lose. Darya Alexandrovna had to drive home again to fetch her curled and pomaded son, who was to carry the holy pictures after the bride. Then a carriage had to be sent for the best man, and another that would take Sergey Ivanovitch away would have to be sent back.... Altogether there were a great many most complicated matters to be considered and arranged. One thing was unmistakable, that there must be no delay, as it was already half-past six.

Nothing special happened at the ceremony of benediction with the holy picture. Stepan Arkadyevitch stood in a comically solemn pose beside his wife, took the holy picture, and telling Levin to bow down to the ground, he blessed him with his kindly, ironical smile, and kissed him three times; Darya Alexandrovna did the same, and immediately was in a hurry to get off, and again plunged into the intricate question of the destinations of the various carriages.

"Come, I'll tell you how we'll manage: you drive in our carriage to fetch him, and Sergey Ivanovitch, if he'll be so good, will drive there and then send his carriage."

"Of course; I shall be delighted."

"We'll come on directly with him. Are your things sent off?" said Stepan Arkadyevitch.

"Yes," answered Levin, and he told Kouzma to put out his clothes for him to dress.

A crowd of people, principally women, was thronging round the church lighted up for the wedding. Those who had not succeeded in getting into the main entrance were crowding about the windows, pushing, wrangling, and peeping through the gratings.

More than twenty carriages had already been drawn up in ranks along the street by the police. A police officer, regardless of the frost, stood at the entrance, gorgeous in his uniform. More carriages were continually driving up, and ladies wearing flowers and carrying their trains, and men taking off their helmets or black hats kept walking into the church. Inside the church both lusters were already lighted, and all the candles before the holy pictures. The gilt on the red ground of the holy picture-stand, and the gilt relief on the pictures, and the silver of the lusters and candlesticks, and the stones of the floor, and the rugs, and the banners above in the choir, and the steps of the altar, and the old blackened books, and the cassocks and surplices—all were flooded with light. On the right side of the warm church, in the crowd of frock coats and white ties, uniforms and broadcloth, velvet, satin, hair and flowers, bare shoulders and arms and long gloves, there was discreet but lively conversation that echoed strangely in the high cupola. Every time there was heard the creak of the opened door the conversation in the crowd died away, and everybody looked round expecting to see the bride and bridegroom come in. But the door had opened more than ten times, and each time it was either a belated guest or guests, who joined the circle of the invited on the right, or a spectator, who had eluded or softened the police officer, and went to join the crowd of outsiders on the left. Both the guests and the outside public had by now passed through all the phases of anticipation.

At first they imagined that the bride and bridegroom would arrive immediately, and attached no importance at all to their being late. Then they began to look more and more often towards the door, and to talk of whether anything could have happened. Then the long delay began to be positively discomforting, and relations and guests tried to look as if they were not thinking of the bridegroom but were engrossed in conversation.

The head deacon, as though to remind them of the value of his time, coughed impatiently, making the window-panes quiver in their frames. In the choir the bored choristers could be heard trying their voices and blowing their noses. The priest was continually sending first the beadle and then the deacon to find out whether the bridegroom had not come, more and more often he went himself, in a lilac vestment and an embroidered sash, to the side door, expecting to see the bridegroom. At last one of the ladies, glancing at her watch, said, "It really is strange, though!" and all the guests became uneasy and began loudly expressing their wonder and dissatisfaction. One of the bridegroom's best men went to find out what had happened. Kitty meanwhile had long ago been quite ready, and in her white dress and long veil and wreath of orange blossoms she was standing in the drawing-room of the Shtcherbatskys' house with her sister, Madame Lvova, who was her bridal-mother. She was looking out of the window, and had been for over half an hour anxiously expecting to hear from the best man that her bridegroom was at the church.

Levin meanwhile, in his trousers, but without his coat and waistcoat, was walking to and fro in his room at the hotel, continually putting his head out of the door and looking up and down the corridor. But in the corridor there was no sign of the person he was looking for and he came back in despair, and frantically waving his hands addressed Stepan Arkadyevitch, who was smoking serenely.

"Was ever a man in such a fearful fool's position?" he said.

"Yes, it is stupid," Stepan Arkadyevitch assented, smiling soothingly. "But don't worry, it'll be brought directly."

"No, what is to be done!" said Levin, with smothered fury. "And these fools of open waistcoats! Out of the question!" he said, looking at the crumpled front of his shirt. "And what if the things have been taken on to the railway station!" he roared in desperation.

"Then you must put on mine."

"I ought to have done so long ago, if at all."

"It's not nice to look ridiculous.... Wait a bit! it will *come round*."

The point was that when Levin asked for his evening suit, Kouzma, his old servant, had brought him the coat, waistcoat, and everything that was wanted.

"But the shirt!" cried Levin.

"You've got a shirt on," Kouzma answered, with a placid smile.

Kouzma had not thought of leaving out a clean shirt, and on receiving instructions to pack up everything and send it round to the Shtcherbatskys' house, from which the young people were to set out the same evening, he had done so, packing everything but the dress suit. The shirt worn since the morning was crumpled and out of the question with the fashionable open waistcoat. It was a long way to send to the Shtcherbatskys'. They sent out to buy a shirt. The servant came back; everything was shut up—it was Sunday. They sent to Stepan Arkadyevitch's and brought a shirt—it was impossibly wide and short. They sent finally to the Shtcherbatskys' to unpack the things. The bridegroom was expected at the church while he was pacing up and down his room like a wild beast in a cage, peeping out into the corridor, and with horror and despair recalling what absurd things he had said to Kitty and what she might be thinking now.

At last the guilty Kouzma flew panting into the room with the shirt.

"Only just in time. They were just lifting it into the van," said Kouzma.

Three minutes later Levin ran full speed into the corridor, not looking at his watch for fear of aggravating his sufferings.

"You won't help matters like this," said Stepan Arkadyevitch with a smile, hurrying with more deliberation after him. "It will come round, it will come round...I tell you."

"They've come!" "Here he is!" "Which one?" "Rather young, eh?" "Why, my dear soul, she looks more dead than alive!" were the comments in the crowd, when Levin, meeting his bride in the entrance, walked with her into the church.

Stepan Arkadyevitch told his wife the cause of the delay, and the guests were whispering it with smiles to one another. Levin saw nothing and no one; he did not take his eyes off his bride.

Everyone said she had lost her looks dreadfully of late, and was not nearly so pretty on her wedding day as usual; but Levin did not think so. He looked at her hair done up high, with the long white veil and white flowers and the high, stand-up, scalloped collar, that in such a maidenly fashion hid her long neck at the sides and only showed it in front, her strikingly slender figure, and it seemed to him that she looked better than ever—not because these flowers, this veil, this gown from Paris added anything to her beauty; but because, in spite of the elaborate sumptuousness of her attire, the expression of her sweet face, of her eyes, of her lips was still her own characteristic expression of guileless truthfulness.

"I was beginning to think you meant to run away," she said, and smiled to him.

"It's so stupid, what happened to me, I'm ashamed to speak of it!" he said, reddening, and he was obliged to turn to Sergey Ivanovitch, who came up to him.

"This is a pretty story of yours about the shirt!" said Sergey Ivanovitch, shaking his head and smiling.

"Yes, yes!" answered Levin, without an idea of what they were talking about.

"Now, Kostya, you have to decide," said Stepan Arkadyevitch with an air of mock dismay, "a weighty question. You are at this moment just in the humor to appreciate all its gravity. They ask me, are they to light the candles that have been lighted before or candles that have never been lighted? It's a matter of ten roubles," he added, relaxing his lips into a smile. "I have decided, but I was afraid you might not agree."

Levin saw it was a joke, but he could not smile.

"Well, how's it to be then?—unlighted or lighted candles? that's the question."

"Yes, yes, unlighted."

"Oh, I'm very glad. The question's decided!" said Stepan Arkadyevitch, smiling. "How silly men are, though, in this position," he said to Tchirikov, when Levin, after looking absently at him, had moved back to his bride.

"Kitty, mind you're the first to step on the carpet," said Countess Nordston, coming up. "You're a nice person!" she said to Levin.

"Aren't you frightened, eh?" said Marya Dmitrievna, an old aunt.

"Are you cold? You're pale. Stop a minute, stoop down," said Kitty's sister, Madame Lvova, and with her plump, handsome arms she smilingly set straight the flowers on her head.

Dolly came up, tried to say something, but could not speak, cried, and then laughed unnaturally.

Kitty looked at all of them with the same absent eyes as Levin.

Meanwhile the officiating clergy had got into their vestments, and the priest and deacon came out to the lectern, which stood in the forepart of the church. The priest turned to Levin saying something. Levin did not hear what the priest said.

"Take the bride's hand and lead her up," the best man said to Levin.

It was a long while before Levin could make out what was expected of him. For a long time they tried to set him right and made him begin again—because he kept taking Kitty by the wrong arm or with the wrong arm—till he understood at last that what he had to do was, without changing his position, to take her right hand in his right hand. When at last he had taken the bride's hand in the correct way, the priest walked a few paces in front of them and stopped at the lectern. The crowd of friends and relations moved after them, with a buzz of talk and a rustle of skirts. Someone stooped down and pulled out the bride's train. The church became so still that the drops of wax could be heard falling from the candles.

The little old priest in his ecclesiastical cap, with his long silvery-gray locks of hair parted behind his ears, was fumbling with something at the lectern, putting out his little old hands from under the heavy silver vestment with the gold cross on the back of it.

Stepan Arkadyevitch approached him cautiously, whispered something, and making a sign to Levin, walked back again.

The priest lighted two candles, wreathed with flowers, and holding them sideways so that the wax dropped slowly from them he turned, facing the bridal pair. The priest was the same old man that had confessed Levin. He looked with weary and melancholy eyes at the bride and bridegroom, sighed, and putting his right hand out from his vestment, blessed the bridegroom with it, and also with a shade of solicitous tenderness laid the crossed fingers on the bowed head of Kitty. Then he gave them the candles, and taking the censer, moved slowly away from them.

"Can it be true?" thought Levin, and he looked round at his bride. Looking down at her he saw her face in profile, and from the scarcely perceptible quiver of her lips and eyelashes he knew she was aware of his eyes upon her. She did not look round, but the high scalloped collar, that reached her little pink ear, trembled faintly. He saw that a sigh was held back in her throat, and the little hand in the long glove shook as it held the candle.

All the fuss of the shirt, of being late, all the talk of friends and relations, their annoyance, his ludicrous position—all suddenly passed away and he was filled with joy and dread.

The handsome, stately head-deacon wearing a silver robe and his curly locks standing out at each side of his head, stepped smartly forward, and lifting his stole on two fingers, stood opposite the priest.

"Blessed be the name of the Lord," the solemn syllables rang out slowly one after another, setting the air quivering with waves of sound.

"Blessed is the name of our God, from the beginning, is now, and ever shall be," the little old priest answered in a submissive, piping voice, still fingering something at the lectern. And the full chorus of the unseen choir rose up, filling the whole church, from the windows to the vaulted roof, with broad waves of melody. It grew stronger, rested for an instant, and slowly died away.

They prayed, as they always do, for peace from on high and for salvation, for the Holy Synod, and for the Tsar; they prayed, too, for the servants of God, Konstantin and Ekaterina, now plighting their troth.

"Vouchsafe to them love made perfect, peace and help, O Lord, we beseech Thee," the whole church seemed to breathe with the voice of the head deacon.

Levin heard the words, and they impressed him. "How did they guess that it is help, just help that one wants?" he thought, recalling all his fears and doubts of late. "What do I know? what can I do in this fearful business," he thought, "without help? Yes, it is help I want now."

When the deacon had finished the prayer for the Imperial family, the priest turned to the bridal pair with a book: "Eternal God, that joinest together in love them that were separate," he read in a gentle, piping voice: "who hast ordained the union of holy wedlock that cannot be set asunder, Thou who didst bless Isaac and Rebecca and their descendants, according to Thy Holy Covenant; bless Thy servants, Konstantin and Ekaterina, leading them in the path of all good works. For gracious and merciful art Thou, our Lord, and glory be to Thee, the Father, the Son, and the Holy Ghost, now and ever shall be."

"Amen!" the unseen choir sent rolling again upon the air.

"'Joinest together in love them that were separate.' What deep meaning in those words, and how they correspond with what one feels at this moment," thought Levin. "Is she feeling the same as I?"

And looking round, he met her eyes, and from their expression he concluded that she was understanding it just as he was. But this was a mistake; she almost completely missed the meaning of the words of the service; she had not heard them, in fact. She could not listen to them and take them in, so strong was the one feeling that filled her breast and grew stronger and stronger. That feeling was joy at the completion of the process that for the last month and a half had been going on in her soul, and had during those six weeks been a joy and a torture to her. On the day when in the drawing room of the house in Arbaty Street she had gone up to him in her brown dress, and given herself to him without a word—on that day, at that hour, there took place in her heart a complete severance from all her old life, and a quite different, new, utterly strange life had begun for her, while the old life was actually going on as before. Those six weeks had for her been a time of the utmost bliss and the utmost misery. All her life, all her desires and hopes were concentrated on this one man, still uncomprehended by her, to whom she was bound by a feeling of alternate attraction and repulsion, even less comprehended than the man himself, and all the while she was going on living in the outward conditions of her old life. Living the old life, she was horrified at herself, at her utter insurmountable callousness to all her own past, to things, to habits, to the people she had loved, who loved her—to her mother, who was wounded by her indifference, to her kind, tender father, till then dearer than all the world. At one moment she was horrified at this indifference, at another she rejoiced at what had brought her to this indifference. She could not frame a thought, not a wish apart from life with this man; but this new life was not yet, and she could not even picture it clearly to herself. There was only anticipation, the dread and joy of the new and the unknown. And now behold—anticipation and uncertainty and remorse at the abandonment of the old life—all was ending, and the new was beginning. This new life could not but have terrors for her inexperience; but, terrible or not, the change had been wrought six weeks before in her soul, and this was merely the final sanction of what had long been completed in her heart.

Turning again to the lectern, the priest with some difficulty took Kitty's little ring, and asking Levin for his hand, put it on the first joint of his finger. "The servant of God, Konstantin, plights his troth to the servant of God, Ekaterina." And putting his big ring on Kitty's touchingly weak, pink little finger, the priest said the same thing.

And the bridal pair tried several times to understand what they had to do, and each time made some mistake and were corrected by the priest in a whisper. At last, having duly performed the ceremony, having signed the rings with the cross, the priest handed Kitty the big ring, and Levin the little one. Again they were puzzled, and passed the rings from hand to hand, still without doing what was expected.

Dolly, Tchirikov, and Stepan Arkadyevitch stepped forward to set them right. There was an interval of hesitation, whispering, and smiles; but the expression of solemn emotion on the faces of the betrothed pair did not change: on the contrary, in their perplexity over their hands they looked more grave and deeply moved than before, and the smile with which Stepan Arkadyevitch whispered to them that now they would each put on their own ring died away on his lips. He had a feeling that any smile would jar on them.

"Thou who didst from the beginning create male and female," the priest read after the exchange of rings, "from Thee woman was given to man to be a helpmeet to him, and for the procreation of children. O Lord, our God, who hast poured down the blessings of Thy Truth according to Thy Holy Covenant upon Thy chosen servants, our fathers, from generation to generation, bless Thy servants Konstantin and Ekaterina, and make their troth fast in faith, and union of hearts, and truth, and love...."

Levin felt more and more that all his ideas of marriage, all his dreams of how he would order his life, were mere childishness, and that it was something he had not understood hitherto, and now understood less than ever, though it was being performed upon him. The lump in his throat rose higher and higher, tears that would not be checked came into his eyes.

In the church there was all Moscow, all the friends and relations; and during the ceremony of plighting troth, in the brilliantly lighted church, there was an incessant flow of discreetly subdued talk in the circle of gaily dressed women and girls, and men in white ties, frockcoats, and uniforms. The talk was principally kept up by the men, while the women were absorbed in watching every detail of the ceremony, which always means so much to them.

In the little group nearest to the bride were her two sisters: Dolly, and the other one, the self-possessed beauty, Madame Lvova, who had just arrived from abroad.

"Why is it Marie's in lilac, as bad as black, at a wedding?" said Madame Korsunskaya.

"With her complexion, it's the one salvation," responded Madame Trubetskaya. "I wonder why they had the wedding in the evening? It's like shop-people..."

"So much prettier. I was married in the evening too..." answered Madame Korsunskaya, and she sighed, remembering how charming she had been that day, and how absurdly in love her husband was, and how different it all was now.

"They say if anyone's best man more than ten times, he'll never be married. I wanted to be for the tenth time, but the post was taken," said Count Siniavin to the pretty Princess Tcharskaya, who had designs on him.

Princess Tcharskaya only answered with a smile. She looked at Kitty, thinking how and when she would stand with Count Siniavin in Kitty's place, and how she would remind him then of his joke today.

Shtcherbatsky told the old maid of honor, Madame Nikolaeva, that he meant to put the crown on Kitty's chignon for luck.

"She ought not to have worn a chignon," answered Madame Nikolaeva, who had long ago made up her mind that if the elderly widower she was angling for married her, the wedding should be of the simplest. "I don't like such grandeur."

Sergey Ivanovitch was talking to Darya Dmitrievna, jestingly assuring her that the custom of going away after the wedding was becoming common because newly married people always felt a little ashamed of themselves.

"Your brother may feel proud of himself. She's a marvel of sweetness. I believe you're envious."

"Oh, I've got over that, Darya Dmitrievna," he answered, and a melancholy and serious expression suddenly came over his face.

Stepan Arkadyevitch was telling his sister-in-law his joke about divorce.

"The wreath wants setting straight," she answered, not hearing him.

"What a pity she's lost her looks so," Countess Nordston said to Madame Lvova. "Still he's not worth her little finger, is he?"

"Oh, I like him so—not because he's my future *beau-frère*," answered Madame Lvova. "And how well he's behaving! It's so difficult, too, to look well in such a position, not to be ridiculous. And he's not ridiculous, and not affected; one can see he's moved."

"You expected it, I suppose?"

"Almost. She always cared for him."

"Well, we shall see which of them will step on the rug first. I warned Kitty."

"It will make no difference," said Madame Lvova; "we're all obedient wives; it's in our family."

"Oh, I stepped on the rug before Vassily on purpose. And you, Dolly?"

Dolly stood beside them; she heard them, but she did not answer. She was deeply moved. The tears stood in her eyes, and she could not have spoken without crying. She was rejoicing over Kitty and Levin; going back in thought to her own wedding, she glanced at the radiant figure of Stepan Arkadyevitch, forgot all the present, and remembered only her own innocent love. She recalled not herself only, but all her women-friends and acquaintances. She thought of them on the one day of their triumph, when they had stood like Kitty under the wedding crown, with love and hope and dread in their hearts, renouncing the past, and stepping forward into the mysterious future. Among the brides that came back to her memory, she thought too of her darling Anna, of whose proposed divorce she had just been hearing. And she had stood just as innocent in orange flowers and bridal veil. And now? "It's terribly strange," she said to herself. It was not merely the sisters, the women-friends and female relations of the bride who were following every detail of the ceremony. Women who were quite strangers, mere spectators, were watching it excitedly, holding their breath, in fear of losing a single movement or expression of the bride and bridegroom, and angrily not answering, often not hearing, the remarks of the callous men, who kept making joking or irrelevant observations.

"Why has she been crying? Is she being married against her will?"

"Against her will to a fine fellow like that? A prince, isn't he?"

"Is that her sister in the white satin? Just listen how the deacon booms out, 'And fearing her husband.'"

"Are the choristers from Tchudovo?"

"No, from the Synod."

"I asked the footman. He says he's going to take her home to his country place at once. Awfully rich, they say. That's why she's being married to him."

"No, they're a well-matched pair."

"I say, Marya Vassilievna, you were making out those fly-away crinolines were not being worn. Just look at her in the puce dress—an ambassador's wife they say she is—how her skirt bounces out from side to side!"

"What a pretty dear the bride is—like a lamb decked with flowers! Well, say what you will, we women feel for our sister."

Such were the comments in the crowd of gazing women who had succeeded in slipping in at the church doors.

Vronsky and Anna had been traveling for three months together in Europe. They had visited Venice, Rome, and Naples, and had just arrived at a small Italian town where they meant to stay some time. A handsome head waiter, with thick pomaded hair parted from the neck upwards, an evening coat, a broad white cambric shirt front, and a bunch of trinkets hanging above his rounded stomach, stood with his hands in the full curve of his pockets, looking contemptuously from under his eyelids while he gave some frigid reply to a gentleman who had stopped him. Catching the sound of footsteps coming from the other side of the entry towards the staircase, the head waiter turned round, and seeing the Russian count, who had taken their best rooms, he took his hands out of his pockets deferentially, and with a bow informed him that a courier had been, and that the business about the palazzo had been arranged. The steward was prepared to sign the agreement.

"Ah! I'm glad to hear it," said Vronsky. "Is madame at home or not?"

"Madame has been out for a walk but has returned now," answered the waiter.

Vronsky took off his soft, wide-brimmed hat and passed his handkerchief over his heated brow and hair, which had grown half over his ears, and was brushed back covering the bald patch on his head. And glancing casually at the gentleman, who still stood there gazing intently at him, he would have gone on.

"This gentleman is a Russian, and was inquiring after you," said the head waiter.

With mingled feelings of annoyance at never being able to get away from acquaintances anywhere, and longing to find some sort of diversion from the monotony of his life, Vronsky looked once more at the gentleman, who had retreated and stood still again, and at the same moment a light came into the eyes of both.

"Golenishtchev!"

"Vronsky!"

It really was Golenishtchev, a comrade of Vronsky's in the Corps of Pages. In the corps Golenishtchev had belonged to the liberal party; he left the corps without entering the army, and had never taken office under the government. Vronsky and he had gone completely different ways on leaving the corps, and had only met once since.

At that meeting Vronsky perceived that Golenishtchev had taken up a sort of lofty, intellectually liberal line, and was consequently disposed to look down upon Vronsky's interests and calling in life. Hence Vronsky had met him with the chilling and haughty manner he so well knew how to assume, the meaning of which was: "You may like or dislike my way of life, that's a matter of the most perfect indifference to me; you will have to treat me with respect if you want to know me." Golenishtchev had been contemptuously indifferent to the tone taken by Vronsky. This second meeting might have been expected, one would have supposed, to estrange them still more. But now they beamed and exclaimed with delight on recognizing one another. Vronsky would never have expected to be so pleased to see Golenishtchev, but probably he was not himself aware how bored he was. He forgot the disagreeable impression of their last meeting, and with a face of frank delight held out his hand to his old comrade. The same expression of delight replaced the look of uneasiness on Golenishtchev's face.

"How glad I am to meet you!" said Vronsky, showing his strong white teeth in a friendly smile.

"I heard the name Vronsky, but I didn't know which one. I'm very, very glad!"

"Let's go in. Come, tell me what you're doing."

"I've been living here for two years. I'm working."

"Ah!" said Vronsky, with sympathy; "let's go in." And with the habit common with Russians, instead of saying in Russian what he wanted to keep from the servants, he began to speak in French.

"Do you know Madame Karenina? We are traveling together. I am going to see her now," he said in French, carefully scrutinizing Golenishtchev's face.

"Ah! I did not know" (though he did know), Golenishtchev answered carelessly. "Have you been here long?" he added.

"Four days," Vronsky answered, once more scrutinizing his friend's face intently.

"Yes, he's a decent fellow, and will look at the thing properly," Vronsky said to himself, catching the significance of Golenishtchev's face and the change of subject. "I can introduce him to Anna, he looks at it properly."

During those three months that Vronsky had spent abroad with Anna, he had always on meeting new people asked himself how the new person would look at his relations with Anna, and for the most part, in men, he had met with the "proper" way of looking at it. But if he had been asked, and those who looked at it "properly" had been asked, exactly how they did look at it, both he and they would have been greatly puzzled to answer.

In reality, those who in Vronsky's opinion had the "proper" view had no sort of view at all, but behaved in general as well-bred persons do behave in regard to all the complex and insoluble problems with which life is encompassed on all sides; they behaved with propriety, avoiding allusions and unpleasant questions. They assumed an air of fully comprehending the import and force of the situation, of accepting and even approving of it, but of considering it superfluous and uncalled for to put all this into words.

Vronsky at once divined that Golenishtchev was of this class, and therefore was doubly pleased to see him. And in fact, Golenishtchev's manner to Madame Karenina, when he was taken to call on her, was all that Vronsky could have desired. Obviously without the slightest effort he steered clear of all subjects which might lead to embarrassment.

He had never met Anna before, and was struck by her beauty, and still more by the frankness with which she accepted her position. She blushed when Vronsky brought in Golenishtchev, and he was extremely charmed by this childish blush overspreading her candid and handsome face. But what he liked particularly was the way in which at once, as though on purpose that there might be no misunderstanding with an outsider, she called Vronsky simply Alexey, and said they were moving into a house they had just taken, what was here called a palazzo. Golenishtchev liked this direct and simple attitude to her own position. Looking at Anna's manner of simple-hearted, spirited gaiety, and knowing Alexey Alexandrovitch and Vronsky, Golenishtchev fancied that he understood her perfectly. He fancied that he understood what she was utterly unable to understand: how it was that, having made her husband wretched, having abandoned him and her son and lost her good name, she yet felt full of spirits, gaiety, and happiness.

"It's in the guide-book," said Golenishtchev, referring to the palazzo Vronsky had taken. "There's a first-rate Tintoretto there. One of his latest period."

"I tell you what: it's a lovely day, let's go and have another look at it," said Vronsky, addressing Anna.

"I shall be very glad to; I'll go and put on my hat. Would you say it's hot?" she said, stopping short in the doorway and looking inquiringly at Vronsky. And again a vivid flush overspread her face.

Vronsky saw from her eyes that she did not know on what terms he cared to be with Golenishtchev, and so was afraid of not behaving as he would wish.

He looked a long, tender look at her.

"No, not very," he said.

And it seemed to her that she understood everything, most of all, that he was pleased with her; and smiling to him, she walked with her rapid step out at the door.

The friends glanced at one another, and a look of hesitation came into both faces, as though Golenishtchev, unmistakably admiring her, would have liked to say something about her, and could not find the right thing to say, while Vronsky desired and dreaded his doing so.

"Well then," Vronsky began to start a conversation of some sort; "so you're settled here? You're still at the same work, then?" he went on, recalling that he had been told Golenishtchev was writing something.

"Yes, I'm writing the second part of the *Two Elements*," said Golenishtchev, coloring with pleasure at the question—"that is, to be exact, I am not writing it yet; I am preparing, collecting materials. It will be of far wider scope, and will touch on almost all questions. We in Russia refuse to see that we are the heirs of Byzantium," and he launched into a long and heated explanation of his views.

Vronsky at the first moment felt embarrassed at not even knowing of the first part of the *Two Elements*, of which the author spoke as something well known. But as Golenishtchev began to lay down his opinions and Vronsky was able to follow them even without knowing the *Two Elements*, he listened to him with some interest, for Golenishtchev spoke well. But Vronsky was startled and annoyed by the nervous irascibility with which Golenishtchev talked of the subject that engrossed him. As he went on talking, his eyes glittered more and more angrily; he was more and more hurried in his replies to imaginary opponents, and his face grew more and more excited and worried. Remembering Golenishtchev, a thin, lively, good-natured and well-bred boy, always at the head of the class, Vronsky could not make out the reason of his irritability, and he did not like it. What he particularly disliked was that Golenishtchev, a man belonging to a good set, should put himself on a level with some scribbling fellows, with whom he was irritated and angry. Was it worth it? Vronsky disliked it, yet he felt that Golenishtchev was unhappy, and was sorry for him. Unhappiness, almost mental derangement, was visible on his mobile, rather handsome face, while without even noticing Anna's coming in, he went on hurriedly and hotly expressing his views.

When Anna came in in her hat and cape, and her lovely hand rapidly swinging her parasol, and stood beside him, it was with a feeling of relief that Vronsky broke away from the plaintive eyes of Golenishtchev which fastened persistently upon him, and with a fresh rush of love looked at his charming companion, full of life and happiness. Golenishtchev recovered himself with an effort, and at first was dejected and gloomy, but Anna, disposed to feel friendly with everyone as she was at that time, soon revived his spirits by her direct and lively manner. After trying various subjects of conversation, she got him upon painting, of which he talked very well, and she listened to him attentively. They walked to the house they had taken, and looked over it.

"I am very glad of one thing," said Anna to Golenishtchev when they were on their way back, "Alexey will have a capital *atelier*. You must certainly take that room," she said to Vronsky in Russian, using the affectionately familiar form as though she saw that Golenishtchev would become intimate with them in their isolation, and that there was no need of reserve before him.

"Do you paint?" said Golenishtchev, turning round quickly to Vronsky.

"Yes, I used to study long ago, and now I have begun to do a little," said Vronsky, reddening.

"He has great talent," said Anna with a delighted smile. "I'm no judge, of course. But good judges have said the same."

Anna, in that first period of her emancipation and rapid return to health, felt herself unpardonably happy and full of the joy of life. The thought of her husband's unhappiness did not poison her happiness. On one side that memory was too awful to be thought of. On the other side her husband's unhappiness had given her too much happiness to be regretted. The memory of all that had happened after her illness: her reconciliation with her husband, its breakdown, the news of Vronsky's wound, his visit, the preparations for divorce, the departure from her husband's house, the parting from her son—all that seemed to her like a delirious dream, from which she had waked up alone with Vronsky abroad. The thought of the harm caused to her husband aroused in her a feeling like repulsion, and akin to what a drowning man might feel who has shaken off another man clinging to him. That man did drown. It was an evil action, of course, but it was the sole means of escape, and better not to brood over these fearful facts.

One consolatory reflection upon her conduct had occurred to her at the first moment of the final rupture, and when now she recalled all the past, she remembered that one reflection. "I have inevitably made that man wretched," she thought; "but I don't want to profit by his misery. I too am suffering, and shall suffer; I am losing what I prized above everything—I am losing my good name and my son. I have done wrong, and so I don't want happiness, I don't want a divorce, and shall suffer from my shame and the separation from my child." But, however sincerely Anna had meant to suffer, she was not suffering. Shame there was not. With the tact of which both had such a large share, they had succeeded in avoiding Russian ladies abroad, and so had never placed themselves in a false position, and everywhere they had met people who pretended that they perfectly understood their position, far better indeed than they did themselves. Separation from the son she loved—even that did not cause her anguish in these early days. The baby girl—*his* child—was so sweet, and had so won Anna's heart, since she was all that was left her, that Anna rarely thought of her son.

The desire for life, waxing stronger with recovered health, was so intense, and the conditions of life were so new and pleasant, that Anna felt unpardonably happy. The more she got to know Vronsky, the more she loved him. She loved him for himself, and for his love for her. Her complete ownership of him was a continual joy to her. His presence was always sweet to her. All the traits of his character, which she learned to know better and better, were unutterably dear to her. His appearance, changed by his civilian dress, was as fascinating to her as though she were some young girl in love. In everything he said, thought, and did, she saw something particularly noble and elevated. Her adoration of him alarmed her indeed; she sought and could not find in him anything not fine. She dared not show him her sense of her own insignificance beside him. It seemed to her that, knowing this, he might sooner cease to love her; and she dreaded nothing now so much as losing his love, though she had no grounds for fearing it. But she could not help being grateful to him for his attitude to her, and showing that she appreciated it. He, who had in her opinion such a marked aptitude for a political career, in which he would have been certain to play a leading part—he had sacrificed his ambition for her sake, and never betrayed the slightest regret. He was more lovingly respectful to her than ever, and the constant care that she should not feel the awkwardness of her position never deserted him for a single instant. He, so manly a man, never opposed her, had indeed, with her, no will of his own, and was anxious, it seemed, for nothing but to anticipate her wishes. And she could not but appreciate this, even though the very intensity of his solicitude for her, the atmosphere of care with which he surrounded her, sometimes weighed upon her.

Vronsky, meanwhile, in spite of the complete realization of what he had so long desired, was not perfectly happy. He soon felt that the realization of his desires gave him no more than a grain of sand out of the mountain of happiness he had expected. It showed him the mistake men make in picturing to themselves happiness as the realization of their desires. For a time after joining his life to hers, and putting on civilian dress, he had felt all the delight of freedom in general of which he had known nothing before, and of freedom in his love,—and he was content, but not for long. He was soon aware that there was springing up in his heart a desire for desires—*ennui*. Without conscious intention he began to clutch at every passing caprice, taking it for a desire and an object. Sixteen hours of the day must be occupied in some way, since they were living abroad in complete freedom, outside the conditions of social life which filled up time in Petersburg. As for the amusements of bachelor existence, which had provided Vronsky with entertainment on previous tours abroad, they could not be thought of, since the sole attempt of the sort had led to a sudden attack of depression in Anna, quite out of proportion with the cause—a late supper with bachelor friends. Relations with the society of the place—foreign and Russian—were equally out of the question owing to the irregularity of their position. The inspection of objects of interest, apart from the fact that everything had been seen already, had not for Vronsky, a Russian and a sensible man, the immense significance Englishmen are able to attach to that pursuit.

And just as the hungry stomach eagerly accepts every object it can get, hoping to find nourishment in it, Vronsky quite unconsciously clutched first at politics, then at new books, and then at pictures.

As he had from a child a taste for painting, and as, not knowing what to spend his money on, he had begun collecting engravings, he came to a stop at painting, began to take interest in it, and concentrated upon it the unoccupied mass of desires which demanded satisfaction.

He had a ready appreciation of art, and probably, with a taste for imitating art, he supposed himself to have the real thing essential for an artist, and after hesitating for some time which style of painting to select—religious, historical, realistic, or genre painting—he set to work to paint. He appreciated all kinds, and could have felt inspired by any one of them; but he had no conception of the possibility of knowing nothing at all of any school of painting, and of being inspired directly by what is within the soul, without caring whether what is painted will belong to any recognized school. Since he knew nothing of this, and drew his inspiration, not directly from life, but indirectly from life embodied in art, his inspiration came very quickly and easily, and as quickly and easily came his success in painting something very similar to the sort of painting he was trying to imitate.

More than any other style he liked the French—graceful and effective—and in that style he began to paint Anna's portrait in Italian costume, and the portrait seemed to him, and to everyone who saw it, extremely successful.

figure in all its force and vigor, as it had suddenly come to him from the spot of tallow. He was carefully finishing the figure when the cards were brought him.

"Coming, coming!"

He went in to his wife.

"Come, Sasha, don't be cross!" he said, smiling timidly and affectionately at her. "You were to blame. I was to blame. I'll make it all right." And having made peace with his wife he put on an olive-green overcoat with a velvet collar and a hat, and went towards his studio. The successful figure he had already forgotten. Now he was delighted and excited at the visit of these people of consequence, Russians, who had come in their carriage.

Of his picture, the one that stood now on his easel, he had at the bottom of his heart one conviction—that no one had ever painted a picture like it. He did not believe that his picture was better than all the pictures of Raphael, but he knew that what he tried to convey in that picture, no one ever had conveyed. This he knew positively, and had known a long while, ever since he had begun to paint it. But other people's criticisms, whatever they might be, had yet immense consequence in his eyes, and they agitated him to the depths of his soul. Any remark, the most insignificant, that showed that the critic saw even the tiniest part of what he saw in the picture, agitated him to the depths of his soul. He always attributed to his critics a more profound comprehension than he had himself, and always expected from them something he did not himself see in the picture. And often in their criticisms he fancied that he had found this.

He walked rapidly to the door of his studio, and in spite of his excitement he was struck by the soft light on Anna's figure as she stood in the shade of the entrance listening to Golenishtchev, who was eagerly telling her something, while she evidently wanted to look round at the artist. He was himself unconscious how, as he approached them, he seized on this impression and absorbed it, as he had the chin of the shopkeeper who had sold him the cigars, and put it away somewhere to be brought out when he wanted it. The visitors, not agreeably impressed beforehand by Golenishtchev's account of the artist, were still less so by his personal appearance. Thick-set and of middle height, with nimble movements, with his brown hat, olive-green coat and narrow trousers—though wide trousers had been a long while in fashion,—most of all, with the ordinariness of his broad face, and the combined expression of timidity and anxiety to keep up his dignity, Mihailov made an unpleasant impression.

"Please step in," he said, trying to look indifferent, and going into the passage he took a key out of his pocket and opened the door.

Anna and Vronsky had long been exchanging glances, regretting their friend's flow of cleverness. At last Vronsky, without waiting for the artist, walked away to another small picture.

"Oh, how exquisite! What a lovely thing! A gem! How exquisite!" they cried with one voice.

"What is it they're so pleased with?" thought Mihailov. He had positively forgotten that picture he had painted three years ago. He had forgotten all the agonies and the ecstasies he had lived through with that picture when for several months it had been the one thought haunting him day and night. He had forgotten, as he always forgot, the pictures he had finished. He did not even like to look at it, and had only brought it out because he was expecting an Englishman who wanted to buy it.

"Oh, that's only an old study," he said.

"How fine!" said Golenishtchev, he too, with unmistakable sincerity, falling under the spell of the picture.

Two boys were angling in the shade of a willow-tree. The elder had just dropped in the hook, and was carefully pulling the float from behind a bush, entirely absorbed in what he was doing. The other, a little younger, was lying in the grass leaning on his elbows, with his tangled, flaxen head in his hands, staring at the water with his dreamy blue eyes. What was he thinking of?

The enthusiasm over this picture stirred some of the old feeling for it in Mihailov, but he feared and disliked this waste of feeling for things past, and so, even though this praise was grateful to him, he tried to draw his visitors away to a third picture.

But Vronsky asked whether the picture was for sale. To Mihailov at that moment, excited by visitors, it was extremely distasteful to speak of money matters.

"It is put up there to be sold," he answered, scowling gloomily.

When the visitors had gone, Mihailov sat down opposite the picture of Pilate and Christ, and in his mind went over what had been said, and what, though not said, had been implied by those visitors. And, strange to say, what had had such weight with him, while they were there and while he mentally put himself at their point of view, suddenly lost all importance for him. He began to look at his picture with all his own full artist vision, and was soon in that mood of conviction of the perfectibility, and so of the significance, of his picture—a conviction essential to the most intense fervor, excluding all other interests—in which alone he could work.

Christ's foreshortened leg was not right, though. He took his palette and began to work. As he corrected the leg he looked continually at the figure of John in the background, which his visitors had not even noticed, but which he knew was beyond perfection. When he had finished the leg he wanted to touch that figure, but he felt too much excited for it. He was equally unable to work when he was cold and when he was too much affected and saw everything too much. There was only one stage in the transition from coldness to inspiration, at which work was possible. Today he was too much agitated. He would have covered the picture, but he stopped, holding the cloth in his hand, and, smiling blissfully, gazed a long while at the figure of John. At last, as it were regretfully tearing himself away, he dropped the cloth, and, exhausted but happy, went home.

Vronsky, Anna, and Golenishtchev, on their way home, were particularly lively and cheerful. They talked of Mihailov and his pictures. The word *talent*, by which they meant an inborn, almost physical, aptitude apart from brain and heart, and in which they tried to find an expression for all the artist had gained from life, recurred particularly often in their talk, as though it were necessary for them to sum up what they had no conception of, though they wanted to talk of it. They said that there was no denying his talent, but that his talent could not develop for want of education—the common defect of our Russian artists. But the picture of the boys had imprinted itself on their memories, and they were continually coming back to it. "What an exquisite thing! How he has succeeded in it, and how simply! He doesn't even comprehend how good it is. Yes, I mustn't let it slip; I must buy it," said Vronsky.

Mihailov sold Vronsky his picture, and agreed to paint a portrait of Anna. On the day fixed he came and began the work.

From the fifth sitting the portrait impressed everyone, especially Vronsky, not only by its resemblance, but by its characteristic beauty. It was strange how Mihailov could have discovered just her characteristic beauty. "One needs to know and love her as I have loved her to discover the very sweetest expression of her soul," Vronsky thought, though it was only from this portrait that he had himself learned this sweetest expression of her soul. But the expression was so true that he, and others too, fancied they had long known it.

"I have been struggling on for ever so long without doing anything," he said of his own portrait of her, "and he just looked and painted it. That's where technique comes in."

"That will come," was the consoling reassurance given him by Golenishtchev, in whose view Vronsky had both talent, and what was most important, culture, giving him a wider outlook on art. Golenishtchev's faith in Vronsky's talent was propped up by his own need of Vronsky's sympathy and approval for his own articles and ideas, and he felt that the praise and support must be mutual.

In another man's house, and especially in Vronsky's palazzo, Mihailov was quite a different man from what he was in his studio. He behaved with hostile courtesy, as though he were afraid of coming closer to people he did not respect. He called Vronsky "your excellency," and notwithstanding Anna's and Vronsky's invitations, he would never stay to dinner, nor come except for the sittings. Anna was even more friendly to him than to other people, and was very grateful for her portrait. Vronsky was more than cordial with him, and was obviously interested to know the artist's opinion of his picture. Golenishtchev never let slip an opportunity of instilling sound ideas about art into Mihailov. But Mihailov remained equally chilly to all of them. Anna was aware from his eyes that he liked looking at her, but he avoided conversation with her. Vronsky's talk about his painting he met with stubborn silence, and he was as stubbornly silent when he was shown Vronsky's picture. He was unmistakably bored by Golenishtchev's conversation, and he did not attempt to oppose him.

Altogether Mihailov, with his reserved and disagreeable, as it were, hostile attitude, was quite disliked by them as they got to know him better; and they were glad when the sittings were over, and they were left with a magnificent portrait in their possession, and he gave up coming. Golenishtchev was the first to give expression to an idea that had occurred to all of them, which was that Mihailov was simply jealous of Vronsky.

"Not envious, let us say, since he has *talent*; but it annoys him that a wealthy man of the highest society, and a count, too (you know they all detest a title), can, without any particular trouble, do as well, if not better, than he who has devoted all his life to it. And more than all, it's a question of culture, which he is without."

Vronsky defended Mihailov, but at the bottom of his heart he believed it, because in his view a man of a different, lower world would be sure to be envious.

Anna's portrait—the same subject painted from nature both by him and by Mihailov—ought to have shown Vronsky the difference between him and Mihailov; but he did not see it. Only after Mihailov's portrait was painted he left off painting his portrait of Anna, deciding that it was now not needed. His picture of mediaeval life he went on with. And he himself, and Golenishtchev, and still more Anna, thought it very good, because it was far more like the celebrated pictures they knew than Mihailov's picture.

Mihailov meanwhile, although Anna's portrait greatly fascinated him, was even more glad than they were when the sittings were over, and he had no longer to listen to Golenishtchev's disquisitions upon art, and could forget about Vronsky's painting. He knew that Vronsky could not be prevented from amusing himself with painting; he knew that he and all dilettanti had a perfect right to paint what they liked, but it was distasteful to him. A man could not be prevented from making himself a big wax doll, and kissing it. But if the man were to come with the doll and sit before a man in love, and begin caressing his doll as the lover caressed the woman he loved, it would be distasteful to the lover. Just such a distasteful sensation was what Mihailov felt at the sight of Vronsky's painting: he felt it both ludicrous and irritating, both pitiable and offensive.

Vronsky's interest in painting and the Middle Ages did not last long. He had enough taste for painting to be unable to finish his picture. The picture came to a standstill. He was vaguely aware that its defects, inconspicuous at first, would be glaring if he were to go on with it. The same experience befell him as Golenishtchev, who felt that he had nothing to say, and continually deceived himself with the theory that his idea was not yet mature, that he was working it out and collecting materials. This exasperated and tortured Golenishtchev, but Vronsky was incapable of deceiving and torturing himself, and even more incapable of exasperation. With his characteristic decision, without explanation or apology, he simply ceased working at painting.

But without this occupation, the life of Vronsky and of Anna, who wondered at his loss of interest in it, struck them as intolerably tedious in an Italian town. The palazzo suddenly seemed so obtrusively old and dirty, the spots on the curtains, the cracks in the floors, the broken plaster on the cornices became so disagreeably obvious, and the everlasting sameness of Golenishtchev, and the Italian professor and the German traveler became so wearisome, that they had to make some change. They resolved to go to Russia, to the country. In Petersburg Vronsky intended to arrange a partition of the land with his brother, while Anna meant to see her son. The summer they intended to spend on Vronsky's great family estate.

Levin had been married three months. He was happy, but not at all in the way he had expected to be. At every step he found his former dreams disappointed, and new, unexpected surprises of happiness. He was happy; but on entering upon family life he saw at every step that it was utterly different from what he had imagined. At every step he experienced what a man would experience who, after admiring the smooth, happy course of a little boat on a lake, should get himself into that little boat. He saw that it was not all sitting still, floating smoothly; that one had to think too, not for an instant to forget where one was floating; and that there was water under one, and that one must row; and that his unaccustomed hands would be sore; and that it was only to look at it that was easy; but that doing it, though very delightful, was very difficult.

As a bachelor, when he had watched other people's married life, seen the petty cares, the squabbles, the jealousy, he had only smiled contemptuously in his heart. In his future married life there could be, he was convinced, nothing of that sort; even the external forms, indeed, he fancied, must be utterly unlike the life of others in everything. And all of a sudden, instead of his life with his wife being made on an individual pattern, it was, on the contrary, entirely made up of the pettiest details, which he had so despised before, but which now, by no will of his own, had gained an extraordinary importance that it was useless to contend against. And Levin saw that the organization of all these details was by no means so easy as he had fancied before. Although Levin believed himself to have the most exact conceptions of domestic life, unconsciously, like all men, he pictured domestic life as the happiest enjoyment of love, with nothing to hinder and no petty cares to distract. He ought, as he conceived the position, to do his work, and to find repose from it in the happiness of love. She ought to be beloved, and nothing more. But, like all men, he forgot that she too would want work. And he was surprised that she, his poetic, exquisite Kitty, could, not merely in the first weeks, but even in the first days of their married life, think, remember, and busy herself about tablecloths, and furniture, about mattresses for visitors, about a tray, about the cook, and the dinner, and so on. While they were still engaged, he had been struck by the definiteness with which she had declined the tour abroad and decided to go into the country, as though she knew of something she wanted, and could still think of something outside her love. This had jarred upon him then, and now her trivial cares and anxieties jarred upon him several times. But he saw that this was essential for her. And, loving her as he did, though he did not understand the reason of them, and jeered at these domestic pursuits, he could not help admiring them. He jeered at the way in which she arranged the furniture they had brought from Moscow; rearranged their room; hung up curtains; prepared rooms for visitors; a room for Dolly; saw after an abode for her new maid; ordered dinner of the old cook; came into collision with Agafea Mihalovna, taking from her the charge of the stores. He saw how the old cook smiled, admiring her, and listening to her inexperienced, impossible orders, how mournfully and tenderly Agafea Mihalovna shook her head over the young mistress's new arrangements. He saw that Kitty was extraordinarily sweet when, laughing and crying, she came to tell him that her maid, Masha, was used to looking upon her as her young lady, and so no one obeyed her. It seemed to him sweet, but strange, and he thought it would have been better without this.

He did not know how great a sense of change she was experiencing; she, who at home had sometimes wanted some favorite dish, or sweets, without the possibility of getting either, now could order what she liked, buy pounds of sweets, spend as much money as she liked, and order any puddings she pleased.

She was dreaming with delight now of Dolly's coming to them with her children, especially because she would order for the children their favorite puddings and Dolly would appreciate all her new housekeeping. She did not know herself why and wherefore, but the arranging of her house had an irresistible attraction for her. Instinctively feeling the approach of spring, and knowing that there would be days of rough weather too, she built her nest as best she could, and was in haste at the same time to build it and to learn how to do it.

This care for domestic details in Kitty, so opposed to Levin's ideal of exalted happiness, was at first one of the disappointments; and this sweet care of her household, the aim of which he did not understand, but could not help loving, was one of the new happy surprises.

Another disappointment and happy surprise came in their quarrels. Levin could never have conceived that between him and his wife any relations could arise other than tender, respectful and loving, and all at once in the very early days they quarreled, so that she said he did not care for her, that he cared for no one but himself, burst into tears, and wrung her arms.

This first quarrel arose from Levin's having gone out to a new farmhouse and having been away half an hour too long, because he had tried to get home by a short cut and had lost his way. He drove home thinking of nothing but her, of her love, of his own happiness, and the nearer he drew to home, the warmer was his tenderness for her. He ran into the room with the same feeling, with an even stronger feeling than he had had when he reached the Shtcherbatskys' house to make his offer. And suddenly he was met by a lowering expression he had never seen in her. He would have kissed her; she pushed him away.

"What is it?"

"You've been enjoying yourself," she began, trying to be calm and spiteful. But as soon as she opened her mouth, a stream of reproach, of senseless jealousy, of all that had been torturing her during that half hour which she had spent sitting motionless at the window, burst from her. It was only then, for the first time, that he clearly understood what he had not understood when he led her out of the church after the wedding. He felt now that he was not simply close to her, but that he did not know where he ended and she began. He felt this from the agonizing sensation of division that he experienced at that instant. He was offended for the first instant, but the very same second he felt that he could not be offended by her, that she was himself. He felt for the first moment as a man feels when, having suddenly received a violent blow from behind, he turns round, angry and eager to avenge himself, to look for his antagonist, and finds that it is he himself who has accidentally struck himself, that there is no one to be angry with, and that he must put up with and try to soothe the pain.

Never afterwards did he feel it with such intensity, but this first time he could not for a long while get over it. His natural feeling urged him to defend himself, to prove to her she was wrong; but to prove her wrong would mean irritating her still more and making the rupture greater that was the cause of all his suffering. One habitual feeling impelled him to get rid of the blame and to pass it on to her. Another feeling, even stronger, impelled him as quickly as possible to smooth over the rupture without letting it grow greater. To remain under such undeserved reproach was wretched, but to make her suffer by justifying himself was worse still. Like a man half-awake in an agony of pain, he wanted to tear out, to fling away the aching place, and coming to his senses, he felt that the aching place was himself. He could do nothing but try to help the aching place to bear it, and this he tried to do.

They made peace. She, recognizing that she was wrong, though she did not say so, became tenderer to him, and they experienced new, redoubled happiness in their love. But that did not prevent such quarrels from happening again, and exceedingly often too, on the most unexpected and trivial grounds. These quarrels frequently arose from the fact that they did not yet know what was of importance to each other and that all this early period they were both often in a bad temper. When one was in a good temper, and the other in a bad temper, the peace was not broken; but when both happened to be in an ill-humor, quarrels sprang up from such incomprehensibly trifling causes, that they could never remember afterwards what they had quarreled about. It is true that when they were both in a good temper their enjoyment of life was redoubled. But still this first period of their married life was a difficult time for them.

During all this early time they had a peculiarly vivid sense of tension, as it were, a tugging in opposite directions of the chain by which they were bound. Altogether their honeymoon—that is to say, the month after their wedding—from which from tradition Levin expected so much, was not merely not a time of sweetness, but remained in the memories of both as the bitterest and most humiliating period in their lives. They both alike tried in later life to blot out from their memories all the monstrous, shameful incidents of that morbid period, when both were rarely in a normal frame of mind, both were rarely quite themselves.

It was only in the third month of their married life, after their return from Moscow, where they had been staying for a month, that their life began to go more smoothly.

They had just come back from Moscow, and were glad to be alone. He was sitting at the writing table in his study, writing. She, wearing the dark lilac dress she had worn during the first days of their married life, and put on again today, a dress particularly remembered and loved by him, was sitting on the sofa, the same old-fashioned leather sofa which had always stood in the study in Levin's father's and grandfather's days. She was sewing at *broderie anglaise*. He thought and wrote, never losing the happy consciousness of her presence. His work, both on the land and on the book, in which the principles of the new land system were to be laid down, had not been abandoned; but just as formerly these pursuits and ideas had seemed to him petty and trivial in comparison with the darkness that overspread all life, now they seemed as unimportant and petty in comparison with the life that lay before him suffused with the brilliant light of happiness. He went on with his work, but he felt now that the center of gravity of his attention had passed to something else, and that consequently he looked at his work quite differently and more clearly. Formerly this work had been for him an escape from life. Formerly he had felt that without this work his life would be too gloomy. Now these pursuits were necessary for him that life might not be too uniformly bright. Taking up his manuscript, reading through what he had written, he found with pleasure that the work was worth his working at. Many of his old ideas seemed to him superfluous and extreme, but many blanks became distinct to him when he reviewed the whole thing in his memory. He was writing now a new chapter on the causes of the present disastrous condition of agriculture in Russia. He maintained that the poverty of Russia arises not merely from the anomalous distribution of landed property and misdirected reforms, but that what had contributed of late years to this result was the civilization from without abnormally grafted upon Russia, especially facilities of communication, as railways, leading to centralization in towns, the development of luxury, and the consequent development of manufactures, credit and its accompaniment of speculation—all to the detriment of agriculture. It seemed to him that in a normal development of wealth in a state all these phenomena would arise only when a considerable amount of labor had been put into agriculture, when it had come under regular, or at least definite, conditions; that the wealth of a country ought to increase proportionally, and especially in such a way that other sources of wealth should not outstrip agriculture; that in harmony with a certain stage of agriculture there should be means of communication corresponding to it, and that in our unsettled condition of the land, railways, called into being by political and not by economic needs, were premature, and instead of promoting agriculture, as was expected of them, they were competing with agriculture and promoting the development of manufactures and credit, and so arresting its progress; and that just as the one-sided and premature development of one organ in an animal would hinder its general development, so in the general development of wealth in Russia, credit, facilities of communication, manufacturing activity, indubitably necessary in Europe, where they had arisen in their proper time, had with us only done harm, by throwing into the background the chief question calling for settlement—the question of the organization of agriculture.

While he was writing his ideas she was thinking how unnaturally cordial her husband had been to young Prince Tcharsky, who had, with great want of tact, flirted with her the day before they left Moscow. "He's jealous," she thought. "Goodness! how sweet and silly he is! He's jealous of me! If he knew that I think no more of them than of Piotr the cook," she thought, looking at his head and red neck with a feeling of possession strange to herself. "Though it's a pity to take him from his work (but he has plenty of time!), I must look at his face; will he feel I'm looking at him? I wish he'd turn round...I'll *will* him to!" and she opened her eyes wide, as though to intensify the influence of her gaze.

"Yes, they draw away all the sap and give a false appearance of prosperity," he muttered, stopping to write, and, feeling that she was looking at him and smiling, he looked round.

"Well?" he queried, smiling, and getting up.

"He looked round," she thought.

"It's nothing; I wanted you to look round," she said, watching him, and trying to guess whether he was vexed at being interrupted or not.

"How happy we are alone together!—I am, that is," he said, going up to her with a radiant smile of happiness.

"I'm just as happy. I'll never go anywhere, especially not to Moscow."

"And what were you thinking about?"

"I? I was thinking.... No, no, go along, go on writing; don't break off," she said, pursing up her lips, "and I must cut out these little holes now, do you see?"

She took up her scissors and began cutting them out.

"No; tell me, what was it?" he said, sitting down beside her and watching the tiny scissors moving round.

"Oh! what was I thinking about? I was thinking about Moscow, about the back of your head."

"Why should I, of all people, have such happiness! It's unnatural, too good," he said, kissing her hand.

"I feel quite the opposite; the better things are, the more natural it seems to me."

"And you've got a little curl loose," he said, carefully turning her head round.

"A little curl, oh yes. No, no, we are busy at our work!"

Work did not progress further, and they darted apart from one another like culprits when Kouzma came in to announce that tea was ready.

"Have they come from the town?" Levin asked Kouzma.

"They've just come; they're unpacking the things."

"Come quickly," she said to him as she went out of the study, "or else I shall read your letters without you."

Left alone, after putting his manuscripts together in the new portfolio bought by her, he washed his hands at the new washstand with the elegant fittings, that had all made their appearance with her. Levin smiled at his own thoughts, and shook his head disapprovingly at those thoughts; a feeling akin to remorse fretted him. There was something shameful, effeminate, Capuan, as he called it to himself, in his present mode of life. "It's not right to go on like this," he thought. "It'll soon be three months, and I'm doing next to nothing. Today, almost for the first time, I set to work seriously, and what happened? I did nothing but begin and throw it aside. Even my ordinary pursuits I have almost given up. On the land I scarcely walk or drive about at all to look after things. Either I am loath to leave her, or I see she's dull alone. And I used to think that, before marriage, life was nothing much, somehow didn't count, but that after marriage, life began in earnest. And here almost three months have passed, and I have spent my time so idly and unprofitably. No, this won't do; I must begin. Of course, it's not her fault. She's not to blame in any way. I ought myself to be firmer, to maintain my masculine independence of action; or else I shall get into such ways, and she'll get used to them too.... Of course she's not to blame," he told himself.

But it is hard for anyone who is dissatisfied not to blame someone else, and especially the person nearest of all to him, for the ground of his dissatisfaction. And it vaguely came into Levin's mind that she herself was not to blame (she could not be to blame for anything), but what was to blame was her education, too superficial and frivolous. ("That fool Tcharsky: she wanted, I know, to stop him, but didn't know how to.") "Yes, apart from her interest in the house (that she has), apart from dress and *broderie anglaise*, she has no serious interests. No interest in her work, in the estate, in the peasants, nor in music, though she's rather good at it, nor in reading. She does nothing, and is perfectly satisfied." Levin, in his heart, censured this, and did not as yet understand that she was preparing for that period of activity which was to come for her when she would at once be the wife of her husband and mistress of the house, and would bear, and nurse, and bring up children. He knew not that she was instinctively aware of this, and preparing herself for this time of terrible toil, did not reproach herself for the moments of carelessness and happiness in her love that she enjoyed now while gaily building her nest for the future.

When Levin went upstairs, his wife was sitting near the new silver samovar behind the new tea service, and, having settled old Agafea Mihalovna at a little table with a full cup of tea, was reading a letter from Dolly, with whom they were in continual and frequent correspondence.

"You see, your good lady's settled me here, told me to sit a bit with her," said Agafea Mihalovna, smiling affectionately at Kitty.

In these words of Agafea Mihalovna, Levin read the final act of the drama which had been enacted of late between her and Kitty. He saw that, in spite of Agafea Mihalovna's feelings being hurt by a new mistress taking the reins of government out of her hands, Kitty had yet conquered her and made her love her.

"Here, I opened your letter too," said Kitty, handing him an illiterate letter. "It's from that woman, I think, your brother's..." she said. "I did not read it through. This is from my people and from Dolly. Fancy! Dolly took Tanya and Grisha to a children's ball at the Sarmatskys': Tanya was a French marquise."

But Levin did not hear her. Flushing, he took the letter from Marya Nikolaevna, his brother's former mistress, and began to read it. This was the second letter he had received from Marya Nikolaevna. In the first letter, Marya Nikolaevna wrote that his brother had sent her away for no fault of hers, and, with touching simplicity, added that though she was in want again, she asked for nothing, and wished for nothing, but was only tormented by the thought that Nikolay Dmitrievitch would come to grief without her, owing to the weak state of his health, and begged his brother to look after him. Now she wrote quite differently. She had found Nikolay Dmitrievitch, had again made it up with him in Moscow, and had moved with him to a provincial town, where he had received a post in the government service. But that he had quarreled with the head official, and was on his way back to Moscow, only he had been taken so ill on the road that it was doubtful if he would ever leave his bed again, she wrote. "It's always of you he has talked, and, besides, he has no more money left."

"Read this; Dolly writes about you," Kitty was beginning, with a smile; but she stopped suddenly, noticing the changed expression on her husband's face.

"What is it? What's the matter?"

"She writes to me that Nikolay, my brother, is at death's door. I shall go to him."

Kitty's face changed at once. Thoughts of Tanya as a marquise, of Dolly, all had vanished.

"When are you going?" she said.

"Tomorrow."

"And I will go with you, can I?" she said.

"Kitty! What are you thinking of?" he said reproachfully.

"How do you mean?" offended that he should seem to take her suggestion unwillingly and with vexation. "Why shouldn't I go? I shan't be in your way. I..."

"I'm going because my brother is dying," said Levin. "Why should you..."

"Why? For the same reason as you."

"And, at a moment of such gravity for me, she only thinks of her being dull by herself," thought Levin. And this lack of candor in a matter of such gravity infuriated him.

"It's out of the question," he said sternly.

Agafea Mihalovna, seeing that it was coming to a quarrel, gently put down her cup and withdrew. Kitty did not even notice her. The tone in which her husband had said the last words wounded her, especially because he evidently did not believe what she had said.

"I tell you, that if you go, I shall come with you; I shall certainly come," she said hastily and wrathfully. "Why out of the question? Why do you say it's out of the question?"

"Because it'll be going God knows where, by all sorts of roads and to all sorts of hotels. You would be a hindrance to me," said Levin, trying to be cool.

"Not at all. I don't want anything. Where you can go, I can...."

"Well, for one thing then, because this woman's there whom you can't meet."

"I don't know and don't care to know who's there and what. I know that my husband's brother is dying and my husband is going to him, and I go with my husband too...."

"Kitty! Don't get angry. But just think a little: this is a matter of such importance that I can't bear to think that you should bring in a feeling of weakness, of dislike to being left alone. Come, you'll be dull alone, so go and stay at Moscow a little."

"There, you always ascribe base, vile motives to me," she said with tears of wounded pride and fury. "I didn't mean, it wasn't weakness, it wasn't...I feel that it's my duty to be with my husband when he's in trouble, but you try on purpose to hurt me, you try on purpose not to understand...."

"No; this is awful! To be such a slave!" cried Levin, getting up, and unable to restrain his anger any longer. But at the same second he felt that he was beating himself.

"Then why did you marry? You could have been free. Why did you, if you regret it?" she said, getting up and running away into the drawing room.

When he went to her, she was sobbing.

He began to speak, trying to find words not to dissuade but simply to soothe her. But she did not heed him, and would not agree to anything. He bent down to her and took her hand, which resisted him. He kissed her hand, kissed her hair, kissed her hand again—still she was silent. But when he took her face in both his hands and said "Kitty!" she suddenly recovered herself, and began to cry, and they were reconciled.

It was decided that they should go together the next day. Levin told his wife that he believed she wanted to go simply in order to be of use, agreed that Marya Nikolaevna's being with his brother did not make her going improper, but he set off at the bottom of his heart dissatisfied both with her and with himself. He was dissatisfied with her for being unable to make up her mind to let him go when it was necessary (and how strange it was for him to think that he, so lately hardly daring to believe in such happiness as that she could love him— now was unhappy because she loved him too much!), and he was dissatisfied with himself for not showing more strength of will. Even greater was the feeling of disagreement at the bottom of his heart as to her not needing to consider the woman who was with his brother, and he thought with horror of all the contingencies they might meet with. The mere idea of his wife, his Kitty, being in the same room with a common wench, set him shuddering with horror and loathing.

CHAPTER FIVE

DARYA ALEXANDROVNA CARRIED out her intention and went to see Anna. She was sorry to annoy her sister and to do anything Levin disliked. She quite understood how right the Levins were in not wishing to have anything to do with Vronsky. But she felt she must go and see Anna, and show her that her feelings could not be changed, in spite of the change in her position. That she might be independent of the Levins in this expedition, Darya Alexandrovna sent to the village to hire horses for the drive; but Levin learning of it went to her to protest.

"What makes you suppose that I dislike your going? But, even if I did dislike it, I should still more dislike your not taking my horses," he said. "You never told me that you were going for certain. Hiring horses in the village is disagreeable to me, and, what's of more importance, they'll undertake the job and never get you there. I have horses. And if you don't want to wound me, you'll take mine."

Darya Alexandrovna had to consent, and on the day fixed Levin had ready for his sister-in-law a set of four horses and relays, getting them together from the farm- and saddle-horses—not at all a smart-looking set, but capable of taking Darya Alexandrovna the whole distance in a single day. At that moment, when horses were wanted for the princess, who was going, and for the midwife, it was a difficult matter for Levin to make up the number, but the duties of hospitality would not let him allow Darya Alexandrovna to hire horses when staying in his house. Moreover, he was well aware that the twenty roubles that would be asked for the journey were a serious matter for her; Darya Alexandrovna's pecuniary affairs, which were in a very unsatisfactory state, were taken to heart by the Levins as if they were their own.

Darya Alexandrovna, by Levin's advice, started before daybreak. The road was good, the carriage comfortable, the horses trotted along merrily, and on the box, besides the coachman, sat the counting-house clerk, whom Levin was sending instead of a groom for greater security. Darya Alexandrovna dozed and waked up only on reaching the inn where the horses were to be changed.

After drinking tea at the same well-to-do peasant's with whom Levin had stayed on the way to Sviazhsky's, and chatting with the women about their children, and with the old man about Count Vronsky, whom the latter praised very highly, Darya Alexandrovna, at ten o'clock, went on again. At home, looking after her children, she had no time to think. So now, after this journey of four hours, all the thoughts she had suppressed before rushed swarming into her brain, and she thought over all her life as she never had before, and from the most different points of view. Her thoughts seemed strange even to herself. At first she thought about the children, about whom she was uneasy, although the princess and Kitty (she reckoned more upon her) had promised to look after them. "If only Masha does not begin her naughty tricks, if Grisha isn't kicked by a horse, and Lily's stomach isn't upset again!" she thought. But these questions of the present were succeeded by questions of the immediate future. She began thinking how she had to get a new flat in Moscow for the coming winter, to renew the drawing room furniture, and to make her elder girl a cloak. Then questions of the more remote future occurred to her: how she was to place her children in the world. "The girls are all right," she thought; "but the boys?"

"It's very well that I'm teaching Grisha, but of course that's only because I am free myself now, I'm not with child. Stiva, of course, there's no counting on. And with the help of good-natured friends I can bring them up; but if there's another baby coming?..." And the thought struck her how untruly it was said that the curse laid on woman was that in sorrow she should bring forth children.

"The birth itself, that's nothing; but the months of carrying the child—that's what's so intolerable," she thought, picturing to herself her last pregnancy, and the death of the last baby. And she recalled the conversation she had just had with the young woman at the inn. On being asked whether she had any children, the handsome young woman had answered cheerfully:

"I had a girl baby, but God set me free; I buried her last Lent."

"Well, did you grieve very much for her?" asked Darya Alexandrovna.

"Why grieve? The old man has grandchildren enough as it is. It was only a trouble. No working, nor nothing. Only a tie."

This answer had struck Darya Alexandrovna as revolting in spite of the good-natured and pleasing face of the young woman; but now she could not help recalling these words. In those cynical words there was indeed a grain of truth.

"Yes, altogether," thought Darya Alexandrovna, looking back over her whole existence during those fifteen years of her married life, "pregnancy, sickness, mental incapacity, indifference to everything, and most of all—hideousness. Kitty, young and pretty as she is, even Kitty has lost her looks; and I when I'm with child become hideous, I know it. The birth, the agony, the hideous agonies, that last moment...then the nursing, the sleepless nights, the fearful pains...."

Darya Alexandrovna shuddered at the mere recollection of the pain from sore breasts which she had suffered with almost every child. "Then the children's illnesses, that everlasting apprehension; then bringing them up; evil propensities" (she thought of little Masha's crime among the raspberries), "education, Latin—it's all so incomprehensible and difficult. And on the top of it all, the death of these children." And there rose again before her imagination the cruel memory, that always tore her mother's heart, of the death of her last little baby, who had died of croup; his funeral, the callous indifference of all at the little pink coffin, and her own torn heart, and her lonely anguish at the sight of the pale little brow with its projecting temples, and the open, wondering little mouth seen in the coffin at the moment when it was being covered with the little pink lid with a cross braided on it.

"And all this, what's it for? What is to come of it all? That I'm wasting my life, never having a moment's peace, either with child, or nursing a child, forever irritable, peevish, wretched myself and worrying others, repulsive to my husband, while the children are growing up unhappy, badly educated, and penniless. Even now, if it weren't for spending the summer at the Levins', I don't know how we should be managing to live. Of course Kostya and Kitty have so much tact that we don't feel it; but it can't go on. They'll have children, they won't be able to keep us; it's a drag on them as it is. How is papa, who has hardly anything left for himself, to help us? So that I can't even bring the children up by myself, and may find it hard with the help of other people, at the cost of humiliation. Why, even if we suppose the greatest good luck, that the children don't die, and I bring them up somehow. At the very best they'll simply be decent people. That's all I can hope for. And to gain simply that—what agonies, what toil!... One's whole life ruined!" Again she recalled what the young peasant woman had said, and again she was revolted at the thought; but she could not help admitting that there was a grain of brutal truth in the words.

"Is it far now, Mihail?" Darya Alexandrovna asked the counting house clerk, to turn her mind from thoughts that were frightening her.

"From this village, they say, it's five miles." The carriage drove along the village street and onto a bridge. On the bridge was a crowd of peasant women with coils of ties for the sheaves on their shoulders, gaily and noisily chattering. They stood still on the bridge, staring inquisitively at the carriage. All the faces turned to Darya Alexandrovna looked to her healthy and happy, making her envious of their enjoyment of life. "They're all living, they're all enjoying life," Darya Alexandrovna still mused when she had passed the peasant women and was driving uphill again at a trot, seated comfortably on the soft springs of the old carriage, "while I, let out, as it were from prison, from the world of worries that fret me to death, am only looking about me now for an instant. They all live; those peasant women and my sister Natalia and Varenka and Anna, whom I am going to see—all, but not I.

"And they attack Anna. What for? am I any better? I have, anyway, a husband I love—not as I should like to love him, still I do love him, while Anna never loved hers. How is she to blame? She wants to live. God has put that in our hearts. Very likely I should have done the same. Even to this day I don't feel sure I did right in listening to her at that terrible time when she came to me in Moscow. I ought then to have cast off my husband and have begun my life fresh. I might have loved and have been loved in reality. And is it any better as it is? I don't respect him. He's necessary to me," she thought about her husband, "and I put up with him. Is that any better? At that time I could still have been admired, I had beauty left me still," Darya Alexandrovna pursued her thoughts, and she would have liked to look at herself in the looking glass. She had a traveling looking glass in her handbag, and she wanted to take it out; but looking at the backs of the coachman and the swaying counting house clerk, she felt that she would be ashamed if either of them were to look round, and she did not take out the glass.

But without looking in the glass, she thought that even now it was not too late; and she thought of Sergey Ivanovitch, who was always particularly attentive to her, of Stiva's good-hearted friend, Turovtsin, who had helped her nurse her children through the scarlatina, and was in love with her. And there was someone else, a quite young man, who—her husband had told her it as a joke—thought her more beautiful than either of her sisters. And the most passionate and impossible romances rose before Darya Alexandrovna's imagination. "Anna did quite right, and certainly I shall never reproach her for it. She is happy, she makes another person happy, and she's not broken down as I am, but most likely just as she always was, bright, clever, open to every impression," thought Darya Alexandrovna,—and a sly smile curved her lips, for, as she pondered on Anna's love affair, Darya Alexandrovna constructed on parallel lines an almost identical love affair for herself, with an imaginary composite figure, the ideal man who was in love with her. She, like Anna, confessed the whole affair to her husband. And the amazement and perplexity of Stepan Arkadyevitch at this avowal made her smile.

In such daydreams she reached the turning of the highroad that led to Vozdvizhenskoe.

Left alone, Darya Alexandrovna, with a good housewife's eye, scanned her room. All she had seen in entering the house and walking through it, and all she saw now in her room, gave her an impression of wealth and sumptuousness and of that modern European luxury of which she had only read in English novels, but had never seen in Russia and in the country. Everything was new from the new French hangings on the walls to the carpet which covered the whole floor. The bed had a spring mattress, and a special sort of bolster and silk pillowcases on the little pillows. The marble washstand, the dressing table, the little sofa, the tables, the bronze clock on the chimney piece, the window curtains, and the *portières* were all new and expensive.

The smart maid, who came in to offer her services, with her hair done up high, and a gown more fashionable than Dolly's, was as new and expensive as the whole room. Darya Alexandrovna liked her neatness, her deferential and obliging manners, but she felt ill at ease with her. She felt ashamed of her seeing the patched dressing jacket that had unluckily been packed by mistake for her. She was ashamed of the very patches and darned places of which she had been so proud at home. At home it had been so clear that for six dressing jackets there would be needed twenty-four yards of nainsook at sixteen pence the yard, which was a matter of thirty shillings besides the cutting-out and making, and these thirty shillings had been saved. But before the maid she felt, if not exactly ashamed, at least uncomfortable.

Darya Alexandrovna had a great sense of relief when Annushka, whom she had known for years, walked in. The smart maid was sent for to go to her mistress, and Annushka remained with Darya Alexandrovna.

Annushka was obviously much pleased at that lady's arrival, and began to chatter away without a pause. Dolly observed that she was longing to express her opinion in regard to her mistress's position, especially as to the love and devotion of the count to Anna Arkadyevna, but Dolly carefully interrupted her whenever she began to speak about this.

"I grew up with Anna Arkadyevna; my lady's dearer to me than anything. Well, it's not for us to judge. And, to be sure, there seems so much love..."

"Kindly pour out the water for me to wash now, please," Darya Alexandrovna cut her short.

"Certainly. We've two women kept specially for washing small things, but most of the linen's done by machinery. The count goes into everything himself. Ah, what a husband!..."

Dolly was glad when Anna came in, and by her entrance put a stop to Annushka's gossip.

Anna had put on a very simple batiste gown. Dolly scrutinized that simple gown attentively. She knew what it meant, and the price at which such simplicity was obtained.

"An old friend," said Anna of Annushka.

Anna was not embarrassed now. She was perfectly composed and at ease. Dolly saw that she had now completely recovered from the impression her arrival had made on her, and had assumed that superficial, careless tone which, as it were, closed the door on that compartment in which her deeper feelings and ideas were kept.

"Well, Anna, and how is your little girl?" asked Dolly.

"Annie?" (This was what she called her little daughter Anna.) "Very well. She has got on wonderfully. Would you like to see her? Come, I'll show her to you. We had a terrible bother," she began telling her, "over nurses. We had an Italian wet-nurse. A good creature, but so stupid! We wanted to get rid of her, but the baby is so used to her that we've gone on keeping her still."

"But how have you managed?..." Dolly was beginning a question as to what name the little girl would have; but noticing a sudden frown on Anna's face, she changed the drift of her question.

"How did you manage? have you weaned her yet?"

But Anna had understood.

"You didn't mean to ask that? You meant to ask about her surname. Yes? That worries Alexey. She has no name—that is, she's a Karenina," said Anna, dropping her eyelids till nothing could be seen but the eyelashes meeting. "But we'll talk about all that later," her face suddenly brightening. "Come, I'll show you her. *Elle est tres gentille*. She crawls now."

In the nursery the luxury which had impressed Dolly in the whole house struck her still more. There were little go-carts ordered from England, and appliances for learning to walk, and a sofa after the fashion of a billiard table, purposely constructed for crawling, and swings and baths, all of special pattern, and modern. They were all English, solid, and of good make, and obviously very expensive. The room was large, and very light and lofty.

When they went in, the baby, with nothing on but her little smock, was sitting in a little elbow chair at the table, having her dinner of broth, which she was spilling all over her little chest. The baby was being fed, and the Russian nursery maid was evidently sharing her meal. Neither the wet-nurse nor the head nurse were there; they were in the next room, from which came the sound of their conversation in the queer French which was their only means of communication.

Hearing Anna's voice, a smart, tall, English nurse with a disagreeable face and a dissolute expression walked in at the door, hurriedly shaking her fair curls, and immediately began to defend herself though Anna had not found fault with her. At every word Anna said, the English nurse said hurriedly several times, "Yes, my lady."

The rosy baby with her black eyebrows and hair, her sturdy red little body with tight goose-flesh skin, delighted Darya Alexandrovna in spite of the cross expression with which she stared at the stranger. She positively envied the baby's healthy appearance. She was delighted, too, at the baby's crawling. Not one of her own children had crawled like that. When the baby was put on the carpet and its little dress tucked up behind, it was wonderfully charming. Looking round like some little wild animal at the grown-up big people with her bright black eyes, she smiled, unmistakably pleased at their admiring her, and holding her legs sideways, she pressed vigorously on her arms, and rapidly drew her whole back up after, and then made another step forward with her little arms.

But the whole atmosphere of the nursery, and especially the English nurse, Darya Alexandrovna did not like at all. It was only on the supposition that no good nurse would have entered so irregular a household as Anna's that Darya Alexandrovna could explain to herself how Anna with her insight into people could take such an unprepossessing, disreputable-looking woman as nurse to her child.

Besides, from a few words that were dropped, Darya Alexandrovna saw at once that Anna, the two nurses, and the child had no common existence, and that the mother's visit was something exceptional. Anna wanted to get the baby her plaything, and could not find it.

Most amazing of all was the fact that on being asked how many teeth the baby had, Anna answered wrong, and knew nothing about the two last teeth.

"I sometimes feel sorry I'm so superfluous here," said Anna, going out of the nursery and holding up her skirt so as to escape the plaything standing in the doorway. "It was very different with my first child."

"I expected it to be the other way," said Darya Alexandrovna shyly.

"Oh, no! By the way, do you know I saw Seryozha?" said Anna, screwing up her eyes, as though looking at something far away. "But we'll talk about that later. You wouldn't believe it,

I'm like a hungry beggar woman when a full dinner is set before her, and she does not know what to begin on first. The dinner is you, and the talks I have before me with you, which I could never have with anyone else; and I don't know which subject to begin upon first. *Mais je ne vous ferai grace de rien.* I must have everything out with you."

"Oh, I ought to give you a sketch of the company you will meet with us," she went on. "I'll begin with the ladies. Princess Varvara—you know her, and I know your opinion and Stiva's about her. Stiva says the whole aim of her existence is to prove her superiority over Auntie Katerina Pavlovna: that's all true; but she's a good-natured woman, and I am so grateful to her. In Petersburg there was a moment when a chaperon was absolutely essential for me. Then she turned up. But really she is good- natured. She did a great deal to alleviate my position. I see you don't understand all the difficulty of my position...there in Petersburg," she added. "Here I'm perfectly at ease and happy. Well, of that later on, though. Then Sviazhsky— he's the marshal of the district, and he's a very good sort of a man, but he wants to get something out of Alexey. You understand, with his property, now that we are settled in the country, Alexey can exercise great influence. Then there's Tushkevitch—you have seen him, you know—Betsy's admirer. Now he's been thrown over and he's come to see us. As Alexey says, he's one of those people who are very pleasant if one accepts them for what they try to appear to be, *et puis il est comme il faut,* as Princess Varvara says. Then Veslovsky...you know him. A very nice boy," she said, and a sly smile curved her lips. "What's this wild story about him and the Levins? Veslovsky told Alexey about it, and we don't believe it. *Il est très gentil et naïf,*" she said again with the same smile. "Men need occupation, and Alexey needs a circle, so I value all these people. We have to have the house lively and gay, so that Alexey may not long for any novelty. Then you'll see the steward—a German, a very good fellow, and he understands his work. Alexey has a very high opinion of him. Then the doctor, a young man, not quite a Nihilist perhaps, but you know, eats with his knife...but a very good doctor. Then the architect.... *Une petite cour!*"

"Here's Dolly for you, princess, you were so anxious to see her," said Anna, coming out with Darya Alexandrovna onto the stone terrace where Princess Varvara was sitting in the shade at an embroidery frame, working at a cover for Count Alexey Kirillovitch's easy chair. "She says she doesn't want anything before dinner, but please order some lunch for her, and I'll go and look for Alexey and bring them all in."

Princess Varvara gave Dolly a cordial and rather patronizing reception, and began at once explaining to her that she was living with Anna because she had always cared more for her than her sister Katerina Pavlovna, the aunt that had brought Anna up, and that now, when every one had abandoned Anna, she thought it her duty to help her in this most difficult period of transition.

"Her husband will give her a divorce, and then I shall go back to my solitude; but now I can be of use, and I am doing my duty, however difficult it may be for me—not like some other people. And how sweet it is of you, how right of you to have come! They live like the best of married couples; it's for God to judge them, not for us. And didn't Biryuzovsky and Madame Avenieva...and Sam Nikandrov, and Vassiliev and Madame Mamonova, and Liza Neptunova... Did no one say anything about them? And it has ended by their being received by everyone. And then, *c'est un intérieur si joli, si comme il faut. Tout-à-fait à l'anglaise. On se réunit le matin au breakfast, et puis on se sépare.* Everyone does as he pleases till dinnertime. Dinner at seven o'clock. Stiva did very rightly to send you. He needs their support. You know that through his mother and brother he can do anything. And then they do so much good. He didn't tell you about his hospital? *Ce sera admirable*—everything from Paris."

Their conversation was interrupted by Anna, who had found the men of the party in the billiard room, and returned with them to the terrace. There was still a long time before the dinner-hour, it was exquisite weather, and so several different methods of spending the next two hours were proposed. There were very many methods of passing the time at Vozdvizhenskoe, and these were all unlike those in use at Pokrovskoe.

"*Une partie de lawn-tennis,*" Veslovsky proposed, with his handsome smile. "We'll be partners again, Anna Arkadyevna."

"No, it's too hot; better stroll about the garden and have a row in the boat, show Darya Alexandrovna the river banks." Vronsky proposed.

"I agree to anything," said Sviazhsky.

"I imagine that what Dolly would like best would be a stroll— wouldn't you? And then the boat, perhaps," said Anna.

So it was decided. Veslovsky and Tushkevitch went off to the bathing place, promising to get the boat ready and to wait there for them.

They walked along the path in two couples, Anna with Sviazhsky, and Dolly with Vronsky. Dolly was a little embarrassed and anxious in the new surroundings in which she found herself. Abstractly, theoretically, she did not merely justify, she positively approved of Anna's conduct. As is indeed not unfrequent with women of unimpeachable virtue, weary of the monotony of respectable existence, at a distance she not only excused illicit love, she positively envied it. Besides, she loved Anna with all her heart. But seeing Anna in actual life among these strangers, with this fashionable tone that was so new to Darya Alexandrovna, she felt ill at ease. What she disliked particularly was seeing Princess Varvara ready to overlook everything for the sake of the comforts she enjoyed.

As a general principle, abstractly, Dolly approved of Anna's action; but to see the man for whose sake her action had been taken was disagreeable to her. Moreover, she had never liked Vronsky. She thought him very proud, and saw nothing in him of which he could be proud except his wealth. But against her own will, here in his own house, he overawed her more than ever, and she could not be at ease with him. She felt with him the same feeling she had had with the maid about her dressing jacket. Just as with the maid she had felt not exactly ashamed, but embarrassed at her darns, so she felt with him not exactly ashamed, but embarrassed at herself.

Dolly was ill at ease, and tried to find a subject of conversation. Even though she supposed that, through his pride, praise of his house and garden would be sure to be disagreeable to him, she did all the same tell him how much she liked his house.

"Yes, it's a very fine building, and in the good old-fashioned style," he said.

"I like so much the court in front of the steps. Was that always so?"

"Oh, no!" he said, and his face beamed with pleasure. "If you could only have seen that court last spring!"

And he began, at first rather diffidently, but more and more carried away by the subject as he went on, to draw her attention to the various details of the decoration of his house and garden. It was evident that, having devoted a great deal of trouble to improve and beautify his home, Vronsky felt a need to show off the improvements to a new person, and was genuinely delighted at Darya Alexandrovna's praise.

"If you would care to look at the hospital, and are not tired, indeed, it's not far. Shall we go?" he said, glancing into her face to convince himself that she was not bored. "Are you coming, Anna?" he turned to her.

"We will come, won't we?" she said, addressing Sviazhsky. "*Mais il ne faut pas laisser le pauvre Veslovsky et Tushkevitch se morfondre là dans le bateau. We must send and tell them.*"

"Yes, this is a monument he is setting up here," said Anna, turning to Dolly with that sly smile of comprehension with which she had previously talked about the hospital.

"Oh, it's a work of real importance!" said Sviazhsky. But to show he was not trying to ingratiate himself with Vronsky, he promptly added some slightly critical remarks.

"I wonder, though, count," he said, "that while you do so much for the health of the peasants, you take so little interest in the schools."

"*C'est devenu tellement commun les écoles,*" said Vronsky. "You understand it's not on that account, but it just happens so, my interest has been diverted elsewhere. This way then to the hospital," he said to Darya Alexandrovna, pointing to a turning out of the avenue.

The ladies put up their parasols and turned into the side path. After going down several turnings, and going through a little gate, Darya Alexandrovna saw standing on rising ground before her a large pretentious-looking red building, almost finished. The iron roof, which was not yet painted, shone with dazzling brightness in the sunshine. Beside the finished building another had been begun, surrounded by scaffolding. Workmen in aprons, standing on scaffolds, were laying bricks, pouring mortar out of vats, and smoothing it with trowels.

"How quickly work gets done with you!" said Sviazhsky. "When I was here last time the roof was not on."

"By the autumn it will all be ready. Inside almost everything is done," said Anna.

"And what's this new building?"

"That's the house for the doctor and the dispensary," answered Vronsky, seeing the architect in a short jacket coming towards him; and excusing himself to the ladies, he went to meet him.

Going round a hole where the workmen were slaking lime, he stood still with the architect and began talking rather warmly.

"The front is still too low," he said to Anna, who had asked what was the matter.

"I said the foundation ought to be raised," said Anna.

"Yes, of course it would have been much better, Anna Arkadyevna," said the architect, "but now it's too late."

"Yes, I take a great interest in it," Anna answered Sviazhsky, who was expressing his surprise at her knowledge of architecture. "This new building ought to have been in harmony with the hospital. It was an afterthought, and was begun without a plan."

Vronsky, having finished his talk with the architect, joined the ladies, and led them inside the hospital.

Although they were still at work on the cornices outside and were painting on the ground floor, upstairs almost all the rooms were finished. Going up the broad cast-iron staircase to the landing, they walked into the first large room. The walls were stuccoed to look like marble, the huge plate-glass windows were already in, only the parquet floor was not yet finished, and the carpenters, who were planing a block of it, left their work, taking off the bands that fastened their hair, to greet the gentry.

"This is the reception room," said Vronsky. "Here there will be a desk, tables, and benches, and nothing more."

"This way; let us go in here. Don't go near the window," said Anna, trying the paint to see if it were dry. "Alexey, the paint's dry already," she added.

From the reception room they went into the corridor. Here Vronsky showed them the mechanism for ventilation on a novel system. Then he showed them marble baths, and beds with extraordinary springs. Then he showed them the wards one after another, the storeroom, the linen room, then the heating stove of a new pattern, then the trolleys, which would make no noise as they carried everything needed along the corridors, and many other things. Sviazhsky, as a connoisseur in the latest mechanical improvements, appreciated everything fully. Dolly simply wondered at all she had not seen before, and, anxious to understand it all, made minute inquiries about everything, which gave Vronsky great satisfaction.

"Yes, I imagine that this will be the solitary example of a properly fitted hospital in Russia," said Sviazhsky.

"And won't you have a lying-in ward?" asked Dolly. "That's so much needed in the country. I have often..."

In spite of his usual courtesy, Vronsky interrupted her.

"This is not a lying-in home, but a hospital for the sick, and is intended for all diseases, except infectious complaints," he said. "Ah! look at this," and he rolled up to Darya Alexandrovna an invalid chair that had just been ordered for the convalescents. "Look." He sat down in the chair and began moving it. "The patient can't walk—still too weak, perhaps, or something wrong with his legs, but he must have air, and he moves, rolls himself along...."

Darya Alexandrovna was interested by everything. She liked everything very much, but most of all she liked Vronsky himself with his natural, simple-hearted eagerness. "Yes, he's a very nice, good man," she thought several times, not hearing what he said, but looking at him and penetrating into his expression, while she mentally put herself in Anna's place. She liked him so much just now with his eager interest that she saw how Anna could be in love with him.

"No, I think the princess is tired, and horses don't interest her," Vronsky said to Anna, who wanted to go on to the stables, where Sviazhsky wished to see the new stallion. "You go on, while I escort the princess home, and we'll have a little talk," he said, "if you would like that?" he added, turning to her.

"I know nothing about horses, and I shall be delighted," answered Darya Alexandrovna, rather astonished.

She saw by Vronsky's face that he wanted something from her. She was not mistaken. As soon as they had passed through the little gate back into the garden, he looked in the direction Anna had taken, and having made sure that she could neither hear nor see them, he began:

"You guess that I have something I want to say to you," he said, looking at her with laughing eyes. "I am not wrong in believing you to be a friend of Anna's." He took off his hat, and taking out his handkerchief, wiped his head, which was growing bald.

Darya Alexandrovna made no answer, and merely stared at him with dismay. When she was left alone with him, she suddenly felt afraid; his laughing eyes and stern expression scared her.

The most diverse suppositions as to what he was about to speak of to her flashed into her brain. "He is going to beg me to come to stay with them with the children, and I shall have to refuse; or to create a set that will receive Anna in Moscow.... Or isn't it Vassenka Veslovsky and his relations with Anna? Or perhaps about Kitty, that he feels he was to blame?" All her conjectures were unpleasant, but she did not guess what he really wanted to talk about to her.

"You have so much influence with Anna, she is so fond of you," he said; "do help me."

Darya Alexandrovna looked with timid inquiry into his energetic face, which under the lime-trees was continually being lighted up in patches by the sunshine, and then passing into complete shadow again. She waited for him to say more, but he walked in silence beside her, scratching with his cane in the gravel.

"You have come to see us, you, the only woman of Anna's former friends—I don't count Princess Varvara—but I know that you have done this not because you regard our position as normal, but because, understanding all the difficulty of the position, you still love her and want to be a help to her. Have I understood you rightly?" he asked, looking round at her.

"Oh, yes," answered Darya Alexandrovna, putting down her sunshade, "but..."

"No," he broke in, and unconsciously, oblivious of the awkward position into which he was putting his companion, he stopped abruptly, so that she had to stop short too. "No one feels more deeply and intensely than I do all the difficulty of Anna's position; and that you may well understand, if you do me the honor of supposing I have any heart. I am to blame for that position, and that is why I feel it."

"I understand," said Darya Alexandrovna, involuntarily admiring the sincerity and firmness with which he said this. "But just because you feel yourself responsible, you exaggerate it, I am afraid," she said. "Her position in the world is difficult, I can well understand."

"In the world it is hell!" he brought out quickly, frowning darkly. "You can't imagine moral sufferings greater than what she went through in Petersburg in that fortnight...and I beg you to believe it."

"Yes, but here, so long as neither Anna...nor you miss society..."

"Society!" he said contemptuously, "how could I miss society?"

"So far—and it may be so always—you are happy and at peace. I see in Anna that she is happy, perfectly happy, she has had time to tell me so much already," said Darya Alexandrovna, smiling; and involuntarily, as she said this, at the same moment a doubt entered her mind whether Anna really were happy.

But Vronsky, it appeared, had no doubts on that score.

"Yes, yes," he said, "I know that she has revived after all her sufferings; she is happy. She is happy in the present. But I?... I am afraid of what is before us...I beg your pardon, you would like to walk on?"

"No, I don't mind."

"Well, then, let us sit here."

Darya Alexandrovna sat down on a garden seat in a corner of the avenue. He stood up facing her.

"I see that she is happy," he repeated, and the doubt whether she were happy sank more deeply into Darya Alexandrovna's mind. "But can it last? Whether we have acted rightly or wrongly is another question, but the die is cast," he said, passing from Russian to French, "and we are bound together for life. We are united by all the ties of love that we hold most sacred. We have a child, we may have other children. But the law and all the conditions of our position are such that thousands of complications arise which she does not see and does not want to see. And that one can well understand. But I can't help seeing them. My daughter is by law not my daughter, but Karenin's. I cannot bear this falsity!" he said, with a vigorous gesture of refusal, and he looked with gloomy inquiry towards Darya Alexandrovna.

She made no answer, but simply gazed at him. He went on:

"One day a son may be born, my son, and he will be legally a Karenin; he will not be the heir of my name nor of my property, and however happy we may be in our home life and however many children we may have, there will be no real tie between us. They will be Karenins. You can understand the bitterness and horror of this position! I have tried to speak of this to Anna. It irritates her. She does not understand, and to her I cannot speak plainly of all this. Now look at another side. I am happy, happy in her love, but I must have occupation. I have found occupation, and am proud of what I am doing and consider it nobler than the pursuits of my former companions at court and in the army. And most certainly I would not change the work I am doing for theirs. I am working here, settled in my own place, and I am happy and contented, and we need nothing more to make us happy. I love my work here. *Ce n'est pas un pis-aller,* on the contrary..."

Darya Alexandrovna noticed that at this point in his explanation he grew confused, and she did not quite understand this digression, but she felt that having once begun to speak of matters near his heart, of which he could not speak to Anna, he was now making a clean breast of everything, and that the question of his pursuits in the country fell into the same category of matters near his heart, as the question of his relations with Anna.

"Well, I will go on," he said, collecting himself. "The great thing is that as I work I want to have a conviction that what I am doing will not die with me, that I shall have heirs to come after me,—and this I have not. Conceive the position of a man who knows that his children, the children of the woman he loves, will not be his, but will belong to someone who hates them and cares nothing about them! It is awful!"

He paused, evidently much moved.

"Yes, indeed, I see that. But what can Anna do?" queried Darya Alexandrovna.

"Yes, that brings me to the object of my conversation," he said, calming himself with an effort. "Anna can, it depends on her.... Even to petition the Tsar for legitimization, a divorce is essential. And that depends on Anna. Her husband agreed to a divorce—at that time your husband had arranged it completely. And now, I know, he would not refuse it. It is only a matter of writing to him. He said plainly at that time that if she expressed the desire, he would not refuse. Of course," he said gloomily, "it is one of those Pharisaical cruelties of which only such heartless men are capable. He knows what agony any recollection of him must give her, and knowing her, he must have a letter from her. I can understand that it is agony to her. But the matter is of such importance, that one must *passer pardessus toutes ces finesses de sentiment. Il y va du bonheur et de l'existence d'Anne et de ses enfants.* I won't speak of myself, though it's hard for me, very hard," he said, with an expression as though he were threatening someone for its being hard for him. "And so it is, princess, that I am shamelessly clutching at you as an anchor of salvation. Help me to persuade her to write to him and ask for a divorce."

"Yes, of course," Darya Alexandrovna said dreamily, as she vividly recalled her last interview with Alexey Alexandrovitch. "Yes, of course," she repeated with decision, thinking of Anna.

"Use your influence with her, make her write. I don't like—I'm almost unable to speak about this to her."

"Very well, I will talk to her. But how is it she does not think of it herself?" said Darya Alexandrovna, and for some reason she suddenly at that point recalled Anna's strange new habit of half-closing her eyes. And she remembered that Anna drooped her eyelids just when the deeper questions of life were touched upon. "Just as though she half-shut her eyes to her own life, so as not to see everything," thought Dolly. "Yes, indeed, for my own sake and for hers I will talk to her," Dolly said in reply to his look of gratitude.

They got up and walked to the house.

When Anna found Dolly at home before her, she looked intently in her eyes, as though questioning her about the talk she had had with Vronsky, but she made no inquiry in words.

"I believe it's dinner time," she said. "We've not seen each other at all yet. I am reckoning on the evening. Now I want to go and dress. I expect you do too; we all got splashed at the buildings."

Dolly went to her room and she felt amused. To change her dress was impossible, for she had already put on her best dress. But in order to signify in some way her preparation for dinner, she asked the maid to brush her dress, changed her cuffs and tie, and put some lace on her head.

"This is all I can do," she said with a smile to Anna, who came in to her in a third dress, again of extreme simplicity.

"Yes, we are too formal here," she said, as it were apologizing for her magnificence. "Alexey is delighted at your visit, as he rarely is at anything. He has completely lost his heart to you," she added. "You're not tired?"

There was no time for talking about anything before dinner. Going into the drawing room they found Princess Varvara already there, and the gentlemen of the party in black frock-coats. The architect wore a swallow-tail coat. Vronsky presented the doctor and the steward to his guest. The architect he had already introduced to her at the hospital.

A stout butler, resplendent with a smoothly shaven round chin and a starched white cravat, announced that dinner was ready, and the ladies got up. Vronsky asked Sviazhsky to take in Anna Arkadyevna, and himself offered his arm to Dolly. Veslovsky was before Tushkevitch in offering his arm to Princess Varvara, so that Tushkevitch with the steward and the doctor walked in alone.

The dinner, the dining room, the service, the waiting at table, the wine, and the food, were not simply in keeping with the general tone of modern luxury throughout all the house, but seemed even more sumptuous and modern. Darya Alexandrovna watched this luxury which was novel to her, and as a good housekeeper used to managing a household—although she never dreamed of adapting anything she saw to her own household, as it was all in a style of luxury far above her own manner of living—she could not help scrutinizing every detail, and wondering how and by whom it was all done. Vassenka Veslovsky, her husband, and even Sviazhsky, and many other people she knew, would never have considered this question, and would have readily believed what every well-bred host tries to make his guests feel, that is, that all that is well-ordered in his house has cost him, the host, no trouble whatever, but comes of itself. Darya Alexandrovna was well aware that even porridge for the children's breakfast does not come of itself, and that therefore, where so complicated and magnificent a style of luxury was maintained, someone must give earnest attention to its organization. And from the glance with which Alexey Kirillovitch scanned the table, from the way he nodded to the butler, and offered Darya Alexandrovna her choice between cold soup and hot soup, she saw that it was all organized and maintained by the care of the master of the house himself. It was evident that it all rested no more upon Anna than upon Veslovsky. She, Sviazhsky, the princess, and Veslovsky, were equally guests, with light hearts enjoying what had been arranged for them.

Anna was the hostess only in conducting the conversation. The conversation was a difficult one for the lady of the house at a small table with persons present, like the steward and the architect, belonging to a completely different world, struggling not to be overawed by an elegance to which they were unaccustomed, and unable to sustain a large share in the general conversation. But this difficult conversation Anna directed with her usual tact and naturalness, and indeed she did so with actual enjoyment, as Darya Alexandrovna observed. The conversation began about the row Tushkevitch and Veslovsky had taken alone together in the boat, and Tushkevitch began describing the last boat races in Petersburg at the Yacht Club. But Anna, seizing the first pause, at once turned to the architect to draw him out of his silence.

"Nikolay Ivanitch was struck," she said, meaning Sviazhsky, "at the progress the new building had made since he was here last; but I am there every day, and every day I wonder at the rate at which it grows."

"It's first-rate working with his excellency," said the architect with a smile (he was respectful and composed, though with a sense of his own dignity). "It's a very different matter to have to do with the district authorities. Where one would have to write out sheaves of papers, here I call upon the count, and in three words we settle the business."

"The American way of doing business," said Sviazhsky, with a smile.

"Yes, there they build in a rational fashion..."

The conversation passed to the misuse of political power in the United States, but Anna quickly brought it round to another topic, so as to draw the steward into talk.

"Have you ever seen a reaping machine?" she said, addressing Darya Alexandrovna. "We had just ridden over to look at one when we met. It's the first time I ever saw one."

"How do they work?" asked Dolly.

"Exactly like little scissors. A plank and a lot of little scissors. Like this."

Anna took a knife and fork in her beautiful white hands covered with rings, and began showing how the machine worked. It was clear that she saw nothing would be understood from her explanation; but aware that her talk was pleasant and her hands beautiful she went on explaining.

"More like little penknives," Veslovsky said playfully, never taking his eyes off her.

Anna gave a just perceptible smile, but made no answer. "Isn't it true, Karl Fedoritch, that it's just like little scissors?" she said to the steward.

"Oh, ja," answered the German. *"Es it ein ganz einfaches Ding,"* and he began to explain the construction of the machine.

"It's a pity it doesn't bind too. I saw one at the Vienna exhibition, which binds with a wire," said Sviazhsky. "They would be more profitable in use."

"Es kommt drauf an.... Der Preis vom Draht muss ausgerechnet werden." And the German, roused from his taciturnity, turned to Vronsky. *"Das lässt sich ausrechnen, Erlaucht."* The German was just feeling in the pocket where were his pencil and the notebook he always wrote in, but recollecting that he was at a dinner, and observing Vronsky's chilly glance, he checked himself. *"Zu compliziert, macht zu viel Klopot,"* he concluded.

"Wünscht man Dochots, so hat man auch Klopots," said Vassenka Veslovsky, mimicking the German. *"J'adore l'allemand,"* he addressed Anna again with the same smile.

"Cessez," she said with playful severity.

"We expected to find you in the fields, Vassily Semyonitch," she said to the doctor, a sickly-looking man; "have you been there?"

"I went there, but I had taken flight," the doctor answered with gloomy jocoseness.

"Then you've taken a good constitutional?"

"Splendid!"

"Well, and how was the old woman? I hope it's not typhus?"

"Typhus it is not, but it's taking a bad turn."

"What a pity!" said Anna, and having thus paid the dues of civility to her domestic circle, she turned to her own friends.

"It would be a hard task, though, to construct a machine from your description, Anna Arkadyevna," Sviazhsky said jestingly.

"Oh, no, why so?" said Anna with a smile that betrayed that she knew there was something charming in her disquisitions upon the machine that had been noticed by Sviazhsky. This new trait of girlish coquettishness made an unpleasant impression on Dolly.

"But Anna Arkadyevna's knowledge of architecture is marvelous," said Tushkevitch.

"To be sure, I heard Anna Arkadyevna talking yesterday about plinths and damp-courses," said Veslovsky. "Have I got it right?"

"There's nothing marvelous about it, when one sees and hears so much of it," said Anna. "But, I dare say, you don't even know what houses are made of?"

Darya Alexandrovna saw that Anna disliked the tone of raillery that existed between her and Veslovsky, but fell in with it against her will.

Vronsky acted in this matter quite differently from Levin. He obviously attached no significance to Veslovsky's chattering; on the contrary, he encouraged his jests.

"Come now, tell us, Veslovsky, how are the stones held together?"

"By cement, of course."

"Bravo! And what is cement?"

"Oh, some sort of paste...no, putty," said Veslovsky, raising a general laugh.

The company at dinner, with the exception of the doctor, the architect, and the steward, who remained plunged in gloomy silence, kept up a conversation that never paused, glancing off one subject, fastening on another, and at times stinging one or the other to the quick. Once Darya Alexandrovna felt wounded to the quick, and got so hot that she positively flushed and wondered afterwards whether she had said anything extreme or unpleasant. Sviazhsky began talking of Levin, describing his strange view that machinery is simply pernicious in its effects on Russian agriculture.

"I have not the pleasure of knowing this M. Levin," Vronsky said, smiling, "but most likely he has never seen the machines he condemns; or if he has seen and tried any, it must have been after a queer fashion, some Russian imitation, not a machine from abroad. What sort of views can anyone have on such a subject?"

"Turkish views, in general," Veslovsky said, turning to Anna with a smile.

"I can't defend his opinions," Darya Alexandrovna said, firing up; "but I can say that he's a highly cultivated man, and if he were here he would know very well how to answer you, though I am not capable of doing so."

"I like him extremely, and we are great friends," Sviazhsky said, smiling good-naturedly. "*Mais pardon, il est un petit peu toqué;* he maintains, for instance, that district councils and arbitration boards are all of no use, and he is unwilling to take part in anything."

"It's our Russian apathy," said Vronsky, pouring water from an iced decanter into a delicate glass on a high stem; "we've no sense of the duties our privileges impose upon us, and so we refuse to recognize these duties."

"I know no man more strict in the performance of his duties," said Darya Alexandrovna, irritated by Vronsky's tone of superiority.

"For my part," pursued Vronsky, who was evidently for some reason or other keenly affected by this conversation, "such as I am, I am, on the contrary, extremely grateful for the honor they have done me, thanks to Nikolay Ivanitch" (he indicated Sviazhsky), "in electing me a justice of the peace. I consider that for me the duty of being present at the session, of judging some peasants' quarrel about a horse, is as important as anything I can do. And I shall regard it as an honor if they elect me for the district council. It's only in that way I can pay for the advantages I enjoy as a landowner. Unluckily they don't understand the weight that the big landowners ought to have in the state."

It was strange to Darya Alexandrovna to hear how serenely confident he was of being right at his own table. She thought how Levin, who believed the opposite, was just as positive in his opinions at his own table. But she loved Levin, and so she was on his side.

"So we can reckon upon you, count, for the coming elections?" said Sviazhsky. "But you must come a little beforehand, so as to be on the spot by the eighth. If you would do me the honor to stop with me."

"I rather agree with your beau-frère," said Anna, "though not quite on the same ground as he," she added with a smile. "I'm afraid that we have too many of these public duties in these latter days. Just as in old days there were so many government functionaries that one had to call in a functionary for every single thing, so now everyone's doing some sort of public duty. Alexey has been here now six months, and he's a member, I do believe, of five or six different public bodies. *Du train que cela va,* the whole time will be wasted on it. And I'm afraid that with such a multiplicity of these bodies, they'll end in being a mere form. How many are you a member of, Nikolay Ivanitch?" she turned to Sviazhsky—"over twenty, I fancy."

Anna spoke lightly, but irritation could be discerned in her tone. Darya Alexandrovna, watching Anna and Vronsky attentively, detected it instantly. She noticed, too, that as she spoke Vronsky's face had immediately taken a serious and obstinate expression. Noticing this, and that Princess Varvara at once made haste to change the conversation by talking of Petersburg acquaintances, and remembering what Vronsky had without apparent connection said in the garden of his work in the country, Dolly surmised that this question of public activity was connected with some deep private disagreement between Anna and Vronsky.

The dinner, the wine, the decoration of the table were all very good; but it was all like what Darya Alexandrovna had seen at formal dinners and balls which of late years had become quite unfamiliar to her; it all had the same impersonal and constrained character, and so on an ordinary day and in a little circle of friends it made a disagreeable impression on her.

After dinner they sat on the terrace, then they proceeded to play lawn tennis. The players, divided into two parties, stood on opposite sides of a tightly drawn net with gilt poles on the carefully leveled and rolled croquet-ground. Darya Alexandrovna made an attempt to play, but it was a long time before she could understand the game, and by the time she did understand it, she was so tired that she sat down with Princess Varvara and simply looked on at the players. Her partner, Tushkevitch, gave up playing too, but the others kept the game up for a long time. Sviazhsky and Vronsky both played very well and seriously. They kept a sharp lookout on the balls served to them, and without haste or getting in each other's way, they ran adroitly up to them, waited for the rebound, and neatly and accurately returned them over the net. Veslovsky played worse than the others. He was too eager, but he kept the players lively with his high spirits. His laughter and outcries never paused. Like the other men of the party, with the ladies' permission, he took off his coat, and his solid, comely figure in his white shirt-sleeves, with his red perspiring face and his impulsive movements, made a picture that imprinted itself vividly on the memory.

When Darya Alexandrovna lay in bed that night, as soon as she closed her eyes, she saw Vassenka Veslovsky flying about the croquet ground.

During the game Darya Alexandrovna was not enjoying herself. She did not like the light tone of raillery that was kept up all the time between Vassenka Veslovsky and Anna, and the unnaturalness altogether of grown-up people, all alone without children, playing at a child's game. But to avoid breaking up the party and to get through the time somehow, after a rest she joined the game again, and pretended to be enjoying it. All that day it seemed to her as though she were acting in a theater with actors cleverer than she, and that her bad acting was spoiling the whole performance. She had come with the intention of staying two days, if all went well. But in the evening, during the game, she made up her mind that she would go home next day. The maternal cares and worries, which she had so hated on the way, now, after a day spent without them, struck her in quite another light, and tempted her back to them.

When, after evening tea and a row by night in the boat, Darya Alexandrovna went alone to her room, took off her dress, and began arranging her thin hair for the night, she had a great sense of relief.

It was positively disagreeable to her to think that Anna was coming to see her immediately. She longed to be alone with her own thoughts.

Dolly was wanting to go to bed when Anna came in to see her, attired for the night. In the course of the day Anna had several times begun to speak of matters near her heart, and every time after a few words she had stopped: "Afterwards, by ourselves, we'll talk about everything. I've got so much I want to tell you," she said.

Now they were by themselves, and Anna did not know what to talk about. She sat in the window looking at Dolly, and going over in her own mind all the stores of intimate talk which had seemed so inexhaustible beforehand, and she found nothing. At that moment it seemed to her that everything had been said already.

"Well, what of Kitty?" she said with a heavy sigh, looking penitently at Dolly. "Tell me the truth, Dolly: isn't she angry with me?"

"Angry? Oh, no!" said Darya Alexandrovna, smiling.

"But she hates me, despises me?"

"Oh, no! But you know that sort of thing isn't forgiven."

"Yes, yes," said Anna, turning away and looking out of the open window. "But I was not to blame. And who is to blame? What's the meaning of being to blame? Could it have been otherwise? What do you think? Could it possibly have happened that you didn't become the wife of Stiva?"

"Really, I don't know. But this is what I want you to tell me..."

"Yes, yes, but we've not finished about Kitty. Is she happy? He's a very nice man, they say."

"He's much more than very nice. I don't know a better man."

"Ah, how glad I am! I'm so glad! Much more than very nice," she repeated.

Dolly smiled.

"But tell me about yourself. We've a great deal to talk about. And I've had a talk with..." Dolly did not know what to call him. She felt it awkward to call him either the count or Alexey Kirillovitch.

"With Alexey," said Anna, "I know what you talked about. But I wanted to ask you directly what you think of me, of my life?"

"How am I to say like that straight off? I really don't know."

"No, tell me all the same.... You see my life. But you mustn't forget that you're seeing us in the summer, when you have come to us and we are not alone.... But we came here early in the spring, lived quite alone, and shall be alone again, and I desire nothing better. But imagine me living alone without him, alone, and that will be...I see by everything that it will often be repeated, that he will be half the time away from home," she said, getting up and sitting down close by Dolly.

"Of course," she interrupted Dolly, who would have answered, "of course I won't try to keep him by force. I don't keep him indeed. The races are just coming, his horses are running, he will go. I'm very glad. But think of me, fancy my position.... But what's the use of talking about it?" She smiled. "Well, what did he talk about with you?"

"He spoke of what I want to speak about of myself, and it's easy for me to be his advocate; of whether there is not a possibility ...whether you could not..." (Darya Alexandrovna hesitated) "correct, improve your position.... You know how I look at it.... But all the same, if possible, you should get married...."

"Divorce, you mean?" said Anna. "Do you know, the only woman who came to see me in Petersburg was Betsy Tverskaya? You know her, of course? *Au fond, c'est la femme la plus depraveé qui existe.* She had an intrigue with Tushkevitch, deceiving her husband in the basest way. And she told me that she did not care to know me so long as my position was irregular. Don't imagine I would compare...I know you, darling. But I could not help remembering.... Well, so what did he say to you?" she repeated.

"He said that he was unhappy on your account and his own. Perhaps you will say that it's egoism, but what a legitimate and noble egoism. He wants first of all to legitimize his daughter, and to be your husband, to have a legal right to you."

"What wife, what slave can be so utterly a slave as I, in my position?" she put in gloomily.

"The chief thing he desires...he desires that you should not suffer."

"That's impossible. Well?"

"Well, and the most legitimate desire—he wishes that your children should have a name."

"What children?" Anna said, not looking at Dolly, and half closing her eyes.

"Annie and those to come..."

"He need not trouble on that score; I shall have no more children."

"How can you tell that you won't?"

"I shall not, because I don't wish it." And, in spite of all her emotion, Anna smiled, as she caught the naïve expression of curiosity, wonder, and horror on Dolly's face.

"The doctor told me after my illness..."

"Impossible!" said Dolly, opening her eyes wide.

For her this was one of those discoveries the consequences and deductions from which are so immense that all that one feels for the first instant is that it is impossible to take it all in, and that one will have to reflect a great, great deal upon it.

This discovery, suddenly throwing light on all those families of one or two children, which had hitherto been so incomprehensible to her, aroused so many ideas, reflections, and contradictory emotions, that she had nothing to say, and simply gazed with wide-open eyes of wonder at Anna. This was the very thing she had been dreaming of, but now learning that it was possible, she was horrified. She felt that it was too simple a solution of too complicated a problem.

"N'est-ce pas immoral?" was all she said, after a brief pause.

"Why so? Think, I have a choice between two alternatives: either to be with child, that is an invalid, or to be the friend and companion of my husband—practically my husband," Anna said in a tone intentionally superficial and frivolous.

"Yes, yes," said Darya Alexandrovna, hearing the very arguments she had used to herself, and not finding the same force in them as before.

"For you, for other people," said Anna, as though divining her thoughts, "there may be reason to hesitate; but for me.... You must consider, I am not his wife; he loves me as long as he loves me. And how am I to keep his love? Not like this!"

She moved her white hands in a curve before her waist with extraordinary rapidity, as happens during moments of excitement; ideas and memories rushed into Darya Alexandrovna's head. "I," she thought, "did not keep my attraction for Stiva; he left me for others, and the first woman for whom he betrayed me did not keep him by being always pretty and lively. He deserted her and took another. And can Anna attract and keep Count Vronsky in that way? If that is what he looks for, he will find dresses and manners still more attractive and charming. And however white and beautiful her bare arms are, however beautiful her full figure and her eager face under her black curls, he will find something better still, just as my disgusting, pitiful, and charming husband does."

Dolly made no answer, she merely sighed. Anna noticed this sigh, indicating dissent, and she went on. In her armory she had other arguments so strong that no answer could be made to them.

"Do you say that it's not right? But you must consider," she went on; "you forget my position. How can I desire children? I'm not speaking of the suffering, I'm not afraid of that. Think only, what are my children to be? Ill-fated children, who will have to bear a stranger's name. For the very fact of their birth they will be forced to be ashamed of their mother, their father, their birth."

"But that is just why a divorce is necessary." But Anna did not hear her. She longed to give utterance to all the arguments with which she had so many times convinced herself.

"What is reason given me for, if I am not to use it to avoid bringing unhappy beings into the world!" She looked at Dolly, but without waiting for a reply she went on:

"I should always feel I had wronged these unhappy children," she said. "If they are not, at any rate they are not unhappy; while if they are unhappy, I alone should be to blame for it."

These were the very arguments Darya Alexandrovna had used in her own reflections; but she heard them without understanding them. "How can one wrong creatures that don't exist?" she thought. And all at once the idea struck her: could it possibly, under any circumstances, have been better for her favorite Grisha if he had never existed? And this seemed to her so wild, so strange, that she shook her head to drive away this tangle of whirling, mad ideas.

"No, I don't know; it's not right," was all she said, with an expression of disgust on her face.

"Yes, but you mustn't forget that you and I.... And besides that," added Anna, in spite of the wealth of her arguments and the poverty of Dolly's objections, seeming still to admit that it was not right, "don't forget the chief point, that I am not now in the same position as you. For you the question is: do you desire not to have any more children; while for me it is: do I desire to have them? And that's a great difference. You must see that I can't desire it in my position."

Darya Alexandrovna made no reply. She suddenly felt that she had got far away from Anna; that there lay between them a barrier of questions on which they could never agree, and about which it was better not to speak.

Vronsky and Anna spent the whole summer and part of the winter in the country, living in just the same condition, and still taking no steps to obtain a divorce. It was an understood thing between them that they should not go away anywhere; but both felt, the longer they lived alone, especially in the autumn, without guests in the house, that they could not stand this existence, and that they would have to alter it.

Their life was apparently such that nothing better could be desired. They had the fullest abundance of everything; they had a child, and both had occupation. Anna devoted just as much care to her appearance when they had no visitors, and she did a great deal of reading, both of novels and of what serious literature was in fashion. She ordered all the books that were praised in the foreign papers and reviews she received, and read them with that concentrated attention which is only given to what is read in seclusion. Moreover, every subject that was of interest to Vronsky, she studied in books and special journals, so that he often went straight to her with questions relating to agriculture or architecture, sometimes even with questions relating to horse-breeding or sport. He was amazed at her knowledge, her memory, and at first was disposed to doubt it, to ask for confirmation of her facts; and she would find what he asked for in some book, and show it to him.

The building of the hospital, too, interested her. She did not merely assist, but planned and suggested a great deal herself. But her chief thought was still of herself—how far she was dear to Vronsky, how far she could make up to him for all he had given up. Vronsky appreciated this desire not only to please, but to serve him, which had become the sole aim of her existence, but at the same time he wearied of the loving snares in which she tried to hold him fast. As time went on, and he saw himself more and more often held fast in these snares, he had an ever growing desire, not so much to escape from them, as to try whether they hindered his freedom. Had it not been for this growing desire to be free, not to have scenes every time he wanted to go to the town to a meeting or a race, Vronsky would have been perfectly satisfied with his life. The rôle he had taken up, the rôle of a wealthy landowner, one of that class which ought to be the very heart of the Russian aristocracy, was entirely to his taste; and now, after spending six months in that character, he derived even greater satisfaction from it. And his management of his estate, which occupied and absorbed him more and more, was most successful. In spite of the immense sums cost him by the hospital, by machinery, by cows ordered from Switzerland, and many other things, he was convinced that he was not wasting, but increasing his substance. In all matters affecting income, the sales of timber, wheat, and wool, the letting of lands, Vronsky was hard as a rock, and knew well how to keep up prices. In all operations on a large scale on this and his other estates, he kept to the simplest methods involving no risk, and in trifling details he was careful and exacting to an extreme degree. In spite of all the cunning and ingenuity of the German steward, who would try to tempt him into purchases by making his original estimate always far larger than really required, and then representing to Vronsky that he might get the thing cheaper, and so make a profit, Vronsky did not give in. He listened to his steward, cross-examined him, and only agreed to his suggestions when the implement to be ordered or constructed was the very newest, not yet known in Russia, and likely to excite wonder. Apart from such exceptions, he resolved upon an increased outlay only where there was a surplus, and in making such an outlay he went into the minutest details, and insisted on getting the very best for his money; so that by the method on which he managed his affairs, it was clear that he was not wasting, but increasing his substance.

In October there were the provincial elections in the Kashinsky province, where were the estates of Vronsky, Sviazhsky, Koznishev, Oblonsky, and a small part of Levin's land.

These elections were attracting public attention from several circumstances connected with them, and also from the people taking part in them. There had been a great deal of talk about them, and great preparations were being made for them. Persons who never attended the elections were coming from Moscow, from Petersburg, and from abroad to attend these. Vronsky had long before promised Sviazhsky to go to them. Before the elections Sviazhsky, who often visited Vozdvizhenskoe, drove over to fetch Vronsky. On the day before there had been almost a quarrel between Vronsky and Anna over this proposed expedition. It was the very dullest autumn weather, which is so dreary in the country, and so, preparing himself for a struggle, Vronsky, with a hard and cold expression, informed Anna of his departure as he had never spoken to her before. But, to his surprise, Anna accepted the information with great composure, and merely asked when he would be back. He looked intently at her, at a loss to explain this composure. She smiled at his look. He knew that way she had of withdrawing into herself, and knew that it only happened when she had determined upon something without letting him know her plans. He was afraid of this; but he was so anxious to avoid a scene that he kept up appearances, and half sincerely believed in what he longed to believe in—her reasonableness.

"I hope you won't be dull?"

"I hope not," said Anna. "I got a box of books yesterday from Gautier's. No, I shan't be dull."

"She's trying to take that tone, and so much the better," he thought, "or else it would be the same thing over and over again."

And he set off for the elections without appealing to her for a candid explanation. It was the first time since the beginning of their intimacy that he had parted from her without a full explanation. From one point of view this troubled him, but on the other side he felt that it was better so. "At first there will be, as this time, something undefined kept back, and then she will get used to it. In any case I can give up anything for her, but not my masculine independence," he thought.

CHAPTER SIX

THE SIXTH DAY was fixed for the election of the marshal of the province.

The rooms, large and small, were full of noblemen in all sorts of uniforms. Many had come only for that day. Men who had not seen each other for years, some from the Crimea, some from Petersburg, some from abroad, met in the rooms of the Hall of Nobility. There was much discussion around the governor's table under the portrait of the Tsar.

The nobles, both in the larger and the smaller rooms, grouped themselves in camps, and from their hostile and suspicious glances, from the silence that fell upon them when outsiders approached a group, and from the way that some, whispering together, retreated to the farther corridor, it was evident that each side had secrets from the other. In appearance the noblemen were sharply divided into two classes: the old and the new. The old were for the most part either in old uniforms of the nobility, buttoned up closely, with spurs and hats, or in their own special naval, cavalry, infantry, or official uniforms. The uniforms of the older men were embroidered in the old-fashioned way with epaulets on their shoulders; they were unmistakably tight and short in the waist, as though their wearers had grown out of them. The younger men wore the uniform of the nobility with long waists and broad shoulders, unbuttoned over white waistcoats, or uniforms with black collars and with the embroidered badges of justices of the peace. To the younger men belonged the court uniforms that here and there brightened up the crowd.

But the division into young and old did not correspond with the division of parties. Some of the young men, as Levin observed, belonged to the old party; and some of the very oldest noblemen, on the contrary, were whispering with Sviazhsky, and were evidently ardent partisans of the new party.

Levin stood in the smaller room, where they were smoking and taking light refreshments, close to his own friends, and listening to what they were saying, he conscientiously exerted all his intelligence trying to understand what was said. Sergey Ivanovitch was the center round which the others grouped themselves. He was listening at that moment to Sviazhsky and Hliustov, the marshal of another district, who belonged to their party. Hliustov would not agree to go with his district to ask Snetkov to stand, while Sviazhsky was persuading him to do so, and Sergey Ivanovitch was approving of the plan. Levin could not make out why the opposition was to ask the marshal to stand whom they wanted to supersede.

Stepan Arkadyevitch, who had just been drinking and taking some lunch, came up to them in his uniform of a gentleman of the bedchamber, wiping his lips with a perfumed handkerchief of bordered batiste.

"We are placing our forces," he said, pulling out his whiskers, "Sergey Ivanovitch!"

And listening to the conversation, he supported Sviazhsky's contention.

"One district's enough, and Sviazhsky's obviously of the opposition," he said, words evidently intelligible to all except Levin.

"Why, Kostya, you here too! I suppose you're converted, eh?" he added, turning to Levin and drawing his arm through his. Levin would have been glad indeed to be converted, but could not make out what the point was, and retreating a few steps from the speakers, he explained to Stepan Arkadyevitch his inability to understand why the marshal of the province should be asked to stand.

"O sancta simplicitas!" said Stepan Arkadyevitch, and briefly and clearly he explained it to Levin. If, as at previous elections, all the districts asked the marshal of the province to stand, then he would be elected without a ballot. That must not be. Now eight districts had agreed to call upon him: if two refused to do so, Snetkov might decline to stand at all; and then the old party might choose another of their party, which would throw them completely out in their reckoning. But if only one district, Sviazhsky's, did not call upon him to stand, Snetkov would let himself be balloted for. They were even, some of them, going to vote for him, and

purposely to let him get a good many votes, so that the enemy might be thrown off the scent, and when a candidate of the other side was put up, they too might give him some votes. Levin understood to some extent, but not fully, and would have put a few more questions, when suddenly everyone began talking and making a noise and they moved towards the big room.

"What is it? eh? whom?" "No guarantee? whose? what?" "They won't pass him?" "No guarantee?" "They won't let Flerov in?" "Eh, because of the charge against him?" "Why, at this rate, they won't admit anyone. It's a swindle!" "The law!" Levin heard exclamations on all sides, and he moved into the big room together with the others, all hurrying somewhere and afraid of missing something. Squeezed by the crowding noblemen, he drew near the high table where the marshal of the province, Sviazhsky, and the other leaders were hotly disputing about something.

Levin was standing rather far off. A nobleman breathing heavily and hoarsely at his side, and another whose thick boots were creaking, prevented him from hearing distinctly. He could only hear the soft voice of the marshal faintly, then the shrill voice of the malignant gentleman, and then the voice of Sviazhsky. They were disputing, as far as he could make out, as to the interpretation to be put on the act and the exact meaning of the words: "liable to be called up for trial."

The crowd parted to make way for Sergey Ivanovitch approaching the table. Sergey Ivanovitch, waiting till the malignant gentleman had finished speaking, said that he thought the best solution would be to refer to the act itself, and asked the secretary to find the act. The act said that in case of difference of opinion, there must be a ballot.

Sergey Ivanovitch read the act and began to explain its meaning, but at that point a tall, stout, round-shouldered landowner, with dyed whiskers, in a tight uniform that cut the back of his neck, interrupted him. He went up to the table, and striking it with his finger ring, he shouted loudly: "A ballot! Put it to the vote! No need for more talking!" Then several voices began to talk all at once, and the tall nobleman with the ring, getting more and more exasperated, shouted more and more loudly. But it was impossible to make out what he said.

He was shouting for the very course Sergey Ivanovitch had proposed; but it was evident that he hated him and all his party, and this feeling of hatred spread through the whole party and roused in opposition to it the same vindictiveness, though in a more seemly form, on the other side. Shouts were raised, and for a moment all was confusion, so that the marshal of the province had to call for order.

"A ballot! A ballot! Every nobleman sees it! We shed our blood for our country!... The confidence of the monarch.... No checking the accounts of the marshal; he's not a cashier.... But that's not the point.... Votes, please! Beastly!..." shouted furious and violent voices on all sides. Looks and faces were even more violent and furious than their words. They expressed the most implacable hatred. Levin did not in the least understand what was the matter, and he marveled at the passion with which it was disputed whether or not the decision about Flerov should be put to the vote. He forgot, as Sergey Ivanovitch explained to him afterwards, this syllogism: that it was necessary for the public good to get rid of the marshal of the province; that to get rid of the marshal it was necessary to have a majority of votes; that to get a majority of votes it was necessary to secure Flerov's right to vote; that to secure the recognition of Flerov's right to vote they must decide on the interpretation to be put on the act.

"And one vote may decide the whole question, and one must be serious and consecutive, if one wants to be of use in public life," concluded Sergey Ivanovitch. But Levin forgot all that, and it was painful to him to see all these excellent persons, for whom he had a respect, in such an unpleasant and vicious state of excitement. To escape from this painful feeling he went away into the other room where there was nobody except the waiters at the refreshment bar. Seeing the waiters busy over washing up the crockery and setting in order their plates and wine glasses, seeing their calm and cheerful faces, Levin felt an unexpected sense of relief as though he had come out of a stuffy room into the fresh air. He began walking up and down, looking with pleasure at the waiters. He particularly liked the way one gray-whiskered waiter, who showed his scorn for the other younger ones and was jeered at by them, was teaching them how to fold up napkins properly. Levin was just about to enter into conversation with the old waiter, when the secretary of the court of wardship, a little old man whose specialty it was to know all the noblemen of the province by name and patronymic, drew him away.

"Please come, Konstantin Dmitrievitch," he said, "your brother's looking for you. They are voting on the legal point."

Levin walked into the room, received a white ball, and followed his brother, Sergey Ivanovitch, to the table where Sviazhsky was standing with a significant and ironical face, holding his beard in his fist and sniffing at it. Sergey Ivanovitch put his hand into the box, put the ball somewhere, and making room for Levin, stopped. Levin advanced, but utterly forgetting what he was to do, and much embarrassed, he turned to Sergey Ivanovitch with the question, "Where am I to put it?" He asked this softly, at a moment when there was talking going on near, so that he had hoped his question would not be overheard. But the persons speaking paused, and his improper question was overheard. Sergey Ivanovitch frowned.

"That is a matter for each man's own decision," he said severely.

Several people smiled. Levin crimsoned, hurriedly thrust his hand under the cloth, and put the ball to the right as it was in his right hand. Having put it in, he recollected that he ought to have thrust his left hand too, and so he thrust it in though too late, and, still more overcome with confusion, he beat a hasty retreat into the background.

"A hundred and twenty-six for admission! Ninety-eight against!" sang out the voice of the secretary, who could not pronounce the letter r. Then there was a laugh; a button and two nuts were found in the box. The nobleman was allowed the right to vote, and the new party had conquered.

But the old party did not consider themselves conquered. Levin heard that they were asking Snetkov to stand, and he saw that a crowd of noblemen was surrounding the marshal, who was saying something. Levin went nearer. In reply Snetkov spoke of the trust the noblemen of the province had placed in him, the affection they had shown him, which he did not deserve, as his only merit had been his attachment to the nobility, to whom he had devoted twelve years of service. Several times he repeated the words: "I have served to the best of my powers with truth and good faith, I value your goodness and thank you," and suddenly he stopped short from the tears that choked him, and went out of the room. Whether these tears came from a sense of the injustice being done him, from his love for the nobility, or from the strain of the position he was placed in, feeling himself surrounded by enemies, his emotion infected the assembly, the majority were touched, and Levin felt a tenderness for Snetkov.

In the doorway the marshal of the province jostled against Levin.

"Beg pardon, excuse me, please," he said as to a stranger, but recognizing Levin, he smiled timidly. It seemed to Levin that he would have liked to say something, but could not speak for emotion. His face and his whole figure in his uniform with the crosses, and white trousers striped with braid, as he moved hurriedly along, reminded Levin of some hunted beast who sees that he is in evil case. This expression in the marshal's face was particularly touching to Levin, because, only the day before, he had been at his house about his trustee business and had seen him in all his grandeur, a kind-hearted, fatherly man. The big house with the old family furniture; the rather dirty, far from stylish, but respectful footmen, unmistakably old house serfs who had stuck to their master; the stout, good-natured wife in a cap with lace and a Turkish shawl, petting her pretty grandchild, her daughter's daughter; the young son, a sixth form high school boy, coming home from school, and greeting his father, kissing his big hand; the genuine, cordial words and gestures of the old man—all this had the day before roused an instinctive feeling of respect and sympathy in Levin. This old man was a touching and pathetic figure to Levin now, and he longed to say something pleasant to him.

"So you're sure to be our marshal again," he said.

"It's not likely," said the marshal, looking round with a scared expression. "I'm worn out, I'm old. If there are men younger and more deserving than I, let them serve."

And the marshal disappeared through a side door.

The most solemn moment was at hand. They were to proceed immediately to the election. The leaders of both parties were reckoning white and black on their fingers.

The discussion upon Flerov had given the new party not only Flerov's vote, but had also gained time for them, so that they could send to fetch three noblemen who had been rendered unable to take part in the elections by the wiles of the other party. Two noble gentlemen, who had a weakness for strong drink, had been made drunk by the partisans of Snetkov, and a third had been robbed of his uniform.

On learning this, the new party had made haste, during the dispute about Flerov, to send some of their men in a sledge to clothe the stripped gentleman, and to bring along one of the intoxicated to the meeting.

"I've brought one, drenched him with water," said the landowner, who had gone on this errand, to Sviazhsky. "He's all right? he'll do."

"Not too drunk, he won't fall down?" said Sviazhsky, shaking his head.

"No, he's first-rate. If only they don't give him any more here.... I've told the waiter not to give him anything on any account."

The narrow room, in which they were smoking and taking refreshments, was full of noblemen. The excitement grew more intense, and every face betrayed some uneasiness. The excitement was specially keen for the leaders of each party, who knew every detail, and had reckoned up every vote. They were the generals organizing the approaching battle. The rest, like the rank and file before an engagement, though they were getting ready for the fight, sought for other distractions in the interval. Some were lunching, standing at the bar, or sitting at the table; others were walking up and down the long room, smoking cigarettes, and talking with friends whom they had not seen for a long while.

Levin did not care to eat, and he was not smoking; he did not want to join his own friends, that is Sergey Ivanovitch, Stepan Arkadyevitch, Sviazhsky and the rest, because Vronsky in his equerry's uniform was standing with them in eager conversation. Levin had seen him already at the meeting on the previous day, and he had studiously avoided him, not caring to greet him. He went to the window and sat down, scanning the groups, and listening to what was being said around him. He felt depressed, especially because everyone else was, as he saw, eager, anxious, and interested, and he alone, with an old, toothless little man with mumbling lips wearing a naval uniform, sitting beside him, had no interest in it and nothing to do.

"He's such a blackguard! I have told him so, but it makes no difference. Only think of it! He couldn't collect it in three years!" he heard vigorously uttered by a round-shouldered, short, country gentleman, who had pomaded hair hanging on his embroidered collar, and new boots obviously put on for the occasion, with heels that tapped energetically as he spoke. Casting a displeased glance at Levin, this gentleman sharply turned his back.

"Yes, it's a dirty business, there's no denying," a small gentleman assented in a high voice.

Next, a whole crowd of country gentlemen, surrounding a stout general, hurriedly came near Levin. These persons were unmistakably seeking a place where they could talk without being overheard.

"How dare he say I had his breeches stolen! Pawned them for drink, I expect. Damn the fellow, prince indeed! He'd better not say it, the beast!"

"But excuse me! They take their stand on the act," was being said in another group; "the wife must be registered as noble."

"Oh, damn your acts! I speak from my heart. We're all gentlemen, aren't we? Above suspicion."

"Shall we go on, your excellency, *fine champagne?*"

Another group was following a nobleman, who was shouting something in a loud voice; it was one of the three intoxicated gentlemen.

"I always advised Marya Semyonovna to let for a fair rent, for she can never save a profit," he heard a pleasant voice say. The speaker was a country gentleman with gray whiskers, wearing the regimental uniform of an old general staff-officer. It was the very landowner Levin had met at Sviazhsky's. He knew him at once. The landowner too stared at Levin, and they exchanged greetings.

"Very glad to see you! To be sure! I remember you very well. Last year at our district marshal, Nikolay Ivanovitch's."

"Well, and how is your land doing?" asked Levin.

"Oh, still just the same, always at a loss," the landowner answered with a resigned smile, but with an expression of serenity and conviction that so it must be. "And how do you come to be in our province?" he asked. "Come to take part in our *coup d'etat?*" he said, confidently pronouncing the French words with a bad accent. "All Russia's here—gentlemen of the bedchamber, and everything short of the ministry." He pointed to the imposing figure of Stepan Arkadyevitch in white trousers and his court uniform, walking by with a general.

"I ought to own that I don't very well understand the drift of the provincial elections," said Levin.

The landowner looked at him.

"Why, what is there to understand? There's no meaning in it at all. It's a decaying institution that goes on running only by the force of inertia. Just look, the very uniforms tell you that it's an assembly of justices of the peace, permanent members of the court, and so on, but not of noblemen."

"Then why do you come?" asked Levin.

"From habit, nothing else. Then, too, one must keep up connections. It's a moral obligation of a sort. And then, to tell the truth, there's one's own interests. My son-in-law wants to stand as a permanent member; they're not rich people, and he must be brought forward. These gentlemen, now, what do they come for?" he said, pointing to the malignant gentleman, who was talking at the high table.

"That's the new generation of nobility."

"New it may be, but nobility it isn't. They're proprietors of a sort, but we're the landowners. As noblemen, they're cutting their own throats."

"But you say it's an institution that's served its time."

"That it may be, but still it ought to be treated a little more respectfully. Snetkov, now...We may be of use, or we may not, but we're the growth of a thousand years. If we're laying out a garden, planning one before the house, you know, and there you've a tree that's stood for centuries in the very spot.... Old and gnarled it may be, and yet you don't cut down the old fellow to make room for the flowerbeds, but lay out your beds so as to take advantage of the tree. You won't grow him again in a year," he said cautiously, and he immediately changed the conversation. "Well, and how is your land doing?"

"Oh, not very well. I make five per cent."

"Yes, but you don't reckon your own work. Aren't you worth something too? I'll tell you my own case. Before I took to seeing after the land, I had a salary of three hundred pounds from the service. Now I do more work than I did in the service, and like you I get five per cent. on the land, and thank God for that. But one's work is thrown in for nothing."

"Then why do you do it, if it's a clear loss?"

"Oh, well, one does it! What would you have? It's habit, and one knows it's how it should be. And what's more," the landowner went on, leaning his elbows on the window and chatting on, "my son, I must tell you, has no taste for it. There's no doubt he'll be a scientific man. So there'll be no one to keep it up. And yet one does it. Here this year I've planted an orchard."

"Yes, yes," said Levin, "that's perfectly true. I always feel there's no real balance of gain in my work on the land, and yet one does it.... It's a sort of duty one feels to the land."

"But I tell you what," the landowner pursued; "a neighbor of mine, a merchant, was at my place. We walked about the fields and the garden. 'No,' said he, 'Stepan Vassilievitch, everything's well looked after, but your garden's neglected.' But, as a fact, it's well kept up. 'To my thinking, I'd cut down that lime-tree. Here you've thousands of limes, and each would make two good bundles of bark. And nowadays that bark's worth something. I'd cut down the lot.'"

"And with what he made he'd increase his stock, or buy some land for a trifle, and let it out in lots to the peasants," Levin added, smiling. He had evidently more than once come across those commercial calculations. "And he'd make his fortune. But you and I must thank God if we keep what we've got and leave it to our children."

"You're married, I've heard?" said the landowner.

"Yes," Levin answered, with proud satisfaction. "Yes, it's rather strange," he went on. "So we live without making anything, as though we were ancient vestals set to keep in a fire."

The landowner chuckled under his white mustaches.

"There are some among us, too, like our friend Nikolay Ivanovitch, or Count Vronsky, that's settled here lately, who try to carry on their husbandry as though it were a factory; but so far it leads to nothing but making away with capital on it."

"But why is it we don't do like the merchants? Why don't we cut down our parks for timber?" said Levin, returning to a thought that had struck him.

"Why, as you said, to keep the fire in. Besides that's not work for a nobleman. And our work as noblemen isn't done here at the elections, but yonder, each in our corner. There's a class instinct, too, of what one ought and oughtn't to do. There's the peasants, too, I wonder at them sometimes; any good peasant tries to take all the land he can. However bad the land is, he'll work it. Without a return too. At a simple loss."

"Just as we do," said Levin. "Very, very glad to have met you," he added, seeing Sviazhsky approaching him.

"And here we've met for the first time since we met at your place," said the landowner to Sviazhsky, "and we've had a good talk too."

"Well, have you been attacking the new order of things?" said Sviazhsky with a smile.

"That we're bound to do."

"You've relieved your feelings?"

Sviazhsky took Levin's arm, and went with him to his own friends. This time there was no avoiding Vronsky. He was standing with Stepan Arkadyevitch and Sergey Ivanovitch, and looking straight at Levin as he drew near.

"Delighted! I believe I've had the pleasure of meeting you...at Princess Shtcherbatskaya's," he said, giving Levin his hand.

"Yes, I quite remember our meeting," said Levin, and blushing crimson, he turned away immediately, and began talking to his brother.

With a slight smile Vronsky went on talking to Sviazhsky, obviously without the slightest inclination to enter into conversation with Levin. But Levin, as he talked to his brother, was continually looking round at Vronsky, trying to think of something to say to him to gloss over his rudeness.

"What are we waiting for now?" asked Levin, looking at Sviazhsky and Vronsky.

"For Snetkov. He has to refuse or to consent to stand," answered Sviazhsky.

"Well, and what has he done, consented or not?"

"That's the point, that he's done neither," said Vronsky.

"And if he refuses, who will stand then?" asked Levin, looking at Vronsky.

"Whoever chooses to," said Sviazhsky.

"Shall you?" asked Levin.

"Certainly not I," said Sviazhsky, looking confused, and turning an alarmed glance at the malignant gentleman, who was standing beside Sergey Ivanovitch.

"Who then? Nevyedovsky?" said Levin, feeling he was putting his foot into it.

But this was worse still. Nevyedovsky and Sviazhsky were the two candidates.

"I certainly shall not, under any circumstances," answered the malignant gentleman.

This was Nevyedovsky himself. Sviazhsky introduced him to Levin.

"Well, you find it exciting too?" said Stepan Arkadyevitch, winking at Vronsky. "It's something like a race. One might bet on it."

"Yes, it is keenly exciting," said Vronsky. "And once taking the thing up, one's eager to see it through. It's a fight!" he said, scowling and setting his powerful jaws.

"What a capable fellow Sviazhsky is! Sees it all so clearly."

"Oh, yes!" Vronsky assented indifferently.

A silence followed, during which Vronsky—since he had to look at something—looked at Levin, at his feet, at his uniform, then at his face, and noticing his gloomy eyes fixed upon him, he said, in order to say something:

"How is it that you, living constantly in the country, are not a justice of the peace? You are not in the uniform of one."

"It's because I consider that the justice of the peace is a silly institution," Levin answered gloomily. He had been all the time looking for an opportunity to enter into conversation with Vronsky, so as to smooth over his rudeness at their first meeting.

"I don't think so, quite the contrary," Vronsky said, with quiet surprise.

"It's a plaything," Levin cut him short. "We don't want justices of the peace. I've never had a single thing to do with them during eight years. And what I have had was decided wrongly by them. The justice of the peace is over thirty miles from me. For some matter of two roubles I should have to send a lawyer, who costs me fifteen."

And he related how a peasant had stolen some flour from the miller, and when the miller told him of it, had lodged a complaint for slander. All this was utterly uncalled for and stupid, and Levin felt it himself as he said it.

"Oh, this is such an original fellow!" said Stepan Arkadyevitch with his most soothing, almond-oil smile. "But come along; I think they're voting...."

And they separated.

"I can't understand," said Sergey Ivanovitch, who had observed his brother's clumsiness, "I can't understand how anyone can be so absolutely devoid of political tact. That's where we Russians are so deficient. The marshal of the province is our opponent, and with him you're *ami cochon*, and you beg him to stand. Count Vronsky, now ...I'm not making a friend of him; he's asked me to dinner, and I'm not going; but he's one of our side—why make an enemy of him? Then you ask Nevyedovsky if he's going to stand. That's not a thing to do."

"Oh, I don't understand it at all! And it's all such nonsense," Levin answered gloomily.

"You say it's all such nonsense, but as soon as you have anything to do with it, you make a muddle."

Levin did not answer, and they walked together into the big room.

The marshal of the province, though he was vaguely conscious in the air of some trap being prepared for him, and though he had not been called upon by all to stand, had still made up his mind to stand. All was silence in the room. The secretary announced in a loud voice that the captain of the guards, Mihail Stepanovitch Snetkov, would now be balloted for as marshal of the province.

The district marshals walked carrying plates, on which were balls, from their tables to the high table, and the election began.

"Put it in the right side," whispered Stepan Arkadyevitch, as with his brother Levin followed the marshal of his district to the table. But Levin had forgotten by now the calculations that had been explained to him, and was afraid Stepan Arkadyevitch might be mistaken in saying "the right side." Surely Snetkov was the enemy. As he went up, he held the ball in his right hand, but thinking he was wrong, just at the box he changed to the left hand, and undoubtedly put the ball to the left. An adept in the business, standing at the box and seeing by the mere action of the elbow where each put his ball, scowled with annoyance. It was no good for him to use his insight.

Everything was still, and the counting of the balls was heard. Then a single voice rose and proclaimed the numbers for and against. The marshal had been voted for by a considerable majority. All was noise and eager movement towards the doors. Snetkov came in, and the nobles thronged round him, congratulating him.

"Well, now is it over?" Levin asked Sergey Ivanovitch.

"It's only just beginning," Sviazhsky said, replying for Sergey Ivanovitch with a smile. "Some other candidate may receive more votes than the marshal."

Levin had quite forgotten about that. Now he could only remember that there was some sort of trickery in it, but he was too bored to think what it was exactly. He felt depressed, and longed to get out of the crowd.

As no one was paying any attention to him, and no one apparently needed him, he quietly slipped away into the little room where the refreshments were, and again had a great sense of comfort when he saw the waiters. The little old waiter pressed him to have something, and Levin agreed. After eating a cutlet with beans and talking to the waiters of their former masters, Levin, not wishing to go back to the hall, where it was all so distasteful to him, proceeded to walk through the galleries. The galleries were full of fashionably dressed ladies, leaning over the balustrade and trying not to lose a single word of what was being said below. With the ladies were sitting and standing smart lawyers, high school teachers in spectacles, and officers. Everywhere they were talking of the election, and of how worried the marshal was, and how splendid the discussions had been. In one group Levin heard his brother's praises. One lady was telling a lawyer:

"How glad I am I heard Koznishev! It's worth losing one's dinner. He's exquisite! So clear and distinct all of it! There's not one of you in the law courts that speaks like that. The only one is Meidel, and he's not so eloquent by a long way."

Finding a free place, Levin leaned over the balustrade and began looking and listening.

All the noblemen were sitting railed off behind barriers according to their districts. In the middle of the room stood a man in a uniform, who shouted in a loud, high voice:

"As a candidate for the marshalship of the nobility of the province we call upon staff-captain Yevgeney Ivanovitch Apuhtin!" A dead silence followed, and then a weak old voice was heard: "Declined!"

"We call upon the privy councilor Pyotr Petrovitch Bol," the voice began again.

"Declined!" a high boyish voice replied.

Again it began, and again "Declined." And so it went on for about an hour. Levin, with his elbows on the balustrade, looked and listened. At first he wondered and wanted to know what it meant; then feeling sure that he could not make it out he began to be bored. Then recalling all the excitement and vindictiveness he had seen on all the faces, he felt sad; he made up his mind to go, and went downstairs. As he passed through the entry to the galleries he met a dejected high school boy walking up and down with tired-looking eyes. On the stairs he met a couple—a lady running quickly on her high heels and the jaunty deputy prosecutor.

"I told you you weren't late," the deputy prosecutor was saying at the moment when Levin moved aside to let the lady pass.

Levin was on the stairs to the way out, and was just feeling in his waistcoat pocket for the number of his overcoat, when the secretary overtook him.

"This way, please, Konstantin Dmitrievitch; they are voting."

The candidate who was being voted on was Nevyedovsky, who had so stoutly denied all idea of standing. Levin went up to the door of the room; it was locked. The secretary knocked, the door opened, and Levin was met by two red-faced gentlemen, who darted out.

"I can't stand any more of it," said one red-faced gentleman.

After them the face of the marshal of the province was poked out. His face was dreadful-looking from exhaustion and dismay.

"I told you not to let any one out!" he cried to the doorkeeper.

"I let someone in, your excellency!"

"Mercy on us!" and with a heavy sigh the marshal of the province walked with downcast head to the high table in the middle of the room, his legs staggering in his white trousers.

Nevyedovsky had scored a higher majority, as they had planned, and he was the new marshal of the province. Many people were amused, many were pleased and happy, many were in ecstasies, many were disgusted and unhappy. The former marshal of the province was in a state of despair, which he could not conceal. When Nevyedovsky went out of the room, the crowd thronged round him and followed him enthusiastically, just as they had followed the governor who had opened the meetings, and just as they had followed Snetkov when he was elected.

Before Vronsky's departure for the elections, Anna had reflected that the scenes constantly repeated between them each time he left home, might only make him cold to her instead of attaching him to her, and resolved to do all she could to control herself so as to bear the parting with composure. But the cold, severe glance with which he had looked at her when he came to tell her he was going had wounded her, and before he had started her peace of mind was destroyed.

In solitude afterwards, thinking over that glance which had expressed his right to freedom, she came, as she always did, to the same point—the sense of her own humiliation. "He has the right to go away when and where he chooses. Not simply to go away, but to leave me. He has every right, and I have none. But knowing that, he ought not to do it. What has he done, though?... He looked at me with a cold, severe expression. Of course that is something indefinable, impalpable, but it has never been so before, and that glance means a great deal," she thought. "That glance shows the beginning of indifference."

And though she felt sure that a coldness was beginning, there was nothing she could do, she could not in any way alter her relations to him. Just as before, only by love and by charm could she keep him. And so, just as before, only by occupation in the day, by morphine at night, could she stifle the fearful thought of what would be if he ceased to love her. It is true there was still one means; not to keep him—for that she wanted nothing more than his love—but to be nearer to him, to be in such a position that he would not leave her. That means was divorce and marriage. And she began to long for that, and made up her mind to agree to it the first time he or Stiva approached her on the subject.

Absorbed in such thoughts, she passed five days without him, the five days that he was to be at the elections.

Walks, conversation with Princess Varvara, visits to the hospital, and, most of all, reading—reading of one book after another—filled up her time. But on the sixth day, when the coachman came back without him, she felt that now she was utterly incapable of stifling the thought of him and of what he was doing there, just at that time her little girl was taken ill. Anna began to look after her, but even that did not distract her mind, especially as the illness was not serious. However hard she tried, she could not love this little child, and to feign love was beyond her powers. Towards the evening of that day, still alone, Anna was in such a panic about him that she decided to start for the town, but on second thoughts wrote him the contradictory letter that Vronsky received, and without reading it through, sent it off by a special messenger. The next morning she received his letter and regretted her own. She dreaded a repetition of the severe look he had flung at her at parting, especially when he knew that the baby was not dangerously ill. But still she was glad she had written to him. At this moment Anna was positively admitting to herself that she was a burden to him, that he would relinquish his freedom regretfully to return to her, and in spite of that she was glad he was coming. Let him weary of her, but he would be here with her, so that she would see him, would know of every action he took.

She was sitting in the drawing room near a lamp, with a new volume of Taine, and as she read, listening to the sound of the wind outside, and every minute expecting the carriage to arrive. Several times she had fancied she heard the sound of wheels, but she had been mistaken. At last she heard not the sound of wheels, but the coachman's shout and the dull rumble in the covered entry. Even Princess Varvara, playing patience, confirmed this, and Anna, flushing hotly, got up; but instead of going down, as she had done twice before, she stood still. She suddenly felt ashamed of her duplicity, but even more she dreaded how he might meet her. All feeling of wounded pride had passed now; she was only afraid of the expression of his displeasure. She remembered that her child had been perfectly well again for the last two days. She felt positively vexed with her for getting better from the very moment her letter was sent off. Then she thought of him, that he was here, all of him, with his hands, his eyes. She heard his voice. And forgetting everything, she ran joyfully to meet him.

"Well, how is Annie?" he said timidly from below, looking up to Anna as she ran down to him.

He was sitting on a chair, and a footman was pulling off his warm over-boot.

"Oh, she is better."

"And you?" he said, shaking himself.

She took his hand in both of hers, and drew it to her waist, never taking her eyes off him.

"Well, I'm glad," he said, coldly scanning her, her hair, her dress, which he knew she had put on for him. All was charming, but how many times it had charmed him! And the stern, stony expression that she so dreaded settled upon his face.

"Well, I'm glad. And are you well?" he said, wiping his damp beard with his handkerchief and kissing her hand.

"Never mind," she thought, "only let him be here, and so long as he's here he cannot, he dare not, cease to love me."

The evening was spent happily and gaily in the presence of Princess Varvara, who complained to him that Anna had been taking morphine in his absence.

"What am I to do? I couldn't sleep.... My thoughts prevented me. When he's here I never take it—hardly ever."

He told her about the election, and Anna knew how by adroit questions to bring him to what gave him most pleasure—his own success. She told him of everything that interested him at home; and all that she told him was of the most cheerful description.

But late in the evening, when they were alone, Anna, seeing that she had regained complete possession of him, wanted to erase the painful impression of the glance he had given her for her letter. She said:

"Tell me frankly, you were vexed at getting my letter, and you didn't believe me?"

As soon as she had said it, she felt that however warm his feelings were to her, he had not forgiven her for that.

"Yes," he said, "the letter was so strange. First, Annie ill, and then you thought of coming yourself."

"It was all the truth."

"Oh, I don't doubt it."

"Yes, you do doubt it. You are vexed, I see."

"Not for one moment. I'm only vexed, that's true, that you seem somehow unwilling to admit that there are duties..."

"The duty of going to a concert..."

"But we won't talk about it," he said.

"Why not talk about it?" she said.

"I only meant to say that matters of real importance may turn up. Now, for instance, I shall have to go to Moscow to arrange about the house.... Oh, Anna, why are you so irritable? Don't you know that I can't live without you?"

"If so," said Anna, her voice suddenly changing, "it means that you are sick of this life.... Yes, you will come for a day and go away, as men do..."

"Anna, that's cruel. I am ready to give up my whole life."

But she did not hear him.

"If you go to Moscow, I will go too. I will not stay here. Either we must separate or else live together."

"Why, you know, that's my one desire. But for that..."

"We must get a divorce. I will write to him. I see I cannot go on like this.... But I will come with you to Moscow."

"You talk as if you were threatening me. But I desire nothing so much as never to be parted from you," said Vronsky, smiling.

But as he said these words there gleamed in his eyes not merely a cold look, but the vindictive look of a man persecuted and made cruel.

She saw the look and correctly divined its meaning.

"If so, it's a calamity!" that glance told her. It was a moment's impression, but she never forgot it.

Anna wrote to her husband asking him about a divorce, and towards the end of November, taking leave of Princess Varvara, who wanted to go to Petersburg, she went with Vronsky to Moscow. Expecting every day an answer from Alexey Alexandrovitch, and after that the divorce, they now established themselves together like married people.

CHAPTER SEVEN

THE LEVINS HAD been three months in Moscow. The date had long passed on which, according to the most trustworthy calculations of people learned in such matters, Kitty should have been confined. But she was still about, and there was nothing to show that her time was any nearer than two months ago. The doctor, the monthly nurse, and Dolly and her mother, and most of all Levin, who could not think of the approaching event without terror, began to be impatient and uneasy. Kitty was the only person who felt perfectly calm and happy.

She was distinctly conscious now of the birth of a new feeling of love for the future child, for her to some extent actually existing already, and she brooded blissfully over this feeling. He was not by now altogether a part of herself, but sometimes lived his own life independently of her. Often this separate being gave her pain, but at the same time she wanted to laugh with a strange new joy.

All the people she loved were with her, and all were so good to her, so attentively caring for her, so entirely pleasant was everything presented to her, that if she had not known and felt that it must all soon be over, she could not have wished for a better and pleasanter life. The only thing that spoiled the charm of this manner of life was that her husband was not here as she loved him to be, and as he was in the country.

She liked his serene, friendly, and hospitable manner in the country. In the town he seemed continually uneasy and on his guard, as though he were afraid someone would be rude to him, and still more to her. At home in the country, knowing himself distinctly to be in his right place, he was never in haste to be off elsewhere. He was never unoccupied. Here in town he was in a continual hurry, as though afraid of missing something, and yet he had nothing to do. And she felt sorry for him. To others, she knew, he did not appear an object of pity. On the contrary, when Kitty looked at him in society, as one sometimes looks at those one loves, trying to see him as if he were a stranger, so as to catch the impression he must make on others, she saw with a panic even of jealous fear that he was far indeed from being a pitiable figure, that he was very attractive with his fine breeding, his rather old-fashioned, reserved courtesy with women, his powerful figure, and striking, as she thought, and expressive face. But she saw him not from without, but from within; she saw that here he was not himself; that was the only way she could define his condition to herself. Sometimes she inwardly reproached him for his inability to live in the town; sometimes she recognized that it was really hard for him to order his life here so that he could be satisfied with it.

What had he to do, indeed? He did not care for cards; he did not go to a club. Spending the time with jovial gentlemen of Oblonsky's type—she knew now what that meant...it meant drinking and going somewhere after drinking. She could not think without horror of where men went on such occasions. Was he to go into society? But she knew he could only find satisfaction in that if he took pleasure in the society of young women, and that she could not wish for. Should he stay at home with her, her mother and her sisters? But much as she liked and enjoyed their conversations forever on the same subjects—"Aline-Nadine," as the old prince called the sisters' talks—she knew it must bore him. What was there left for him to do? To go on writing at his book he had indeed attempted, and at first he used to go to the library and make extracts and look up references for his book. But, as he told her, the more he did nothing, the less time he had to do anything. And besides, he complained that he had talked too much about his book here, and that consequently all his ideas about it were muddled and had lost their interest for him.

One advantage in this town life was that quarrels hardly ever happened between them here in town. Whether it was that their conditions were different, or that they had both become more careful and sensible in that respect, they had no quarrels in Moscow from jealousy, which they had so dreaded when they moved from the country.

One event, an event of great importance to both from that point of view, did indeed happen—that was Kitty's meeting with Vronsky.

The old Princess Marya Borissovna, Kitty's godmother, who had always been very fond of her, had insisted on seeing her. Kitty, though she did not go into society at all on account of her condition, went with her father to see the venerable old lady, and there met Vronsky.

The only thing Kitty could reproach herself for at this meeting was that at the instant when she recognized in his civilian dress the features once so familiar to her, her breath failed her, the blood rushed to her heart, and a vivid blush—she felt it— overspread her face. But this lasted only a few seconds. Before her father, who purposely began talking in a loud voice to Vronsky, had finished, she was perfectly ready to look at Vronsky, to speak to him, if necessary, exactly as she spoke to Princess Marya Borissovna, and more than that, to do so in such a way that everything to the faintest intonation and smile would have been approved by her husband, whose unseen presence she seemed to feel about her at that instant.

She said a few words to him, even smiled serenely at his joke about the elections, which he called "our parliament." (She had to smile to show she saw the joke.) But she turned away immediately to Princess Marya Borissovna, and did not once glance at him till he got up to go; then she looked at him, but evidently only because it would be uncivil not to look at a man when he is saying good-bye.

She was grateful to her father for saying nothing to her about their meeting Vronsky, but she saw by his special warmth to her after the visit during their usual walk that he was pleased with her. She was pleased with herself. She had not expected she would have had the power, while keeping somewhere in the bottom of her heart all the memories of her old feeling for Vronsky, not only to seem but to be perfectly indifferent and composed with him.

Levin flushed a great deal more than she when she told him she had met Vronsky at Princess Marya Borissovna's. It was very hard for her to tell him this, but still harder to go on speaking of the details of the meeting, as he did not question her, but simply gazed at her with a frown.

"I am very sorry you weren't there," she said. "Not that you weren't in the room...I couldn't have been so natural in your presence...I am blushing now much more, much, much more," she said, blushing till the tears came into her eyes. "But that you couldn't see through a crack."

The truthful eyes told Levin that she was satisfied with herself, and in spite of her blushing he was quickly reassured and began questioning her, which was all she wanted. When he had heard everything, even to the detail that for the first second she could not help flushing, but that afterwards she was just as direct and as much at her ease as with any chance acquaintance, Levin was quite happy again and said he was glad of it, and would not now behave as stupidly as he had done at the election, but would try the first time he met Vronsky to be as friendly as possible.

"It's so wretched to feel that there's a man almost an enemy whom it's painful to meet," said Levin. "I'm very, very glad."

Levin had on this visit to town seen a great deal of his old friend at the university, Professor Katavasov, whom he had not seen since his marriage. He liked in Katavasov the clearness and simplicity of his conception of life. Levin thought that the clearness of Katavasov's conception of life was due to the poverty of his nature; Katavasov thought that the disconnectedness of Levin's ideas was due to his lack of intellectual discipline; but Levin enjoyed Katavasov's clearness, and Katavasov enjoyed the abundance of Levin's untrained ideas, and they liked to meet and to discuss.

Levin had read Katavasov some parts of his book, and he had liked them. On the previous day Katavasov had met Levin at a public lecture and told him that the celebrated Metrov, whose article Levin had so much liked, was in Moscow, that he had been much interested by what Katavasov had told him about Levin's work, and that he was coming to see him tomorrow at eleven, and would be very glad to make Levin's acquaintance.

"You're positively a reformed character, I'm glad to see," said Katavasov, meeting Levin in the little drawing room. "I heard the bell and thought: Impossible that it can be he at the exact time!... Well, what do you say to the Montenegrins now? They're a race of warriors."

"Why, what's happened?" asked Levin.

Katavasov in a few words told him the last piece of news from the war, and going into his study, introduced Levin to a short, thick-set man of pleasant appearance. This was Metrov. The conversation touched for a brief space on politics and on how recent events were looked at in the higher spheres in Petersburg. Metrov repeated a saying that had reached him through a most trustworthy source, reported as having been uttered on this subject by the Tsar and one of the ministers. Katavasov had heard also on excellent authority that the Tsar had said something quite different. Levin tried to imagine circumstances in which both sayings might have been uttered, and the conversation on that topic dropped.

"Yes, here he's written almost a book on the natural conditions of the laborer in relation to the land," said Katavasov; "I'm not a specialist, but I, as a natural science man, was pleased at his not taking mankind as something outside biological laws; but, on the contrary, seeing his dependence on his surroundings, and in that dependence seeking the laws of his development."

"That's very interesting," said Metrov.

"What I began precisely was to write a book on agriculture; but studying the chief instrument of agriculture, the laborer," said Levin, reddening, "I could not help coming to quite unexpected results."

And Levin began carefully, as it were, feeling his ground, to expound his views. He knew Metrov had written an article against the generally accepted theory of political economy, but to what extent he could reckon on his sympathy with his own new views he did not know and could not guess from the clever and serene face of the learned man.

"But in what do you see the special characteristics of the Russian laborer?" said Metrov; "in his biological characteristics, so to speak, or in the condition in which he is placed?"

Levin saw that there was an idea underlying this question with which he did not agree. But he went on explaining his own idea that the Russian laborer has a quite special view of the land, different from that of other people; and to support this proposition he made haste to add that in his opinion this attitude of the Russian peasant was due to the consciousness of his vocation to people vast unoccupied expanses in the East.

"One may easily be led into error in basing any conclusion on the general vocation of a people," said Metrov, interrupting Levin. "The condition of the laborer will always depend on his relation to the land and to capital."

And without letting Levin finish explaining his idea, Metrov began expounding to him the special point of his own theory.

In what the point of his theory lay, Levin did not understand, because he did not take the trouble to understand. He saw that Metrov, like other people, in spite of his own article, in which he had attacked the current theory of political economy, looked at the position of the Russian peasant simply from the point of view of capital, wages, and rent. He would indeed have been obliged to admit that in the eastern—much the larger—part of Russia rent was as yet nil, that for nine-tenths of the eighty millions of the Russian peasants wages took the form simply of food provided for themselves, and that capital does not so far exist except in the form of the most primitive tools. Yet it was only from that point of view that he considered every laborer, though in many points he differed from the economists and had his own theory of the wage-fund, which he expounded to Levin.

Levin listened reluctantly, and at first made objections. He would have liked to interrupt Metrov, to explain his own thought, which in his opinion would have rendered further exposition of Metrov's theories superfluous. But later on, feeling convinced that they looked at the matter so differently, that they could never understand one another, he did not even oppose his statements, but simply listened. Although what Metrov was saying was by now utterly devoid of interest for him, he yet experienced a certain satisfaction in listening to him. It flattered his vanity that such a learned man should explain his ideas to him so eagerly, with such intensity and confidence in Levin's understanding of the subject, sometimes with a mere hint referring him to a whole aspect of the subject. He put this down to his own credit, unaware that Metrov, who had already discussed his theory over and over again with all his intimate friends, talked of it with special eagerness to every new person, and in general was eager to talk to anyone of any subject that interested him, even if still obscure to himself.

"We are late though," said Katavasov, looking at his watch directly Metrov had finished his discourse.

"Yes, there's a meeting of the Society of Amateurs today in commemoration of the jubilee of Svintitch," said Katavasov in answer to Levin's inquiry. "Pyotr Ivanovitch and I were going.

I've promised to deliver an address on his labors in zoology. Come along with us, it's very interesting."

"Yes, and indeed it's time to start," said Metrov. "Come with us, and from there, if you care to, come to my place. I should very much like to hear your work."

"Oh, no! It's no good yet, it's unfinished. But I shall be very glad to go to the meeting."

"I say, friends, have you heard? He has handed in the separate report," Katavasov called from the other room, where he was putting on his frock coat.

And a conversation sprang up upon the university question, which was a very important event that winter in Moscow. Three old professors in the council had not accepted the opinion of the younger professors. The young ones had registered a separate resolution. This, in the judgment of some people, was monstrous, in the judgment of others it was the simplest and most just thing to do, and the professors were split up into two parties.

One party, to which Katavasov belonged, saw in the opposite party a scoundrelly betrayal and treachery, while the opposite party saw in them childishness and lack of respect for the authorities. Levin, though he did not belong to the university, had several times already during his stay in Moscow heard and talked about this matter, and had his own opinion on the subject. He took part in the conversation that was continued in the street, as they all three walked to the buildings of the old university.

The meeting had already begun. Round the cloth-covered table, at which Katavasov and Metrov seated themselves, there were some half-dozen persons, and one of these was bending close over a manuscript, reading something aloud. Levin sat down in one of the empty chairs that were standing round the table, and in a whisper asked a student sitting near what was being read. The student, eyeing Levin with displeasure, said:

"Biography."

Though Levin was not interested in the biography, he could not help listening, and learned some new and interesting facts about the life of the distinguished man of science.

When the reader had finished, the chairman thanked him and read some verses of the poet Ment sent him on the jubilee, and said a few words by way of thanks to the poet. Then Katavasov in his loud, ringing voice read his address on the scientific labors of the man whose jubilee was being kept.

When Katavasov had finished, Levin looked at his watch, saw it was past one, and thought that there would not be time before the concert to read Metrov his book, and indeed, he did not now care to do so. During the reading he had thought over their conversation. He saw distinctly now that though Metrov's ideas might perhaps have value, his own ideas had a value too, and their ideas could only be made clear and lead to something if each worked separately in his chosen path, and that nothing would be gained by putting their ideas together. And having made up his mind to refuse Metrov's invitation, Levin went up to him at the end of the meeting. Metrov introduced Levin to the chairman, with whom he was talking of the political news. Metrov told the chairman what he had already told Levin, and Levin made the same remarks on his news that he had already made that morning, but for the sake of variety he expressed also a new opinion which had only just struck him. After that the conversation turned again on the university question. As Levin had already heard it all, he made haste to tell Metrov that he was sorry he could not take advantage of his invitation, and took leave.

"Perhaps they're not at home?" said Levin, as he went into the hall of Countess Bola's house.

"At home; please walk in," said the porter, resolutely removing his overcoat.

"How annoying!" thought Levin with a sigh, taking off one glove and stroking his hat. "What did I come for? What have I to say to them?"

As he passed through the first drawing room Levin met in the doorway Countess Bola, giving some order to a servant with a care-worn and severe face. On seeing Levin she smiled, and asked him to come into the little drawing room, where he heard voices. In this room there were sitting in armchairs the two daughters of the countess, and a Moscow colonel, whom Levin knew. Levin went up, greeted them, and sat down beside the sofa with his hat on his knees.

"How is your wife? Have you been at the concert? We couldn't go. Mamma had to be at the funeral service."

"Yes, I heard.... What a sudden death!" said Levin.

The countess came in, sat down on the sofa, and she too asked after his wife and inquired about the concert.

Levin answered, and repeated an inquiry about Madame Apraksina's sudden death.

"But she was always in weak health."

"Were you at the opera yesterday?"

"Yes, I was."

"Lucca was very good."

"Yes, very good," he said, and as it was utterly of no consequence to him what they thought of him, he began repeating what they had heard a hundred times about the characteristics of the singer's talent. Countess Bola pretended to be listening. Then, when he had said enough and paused, the colonel, who had been silent till then, began to talk. The colonel too talked of the opera, and about culture. At last, after speaking of the proposed *folle journée* at Turin's, the colonel laughed, got up noisily, and went away. Levin too rose, but he saw by the face of the countess that it was not yet time for him to go. He must stay two minutes longer. He sat down.

But as he was thinking all the while how stupid it was, he could not find a subject for conversation, and sat silent.

"You are not going to the public meeting? They say it will be very interesting," began the countess.

"No, I promised my belle-soeur to fetch her from it," said Levin.

A silence followed. The mother once more exchanged glances with a daughter.

"Well, now I think the time has come," thought Levin, and he got up. The ladies shook hands with him, and begged him to say *mille choses* to his wife for them.

The porter asked him, as he gave him his coat, "Where is your honor staying?" and immediately wrote down his address in a big handsomely bound book.

"Of course I don't care, but still I feel ashamed and awfully stupid," thought Levin, consoling himself with the reflection that everyone does it. He drove to the public meeting, where he was to find his sister-in-law, so as to drive home with her.

At the public meeting of the committee there were a great many people, and almost all the highest society. Levin was in time for the report which, as everyone said, was very interesting. When the reading of the report was over, people moved about, and Levin met Sviazhsky, who invited him very pressingly to come that evening to a meeting of the Society of Agriculture, where a celebrated lecture was to be delivered, and Stepan Arkadyevitch, who had only just come from the races, and many other acquaintances; and Levin heard and uttered various criticisms on the meeting, on the new fantasia, and on a public trial. But, probably from the mental fatigue he was beginning to feel, he made a blunder in speaking of the trial, and this blunder he recalled several times with vexation. Speaking of the sentence upon a foreigner who had been condemned in Russia, and of how unfair it would be to punish him by exile abroad, Levin repeated what he had heard the day before in conversation from an acquaintance.

"I think sending him abroad is much the same as punishing a carp by putting it into the water," said Levin. Then he recollected that this idea, which he had heard from an acquaintance and uttered as his own, came from a fable of Krilov's, and that the acquaintance had picked it up from a newspaper article.

After driving home with his sister-in-law, and finding Kitty in good spirits and quite well, Levin drove to the club.

Levin reached the club just at the right time. Members and visitors were driving up as he arrived. Levin had not been at the club for a very long while—not since he lived in Moscow, when he was leaving the university and going into society. He remembered the club, the external details of its arrangement, but he had completely forgotten the impression it had made on him in old days. But as soon as, driving into the wide semicircular court and getting out of the sledge, he mounted the steps, and the hall porter, adorned with a crossway scarf, noiselessly opened the door to him with a bow; as soon as he saw in the porter's room the cloaks and galoshes of members who thought it less trouble to take them off downstairs; as soon as he heard the mysterious ringing bell that preceded him as he ascended the easy, carpeted staircase, and saw the statue on the landing, and the third porter at the top doors, a familiar figure grown older, in the club livery, opening the door without haste or delay, and scanning the visitors as they passed in—Levin felt the old impression of the club come back in a rush, an impression of repose, comfort, and propriety.

"Your hat, please," the porter said to Levin, who forgot the club rule to leave his hat in the porter's room. "Long time since you've been. The prince put your name down yesterday. Prince Stepan Arkadyevitch is not here yet."

The porter did not only know Levin, but also all his ties and relationships, and so immediately mentioned his intimate friends.

Passing through the outer hall, divided up by screens, and the room partitioned on the right, where a man sits at the fruit buffet, Levin overtook an old man walking slowly in, and entered the dining room full of noise and people.

He walked along the tables, almost all full, and looked at the visitors. He saw people of all sorts, old and young; some he knew a little, some intimate friends. There was not a single cross or worried-looking face. All seemed to have left their cares and anxieties in the porter's room with their hats, and were all deliberately getting ready to enjoy the material blessings of life. Sviazhsky was here and Shtcherbatsky, Nevyedovsky and the old prince, and Vronsky and Sergey Ivanovitch.

"Ah! why are you late?" the prince said smiling, and giving him his hand over his own shoulder. "How's Kitty?" he added, smoothing out the napkin he had tucked in at his waistcoat buttons.

"All right; they are dining at home, all the three of them."

"Ah, 'Aline-Nadine,' to be sure! There's no room with us. Go to that table, and make haste and take a seat," said the prince, and turning away he carefully took a plate of eel soup.

"Levin, this way!" a good-natured voice shouted a little farther on. It was Turovtsin. He was sitting with a young officer, and beside them were two chairs turned upside down. Levin gladly went up to them. He had always liked the good-hearted rake, Turovtsin—he was associated in his mind with memories of his courtship—and at that moment, after the strain of intellectual conversation, the sight of Turovtsin's good-natured face was particularly welcome.

"For you and Oblonsky. He'll be here directly."

The young man, holding himself very erect, with eyes forever twinkling with enjoyment, was an officer from Petersburg, Gagin. Turovtsin introduced them.

"Oblonsky's always late."

"Ah, here he is!"

"Have you only just come?" said Oblonsky, coming quickly towards them. "Good day. Had some vodka? Well, come along then."

Levin got up and went with him to the big table spread with spirits and appetizers of the most various kinds. One would have thought that out of two dozen delicacies one might find something to one's taste, but Stepan Arkadyevitch asked for something special, and one of the liveried waiters standing by immediately brought what was required. They drank a wine glassful and returned to their table.

At once, while they were still at the soup, Gagin was served with champagne, and told the waiter to fill four glasses. Levin did not refuse the wine, and asked for a second bottle. He was very hungry, and ate and drank with great enjoyment, and with still greater enjoyment took part in the lively and simple conversation of his companions. Gagin, dropping his voice, told the last good story from Petersburg, and the story, though improper and stupid, was so ludicrous that Levin broke into roars of laughter so loud that those near looked round.

"That's in the same style as, 'that's a thing I can't endure!' You know the story?" said Stepan Arkadyevitch. "Ah, that's exquisite! Another bottle," he said to the waiter, and he began to relate his good story.

"Pyotr Illyitch Vinovsky invites you to drink with him," a little old waiter interrupted Stepan Arkadyevitch, bringing two delicate glasses of sparkling champagne, and addressing Stepan Arkadyevitch and Levin. Stepan Arkadyevitch took the glass, and looking towards a bald man with red mustaches at the other end of the table, he nodded to him, smiling.

"Who's that?" asked Levin.

"You met him once at my place, don't you remember? A good-natured fellow."

Levin did the same as Stepan Arkadyevitch and took the glass.

Stepan Arkadyevitch's anecdote too was very amusing. Levin told his story, and that too was successful. Then they talked of horses, of the races, of what they had been doing that day, and of how smartly Vronsky's Atlas had won the first prize. Levin did not notice how the time passed at dinner.

"Ah! and here they are!" Stepan Arkadyevitch said towards the end of dinner, leaning over the back of his chair and holding out his hand to Vronsky, who came up with a tall officer of the Guards. Vronsky's face too beamed with the look of good-humored enjoyment that was general in the club. He propped his elbow playfully on Stepan Arkadyevitch's shoulder, whispering something to him, and he held out his hand to Levin with the same good-humored smile.

"Very glad to meet you," he said. "I looked out for you at the election, but I was told you had gone away."

"Yes, I left the same day. We've just been talking of your horse. I congratulate you," said Levin. "It was very rapidly run."

"Yes; you've race horses too, haven't you?"

"No, my father had; but I remember and know something about it."

"Where have you dined?" asked Stepan Arkadyevitch.

"We were at the second table, behind the columns."

"We've been celebrating his success," said the tall colonel. "It's his second Imperial prize. I wish I might have the luck at cards he has with horses. Well, why waste the precious time? I'm going to the 'infernal regions,'" added the colonel, and he walked away.

"That's Yashvin," Vronsky said in answer to Turovtsin, and he sat down in the vacated seat beside them. He drank the glass offered him, and ordered a bottle of wine. Under the influence of the club atmosphere or the wine he had drunk, Levin chatted away to Vronsky of the best breeds of cattle, and was very glad not to feel the slightest hostility to this man. He even told him, among other things, that he had heard from his wife that she had met him at Princess Marya Borissovna's.

"Ah, Princess Marya Borissovna, she's exquisite!" said Stepan Arkadyevitch, and he told an anecdote about her which set them all laughing. Vronsky particularly laughed with such simplehearted amusement that Levin felt quite reconciled to him.

"Well, have we finished?" said Stepan Arkadyevitch, getting up with a smile. "Let us go."

Getting up from the table, Levin walked with Gagin through the lofty room to the billiard room, feeling his arms swing as he walked with a peculiar lightness and ease. As he crossed the big room, he came upon his father-in-law.

"Well, how do you like our Temple of Indolence?" said the prince, taking his arm. "Come along, come along!"

"Yes, I wanted to walk about and look at everything. It's interesting."

"Yes, it's interesting for you. But its interest for me is quite different. You look at those little old men now," he said, pointing to a club member with bent back and projecting lip, shuffling towards them in his soft boots, "and imagine that they were *shlupiks* like that from their birth up."

"How *shlupiks*?"

"I see you don't know that name. That's our club designation. You know the game of rolling eggs: when one's rolled a long while it becomes a *shlupik*. So it is with us; one goes on coming and coming to the club, and ends by becoming a *shlupik*. Ah, you laugh! but we look out, for fear of dropping into it ourselves. You know Prince Tchetchensky?" inquired the prince; and Levin saw by his face that he was just going to relate something funny.

"No, I don't know him."

"You don't say so! Well, Prince Tchetchensky is a well-known figure. No matter, though. He's always playing billiards here. Only three years ago he was not a *shlupik* and kept up his spirits and even used to call other people *shlupiks*. But one day he turns up, and our porter...you know Vassily? Why, that fat one; he's famous for his *bon mots*. And so Prince Tchetchensky asks him, 'Come, Vassily, who's here? Any *shlupiks* here yet?' And he says, 'You're the third.' Yes, my dear boy, that he did!"

Talking and greeting the friends they met, Levin and the prince walked through all the rooms: the great room where tables had already been set, and the usual partners were playing for small stakes; the divan room, where they were playing chess, and Sergey Ivanovitch was sitting talking to somebody; the billiard room, where, about a sofa in a recess, there was a lively party drinking champagne—Gagin was one of them. They peeped into the "infernal regions," where a good many men were crowding round one table, at which Yashvin was sitting. Trying not to make a noise, they walked into the dark reading room, where under the shaded lamps there sat a young man with a wrathful countenance, turning over one journal after another, and a bald general buried in a book. They went, too, into what the prince called the intellectual room, where three gentlemen were engaged in a heated discussion of the latest political news.

"Prince, please come, we're ready," said one of his card party, who had come to look for him, and the prince went off. Levin sat down and listened, but recalling all the conversation of the morning he felt all of a sudden fearfully bored. He got up hurriedly, and went to look for Oblonsky and Turovtsin, with whom it had been so pleasant.

Turovtsin was one of the circle drinking in the billiard room, and Stepan Arkadyevitch was talking with Vronsky near the door at the farther corner of the room.

"It's not that she's dull; but this undefined, this unsettled position," Levin caught, and he was hurrying away, but Stepan Arkadyevitch called to him.

"Levin," said Stepan Arkadyevitch, and Levin noticed that his eyes were not full of tears exactly, but moist, which always happened when he had been drinking, or when he was touched. Just now it was due to both causes. "Levin, don't go," he said, and he warmly squeezed his arm above the elbow, obviously not at all wishing to let him go.

"This is a true friend of mine—almost my greatest friend," he said to Vronsky. "You have become even closer and dearer to me. And I want you, and I know you ought to be friends, and great friends, because you're both splendid fellows."

"Well, there's nothing for us now but to kiss and be friends," Vronsky said, with good-natured playfulness, holding out his hand.

Levin quickly took the offered hand, and pressed it warmly.

"I'm very, very glad," said Levin.

"Waiter, a bottle of champagne," said Stepan Arkadyevitch.

"And I'm very glad," said Vronsky.

But in spite of Stepan Arkadyevitch's desire, and their own desire, they had nothing to talk about, and both felt it.

"Do you know, he has never met Anna?" Stepan Arkadyevitch said to Vronsky. "And I want above everything to take him to see her. Let us go, Levin!"

"Really?" said Vronsky. "She will be very glad to see you. I should be going home at once," he added, "but I'm worried about Yashvin, and I want to stay on till he finishes."

"Why, is he losing?"

"He keeps losing, and I'm the only friend that can restrain him."

"Well, what do you say to pyramids? Levin, will you play? Capital!" said Stepan Arkadyevitch. "Get the table ready," he said to the marker.

"It has been ready a long while," answered the marker, who had already set the balls in a triangle, and was knocking the red one about for his own diversion.

"Well, let us begin."

After the game Vronsky and Levin sat down at Gagin's table, and at Stepan Arkadyevitch's suggestion Levin took a hand in the game.

Vronsky sat down at the table, surrounded by friends, who were incessantly coming up to him. Every now and then he went to the "infernal" to keep an eye on Yashvin. Levin was enjoying a delightful sense of repose after the mental fatigue of the morning. He was glad that all hostility was at an end with Vronsky, and the sense of peace, decorum, and comfort never left him.

When the game was over, Stepan Arkadyevitch took Levin's arm.

"Well, let us go to Anna's, then. At once? Eh? She is at home. I promised her long ago to bring you. Where were you meaning to spend the evening?"

"Oh, nowhere specially. I promised Sviazhsky to go to the Society of Agriculture. By all means, let us go," said Levin.

"Very good; come along. Find out if my carriage is here," Stepan Arkadyevitch said to the waiter.

Levin went up to the table, paid the forty roubles he had lost; paid his bill, the amount of which was in some mysterious way ascertained by the little old waiter who stood at the counter, and swinging his arms he walked through all the rooms to the way out.

She had risen to meet him, not concealing her pleasure at seeing him; and in the quiet ease with which she held out her little vigorous hand, introduced him to Vorkuev and indicated a red-haired, pretty little girl who was sitting at work, calling her her pupil, Levin recognized and liked the manners of a woman of the great world, always self-possessed and natural.

"I am delighted, delighted," she repeated, and on her lips these simple words took for Levin's ears a special significance. "I have known you and liked you for a long while, both from your friendship with Stiva and for your wife's sake.... I knew her for a very short time, but she left on me the impression of an exquisite flower, simply a flower. And to think she will soon be a mother!"

She spoke easily and without haste, looking now and then from Levin to her brother, and Levin felt that the impression he was making was good, and he felt immediately at home, simple and happy with her, as though he had known her from childhood.

"Ivan Petrovitch and I settled in Alexey's study," she said in answer to Stepan Arkadyevitch's question whether he might smoke, "just so as to be able to smoke"—and glancing at Levin, instead of asking whether he would smoke, she pulled closer a tortoise-shell cigar-case and took a cigarette.

"How are you feeling today?" her brother asked her.

"Oh, nothing. Nerves, as usual."

"Yes, isn't it extraordinarily fine?" said Stepan Arkadyevitch, noticing that Levin was scrutinizing the picture.

"I have never seen a better portrait."

"And extraordinarily like, isn't it?" said Vorkuev.

Levin looked from the portrait to the original. A peculiar brilliance lighted up Anna's face when she felt his eyes on her. Levin flushed, and to cover his confusion would have asked whether she had seen Darya Alexandrovna lately; but at that moment Anna spoke. "We were just talking, Ivan Petrovitch and I, of Vashtchenkov's last pictures. Have you seen them?"

"Yes, I have seen them," answered Levin.

"But, I beg your pardon, I interrupted you...you were saying?..."

Levin asked if she had seen Dolly lately.

"She was here yesterday. She was very indignant with the high school people on Grisha's account. The Latin teacher, it seems, had been unfair to him."

"Yes, I have seen his pictures. I didn't care for them very much," Levin went back to the subject she had started.

Levin talked now not at all with that purely businesslike attitude to the subject with which he had been talking all the morning. Every word in his conversation with her had a special significance. And talking to her was pleasant; still pleasanter it was to listen to her.

Anna talked not merely naturally and cleverly, but cleverly and carelessly, attaching no value to her own ideas and giving great weight to the ideas of the person she was talking to.

The conversation turned on the new movement in art, on the new illustrations of the Bible by a French artist. Vorkuev attacked the artist for a realism carried to the point of coarseness.

Levin said that the French had carried conventionality further than anyone, and that consequently they see a great merit in the return to realism. In the fact of not lying they see poetry.

Never had anything clever said by Levin given him so much pleasure as this remark. Anna's face lighted up at once, as at once she appreciated the thought. She laughed.

"I laugh," she said, "as one laughs when one sees a very true portrait. What you said so perfectly hits off French art now, painting and literature too, indeed—Zola, Daudet. But perhaps it is always so, that men form their conceptions from fictitious, conventional types, and then—all the *combinaisons* made—they are tired of the fictitious figures and begin to invent more natural, true figures."

"That's perfectly true," said Vorknev.

"So you've been at the club?" she said to her brother.

"Yes, yes, this is a woman!" Levin thought, forgetting himself and staring persistently at her lovely, mobile face, which at that moment was all at once completely transformed. Levin did not hear what she was talking of as she leaned over to her brother, but he was struck by the change of her expression. Her face—so handsome a moment before in its repose—suddenly wore a look of strange curiosity, anger, and pride. But this lasted only an instant. She dropped her eyelids, as though recollecting something.

"Oh, well, but that's of no interest to anyone," she said, and she turned to the English girl.

"Please order the tea in the drawing room," she said in English.

The girl got up and went out.

"Well, how did she get through her examination?" asked Stepan Arkadyevitch.

"Splendidly! She's a very gifted child and a sweet character."

"It will end in your loving her more than your own."

"There a man speaks. In love there's no more nor less. I love my daughter with one love, and her with another."

"I was just telling Anna Arkadyevna," said Vorkuev, "that if she were to put a hundredth part of the energy she devotes to this English girl to the public question of the education of Russian children, she would be doing a great and useful work."

"Yes, but I can't help it; I couldn't do it. Count Alexey Kirillovitch urged me very much" (as she uttered the words *Count Alexey Kirillovitch* she glanced with appealing timidity at Levin, and he unconsciously responded with a respectful and reassuring look); "he urged me to take up the school in the village. I visited it several times. The children were very nice, but I could not feel drawn to the work. You speak of energy. Energy rests upon love; and come as it will, there's no forcing it. I took to this child—I could not myself say why."

And she glanced again at Levin. And her smile and her glance— all told him that it was to him only she was addressing her words, valuing his good opinion, and at the same time sure beforehand that they understood each other.

"I quite understand that," Levin answered. "It's impossible to give one's heart to a school or such institutions in general, and I believe that's just why philanthropic institutions always give such poor results."

She was silent for a while, then she smiled.

"Yes, yes," she agreed; "I never could. *Je n'ai pas le coeur assez* large to love a whole asylum of horrid little girls. *Cela ne m'a jamais réussi.* There are so many women who have made themselves *une position sociale* in that way. And now more than ever," she said with a mournful, confiding expression, ostensibly addressing her brother, but unmistakably intending her words only for Levin, "now when I have such need of some occupation, I cannot." And suddenly frowning (Levin saw that she was frowning at herself for talking about herself) she changed the subject. "I know about you," she said to Levin; "that you're not a public-spirited citizen, and I have defended you to the best of my ability."

"How have you defended me?"

"Oh, according to the attacks made on you. But won't you have some tea?" She rose and took up a book bound in morocco.

"Give it to me, Anna Arkadyevna," said Vorkuev, indicating the book. "It's well worth taking up."

"Oh, no, it's all so sketchy."

"I told him about it," Stepan Arkadyevitch said to his sister, nodding at Levin.

"You shouldn't have. My writing is something after the fashion of those little baskets and carving which Liza Mertsalova used to sell me from the prisons. She had the direction of the prison department in that society," she turned to Levin; "and they were miracles of patience, the work of those poor wretches."

And Levin saw a new trait in this woman, who attracted him so extraordinarily. Besides wit, grace, and beauty, she had truth. She had no wish to hide from him all the bitterness of her position. As she said that she sighed, and her face suddenly taking a hard expression, looked as it were turned to stone. With that expression on her face she was more beautiful than ever; but the expression was new; it was utterly unlike that expression, radiant with happiness and creating happiness, which had been caught by the painter in her portrait. Levin looked more than once at the portrait and at her figure, as taking her brother's arm she walked with him to the high doors and he felt for her a tenderness and pity at which he wondered himself.

She asked Levin and Vorkuev to go into the drawing room, while she stayed behind to say a few words to her brother. "About her divorce, about Vronsky, and what he's doing at the club, about me?" wondered Levin. And he was so keenly interested by the question of what she was saying to Stepan Arkadyevitch, that he scarcely heard what Vorkuev was telling him of the qualities of the story for children Anna Arkadyevna had written.

At tea the same pleasant sort of talk, full of interesting matter, continued. There was not a single instant when a subject for conversation was to seek; on the contrary, it was felt that one had hardly time to say what one had to say, and eagerly held back to hear what the others were saying. And all that was said, not only by her, but by Vorkuev and Stepan Arkadyevitch— all, so it seemed to Levin, gained peculiar significance from her appreciation and her criticism. While he followed this interesting conversation, Levin was all the time admiring her— her beauty, her intelligence, her culture, and at the same time her directness and genuine depth of feeling. He listened and talked, and all the while he was thinking of her inner life, trying to divine her feelings. And though he had judged her so severely hitherto, now by some strange chain of reasoning he was justifying her and was also sorry for her, and afraid that Vronsky did not fully understand her. At eleven o'clock, when Stepan Arkadyevitch got up to go (Vorkuev had left earlier), it seemed to Levin that he had only just come. Regretfully Levin too rose.

"Good-bye," she said, holding his hand and glancing into his face with a winning look. "I am very glad *que la glace est rompue*."

She dropped his hand, and half closed her eyes.

"Tell your wife that I love her as before, and that if she cannot pardon me my position, then my wish for her is that she may never pardon it. To pardon it, one must go through what I have gone through, and may God spare her that."

"Certainly, yes, I will tell her..." Levin said, blushing.

"What a marvelous, sweet and unhappy woman!" he was thinking, as he stepped out into the frosty air with Stepan Arkadyevitch.

"Well, didn't I tell you?" said Stepan Arkadyevitch, seeing that Levin had been completely won over.

"Yes," said Levin dreamily, "an extraordinary woman! It's not her cleverness, but she has such wonderful depth of feeling. I'm awfully sorry for her!"

"Now, please God, everything will soon be settled. Well, well, don't be hard on people in future," said Stepan Arkadyevitch, opening the carriage door. "Good-bye; we don't go the same way."

Still thinking of Anna, of everything, even the simplest phrase in their conversation with her, and recalling the minutest changes in her expression, entering more and more into her position, and feeling sympathy for her, Levin reached home.

At home Kouzma told Levin that Katerina Alexandrovna was quite well, and that her sisters had not long been gone, and he handed him two letters. Levin read them at once in the hall, that he might not over look them later. One was from Sokolov, his bailiff. Sokolov wrote that the corn could not be sold, that it was fetching only five and a half roubles, and that more than that could not be got for it. The other letter was from his sister. She scolded him for her business being still unsettled.

"Well, we must sell it at five and a half if we can't get more," Levin decided the first question, which had always before seemed such a weighty one, with extraordinary facility on the spot. "It's extraordinary how all one's time is taken up here," he thought, considering the second letter. He felt himself to blame for not having got done what his sister had asked him to do for her. "Today, again, I've not been to the court, but today I've certainly not had time." And resolving that he would not fail to do it next day, he went up to his wife. As he went in, Levin rapidly ran through mentally the day he had spent. All the events of the day were conversations, conversations he had heard and taken part in. All the conversations were upon subjects which, if he had been alone at home, he would never have taken up, but here they were very interesting. And all these conversations were right enough, only in two places there was something not quite right. One was what he had said about the carp, the other was something not "quite the thing" in the tender sympathy he was feeling for Anna.

Levin found his wife low-spirited and dull. The dinner of the three sisters had gone off very well, but then they had waited and waited for him, all of them had felt dull, the sisters had departed, and she had been left alone.

"Well, and what have you been doing?" she asked him, looking straight into his eyes, which shone with rather a suspicious brightness. But that she might not prevent his telling her everything, she concealed her close scrutiny of him, and with an approving smile listened to his account of how he had spent the evening.

"Well, I'm very glad I met Vronsky. I felt quite at ease and natural with him. You understand, I shall try not to see him, but I'm glad that this awkwardness is all over," he said, and remembering that by way of trying not to see him, he had immediately gone to call on

Anna, he blushed. "We talk about the peasants drinking; I don't know which drinks most, the peasantry or our own class; the peasants do on holidays, but..."

But Kitty took not the slightest interest in discussing the drinking habits of the peasants. She saw that he blushed, and she wanted to know why.

"Well, and then where did you go?"

"Stiva urged me awfully to go and see Anna Arkadyevna."

And as he said this, Levin blushed even more, and his doubts as to whether he had done right in going to see Anna were settled once for all. He knew now that he ought not to have done so.

Kitty's eyes opened in a curious way and gleamed at Anna's name, but controlling herself with an effort, she concealed her emotion and deceived him.

"Oh!" was all she said.

"I'm sure you won't be angry at my going. Stiva begged me to, and Dolly wished it," Levin went on.

"Oh, no!" she said, but he saw in her eyes a constraint that boded him no good.

"She is a very sweet, very, very unhappy, good woman," he said, telling her about Anna, her occupations, and what she had told him to say to her.

"Yes, of course, she is very much to be pitied," said Kitty, when he had finished. "Whom was your letter from?"

He told her, and believing in her calm tone, he went to change his coat.

Coming back, he found Kitty in the same easy chair. When he went up to her, she glanced at him and broke into sobs.

"What? what is it?" he asked, knowing beforehand what.

"You're in love with that hateful woman; she has bewitched you! I saw it in your eyes. Yes, yes! What can it all lead to? You were drinking at the club, drinking and gambling, and then you went...to her of all people! No, we must go away.... I shall go away tomorrow."

It was a long while before Levin could soothe his wife. At last he succeeded in calming her, only by confessing that a feeling of pity, in conjunction with the wine he had drunk, had been too much for him, that he had succumbed to Anna's artful influence, and that he would avoid her. One thing he did with more sincerity confess to was that living so long in Moscow, a life of nothing but conversation, eating and drinking, he was degenerating. They talked till three o'clock in the morning. Only at three o'clock were they sufficiently reconciled to be able to go to sleep.

After taking leave of her guests, Anna did not sit down, but began walking up and down the room. She had unconsciously the whole evening done her utmost to arouse in Levin a feeling of love—as of late she had fallen into doing with all young men— and she knew she had attained her aim, as far as was possible in one evening, with a married and conscientious man. She liked him indeed extremely, and, in spite of the striking difference, from the masculine point of view, between Vronsky and Levin, as a woman she saw something they had in common, which had made Kitty able to love both. Yet as soon as he was out of the room, she ceased to think of him.

One thought, and one only, pursued her in different forms, and refused to be shaken off. "If I have so much effect on others, on this man, who loves his home and his wife, why is it *he* so cold to me?...not cold exactly, he loves me, I know that! But something new is drawing us apart now. Why wasn't he here all the evening? He told Stiva to say he could not leave Yashvin, and must watch over his play. Is Yashvin a child? But supposing it's true. He never tells a lie. But there's something else in it if it's true. He is glad of an opportunity of showing me that he has other duties; I know that, I submit to that. But why prove that to me? He wants to show me that his love for me is not to interfere with his freedom. But I need no proofs, I need love. He ought to understand all the bitterness of this life for me here in Moscow. Is this life? I am not living, but waiting for an event, which is continually put off and put off. No answer again! And Stiva says he cannot go to Alexey Alexandrovitch. And I can't write again. I can do nothing, can begin nothing, can alter nothing; I hold myself in, I wait, inventing amusements for myself—the English family, writing, reading—but it's all nothing but a sham, it's all the same as morphine. He ought to feel for me," she said, feeling tears of self-pity coming into her eyes.

She heard Vronsky's abrupt ring and hurriedly dried her tears— not only dried her tears, but sat down by a lamp and opened a book, affecting composure. She wanted to show him that she was displeased that he had not come home as he had promised— displeased only, and not on any account to let him see her distress, and least of all, her self-pity. She might pity herself, but he must not pity her. She did not want strife, she blamed him for wanting to quarrel, but unconsciously put herself into an attitude of antagonism.

"Well, you've not been dull?" he said, eagerly and good-humoredly, going up to her. "What a terrible passion it is—gambling!"

"No, I've not been dull; I've learned long ago not to be dull. Stiva has been here and Levin."

"Yes, they meant to come and see you. Well, how did you like Levin?" he said, sitting down beside her.

"Very much. They have not long been gone. What was Yashvin doing?"

"He was winning—seventeen thousand. I got him away. He had really started home, but he went back again, and now he's losing."

"Then what did you stay for?" she asked, suddenly lifting her eyes to him. The expression of her face was cold and ungracious. "You told Stiva you were staying on to get Yashvin away. And you have left him there."

The same expression of cold readiness for the conflict appeared on his face too.

"In the first place, I did not ask him to give you any message; and secondly, I never tell lies. But what's the chief point, I wanted to stay, and I stayed," he said, frowning. "Anna, what is it for, why will you?" he said after a moment's silence, bending over towards her, and he opened his hand, hoping she would lay hers in it.

She was glad of this appeal for tenderness. But some strange force of evil would not let her give herself up to her feelings, as though the rules of warfare would not permit her to surrender.

"Of course you wanted to stay, and you stayed. You do everything you want to. But what do you tell me that for? With what object?" she said, getting more and more excited. "Does anyone contest your rights? But you want to be right, and you're welcome to be right."

His hand closed, he turned away, and his face wore a still more obstinate expression.

"For you it's a matter of obstinacy," she said, watching him intently and suddenly finding the right word for that expression that irritated her, "simply obstinacy. For you it's a question of whether you keep the upper hand of me, while for me...." Again she felt sorry for herself, and she almost burst into tears. "If you knew what it is for me! When I feel as I do now that you are hostile, yes, hostile to me, if you knew what this means for me! If you knew how I feel on the brink of calamity at this instant, how afraid I am of myself!" And she turned away, hiding her sobs.

"But what are you talking about?" he said, horrified at her expression of despair, and again bending over her, he took her hand and kissed it. "What is it for? Do I seek amusements outside our home? Don't I avoid the society of women?"

"Well, yes! If that were all!" she said.

"Come, tell me what I ought to do to give you peace of mind? I am ready to do anything to make you happy," he said, touched by her expression of despair; "what wouldn't I do to save you from distress of any sort, as now, Anna!" he said.

"It's nothing, nothing!" she said. "I don't know myself whether it's the solitary life, my nerves.... Come, don't let us talk of it. What about the race? You haven't told me!" she inquired, trying to conceal her triumph at the victory, which had anyway been on her side.

He asked for supper, and began telling her about the races; but in his tone, in his eyes, which became more and more cold, she saw that he did not forgive her for her victory, that the feeling of obstinacy with which she had been struggling had asserted itself again in him. He was colder to her than before, as though he were regretting his surrender. And she, remembering the words that had given her the victory, "how I feel on the brink of calamity, how afraid I am of myself," saw that this weapon was a dangerous one, and that it could not be used a second time. And she felt that beside the love that bound them together there had grown up between them some evil spirit of strife, which she could not exorcise from his, and still less from her own heart.

There are no conditions to which a man cannot become used, especially if he sees that all around him are living in the same way. Levin could not have believed three months before that he could have gone quietly to sleep in the condition in which he was that day, that leading an aimless, irrational life, living too beyond his means, after drinking to excess (he could not call what happened at the club anything else), forming inappropriately friendly relations with a man with whom his wife had once been in love, and a still more inappropriate call upon a woman who could only be called a lost woman, after being fascinated by that woman and causing his wife distress—he could still go quietly to sleep. But under the influence of fatigue, a sleepless night, and the wine he had drunk, his sleep was sound and untroubled.

At five o'clock the creak of a door opening waked him. He jumped up and looked round. Kitty was not in bed beside him. But there was a light moving behind the screen, and he heard her steps.

"What is it?...what is it?" he said, half-asleep. "Kitty! What is it?"

"Nothing," she said, coming from behind the screen with a candle in her hand. "I felt unwell," she said, smiling a particularly sweet and meaning smile.

"What? has it begun?" he said in terror. "We ought to send..." and hurriedly he reached after his clothes.

"No, no," she said, smiling and holding his hand. "It's sure to be nothing. I was rather unwell, only a little. It's all over now."

And getting into bed, she blew out the candle, lay down and was still. Though he thought her stillness suspicious, as though she were holding her breath, and still more suspicious the expression of peculiar tenderness and excitement with which, as she came from behind the screen, she said "nothing," he was so sleepy that he fell asleep at once. Only later he remembered the stillness of her breathing, and understood all that must have been passing in her sweet, precious heart while she lay beside him, not stirring, in anticipation of the greatest event in a woman's life. At seven o'clock he was waked by the touch of her hand on his shoulder, and a gentle whisper. She seemed struggling between regret at waking him, and the desire to talk to him.

"Kostya, don't be frightened. It's all right. But I fancy.... We ought to send for Lizaveta Petrovna."

The candle was lighted again. She was sitting up in bed, holding some knitting, which she had been busy upon during the last few days.

"Please, don't be frightened, it's all right. I'm not a bit afraid," she said, seeing his scared face, and she pressed his hand to her bosom and then to her lips.

He hurriedly jumped up, hardly awake, and kept his eyes fixed on her, as he put on his dressing gown; then he stopped, still looking at her. He had to go, but he could not tear himself from her eyes. He thought he loved her face, knew her expression, her eyes, but never had he seen it like this. How hateful and horrible he seemed to himself, thinking of the distress he had caused her yesterday. Her flushed face, fringed with soft curling hair under her night cap, was radiant with joy and courage.

Though there was so little that was complex or artificial in Kitty's character in general, Levin was struck by what was revealed now, when suddenly all disguises were thrown off and the very kernel of her soul shone in her eyes. And in this simplicity and nakedness of her soul, she, the very woman he loved in her, was more manifest than ever. She looked at him, smiling; but all at once her brows twitched, she threw up her head, and going quickly up to him, clutched his hand and pressed close up to him, breathing her hot breath upon him. She was in pain and was, as it were, complaining to him of her suffering. And for the first minute, from habit, it seemed to him that he was to blame. But in her eyes there was a tenderness that told him that she was far from reproaching him, that she loved him for her sufferings. "If not I, who is to blame for it?" he thought unconsciously, seeking someone responsible for this suffering for him to punish; but there was no one responsible. She was suffering, complaining, and triumphing in her sufferings, and rejoicing in them, and loving them. He saw that something sublime was being accomplished in her soul, but what? He could not make it out. It was beyond his understanding.

"I have sent to mamma. You go quickly to fetch Lizaveta Petrovna ...Kostya!... Nothing, it's over."

She moved away from him and rang the bell.

"Well, go now; Pasha's coming. I am all right."

And Levin saw with astonishment that she had taken up the knitting she had brought in in the night and begun working at it again.

As Levin was going out of one door, he heard the maid-servant come in at the other. He stood at the door and heard Kitty giving exact directions to the maid, and beginning to help her move the bedstead.

He dressed, and while they were putting in his horses, as a hired sledge was not to be seen yet, he ran again up to the bedroom, not on tiptoe, it seemed to him, but on wings. Two maid-servants were carefully moving something in the bedroom.

Kitty was walking about knitting rapidly and giving directions.

"I'm going for the doctor. They have sent for Lizaveta Petrovna, but I'll go on there too. Isn't there anything wanted? Yes, shall I go to Dolly's?"

She looked at him, obviously not hearing what he was saying.

"Yes, yes. Do go," she said quickly, frowning and waving her hand to him.

He had just gone into the drawing room, when suddenly a plaintive moan sounded from the bedroom, smothered instantly. He stood still, and for a long while he could not understand.

"Yes, that is she," he said to himself, and clutching at his head he ran downstairs.

"Lord have mercy on us! pardon us! aid us!" he repeated the words that for some reason came suddenly to his lips. And he, an unbeliever, repeated these words not with his lips only. At that instant he knew that all his doubts, even the impossibility of believing with his reason, of which he was aware in himself, did not in the least hinder his turning to God. All of that now floated out of his soul like dust. To whom was he to turn if not to Him in whose hands he felt himself, his soul, and his love?

The horse was not yet ready, but feeling a peculiar concentration of his physical forces and his intellect on what he had to do, he started off on foot without waiting for the horse, and told Kouzma to overtake him.

At the corner he met a night cabman driving hurriedly. In the little sledge, wrapped in a velvet cloak, sat Lizaveta Petrovna with a kerchief round her head. "Thank God! thank God!" he said, overjoyed to recognize her little fair face which wore a peculiarly serious, even stern expression. Telling the driver not to stop, he ran along beside her.

"For two hours, then? Not more?" she inquired. "You should let Pyotr Dmitrievitch know, but don't hurry him. And get some opium at the chemist's."

"So you think that it may go on well? Lord have mercy on us and help us!" Levin said, seeing his own horse driving out of the gate. Jumping into the sledge beside Kouzma, he told him to drive to the doctor's.

From the moment when he had waked up and understood what was going on, Levin had prepared his mind to bear resolutely what was before him, and without considering or anticipating anything, to avoid upsetting his wife, and on the contrary to soothe her and keep up her courage. Without allowing himself even to think of what was to come, of how it would end, judging from his inquiries as to the usual duration of these ordeals, Levin had in his imagination braced himself to bear up and to keep a tight rein on his feelings for five hours, and it had seemed to him he could do this. But when he came back from the doctor's and saw her sufferings again, he fell to repeating more and more frequently: "Lord, have mercy on us, and succor us!" He sighed, and flung his head up, and began to feel afraid he could not bear it, that he would burst into tears or run away. Such agony it was to him. And only one hour had passed.

But after that hour there passed another hour, two hours, three, the full five hours he had fixed as the furthest limit of his sufferings, and the position was still unchanged; and he was still bearing it because there was nothing to be done but bear it; every instant feeling that he had reached the utmost limits of his endurance, and that his heart would break with sympathy and pain.

But still the minutes passed by and the hours, and still hours more, and his misery and horror grew and were more and more intense.

All the ordinary conditions of life, without which one can form no conception of anything, had ceased to exist for Levin. He lost all sense of time. Minutes—those minutes when she sent for him and he held her moist hand, that would squeeze his hand with extraordinary violence and then push it away—seemed to him hours, and hours seemed to him minutes. He was surprised when Lizaveta Petrovna asked him to light a candle behind a screen, and he found that it was five o'clock in the afternoon. If he had been told it was only ten o'clock in the morning, he would not have been more surprised. Where he was all this time, he knew as little as the time of anything. He saw her swollen face, sometimes bewildered and in agony, sometimes smiling and trying to reassure him. He saw the old princess too, flushed and overwrought, with her gray curls in disorder, forcing herself to gulp down her tears, biting her lips; he saw Dolly too and the doctor, smoking fat cigarettes, and Lizaveta Petrovna with a firm, resolute, reassuring face, and the old prince walking up and down the hall with a frowning face. But why they came in and went out, where they were, he did not know. The princess was with the doctor in the bedroom, then in the study, where a table set for dinner suddenly appeared; then she was not there, but Dolly was. Then Levin remembered he had been sent somewhere. Once he had been sent to move a table and sofa. He had done this eagerly, thinking it had to be done for her sake, and only later on he found it was his own bed he had been getting ready. Then he had been sent to the study to ask the doctor something. The doctor had answered and then had said something about the irregularities in the municipal council. Then he had been sent to the bedroom to help the old princess to move the holy picture in its silver and gold setting, and with the princess's old waiting maid he had clambered on a shelf to reach it and had broken the little lamp, and the old servant had tried to reassure him about the lamp and about his wife, and he carried the holy picture and set it at Kitty's head, carefully tucking it in behind the pillow. But where, when, and why all this had happened, he could not tell. He did not understand why the old princess took his hand, and looking compassionately at him, begged him not to worry himself, and Dolly persuaded him to eat something and led him out of the room, and even the doctor looked seriously and with commiseration at him and offered him a drop of something.

All he knew and felt was that what was happening was what had happened nearly a year before in the hotel of the country town at the deathbed of his brother Nikolay. But that had been grief— this was joy. Yet that grief and this joy were alike outside all the ordinary conditions of life; they were loop-holes, as it were, in that ordinary life through which there came glimpses of something sublime. And in the contemplation of this sublime something the soul was exalted to inconceivable heights of which it had before had no conception, while reason lagged behind, unable to keep up with it.

"Lord, have mercy on us, and succor us!" he repeated to himself incessantly, feeling, in spite of his long and, as it seemed, complete alienation from religion, that he turned to God just as trustfully and simply as he had in his childhood and first youth.

All this time he had two distinct spiritual conditions. One was away from her, with the doctor, who kept smoking one fat cigarette after another and extinguishing them on the edge of a full ash tray, with Dolly, and with the old prince, where there was talk about dinner, about politics, about Marya Petrovna's illness, and where Levin suddenly forgot for a minute what was happening, and felt as though he had waked up from sleep; the other was in her presence, at her pillow, where his heart seemed breaking and still did not break from sympathetic suffering, and he prayed to God without ceasing. And every time he was brought back from a moment of oblivion by a scream reaching him from the bedroom, he fell into the same strange terror that had come upon him the first minute. Every time he heard a shriek, he jumped up, ran to justify himself, remembered on the way that he was not to blame, and he longed to defend her, to help her. But as he looked at her, he saw again that help was impossible, and he was filled with terror and prayed: "Lord, have mercy on us, and help us!" And as time went on, both these conditions became more intense; the calmer he became away from her, completely forgetting her, the more agonizing became both her sufferings and his feeling of helplessness before them. He jumped up, would have liked to run away, but ran to her.

Sometimes, when again and again she called upon him, he blamed her; but seeing her patient, smiling face, and hearing the words, "I am worrying you," he threw the blame on God; but thinking of God, at once he fell to beseeching God to forgive him and have mercy.

He did not know whether it was late or early. The candles had all burned out. Dolly had just been in the study and had suggested to the doctor that he should lie down. Levin sat listening to the doctor's stories of a quack mesmerizer and looking at the ashes of his cigarette. There had been a period of repose, and he had sunk into oblivion. He had completely forgotten what was going on now. He heard the doctor's chat and understood it. Suddenly there came an unearthly shriek. The shriek was so awful that Levin did not even jump up, but holding his breath, gazed in terrified inquiry at the doctor. The doctor put his head on one side, listened, and smiled approvingly. Everything was so extraordinary that nothing could strike Levin as strange. "I suppose it must be so," he thought, and still sat where he was. Whose scream was this? He jumped up, ran on tiptoe to the bedroom, edged round Lizaveta Petrovna and the princess, and took up his position at Kitty's pillow. The scream had subsided, but there was some change now. What it was he did not see and did not comprehend, and he had no wish to see or comprehend. But he saw it by the face of Lizaveta Petrovna. Lizaveta Petrovna's face was stern and pale, and still as resolute, though her jaws were twitching, and her eyes were fixed intently on Kitty. Kitty's swollen and agonized face, a tress of hair clinging to her moist brow, was turned to him and sought his eyes. Her lifted hands asked for his hands. Clutching his chill hands in her moist ones, she began squeezing them to her face.

"Don't go, don't go! I'm not afraid, I'm not afraid!" she said rapidly. "Mamma, take my earrings. They bother me. You're not afraid? Quick, quick, Lizaveta Petrovna..."

She spoke quickly, very quickly, and tried to smile. But suddenly her face was drawn, she pushed him away.

"Oh, this is awful! I'm dying, I'm dying! Go away!" she shrieked, and again he heard that unearthly scream.

Levin clutched at his head and ran out of the room.

"It's nothing, it's nothing, it's all right," Dolly called after him.

But they might say what they liked, he knew now that all was over. He stood in the next room, his head leaning against the door post, and heard shrieks, howls such as he had never heard before, and he knew that what had been Kitty was uttering these shrieks. He had long ago ceased to wish for the child. By now he loathed this child. He did not even wish for her life now, all he longed for was the end of this awful anguish.

"Doctor! What is it? What is it? By God!" he said, snatching at the doctor's hand as he came up.

"It's the end," said the doctor. And the doctor's face was so grave as he said it that Levin took *the end* as meaning her death.

Beside himself, he ran into the bedroom. The first thing he saw was the face of Lizaveta Petrovna. It was even more frowning and stern. Kitty's face he did not know. In the place where it had been was something that was fearful in its strained distortion and in the sounds that came from it. He fell down with his head on the wooden framework of the bed, feeling that his heart was bursting. The awful scream never paused, it became still more awful, and as though it had reached the utmost limit of terror, suddenly it ceased. Levin could not believe his ears, but there could be no doubt; the scream had ceased and he heard a subdued stir and bustle, and hurried breathing, and her voice, gasping, alive, tender, and blissful, uttered softly, "It's over!"

He lifted his head. With her hands hanging exhausted on the quilt, looking extraordinarily lovely and serene, she looked at him in silence and tried to smile, and could not.

And suddenly, from the mysterious and awful far-away world in which he had been living for the last twenty-two hours, Levin felt himself all in an instant borne back to the old every-day world, glorified though now, by such a radiance of happiness that he could not bear it. The strained chords snapped, sobs and tears of joy which he had never foreseen rose up with such violence that his whole body shook, that for long they prevented him from speaking.

Falling on his knees before the bed, he held his wife's hand before his lips and kissed it, and the hand, with a weak movement of the fingers, responded to his kiss. And meanwhile, there at the foot of the bed, in the deft hands of Lizaveta Petrovna, like a flickering light in a lamp, lay the life of a human creature, which had never existed before, and which would now with the same right, with the same importance to itself, live and create in its own image.

"Alive! alive! And a boy too! Set your mind at rest!" Levin heard Lizaveta Petrovna saying, as she slapped the baby's back with a shaking hand.

"Mamma, is it true?" said Kitty's voice.

The princess's sobs were all the answers she could make. And in the midst of the silence there came in unmistakable reply to the mother's question, a voice quite unlike the subdued voices speaking in the room. It was the bold, clamorous, self-assertive squall of the new human being, who had so incomprehensibly appeared.

If Levin had been told before that Kitty was dead, and that he had died with her, and that their children were angels, and that God was standing before him, he would have been surprised at nothing. But now, coming back to the world of reality, he had to make great mental efforts to take in that she was alive and well, and that the creature squalling so desperately was his son. Kitty was alive, her agony was over. And he was unutterably happy. That he understood; he was completely happy in it. But the baby? Whence, why, who was he?... He could not get used to the idea. It seemed to him something extraneous, superfluous, to which he could not accustom himself.

At ten o'clock the old prince, Sergey Ivanovitch, and Stepan Arkadyevitch were sitting at Levin's. Having inquired after Kitty, they had dropped into conversation upon other subjects. Levin heard them, and unconsciously, as they talked, going over the past, over what had been up to that morning, he thought of himself as he had been yesterday till that point. It was as though a hundred years had passed since then. He felt himself exalted to unattainable heights, from which he studiously lowered himself so as not to wound the people he was talking to. He talked, and was all the time thinking of his wife, of her condition now, of his son, in whose existence he tried to school himself into believing. The whole world of woman, which had taken for him since his marriage a new value he had never suspected before, was now so exalted that he could not take it in in his imagination. He heard them talk of yesterday's dinner at the club, and thought: "What is happening with her now? Is she asleep? How is she? What is she thinking of? Is he crying, my son Dmitri?" And in the middle of the conversation, in the middle of a sentence, he jumped up and went out of the room.

"Send me word if I can see her," said the prince.

"Very well, in a minute," answered Levin, and without stopping, he went to her room.

She was not asleep, she was talking gently with her mother, making plans about the christening.

Carefully set to rights, with hair well-brushed, in a smart little cap with some blue in it, her arms out on the quilt, she was lying on her back. Meeting his eyes, her eyes drew him to her. Her face, bright before, brightened still more as he drew near her. There was the same change in it from earthly to unearthly that is seen in the face of the dead. But then it means farewell, here it meant welcome. Again a rush of emotion, such as he had felt at the moment of the child's birth, flooded his heart. She took his hand and asked him if he had slept. He could not answer, and turned away, struggling with his weakness.

"I have had a nap, Kostya!" she said to him; "and I am so comfortable now."

She looked at him, but suddenly her expression changed.

"Give him to me," she said, hearing the baby's cry. "Give him to me, Lizaveta Petrovna, and he shall look at him."

"To be sure, his papa shall look at him," said Lizaveta Petrovna, getting up and bringing something red, and queer, and wriggling. "Wait a minute, we'll make him tidy first," and Lizaveta Petrovna laid the red wobbling thing on the bed, began untrussing and trussing up the baby, lifting it up and turning it over with one finger and powdering it with something.

Levin, looking at the tiny, pitiful creature, made strenuous efforts to discover in his heart some traces of fatherly feeling for it. He felt nothing towards it but disgust. But when it was undressed and he caught a glimpse of wee, wee, little hands, little feet, saffron-colored, with little toes, too, and positively with a little big toe different from the rest, and when he saw Lizaveta Petrovna closing the wide-open little hands, as though they were soft springs, and putting them into linen garments, such pity for the little creature came upon him, and such terror that she would hurt it, that he held her hand back.

Lizaveta Petrovna laughed.

"Don't be frightened, don't be frightened!"

When the baby had been put to rights and transformed into a firm doll, Lizaveta Petrovna dandled it as though proud of her handiwork, and stood a little away so that Levin might see his son in all his glory.

Kitty looked sideways in the same direction, never taking her eyes off the baby. "Give him to me! give him to me!" she said, and even made as though she would sit up.

"What are you thinking of, Katerina Alexandrovna, you mustn't move like that! Wait a minute. I'll give him to you. Here we're showing papa what a fine fellow we are!"

And Lizaveta Petrovna, with one hand supporting the wobbling head, lifted up on the other arm the strange, limp, red creature, whose head was lost in its swaddling clothes. But it had a nose, too, and slanting eyes and smacking lips.

"A splendid baby!" said Lizaveta Petrovna.

Levin sighed with mortification. This splendid baby excited in him no feeling but disgust and compassion. It was not at all the feeling he had looked forward to.

He turned away while Lizaveta Petrovna put the baby to the unaccustomed breast.

Suddenly laughter made him look round. The baby had taken the breast.

"Come, that's enough, that's enough!" said Lizaveta Petrovna, but Kitty would not let the baby go. He fell asleep in her arms.

"Look, now," said Kitty, turning the baby so that he could see it. The aged-looking little face suddenly puckered up still more and the baby sneezed.

Smiling, hardly able to restrain his tears, Levin kissed his wife and went out of the dark room. What he felt towards this little creature was utterly unlike what he had expected. There was nothing cheerful and joyous in the feeling; on the contrary, it was a new torture of apprehension. It was the consciousness of a new sphere of liability to pain. And this sense was so painful at first, the apprehension lest this helpless creature should suffer was so intense, that it prevented him from noticing the strange thrill of senseless joy and even pride that he had felt when the baby sneezed.

Stepan Arkadyevitch's affairs were in a very bad way.

The money for two-thirds of the forest had all been spent already, and he had borrowed from the merchant in advance at ten per cent discount, almost all the remaining third. The merchant would not give more, especially as Darya Alexandrovna, for the first time that winter insisting on her right to her own property, had refused to sign the receipt for the payment of the last third of the forest. All his salary went on household expenses and in payment of petty debts that could not be put off. There was positively no money.

This was unpleasant and awkward, and in Stepan Arkadyevitch's opinion things could not go on like this. The explanation of the position was, in his view, to be found in the fact that his salary was too small. The post he filled had been unmistakably very good five years ago, but it was so no longer.

Petrov, the bank director, had twelve thousand; Sventitsky, a company director, had seventeen thousand; Mitin, who had founded a bank, received fifty thousand.

"Clearly I've been napping, and they've overlooked me," Stepan Arkadyevitch thought about himself. And he began keeping his eyes and ears open, and towards the end of the winter he had discovered a very good berth and had formed a plan of attack upon it, at first from Moscow through aunts, uncles, and friends, and then, when the matter was well advanced, in the spring, he went himself to Petersburg. It was one of those snug, lucrative berths of which there are so many more nowadays than there used to be, with incomes ranging from one thousand to fifty thousand roubles. It was the post of secretary of the committee of the amalgamated agency of the southern railways, and of certain banking companies. This position, like all such appointments, called for such immense energy and such varied qualifications, that it was difficult for them to be found united in any one man. And since a man combining all the qualifications was not to be found, it was at least better that the post be filled by an honest than by a dishonest man. And Stepan Arkadyevitch was not merely an honest man—unemphatically—in the common acceptation of the words, he was an honest man—emphatically—in that special sense which the word has in Moscow, when they talk of an "honest" politician, an "honest" writer, an "honest" newspaper, an "honest" institution, an "honest" tendency, meaning not simply that the man or the institution is not dishonest, but that they are capable on occasion of taking a line of their own in opposition to the authorities.

Stepan Arkadyevitch moved in those circles in Moscow in which that expression had come into use, was regarded there as an honest man, and so had more right to this appointment than others.

The appointment yielded an income of from seven to ten thousand a year, and Oblonsky could fill it without giving up his government position. It was in the hands of two ministers, one lady, and two Jews, and all these people, though the way had been paved already with them, Stepan Arkadyevitch had to see in Petersburg. Besides this business, Stepan Arkadyevitch had promised his sister Anna to obtain from Karenin a definite answer on the question of divorce. And begging fifty roubles from Dolly, he set off for Petersburg.

Stepan Arkadyevitch sat in Karenin's study listening to his report on the causes of the unsatisfactory position of Russian finance, and only waiting for the moment when he would finish to speak about his own business or about Anna.

"Yes, that's very true," he said, when Alexey Alexandrovitch took off the pince-nez, without which he could not read now, and looked inquiringly at his former brother-in-law, "that's very true in particular cases, but still the principle of our day is freedom."

"Yes, but I lay down another principle, embracing the principle of freedom," said Alexey Alexandrovitch, with emphasis on the word "embracing," and he put on his pince-nez again, so as to read the passage in which this statement was made. And turning over the beautifully written, wide-margined manuscript, Alexey Alexandrovitch read aloud over again the conclusive passage.

"I don't advocate protection for the sake of private interests, but for the public weal, and for the lower and upper classes equally," he said, looking over his pince-nez at Oblonsky. "But *they* cannot grasp that, *they* are taken up now with personal interests, and carried away by phrases."

Stepan Arkadyevitch knew that when Karenin began to talk of what *they* were doing and thinking, the persons who would not accept his report and were the cause of everything wrong in Russia, that it was coming near the end. And so now he eagerly abandoned the principle of free-trade, and fully agreed. Alexey Alexandrovitch paused, thoughtfully turning over the pages of his manuscript.

"Oh, by the way," said Stepan Arkadyevitch, "I wanted to ask you, some time when you see Pomorsky, to drop him a hint that I should be very glad to get that new appointment of secretary of the committee of the amalgamated agency of the southern railways and banking companies." Stepan Arkadyevitch was familiar by now with the title of the post he coveted, and he brought it out rapidly without mistake.

Alexey Alexandrovitch questioned him as to the duties of this new committee, and pondered. He was considering whether the new committee would not be acting in some way contrary to the views he had been advocating. But as the influence of the new committee was of a very complex nature, and his views were of very wide application, he could not decide this straight off, and taking off his pince-nez, he said:

"Of course, I can mention it to him; but what is your reason precisely for wishing to obtain the appointment?"

"It's a good salary, rising to nine thousand, and my means..."

"Nine thousand!" repeated Alexey Alexandrovitch, and he frowned. The high figure of the salary made him reflect that on that side Stepan Arkadyevitch's proposed position ran counter to the main tendency of his own projects of reform, which always leaned towards economy.

"I consider, and I have embodied my views in a note on the subject, that in our day these immense salaries are evidence of the unsound economic *assiette* of our finances."

"But what's to be done?" said Stepan Arkadyevitch. "Suppose a bank director gets ten thousand—well, he's worth it; or an engineer gets twenty thousand—after all, it's a growing thing, you know!"

"I assume that a salary is the price paid for a commodity, and it ought to conform with the law of supply and demand. If the salary is fixed without any regard for that law, as, for instance, when I see two engineers leaving college together, both equally well trained and efficient, and one getting forty thousand while the other is satisfied with two; or when I see lawyers and hussars, having no special qualifications, appointed directors of banking companies with immense salaries, I conclude that the salary is not fixed in accordance with the law of supply and demand, but simply through personal interest. And this is an abuse of great gravity in itself, and one that reacts injuriously on the government service. I consider..."

Stepan Arkadyevitch made haste to interrupt his brother-in-law.

"Yes; but you must agree that it's a new institution of undoubted utility that's being started. After all, you know, it's a growing thing! What they lay particular stress on is the thing being carried on honestly," said Stepan Arkadyevitch with emphasis.

But the Moscow significance of the word "honest" was lost on Alexey Alexandrovitch.

"Honesty is only a negative qualification," he said.

"Well, you'll do me a great service, anyway," said Stepan Arkadyevitch, "by putting in a word to Pomorsky—just in the way of conversation...."

"But I fancy it's more in Volgarinov's hands," said Alexey Alexandrovitch.

"Volgarinov has fully assented, as far as he's concerned," said Stepan Arkadyevitch, turning red. Stepan Arkadyevitch reddened at the mention of that name, because he had been that morning at the Jew Volgarinov's, and the visit had left an unpleasant recollection.

Stepan Arkadyevitch believed most positively that the committee in which he was trying to get an appointment was a new, genuine, and honest public body, but that morning when Volgarinov had— intentionally, beyond a doubt—kept him two hours waiting with other petitioners in his waiting room, he had suddenly felt uneasy.

Whether he was uncomfortable that he, a descendant of Rurik, Prince Oblonsky, had been kept for two hours waiting to see a Jew, or that for the first time in his life he was not following the example of his ancestors in serving the government, but was turning off into a new career, anyway he was very uncomfortable. During those two hours in Volgarinov's waiting room Stepan Arkadyevitch, stepping jauntily about the room, pulling his whiskers, entering into conversation with the other petitioners, and inventing an epigram on his position, assiduously concealed from others, and even from himself, the feeling he was experiencing.

But all the time he was uncomfortable and angry, he could not have said why—whether because he could not get his epigram just right, or from some other reason. When at last Volgarinov had received him with exaggerated politeness and unmistakable triumph at his humiliation, and had all but refused the favor asked of him, Stepan Arkadyevitch had made haste to forget it all as soon as possible. And now, at the mere recollection, he blushed.

"Now there is something I want to talk about, and you know what it is. About Anna," Stepan Arkadyevitch said, pausing for a brief space, and shaking off the unpleasant impression.

As soon as Oblonsky uttered Anna's name, the face of Alexey Alexandrovitch was completely transformed; all the life was gone out of it, and it looked weary and dead.

"What is it exactly that you want from me?" he said, moving in his chair and snapping his pince-nez.

"A definite settlement, Alexey Alexandrovitch, some settlement of the position. I'm appealing to you" ("not as an injured husband," Stepan Arkadyevitch was going to say, but afraid of wrecking his negotiation by this, he changed the words) "not as a statesman" (which did not sound à propos), "but simply as a man, and a good-hearted man and a Christian. You must have pity on her," he said.

"That is, in what way precisely?" Karenin said softly.

"Yes, pity on her. If you had seen her as I have!—I have been spending all the winter with her—you would have pity on her. Her position is awful, simply awful!"

"I had imagined," answered Alexey Alexandrovitch in a higher, almost shrill voice, "that Anna Arkadyevna had everything she had desired for herself."

"Oh, Alexey Alexandrovitch, for heaven's sake, don't let us indulge in recriminations! What is past is past, and you know what she wants and is waiting for—divorce."

"But I believe Anna Arkadyevna refuses a divorce, if I make it a condition to leave me my son. I replied in that sense, and supposed that the matter was ended. I consider it at an end," shrieked Alexey Alexandrovitch.

"But, for heaven's sake, don't get hot!" said Stepan Arkadyevitch, touching his brother-in-law's knee. "The matter is not ended. If you will allow me to recapitulate, it was like this: when you parted, you were as magnanimous as could possibly be; you were ready to give her everything—freedom, divorce even. She appreciated that. No, don't think that. She did appreciate it—to such a degree that at the first moment, feeling how she had wronged you, she did not consider and could not consider everything. She gave up everything. But experience, time, have shown that her position is unbearable, impossible."

"The life of Anna Arkadyevna can have no interest for me," Alexey Alexandrovitch put in, lifting his eyebrows.

"Allow me to disbelieve that," Stepan Arkadyevitch replied gently. "Her position is intolerable for her, and of no benefit to anyone whatever. She has deserved it, you will say. She knows that and asks you for nothing; she says plainly that she dare not ask you. But I, all of us, her relatives, all who love her, beg you, entreat you. Why should she suffer? Who is any the better for it?"

"Excuse me, you seem to put me in the position of the guilty party," observed Alexey Alexandrovitch.

"Oh, no, oh, no, not at all! please understand me," said Stepan Arkadyevitch, touching his hand again, as though feeling sure this physical contact would soften his brother-in-law. "All I say is this: her position is intolerable, and it might be alleviated by you, and you will lose nothing by it. I will arrange it all for you, so that you'll not notice it. You did promise it, you know."

"The promise was given before. And I had supposed that the question of my son had settled the matter. Besides, I had hoped that Anna Arkadyevna had enough generosity..." Alexey Alexandrovitch articulated with difficulty, his lips twitching and his face white.

"She leaves it all to your generosity. She begs, she implores one thing of you—to extricate her from the impossible position in which she is placed. She does not ask for her son now. Alexey Alexandrovitch, you are a good man. Put yourself in her position for a minute. The question of divorce for her in her position is a question of life and death. If you had not promised it once, she would have reconciled herself to her position, she would have gone on living in the country. But you promised it, and she wrote to you, and moved to Moscow. And here she's been for six months in Moscow, where every chance meeting cuts her to the heart, every day expecting an answer. Why, it's like keeping a condemned criminal for six months with the rope round his neck, promising him perhaps death, perhaps mercy. Have pity on her, and I will undertake to arrange everything. *Vos scrupules...*"

"I am not talking about that, about that..." Alexey Alexandrovitch interrupted with disgust. "But, perhaps, I promised what I had no right to promise."

"So you go back from your promise?"

"I have never refused to do all that is possible, but I want time to consider how much of what I promised is possible."

"No, Alexey Alexandrovitch!" cried Oblonsky, jumping up, "I won't believe that! She's unhappy as only an unhappy woman can be, and you cannot refuse in such..."

"As much of what I promised as is possible. *Vous professez d'être libre penseur.* But I as a believer cannot, in a matter of such gravity, act in opposition to the Christian law."

"But in Christian societies and among us, as far as I'm aware, divorce is allowed," said Stepan Arkadyevitch. "Divorce is sanctioned even by our church. And we see..."

"It is allowed, but not in the sense..."

"Alexey Alexandrovitch, you are not like yourself," said Oblonsky, after a brief pause. "Wasn't it you (and didn't we all appreciate it in you?) who forgave everything, and moved simply by Christian feeling was ready to make any sacrifice? You said yourself: if a man take thy coat, give him thy cloak also, and now..."

"I beg," said Alexey Alexandrovitch shrilly, getting suddenly onto his feet, his face white and his jaws twitching, "I beg you to drop this...to drop...this subject!"

"Oh, no! Oh, forgive me, forgive me if I have wounded you," said Stepan Arkadyevitch, holding out his hand with a smile of embarrassment; "but like a messenger I have simply performed the commission given me."

Alexey Alexandrovitch gave him his hand, pondered a little, and said:

"I must think it over and seek for guidance. The day after tomorrow I will give you a final answer," he said, after considering a moment.

CHAPTER EIGHT

STEPAN ARKADYEVITCH, AS usual, did not waste his time in Petersburg. In Petersburg, besides business, his sister's divorce, and his coveted appointment, he wanted, as he always did, to freshen himself up, as he said, after the mustiness of Moscow.

In spite of its *cafés chantants* and its omnibuses, Moscow was yet a stagnant bog. Stepan Arkadyevitch always felt it. After living for some time in Moscow, especially in close relations with his family, he was conscious of a depression of spirits. After being a long time in Moscow without a change, he reached a point when he positively began to be worrying himself over his wife's ill-humor and reproaches, over his children's health and education, and the petty details of his official work; even the fact of being in debt worried him. But he had only to go and stay a little while in Petersburg, in the circle there in which he moved, where people lived—really lived—instead of vegetating as in Moscow, and all such ideas vanished and melted away at once, like wax before the fire. His wife?... Only that day he had been talking to Prince Tchetchensky. Prince Tchetchensky had a wife and family, grown-up pages in the corps,...and he had another illegitimate family of children also. Though the first family was very nice too, Prince Tchetchensky felt happier in his second family; and he used to take his eldest son with him to his second family, and told Stepan Arkadyevitch that he thought it good for his son, enlarging his ideas. What would have been said to that in Moscow?

His children? In Petersburg children did not prevent their parents from enjoying life. The children were brought up in schools, and there was no trace of the wild idea that prevailed in Moscow, in Lvov's household, for instance, that all the luxuries of life were for the children, while the parents have nothing but work and anxiety. Here people understood that a man is in duty bound to live for himself, as every man of culture should live.

His official duties? Official work here was not the stiff, hopeless drudgery that it was in Moscow. Here there was some interest in official life. A chance meeting, a service rendered, a happy phrase, a knack of facetious mimicry, and a man's career might be made in a trice. So it had been with Bryantsev, whom Stepan Arkadyevitch had met the previous day, and who was one of the highest functionaries in government now. There was some interest in official work like that.

The Petersburg attitude on pecuniary matters had an especially soothing effect on Stepan Arkadyevitch. Bartnyansky, who must spend at least fifty thousand to judge by the style he lived in, had made an interesting comment the day before on that subject.

As they were talking before dinner, Stepan Arkadyevitch said to Bartnyansky:

"You're friendly, I fancy, with Mordvinsky; you might do me a favor: say a word to him, please, for me. There's an appointment I should like to get—secretary of the agency..."

"Oh, I shan't remember all that, if you tell it to me.... But what possesses you to have to do with railways and Jews?... Take it as you will, it's a low business."

Stepan Arkadyevitch did not say to Bartnyansky that it was a "growing thing"— Bartnyansky would not have understood that.

"I want the money, I've nothing to live on."

"You're living, aren't you?"

"Yes, but in debt."

"Are you, though? Heavily?" said Bartnyansky sympathetically.

"Very heavily: twenty thousand."

Bartnyansky broke into good-humored laughter.

"Oh, lucky fellow!" said he. "My debts mount up to a million and a half, and I've nothing, and still I can live, as you see!"

And Stepan Arkadyevitch saw the correctness of this view not in words only but in actual fact. Zhivahov owed three hundred thousand, and hadn't a farthing to bless himself with, and he lived, and in style too! Count Krivtsov was considered a hopeless case by everyone, and yet he kept two mistresses. Petrovsky had run through five millions, and still lived in just the same style, and was even a manager in the financial department with a salary of twenty thousand. But besides this, Petersburg had physically an agreeable effect on Stepan Arkadyevitch. It made him younger. In Moscow he sometimes found a gray hair in his head, dropped asleep after dinner, stretched, walked slowly upstairs, breathing heavily, was bored by the society of young women, and did not dance at balls. In Petersburg he always felt ten years younger.

His experience in Petersburg was exactly what had been described to him on the previous day by Prince Pyotr Oblonsky, a man of sixty, who had just come back from abroad:

"We don't know the way to live here," said Pyotr Oblonsky. "I spent the summer in Baden, and you wouldn't believe it, I felt quite a young man. At a glimpse of a pretty woman, my thoughts.... One dines and drinks a glass of wine, and feels strong and ready for anything. I came home to Russia—had to see my wife, and, what's more, go to my country place; and there, you'd hardly believe it, in a fortnight I'd got into a dressing gown and given up dressing for dinner. Needn't say I had no thoughts left for pretty women. I became quite an old gentleman. There was nothing left for me but to think of my eternal salvation. I went off to Paris—I was as right as could be at once."

Stepan Arkadyevitch felt exactly the difference that Pyotr Oblonsky described. In Moscow he degenerated so much that if he had had to be there for long together, he might in good earnest have come to considering his salvation; in Petersburg he felt himself a man of the world again.

Between Princess Betsy Tverskaya and Stepan Arkadyevitch there had long existed rather curious relations. Stepan Arkadyevitch always flirted with her in jest, and used to say to her, also in jest, the most unseemly things, knowing that nothing delighted her so much. The day after his conversation with Karenin, Stepan Arkadyevitch went to see her, and felt so youthful that in this jesting flirtation and nonsense he recklessly went so far that he did not know how to extricate himself, as unluckily he was so far from being attracted by her that he thought her positively disagreeable. What made it hard to change the conversation was the fact that he was very attractive to her. So that he was considerably relieved at the arrival of Princess Myakaya, which cut short their *tête-à-tête*.

"Ah, so you're here!" said she when she saw him. "Well, and what news of your poor sister? You needn't look at me like that," she added. "Ever since they've all turned against her, all those who're a thousand times worse than she, I've thought she did a very fine thing. I can't forgive Vronsky for not letting me know when she was in Petersburg. I'd have gone to see her and gone about with her everywhere. Please give her my love. Come, tell me about her."

"Yes, her position is very difficult; she..." began Stepan Arkadyevitch, in the simplicity of his heart accepting as sterling coin Princess Myakaya's words "tell me about her." Princess Myakaya interrupted him immediately, as she always did, and began talking herself.

"She's done what they all do, except me—only they hide it. But she wouldn't be deceitful, and she did a fine thing. And she did better still in throwing up that crazy brother-in-law of yours. You must excuse me. Everybody used to say he was so clever, so very clever; I was the only one that said he was a fool. Now that he's so thick with Lidia Ivanovna and Landau, they all say he's crazy, and I should prefer not to agree with everybody, but this time I can't help it."

"Oh, do please explain," said Stepan Arkadyevitch; "what does it mean? Yesterday I was seeing him on my sister's behalf, and I asked him to give me a final answer. He gave me no answer, and said he would think it over. But this morning, instead of an answer, I received an invitation from Countess Lidia Ivanovna for this evening."

"Ah, so that's it, that's it!" said Princess Myakaya gleefully, "they're going to ask Landau what he's to say."

"Ask Landau? What for? Who or what's Landau?"

"What! you don't know Jules Landau, *le fameux Jules Landau, le clairvoyant*? He's crazy too, but on him your sister's fate depends. See what comes of living in the provinces—you know nothing about anything. Landau, do you see, was a *commis* in a shop in Paris, and he went to a doctor's; and in the doctor's waiting room he fell asleep, and in his sleep he began giving advice to all the patients. And wonderful advice it was! Then the wife of Yury Meledinsky—you know, the invalid?—heard of this Landau, and had him to see her husband. And he cured her husband, though I can't say that I see he did him much good, for he's just as feeble a creature as ever he was, but they believed in him, and took him along with them and brought him to Russia. Here there's been a general rush to him, and he's begun doctoring everyone. He cured Countess Bezzubova, and she took such a fancy to him that she adopted him."

"Adopted him?"

"Yes, as her son. He's not Landau any more now, but Count Bezzubov. That's neither here nor there, though; but Lidia—I'm very fond of her, but she has a screw loose somewhere—has lost her heart to this Landau now, and nothing is settled now in her house or Alexey Alexandrovitch's without him, and so your sister's fate is now in the hands of Landau, *alias* Count Bezzubov."

After a capital dinner and a great deal of cognac drunk at Bartnyansky's, Stepan Arkadyevitch, only a little later than the appointed time, went in to Countess Lidia Ivanovna's.

"Who else is with the countess?—a Frenchman?" Stepan Arkadyevitch asked the hall porter, as he glanced at the familiar overcoat of Alexey Alexandrovitch and a queer, rather artless-looking overcoat with clasps.

"Alexey Alexandrovitch Karenin and Count Bezzubov," the porter answered severely.

"Princess Myakaya guessed right," thought Stepan Arkadyevitch, as he went upstairs. "Curious! It would be quite as well, though, to get on friendly terms with her. She has immense influence. If she would say a word to Pomorsky, the thing would be a certainty."

It was still quite light out-of-doors, but in Countess Lidia Ivanovna's little drawing room the blinds were drawn and the lamps lighted. At a round table under a lamp sat the countess and Alexey Alexandrovitch, talking softly. A short, thinnish man, very pale and handsome, with feminine hips and knock-kneed legs, with fine brilliant eyes and long hair lying on the collar of his coat, was standing at the end of the room gazing at the portraits on the wall. After greeting the lady of the house and Alexey Alexandrovitch, Stepan Arkadyevitch could not resist glancing once more at the unknown man.

"Monsieur Landau!" the countess addressed him with a softness and caution that impressed Oblonsky. And she introduced them.

Landau looked round hurriedly, came up, and smiling, laid his moist, lifeless hand in Stepan Arkadyevitch's outstretched hand and immediately walked away and fell to gazing at the portraits again. The countess and Alexey Alexandrovitch looked at each other significantly.

"I am very glad to see you, particularly today," said Countess Lidia Ivanovna, pointing Stepan Arkadyevitch to a seat beside Karenin.

"I introduced you to him as Landau," she said in a soft voice, glancing at the Frenchman and again immediately after at Alexey Alexandrovitch, "but he is really Count Bezzubov, as you're probably aware. Only he does not like the title."

"Yes, I heard so," answered Stepan Arkadyevitch; "they say he completely cured Countess Bezzubova."

"She was here today, poor thing!" the countess said, turning to Alexey Alexandrovitch. "This separation is awful for her. It's such a blow to her!"

"And he positively is going?" queried Alexey Alexandrovitch.

"Yes, he's going to Paris. He heard a voice yesterday," said Countess Lidia Ivanovna, looking at Stepan Arkadyevitch.

"Ah, a voice!" repeated Oblonsky, feeling that he must be as circumspect as he possibly could in this society, where something peculiar was going on, or was to go on, to which he had not the key.

A moment's silence followed, after which Countess Lidia Ivanovna, as though approaching the main topic of conversation, said with a fine smile to Oblonsky:

"I've known you for a long while, and am very glad to make a closer acquaintance with you. *Les amis de nos amis sont nos amis.* But to be a true friend, one must enter into the spiritual state of one's friend, and I fear that you are not doing so in the case of Alexey Alexandrovitch. You understand what I mean?" she said, lifting her fine pensive eyes.

"In part, countess, I understand the position of Alexey Alexandrovitch..." said Oblonsky. Having no clear idea what they were talking about, he wanted to confine himself to generalities.

"The change is not in his external position," Countess Lidia Ivanovna said sternly, following with eyes of love the figure of Alexey Alexandrovitch as he got up and crossed over to Landau;

"his heart is changed, a new heart has been vouchsafed him, and I fear you don't fully apprehend the change that has taken place in him."

"Oh, well, in general outlines I can conceive the change. We have always been friendly, and now..." said Stepan Arkadyevitch, responding with a sympathetic glance to the expression of the countess, and mentally balancing the question with which of the two ministers she was most intimate, so as to know about which to ask her to speak for him.

"The change that has taken place in him cannot lessen his love for his neighbors; on the contrary, that change can only intensify love in his heart. But I am afraid you do not understand me. Won't you have some tea?" she said, with her eyes indicating the footman, who was handing round tea on a tray.

"Not quite, countess. Of course, his misfortune..."

"Yes, a misfortune which has proved the highest happiness, when his heart was made new, was filled full of it," she said, gazing with eyes full of love at Stepan Arkadyevitch.

"I do believe I might ask her to speak to both of them," thought Stepan Arkadyevitch.

"Oh, of course, countess," he said; "but I imagine such changes are a matter so private that no one, even the most intimate friend, would care to speak of them."

"On the contrary! We ought to speak freely and help one another."

"Yes, undoubtedly so, but there is such a difference of convictions, and besides..." said Oblonsky with a soft smile.

"There can be no difference where it is a question of holy truth."

"Oh, no, of course; but..." and Stepan Arkadyevitch paused in confusion. He understood at last that they were talking of religion.

"I fancy he will fall asleep immediately," said Alexey Alexandrovitch in a whisper full of meaning, going up to Lidia Ivanovna.

Stepan Arkadyevitch looked round. Landau was sitting at the window, leaning on his elbow and the back of his chair, his head drooping. Noticing that all eyes were turned on him he raised his head and smiled a smile of childlike artlessness.

"Don't take any notice," said Lidia Ivanovna, and she lightly moved a chair up for Alexey Alexandrovitch. "I have observed..." she was beginning, when a footman came into the room with a letter. Lidia Ivanovna rapidly ran her eyes over the note, and excusing herself, wrote an answer with extraordinary rapidity, handed it to the man, and came back to the table. "I have observed," she went on, "that Moscow people, especially the men, are more indifferent to religion than anyone."

"Oh, no, countess, I thought Moscow people had the reputation of being the firmest in the faith," answered Stepan Arkadyevitch.

"But as far as I can make out, you are unfortunately one of the indifferent ones," said Alexey Alexandrovitch, turning to him with a weary smile.

"How anyone can be indifferent!" said Lidia Ivanovna.

"I am not so much indifferent on that subject as I am waiting in suspense," said Stepan Arkadyevitch, with his most deprecating smile. "I hardly think that the time for such questions has come yet for me."

Alexey Alexandrovitch and Lidia Ivanovna looked at each other.

"We can never tell whether the time has come for us or not," said Alexey Alexandrovitch severely. "We ought not to think whether we are ready or not ready. God's grace is not guided by human considerations: sometimes it comes not to those that strive for it, and comes to those that are unprepared, like Saul."

"No, I believe it won't be just yet," said Lidia Ivanovna, who had been meanwhile watching the movements of the Frenchman. Landau got up and came to them.

"Do you allow me to listen?" he asked.

"Oh, yes; I did not want to disturb you," said Lidia Ivanovna, gazing tenderly at him; "sit here with us."

"One has only not to close one's eyes to shut out the light," Alexey Alexandrovitch went on.

"Ah, if you knew the happiness we know, feeling His presence ever in our hearts!" said Countess Lidia Ivanovna with a rapturous smile.

"But a man may feel himself unworthy sometimes to rise to that height," said Stepan Arkadyevitch, conscious of hypocrisy in admitting this religious height, but at the same time unable to bring himself to acknowledge his free-thinking views before a person who, by a single word to Pomorsky, might procure him the coveted appointment.

"That is, you mean that sin keeps him back?" said Lidia Ivanovna. "But that is a false idea. There is no sin for believers, their sin has been atoned for. *Pardon,*" she added, looking at the footman, who came in again with another letter. She read it and gave a verbal answer: "Tomorrow at the Grand Duchess's, say." "For the believer sin is not," she went on.

"Yes, but faith without works is dead," said Stepan Arkadyevitch, recalling the phrase from the catechism, and only by his smile clinging to his independence.

"There you have it—from the epistle of St. James," said Alexey Alexandrovitch, addressing Lidia Ivanovna, with a certain reproachfulness in his tone. It was unmistakably a subject they had discussed more than once before. "What harm has been done by the false interpretation of that passage! Nothing holds men back from belief like that misinterpretation. 'I have not works, so I cannot believe,' though all the while that is not said. But the very opposite is said."

"Striving for God, saving the soul by fasting," said Countess Lidia Ivanovna, with disgusted contempt, "those are the crude ideas of our monks.... Yet that is nowhere said. It is far simpler and easier," she added, looking at Oblonsky with the same encouraging smile with which at court she encouraged youthful maids of honor, disconcerted by the new surroundings of the court.

"We are saved by Christ who suffered for us. We are saved by faith," Alexey Alexandrovitch chimed in, with a glance of approval at her words.

"Vous comprenez l'anglais?" asked Lidia Ivanovna, and receiving a reply in the affirmative, she got up and began looking through a shelf of books.

"I want to read him 'Safe and Happy,' or 'Under the Wing,'" she said, looking inquiringly at Karenin. And finding the book, and sitting down again in her place, she opened it. "It's very short. In it is described the way by which faith can be reached, and the happiness, above all earthly bliss, with which it fills the soul. The believer cannot be unhappy because he is not alone. But you will see." She was just settling herself to read when the footman came in again. "Madame Borozdina? Tell her, tomorrow at two o'clock. Yes," she said, putting her finger in the place in the book, and gazing before her with her fine pensive eyes, "that is how true faith acts. You know Marie Sanina? You know about her trouble? She lost her only child. She was in despair. And what happened? She found this comforter, and she thanks God now for the death of her child. Such is the happiness faith brings!"

"Oh, yes, that is most..." said Stepan Arkadyevitch, glad they were going to read, and let him have a chance to collect his faculties. "No, I see I'd better not ask her about anything today," he thought. "If only I can get out of this without putting my foot in it!"

"It will be dull for you," said Countess Lidia Ivanovna, addressing Landau; "you don't know English, but it's short."

"Oh, I shall understand," said Landau, with the same smile, and he closed his eyes. Alexey Alexandrovitch and Lidia Ivanovna exchanged meaningful glances, and the reading began.

Stepan Arkadyevitch felt completely nonplussed by the strange talk which he was hearing for the first time. The complexity of Petersburg, as a rule, had a stimulating effect on him, rousing him out of his Moscow stagnation. But he liked these complications, and understood them only in the circles he knew and was at home in. In these unfamiliar surroundings he was puzzled and disconcerted, and could not get his bearings. As he listened to Countess Lidia Ivanovna, aware of the beautiful, artless—or perhaps artful, he could not decide which—eyes of Landau fixed upon him, Stepan Arkadyevitch began to be conscious of a peculiar heaviness in his head.

The most incongruous ideas were in confusion in his head. "Marie Sanina is glad her child's dead.... How good a smoke would be now!... To be saved, one need only believe, and the monks don't know how the thing's to be done, but Countess Lidia Ivanovna does know.... And why is my head so heavy? Is it the cognac, or all this being so queer? Anyway, I fancy I've done nothing unsuitable so far. But anyway, it won't do to ask her now. They say they make one say one's prayers. I only hope they won't make me! That'll be too imbecile. And what stuff it is she's reading! but she has a good accent. Landau—Bezzubov— what's he Bezzubov for?" All at once Stepan Arkadyevitch became aware that his lower jaw was uncontrollably forming a yawn. He pulled his whiskers to cover the yawn, and shook himself together. But soon after he became aware that he was dropping asleep and on the very point of snoring. He recovered himself at the very moment when the voice of Countess Lidia Ivanovna was saying "he's asleep." Stepan Arkadyevitch started with dismay, feeling guilty and caught. But he was reassured at once by seeing that the words "he's asleep" referred not to him, but to Landau. The Frenchman was asleep as well as Stepan Arkadyevitch. But Stepan Arkadyevitch's being asleep would have offended them, as he thought (though even this, he thought, might not be so, as everything seemed so queer), while Landau's being asleep delighted them extremely, especially Countess Lidia Ivanovna.

"Mon ami," said Lidia Ivanovna, carefully holding the folds of her silk gown so as not to rustle, and in her excitement calling Karenin not Alexey Alexandrovitch, but "mon ami," "donnez-lui la main. Vous voyez? Sh!" she hissed at the footman as he came in again. "Not at home."

The Frenchman was asleep, or pretending to be asleep, with his head on the back of his chair, and his moist hand, as it lay on his knee, made faint movements, as though trying to catch something. Alexey Alexandrovitch got up, tried to move carefully, but stumbled against the table, went up and laid his hand in the Frenchman's hand. Stepan Arkadyevitch got up too, and opening his eyes wide, trying to wake himself up if he were asleep, he looked first at one and then at the other. It was all real. Stepan Arkadyevitch felt that his head was getting worse and worse.

"Que la personne qui est arrivee la derniere, celle qui demande, qu'elle sorte! Qu'elle sorte!" articulated the Frenchman, without opening his eyes.

"Vous m'excuserez, mais vous voyez.... Revenez vers dix heures, encore mieux demain."

"Qu'elle sorte!" repeated the Frenchman impatiently.

"C'est moi, n'est-ce pas?" And receiving an answer in the affirmative, Stepan Arkadyevitch, forgetting the favor he had meant to ask of Lidia Ivanovna, and forgetting his sister's affairs, caring for nothing, but filled with the sole desire to get away as soon as possible, went out on tiptoe and ran out into the street as though from a plague-stricken house. For a long while he chatted and joked with his cab-driver, trying to recover his spirits.

At the French theater where he arrived for the last act, and afterwards at the Tatar restaurant after his champagne, Stepan Arkadyevitch felt a little refreshed in the atmosphere he was used to. But still he felt quite unlike himself all that evening.

On getting home to Pyotr Oblonsky's, where he was staying, Stepan Arkadyevitch found a note from Betsy. She wrote to him that she was very anxious to finish their interrupted conversation, and begged him to come next day. He had scarcely read this note, and frowned at its contents, when he heard below the ponderous tramp of the servants, carrying something heavy.

Stepan Arkadyevitch went out to look. It was the rejuvenated Pyotr Oblonsky. He was so drunk that he could not walk upstairs; but he told them to set him on his legs when he saw Stepan Arkadyevitch, and clinging to him, walked with him into his room and there began telling him how he had spent the evening, and fell asleep doing so.

Stepan Arkadyevitch was in very low spirits, which happened rarely with him, and for a long while he could not go to sleep. Everything he could recall to his mind, everything was disgusting; but most disgusting of all, as if it were something shameful, was the memory of the evening he had spent at Countess Lidia Ivanovna's.

Next day he received from Alexey Alexandrovitch a final answer, refusing to grant Anna's divorce, and he understood that this decision was based on what the Frenchman had said in his real or pretended trance.

In order to carry through any undertaking in family life, there must necessarily be either complete division between the husband and wife, or loving agreement. When the relations of a couple are vacillating and neither one thing nor the other, no sort of enterprise can be undertaken.

Many families remain for years in the same place, though both husband and wife are sick of it, simply because there is neither complete division nor agreement between them.

Both Vronsky and Anna felt life in Moscow insupportable in the heat and dust, when the spring sunshine was followed by the glare of summer, and all the trees in the boulevards had long since been in full leaf, and the leaves were covered with dust. But they did not go back to Vozdvizhenskoe, as they had arranged to do long before; they went on staying in Moscow, though they both loathed it, because of late there had been no agreement between them.

The irritability that kept them apart had no external cause, and all efforts to come to an understanding intensified it, instead of removing it. It was an inner irritation, grounded in her mind on the conviction that his love had grown less; in his, on regret that he had put himself for her sake in a difficult position, which she, instead of lightening, made still more difficult. Neither of them gave full utterance to their sense of grievance, but they considered each other in the wrong, and tried on every pretext to prove this to one another.

In her eyes the whole of him, with all his habits, ideas, desires, with all his spiritual and physical temperament, was one thing—love for women, and that love, she felt, ought to be entirely concentrated on her alone. That love was less; consequently, as she reasoned, he must have transferred part of his love to other women or to another woman—and she was jealous. She was jealous not of any particular woman but of the decrease of his love. Not having got an object for her jealousy, she was on the lookout for it. At the slightest hint she transferred her jealousy from one object to another. At one time she was jealous of those low women with whom he might so easily renew his old bachelor ties; then she was jealous of the society women he might meet; then she was jealous of the imaginary girl whom he might want to marry, for whose sake he would break with her. And this last form of jealousy tortured her most of all, especially as he had unwarily told her, in a moment of frankness, that his mother knew him so little that she had had the audacity to try and persuade him to marry the young Princess Sorokina.

And being jealous of him, Anna was indignant against him and found grounds for indignation in everything. For everything that was difficult in her position she blamed him. The agonizing condition of suspense she had passed in Moscow, the tardiness and indecision of Alexey Alexandrovitch, her solitude—she put it all down to him. If he had loved her he would have seen all the bitterness of her position, and would have rescued her from it. For her being in Moscow and not in the country, he was to blame too. He could not live buried in the country as she would have liked to do. He must have society, and he had put her in this awful position, the bitterness of which he would not see. And again, it was his fault that she was forever separated from her son.

Even the rare moments of tenderness that came from time to time did not soothe her; in his tenderness now she saw a shade of complacency, of self-confidence, which had not been of old, and which exasperated her.

It was dusk. Anna was alone, and waiting for him to come back from a bachelor dinner. She walked up and down in his study (the room where the noise from the street was least heard), and thought over every detail of their yesterday's quarrel. Going back from the well-remembered, offensive words of the quarrel to what had been the ground of it, she arrived at last at its origin. For a long while she could hardly believe that their dissension had arisen from a conversation so inoffensive, of so little moment to either. But so it actually had been. It all arose from his laughing at the girls' high schools, declaring they were useless, while she defended them. He had spoken slightingly of women's education in general, and had said that Hannah, Anna's English protégée, had not the slightest need to know anything of physics.

This irritated Anna. She saw in this a contemptuous reference to her occupations. And she bethought her of a phrase to pay him back for the pain he had given her. "I don't expect you to understand me, my feelings, as anyone who loved me might, but simple delicacy I did expect," she said.

And he had actually flushed with vexation, and had said something unpleasant. She could not recall her answer, but at that point, with an unmistakable desire to wound her too, he had said:

"I feel no interest in your infatuation over this girl, that's true, because I see it's unnatural."

The cruelty with which he shattered the world she had built up for herself so laboriously to enable her to endure her hard life, the injustice with which he had accused her of affectation, of artificiality, aroused her.

"I am very sorry that nothing but what's coarse and material is comprehensible and natural to you," she said and walked out of the room.

When he had come in to her yesterday evening, they had not referred to the quarrel, but both felt that the quarrel had been smoothed over, but was not at an end.

Today he had not been at home all day, and she felt so lonely and wretched in being on bad terms with him that she wanted to forget it all, to forgive him, and be reconciled with him; she wanted to throw the blame on herself and to justify him.

"I am myself to blame. I'm irritable, I'm insanely jealous. I will make it up with him, and we'll go away to the country; there I shall be more at peace."

"Unnatural!" She suddenly recalled the word that had stung her most of all, not so much the word itself as the intent to wound her with which it was said. "I know what he meant; he meant— unnatural, not loving my own daughter, to love another person's child. What does he know of love for children, of my love for Seryozha, whom I've sacrificed for him? But that wish to wound me! No, he loves another woman, it must be so."

And perceiving that, while trying to regain her peace of mind, she had gone round the same circle that she had been round so often before, and had come back to her former state of exasperation, she was horrified at herself. "Can it be impossible? Can it be beyond me to control myself?" she said to herself, and began again from the beginning. "He's truthful, he's honest, he loves me. I love him, and in a few days the divorce will come. What more do I want? I want peace of mind and trust, and I will take the blame on myself. Yes, now when he comes in, I will tell him I was wrong, though I was not wrong, and we will go away tomorrow."

And to escape thinking any more, and being overcome by irritability, she rang, and ordered the boxes to be brought up for packing their things for the country.

At ten o'clock Vronsky came in.

"Well, was it nice?" she asked, coming out to meet him with a penitent and meek expression.

"Just as usual," he answered, seeing at a glance that she was in one of her good moods. He was used by now to these transitions, and he was particularly glad to see it today, as he was in a specially good humor himself.

"What do I see? Come, that's good!" he said, pointing to the boxes in the passage.

"Yes, we must go. I went out for a drive, and it was so fine I longed to be in the country. There's nothing to keep you, is there?"

"It's the one thing I desire. I'll be back directly, and we'll talk it over; I only want to change my coat. Order some tea."

And he went into his room.

There was something mortifying in the way he had said "Come, that's good," as one says to a child when it leaves off being naughty, and still more mortifying was the contrast between her penitent and his self-confident tone; and for one instant she felt the lust of strife rising up in her again, but making an effort she conquered it, and met Vronsky as good-humoredly as before.

When he came in she told him, partly repeating phrases she had prepared beforehand, how she had spent the day, and her plans for going away.

"You know it came to me almost like an inspiration," she said. "Why wait here for the divorce? Won't it be just the same in the country? I can't wait any longer! I don't want to go on hoping, I don't want to hear anything about the divorce. I have made up my mind it shall not have any more influence on my life. Do you agree?"

"Oh, yes!" he said, glancing uneasily at her excited face.

"What did you do? Who was there?" she said, after a pause.

Vronsky mentioned the names of the guests. "The dinner was first rate, and the boat race, and it was all pleasant enough, but in Moscow they can never do anything without something *ridicule*. A lady of a sort appeared on the scene, teacher of swimming to the Queen of Sweden, and gave us an exhibition of her skill."

"How? did she swim?" asked Anna, frowning.

"In an absurd red *costume de natation;* she was old and hideous too. So when shall we go?"

"What an absurd fancy! Why, did she swim in some special way, then?" said Anna, not answering.

"There was absolutely nothing in it. That's just what I say, it was awfully stupid. Well, then, when do you think of going?"

Anna shook her head as though trying to drive away some unpleasant idea.

"When? Why, the sooner the better! By tomorrow we shan't be ready. The day after tomorrow."

"Yes...oh, no, wait a minute! The day after to-morrow's Sunday, I have to be at maman's," said Vronsky, embarrassed, because as soon as he uttered his mother's name he was aware of her intent, suspicious eyes. His embarrassment confirmed her suspicion. She flushed hotly and drew away from him. It was now not the Queen of Sweden's swimming-mistress who filled Anna's imagination, but the young Princess Sorokina. She was staying in a village near Moscow with Countess Vronskaya.

"Can't you go tomorrow?" she said.

"Well, no! The deeds and the money for the business I'm going there for I can't get by tomorrow," he answered.

"If so, we won't go at all."

"But why so?"

"I shall not go later. Monday or never!"

"What for?" said Vronsky, as though in amazement. "Why, there's no meaning in it!"

"There's no meaning in it to you, because you care nothing for me. You don't care to understand my life. The one thing that I cared for here was Hannah. You say it's affectation. Why, you said yesterday that I don't love my daughter, that I love this English girl, that it's unnatural. I should like to know what life there is for me that could be natural!"

For an instant she had a clear vision of what she was doing, and was horrified at how she had fallen away from her resolution. But even though she knew it was her own ruin, she could not restrain herself, could not keep herself from proving to him that he was wrong, could not give way to him.

"I never said that; I said I did not sympathize with this sudden passion."

"How is it, though you boast of your straightforwardness, you don't tell the truth?"

"I never boast, and I never tell lies," he said slowly, restraining his rising anger. "It's a great pity if you can't respect..."

"Respect was invented to cover the empty place where love should be. And if you don't love me any more, it would be better and more honest to say so."

"No, this is becoming unbearable!" cried Vronsky, getting up from his chair; and stopping short, facing her, he said, speaking deliberately: "What do you try my patience for?" looking as though he might have said much more, but was restraining himself. "It has limits."

"What do you mean by that?" she cried, looking with terror at the undisguised hatred in his whole face, and especially in his cruel, menacing eyes.

"I mean to say..." he was beginning, but he checked himself. "I must ask what it is you want of me?"

"What can I want? All I can want is that you should not desert me, as you think of doing," she said, understanding all he had not uttered. "But that I don't want; that's secondary. I want love, and there is none. So then all is over."

She turned towards the door.

"Stop! sto-op!" said Vronsky, with no change in the gloomy lines of his brows, though he held her by the hand. "What is it all about? I said that we must put off going for three days, and on that you told me I was lying, that I was not an honorable man."

"Yes, and I repeat that the man who reproaches me with having sacrificed everything for me," she said, recalling the words of a still earlier quarrel, "that he's worse than a dishonorable man— he's a heartless man."

"Oh, there are limits to endurance!" he cried, and hastily let go her hand.

"He hates me, that's clear," she thought, and in silence, without looking round, she walked with faltering steps out of the room. "He loves another woman, that's even clearer," she said to herself as she went into her own room. "I want love, and there is none. So, then, all is over." She repeated the words she had said, "and it must be ended."

"But how?" she asked herself, and she sat down in a low chair before the looking glass.

Thoughts of where she would go now, whether to the aunt who had brought her up, to Dolly, or simply alone abroad, and of what *he* was doing now alone in his study; whether this was the final quarrel, or whether reconciliation were still possible; and of what all her old friends at Petersburg would say of her now; and of how Alexey Alexandrovitch would look at it, and many other ideas of what would happen now after this rupture, came into her head; but she did not give herself up to them with all her heart. At the bottom of her heart was some obscure idea that alone interested her, but she could not get clear sight of it. Thinking once more of Alexey Alexandrovitch, she recalled the time of her illness after her confinement, and the feeling which never left her at that time. "Why didn't I die?" and the words and the feeling of that time came back to her. And all at once she knew what was in her soul. Yes, it was that idea which alone solved all. "Yes, to die!... And the shame and disgrace of Alexey Alexandrovitch and of Seryozha, and my awful shame, it will all be saved by death. To die! and he will feel remorse; will be sorry; will love me; he will suffer on my account." With the trace of a smile of commiseration for herself she sat down in the armchair, taking off and putting on the rings on her left hand, vividly picturing from different sides his feelings after her death.

Approaching footsteps—his steps—distracted her attention. As though absorbed in the arrangement of her rings, she did not even turn to him.

He went up to her, and taking her by the hand, said softly:

"Anna, we'll go the day after tomorrow, if you like. I agree to everything."

She did not speak.

"What is it?" he urged.

"You know," she said, and at the same instant, unable to restrain herself any longer, she burst into sobs.

"Cast me off!" she articulated between her sobs. "I'll go away tomorrow...I'll do more. What am I? An immoral woman! A stone round your neck. I don't want to make you wretched, I don't want to! I'll set you free. You don't love me; you love someone else!"

Vronsky besought her to be calm, and declared that there was no trace of foundation for her jealousy; that he had never ceased, and never would cease, to love her; that he loved her more than ever.

"Anna, why distress yourself and me so?" he said to her, kissing her hands. There was tenderness now in his face, and she fancied she caught the sound of tears in his voice, and she felt them wet on her hand. And instantly Anna's despairing jealousy changed to a despairing passion of tenderness. She put her arms round him, and covered with kisses his head, his neck, his hands.

Feeling that the reconciliation was complete, Anna set eagerly to work in the morning preparing for their departure. Though it was not settled whether they should go on Monday or Tuesday, as they had each given way to the other, Anna packed busily, feeling absolutely indifferent whether they went a day earlier or later. She was standing in her room over an open box, taking things out of it, when he came in to see her earlier than usual, dressed to go out.

"I'm going off at once to see maman; she can send me the money by Yegorov. And I shall be ready to go tomorrow," he said.

Though she was in such a good mood, the thought of his visit to his mother's gave her a pang.

"No, I shan't be ready by then myself," she said; and at once reflected, "so then it was possible to arrange to do as I wished." "No, do as you meant to do. Go into the dining room, I'm coming directly. It's only to turn out those things that aren't wanted," she said, putting something more on the heap of frippery that lay in Annushka's arms.

Vronsky was eating his beefsteak when she came into the dining- room.

"You wouldn't believe how distasteful these rooms have become to me," she said, sitting down beside him to her coffee. "There's nothing more awful than these *chambres garnies.* There's no individuality in them, no soul. These clocks, and curtains, and, worst of all, the wallpapers—they're a nightmare. I think of Vozdvizhenskoe as the promised land. You're not sending the horses off yet?"

"No, they will come after us. Where are you going to?"

"I wanted to go to Wilson's to take some dresses to her. So it's really to be tomorrow?" she said in a cheerful voice; but suddenly her face changed.

Vronsky's valet came in to ask him to sign a receipt for a telegram from Petersburg. There was nothing out of the way in Vronsky's getting a telegram, but he said, as though anxious to conceal something from her, that the receipt was in his study, and he turned hurriedly to her.

"By tomorrow, without fail, I will finish it all."

"From whom is the telegram?" she asked, not hearing him.

"From Stiva," he answered reluctantly.

"Why didn't you show it to me? What secret can there be between Stiva and me?"

Vronsky called the valet back, and told him to bring the telegram.

"I didn't want to show it to you, because Stiva has such a passion for telegraphing: why telegraph when nothing is settled?"

"About the divorce?"

"Yes; but he says he has not been able to come at anything yet. He has promised a decisive answer in a day or two. But here it is; read it."

With trembling hands Anna took the telegram, and read what Vronsky had told her. At the end was added: "Little hope; but I will do everything possible and impossible."

"I said yesterday that it's absolutely nothing to me when I get, or whether I never get, a divorce," she said, flushing crimson. "There was not the slightest necessity to hide it from me." "So he may hide and does hide his correspondence with women from me," she thought.

"Yashvin meant to come this morning with Voytov," said Vronsky; "I believe he's won from Pyevtsov all and more than he can pay, about sixty thousand."

"No," she said, irritated by his so obviously showing by this change of subject that he was irritated, "why did you suppose that this news would affect me so, that you must even try to hide it? I said I don't want to consider it, and I should have liked you to care as little about it as I do."

"I care about it because I like definiteness," he said.

"Definiteness is not in the form but the love," she said, more and more irritated, not by his words, but by the tone of cool composure in which he spoke. "What do you want it for?"

"My God! love again," he thought, frowning.

"Oh, you know what for; for your sake and your children's in the future."

"There won't be children in the future."

"That's a great pity," he said.

"You want it for the children's sake, but you don't think of me?" she said, quite forgetting or not having heard that he had said, "*for your sake* and the children's."

The question of the possibility of having children had long been a subject of dispute and irritation to her. His desire to have children she interpreted as a proof he did not prize her beauty.

"Oh, I said: for your sake. Above all for your sake," he repeated, frowning as though in pain, "because I am certain that the greater part of your irritability comes from the indefiniteness of the position."

"Yes, now he has laid aside all pretense, and all his cold hatred for me is apparent," she thought, not hearing his words, but watching with terror the cold, cruel judge who looked mocking her out of his eyes.

"The cause is not that," she said, "and, indeed, I don't see how the cause of my irritability, as you call it, can be that I am completely in your power. What indefiniteness is there in the position? on the contrary..."

"I am very sorry that you don't care to understand," he interrupted, obstinately anxious to give utterance to his thought. "The indefiniteness consists in your imagining that I am free."

"On that score you can set your mind quite at rest," she said, and turning away from him, she began drinking her coffee.

She lifted her cup, with her little finger held apart, and put it to her lips. After drinking a few sips she glanced at him, and by his expression, she saw clearly that he was repelled by her hand, and her gesture, and the sound made by her lips.

"I don't care in the least what your mother thinks, and what match she wants to make for you," she said, putting the cup down with a shaking hand.

"But we are not talking about that."

"Yes, that's just what we are talking about. And let me tell you that a heartless woman, whether she's old or not old, your mother or anyone else, is of no consequence to me, and I would not consent to know her."

"Anna, I beg you not to speak disrespectfully of my mother."

"A woman whose heart does not tell her where her son's happiness and honor lie has no heart."

"I repeat my request that you will not speak disrespectfully of my mother, whom I respect," he said, raising his voice and looking sternly at her.

She did not answer. Looking intently at him, at his face, his hands, she recalled all the details of their reconciliation the previous day, and his passionate caresses. "There, just such caresses he has lavished, and will lavish, and longs to lavish on other women!" she thought.

"You don't love your mother. That's all talk, and talk, and talk!" she said, looking at him with hatred in her eyes.

"Even if so, you must..."

"Must decide, and I have decided," she said, and she would have gone away, but at that moment Yashvin walked into the room. Anna greeted him and remained.

Why, when there was a tempest in her soul, and she felt she was standing at a turning point in her life, which might have fearful consequences—why, at that minute, she had to keep up appearances before an outsider, who sooner or later must know it all—she did not know. But at once quelling the storm within her, she sat down and began talking to their guest.

"Well, how are you getting on? Has your debt been paid you?" she asked Yashvin.

"Oh, pretty fair; I fancy I shan't get it all, but I shall get a good half. And when are you off?" said Yashvin, looking at Vronsky, and unmistakably guessing at a quarrel.

"The day after tomorrow, I think," said Vronsky.

"You've been meaning to go so long, though."

"But now it's quite decided," said Anna, looking Vronsky straight in the face with a look which told him not to dream of the possibility of reconciliation.

"Don't you feel sorry for that unlucky Pyevtsov?" she went on, talking to Yashvin.

"I've never asked myself the question, Anna Arkadyevna, whether I'm sorry for him or not. You see, all my fortune's here"—he touched his breast pocket—"and just now I'm a wealthy man. But today I'm going to the club, and I may come out a beggar. You see, whoever sits down to play with me—he wants to leave me without a shirt to my back, and so do I him. And so we fight it out, and that's the pleasure of it."

"Well, but suppose you were married," said Anna, "how would it be for your wife?"

Yashvin laughed.

"That's why I'm not married, and never mean to be."

"And Helsingfors?" said Vronsky, entering into the conversation and glancing at Anna's smiling face. Meeting his eyes, Anna's face instantly took a coldly severe expression as though she were saying to him: "It's not forgotten. It's all the same."

"Were you really in love?" she said to Yashvin.

"Oh heavens! ever so many times! But you see, some men can play but only so that they can always lay down their cards when the hour of a *rendezvous* comes, while I can take up love, but only so as not to be late for my cards in the evening. That's how I manage things."

"No, I didn't mean that, but the real thing." She would have said *Helsingfors*, but would not repeat the word used by Vronsky.

Voytov, who was buying the horse, came in. Anna got up and went out of the room.

Before leaving the house, Vronsky went into her room. She would have pretended to be looking for something on the table, but ashamed of making a pretense, she looked straight in his face with cold eyes.

"What do you want?" she asked in French.

"To get the guarantee for Gambetta, I've sold him," he said, in a tone which said more clearly than words, "I've no time for discussing things, and it would lead to nothing."

"I'm not to blame in any way," he thought. "If she will punish herself, *tant pis pour elle.*" But as he was going he fancied that she said something, and his heart suddenly ached with pity for her.

"Eh, Anna?" he queried.

"I said nothing," she answered just as coldly and calmly.

"Oh, nothing, tant pis then," he thought, feeling cold again, and he turned and went out. As he was going out he caught a glimpse in the looking glass of her face, white, with quivering lips. He even wanted to stop and to say some comforting word to her, but his legs carried him out of the room before he could think what to say. The whole of that day he spent away from home, and when he came in late in the evening the maid told him that Anna Arkadyevna had a headache and begged him not to go in to her.

"He has gone! It is over!" Anna said to herself, standing at the window; and in answer to this statement the impression of the darkness when the candle had flickered out, and of her fearful dream mingling into one, filled her heart with cold terror.

"No, that cannot be!" she cried, and crossing the room she rang the bell. She was so afraid now of being alone, that without waiting for the servant to come in, she went out to meet him.

"Inquire where the count has gone," she said. The servant answered that the count had gone to the stable.

"His honor left word that if you cared to drive out, the carriage would be back immediately."

"Very good. Wait a minute. I'll write a note at once. Send Mihail with the note to the stables. Make haste."

She sat down and wrote:

"I was wrong. Come back home; I must explain. For God's sake come! I'm afraid."

She sealed it up and gave it to the servant.

She was afraid of being left alone now; she followed the servant out of the room, and went to the nursery.

"Why, this isn't it, this isn't he! Where are his blue eyes, his sweet, shy smile?" was her first thought when she saw her chubby, rosy little girl with her black, curly hair instead of Seryozha, whom in the tangle of her ideas she had expected to see in the nursery. The little girl sitting at the table was obstinately and violently battering on it with a cork, and staring aimlessly at her mother with her pitch-black eyes. Answering the English nurse that she was quite well, and that she was going to the country tomorrow, Anna sat down by the little girl and began spinning the cork to show her. But the child's loud, ringing laugh, and the motion of her eyebrows, recalled Vronsky so vividly that she got up hurriedly, restraining her sobs, and went away. "Can it be all over? No, it cannot be!" she thought. "He will come back. But how can he explain that smile, that excitement after he had been talking to her? But even if he doesn't explain, I will believe. If I don't believe, there's only one thing left for me, and I can't."

She looked at her watch. Twenty minutes had passed. "By now he has received the note and is coming back. Not long, ten minutes more.... But what if he doesn't come? No, that cannot be. He mustn't see me with tear-stained eyes. I'll go and wash. Yes, yes; did I do my hair or not?" she asked herself. And she could not remember. She felt her head with her hand. "Yes, my hair has been done, but when I did it I can't in the least remember." She could not believe the evidence of her hand, and went up to the pier glass to see whether she really had done her hair. She certainly had, but she could not think when she had done it. "Who's that?" she thought, looking in the looking glass at the swollen face with strangely glittering eyes, that looked in a scared way at her. "Why, it's I!" she suddenly understood, and looking round, she seemed all at once to feel his kisses on her, and twitched her shoulders, shuddering. Then she lifted her hand to her lips and kissed it.

"What is it? Why, I'm going out of my mind!" and she went into her bedroom, where Annushka was tidying the room.

"Annushka," she said, coming to a standstill before her, and she stared at the maid, not knowing what to say to her.

"You meant to go and see Darya Alexandrovna," said the girl, as though she understood.

"Darya Alexandrovna? Yes, I'll go."

"Fifteen minutes there, fifteen minutes back. He's coming, he'll be here soon." She took out her watch and looked at it. "But how could he go away, leaving me in such a state? How can he live, without making it up with me?" She went to the window and began looking into the street. Judging by the time, he might be back now. But her calculations might be wrong, and she began once more to recall when he had started and to count the minutes.

At the moment when she had moved away to the big clock to compare it with her watch, someone drove up. Glancing out of the window, she saw his carriage. But no one came upstairs, and voices could be heard below. It was the messenger who had come back in the carriage. She went down to him.

"We didn't catch the count. The count had driven off on the lower city road."

"What do you say? What!..." she said to the rosy, good-humored Mihail, as he handed her back her note.

"Why, then, he has never received it!" she thought.

"Go with this note to Countess Vronskaya's place, you know? and bring an answer back immediately," she said to the messenger.

"And I, what am I going to do?" she thought. "Yes, I'm going to Dolly's, that's true or else I shall go out of my mind. Yes, and I can telegraph, too." And she wrote a telegram. "I absolutely must talk to you; come at once." After sending off the telegram, she went to dress. When she was dressed and in her hat, she glanced again into the eyes of the plump, comfortable-looking Annushka. There was unmistakable sympathy in those good-natured little gray eyes.

"Annushka, dear, what am I to do?" said Anna, sobbing and sinking helplessly into a chair.

"Why fret yourself so, Anna Arkadyevna? Why, there's nothing out of the way. You drive out a little, and it'll cheer you up," said the maid.

"Yes, I'm going," said Anna, rousing herself and getting up. "And if there's a telegram while I'm away, send it on to Darya Alexandrovna's...but no, I shall be back myself."

"Yes, I mustn't think, I must do something, drive somewhere, and most of all, get out of this house," she said, feeling with terror the strange turmoil going on in her own heart, and she made haste to go out and get into the carriage.

"Where to?" asked Pyotr before getting onto the box.

"To Znamenka, the Oblonskys'."

It was bright and sunny. A fine rain had been falling all the morning, and now it had not long cleared up. The iron roofs, the flags of the roads, the flints of the pavements, the wheels and leather, the brass and the tinplate of the carriages—all glistened brightly in the May sunshine. It was three o'clock, and the very liveliest time in the streets.

As she sat in a corner of the comfortable carriage, that hardly swayed on its supple springs, while the grays trotted swiftly, in the midst of the unceasing rattle of wheels and the changing impressions in the pure air, Anna ran over the events of the last days, and she saw her position quite differently from how it had seemed at home. Now the thought of death seemed no longer so terrible and so clear to her, and death itself no longer seemed so inevitable. Now she blamed herself for the humiliation to which she had lowered herself. "I entreat him to forgive me. I have given in to him. I have owned myself in fault. What for? Can't I live without him?" And leaving unanswered the question how she was going to live without him, she fell to reading the signs on the shops. "Office and warehouse. Dental surgeon. Yes, I'll tell Dolly all about it. She doesn't like Vronsky. I shall be sick and ashamed, but I'll tell her. She loves me, and I'll follow her advice. I won't give in to him; I won't let him train me as he pleases. Filippov, bun shop. They say they send their dough to Petersburg. The Moscow water is so good for it. Ah, the springs at Mitishtchen, and the pancakes!"

And she remembered how, long, long ago, when she was a girl of seventeen, she had gone with her aunt to Troitsa. "Riding, too. Was that really me, with red hands? How much that seemed to me then splendid and out of reach has become worthless, while what I had then has gone out of my reach forever! Could I ever have believed then that I could come to such humiliation? How conceited and self-satisfied he will be when he gets my note! But I will show him.... How horrid that paint smells! Why is it they're always painting and building? *Modes et robes*," she read. A man bowed to her. It was Annushka's husband. "Our parasites"; she remembered how Vronsky had said that. "Our? Why our? What's so awful is that one can't tear up the past by its roots. One can't tear it out, but one can hide one's memory of it. And I'll hide it." And then she thought of her past with Alexey Alexandrovitch, of how she had blotted the memory of it out of her life. "Dolly will think I'm leaving my second husband, and so I certainly must be in the wrong. As if I cared to be right! I can't help it!" she said, and she wanted to cry. But at once she fell to wondering what those two girls could be smiling about. "Love, most likely. They don't know how dreary it is, how low.... The boulevard and the children. Three boys running, playing at horses. Seryozha! And I'm losing everything and not getting him back. Yes, I'm losing everything, if he doesn't return. Perhaps he was late for the train and has come back by now. Longing for humiliation again!" she said to herself. "No, I'll go to Dolly, and say straight out to her, I'm unhappy, I deserve this, I'm to blame, but still I'm unhappy, help me. These horses, this carriage—how loathsome I am to myself in this carriage—all his; but I won't see them again."

Thinking over the words in which she would tell Dolly, and mentally working her heart up to great bitterness, Anna went upstairs.

"Is there anyone with her?" she asked in the hall.

"Katerina Alexandrovna Levin," answered the footman.

"Kitty! Kitty, whom Vronsky was in love with!" thought Anna, "the girl he thinks of with love. He's sorry he didn't marry her. But me he thinks of with hatred, and is sorry he had anything to do with me."

The sisters were having a consultation about nursing when Anna called. Dolly went down alone to see the visitor who had interrupted their conversation.

"Well, so you've not gone away yet? I meant to have come to you," she said; "I had a letter from Stiva today."

"We had a telegram too," answered Anna, looking round for Kitty.

"He writes that he can't make out quite what Alexey Alexandrovitch wants, but he won't go away without a decisive answer."

"I thought you had someone with you. Can I see the letter?"

"Yes; Kitty," said Dolly, embarrassed. "She stayed in the nursery. She has been very ill."

"So I heard. May I see the letter?"

"I'll get it directly. But he doesn't refuse; on the contrary, Stiva has hopes," said Dolly, stopping in the doorway.

"I haven't, and indeed I don't wish it," said Anna.

"What's this? Does Kitty consider it degrading to meet me?" thought Anna when she was alone. "Perhaps she's right, too. But it's not for her, the girl who was in love with Vronsky, it's not for her to show me that, even if it is true. I know that in my position I can't be received by any decent woman. I knew that from the first moment I sacrificed everything to him. And this is my reward! Oh, how I hate him! And what did I come here for? I'm worse here, more miserable." She heard from the next room the sisters' voices in consultation. "And what am I going to say to Dolly now? Amuse Kitty by the sight of my wretchedness, submit to her patronizing? No; and besides, Dolly wouldn't understand. And it would be no good my telling her. It would only be interesting to see Kitty, to show her how I despise everyone and everything, how nothing matters to me now."

Dolly came in with the letter. Anna read it and handed it back in silence.

"I knew all that," she said, "and it doesn't interest me in the least."

"Oh, why so? On the contrary, I have hopes," said Dolly, looking inquisitively at Anna. She had never seen her in such a strangely irritable condition. "When are you going away?" she asked.

Anna, half-closing her eyes, looked straight before her and did not answer.

"Why does Kitty shrink from me?" she said, looking at the door and flushing red.

"Oh, what nonsense! She's nursing, and things aren't going right with her, and I've been advising her.... She's delighted. She'll be here in a minute," said Dolly awkwardly, not clever at lying. "Yes, here she is."

Hearing that Anna had called, Kitty had wanted not to appear, but Dolly persuaded her. Rallying her forces, Kitty went in, walked up to her, blushing, and shook hands.

"I am so glad to see you," she said with a trembling voice.

Kitty had been thrown into confusion by the inward conflict between her antagonism to this bad woman and her desire to be nice to her. But as soon as she saw Anna's lovely and attractive face, all feeling of antagonism disappeared.

"I should not have been surprised if you had not cared to meet me. I'm used to everything. You have been ill? Yes, you are changed," said Anna.

Kitty felt that Anna was looking at her with hostile eyes. She ascribed this hostility to the awkward position in which Anna, who had once patronized her, must feel with her now, and she felt sorry for her.

They talked of Kitty's illness, of the baby, of Stiva, but it was obvious that nothing interested Anna.

"I came to say good-bye to you," she said, getting up.

"Oh, when are you going?"

But again not answering, Anna turned to Kitty.

"Yes, I am very glad to have seen you," she said with a smile. "I have heard so much of you from everyone, even from your husband. He came to see me, and I liked him exceedingly," she said, unmistakably with malicious intent. "Where is he?"

"He has gone back to the country," said Kitty, blushing.

"Remember me to him, be sure you do."

"I'll be sure to!" Kitty said naïvely, looking compassionately into her eyes.

"So good-bye, Dolly." And kissing Dolly and shaking hands with Kitty, Anna went out hurriedly.

"She's just the same and just as charming! She's very lovely!" said Kitty, when she was alone with her sister. "But there's something piteous about her. Awfully piteous!"

"Yes, there's something unusual about her today," said Dolly. "When I went with her into the hall, I fancied she was almost crying."

A bell rang, some young men, ugly and impudent, and at the same time careful of the impression they were making, hurried by. Pyotr, too, crossed the room in his livery and top-boots, with his dull, animal face, and came up to her to take her to the train. Some noisy men were quiet as she passed them on the platform, and one whispered something about her to another— something vile, no doubt. She stepped up on the high step, and sat down in a carriage by herself on a dirty seat that had been white. Her bag lay beside her, shaken up and down by the springiness of the seat. With a foolish smile Pyotr raised his hat, with its colored band, at the window, in token of farewell; an impudent conductor slammed the door and the latch. A grotesque-looking lady wearing a bustle (Anna mentally undressed the woman, and was appalled at her hideousness), and a little girl laughing affectedly ran down the platform.

"Do you wish to get out?"

Anna made no answer. The conductor and her two fellow-passengers did not notice under her veil her panic-stricken face. She went back to her corner and sat down. The couple seated themselves on the opposite side, and intently but surreptitiously scrutinized her clothes. Both husband and wife seemed repulsive to Anna. The husband asked, would she allow him to smoke, obviously not with a view to smoking but to getting into conversation with her. Receiving her assent, he said to his wife in French something about caring less to smoke than to talk. They made inane and affected remarks to one another, entirely for her benefit. Anna saw clearly that they were sick of each other, and hated each other. And no one could have helped hating such miserable monstrosities.

A second bell sounded, and was followed by moving of luggage, noise, shouting and laughter. It was so clear to Anna that there was nothing for anyone to be glad of, that this laughter irritated her agonizingly, and she would have liked to stop up her ears not to hear it. At last the third bell rang, there was a whistle and a hiss of steam, and a clank of chains, and the man in her carriage crossed himself. "It would be interesting to ask him what meaning he attaches to that," thought Anna, looking angrily at him. She looked past the lady out of the window at the people who seemed whirling by as they ran beside the train or stood on the platform. The train, jerking at regular intervals at the junctions of the rails, rolled by the platform, past a stone wall, a signal-box, past other trains; the wheels, moving more smoothly and evenly, resounded with a slight clang on the rails. The window was lighted up by the bright evening sun, and a slight breeze fluttered the curtain. Anna forgot her fellow passengers, and to the light swaying of the train she fell to thinking again, as she breathed the fresh air.

"Yes, what did I stop at? That I couldn't conceive a position in which life would not be a misery, that we are all created to be miserable, and that we all know it, and all invent means of deceiving each other. And when one sees the truth, what is one to do?"

"That's what reason is given man for, to escape from what worries him," said the lady in French, lisping affectedly, and obviously pleased with her phrase.

The words seemed an answer to Anna's thoughts.

"To escape from what worries him," repeated Anna. And glancing at the red-cheeked husband and the thin wife, she saw that the sickly wife considered herself misunderstood, and the husband deceived her and encouraged her in that idea of herself. Anna seemed to see all their history and all the crannies of their souls, as it were turning a light upon them. But there was nothing interesting in them, and she pursued her thought.

"Yes, I'm very much worried, and that's what reason was given me for, to escape; so then one must escape: why not put out the light when there's nothing more to look at, when it's sickening to look at it all? But how? Why did the conductor run along the footboard, why are they shrieking, those young men in that train? why are they talking, why are they laughing? It's all falsehood, all lying, all humbug, all cruelty!..."

When the train came into the station, Anna got out into the crowd of passengers, and moving apart from them as if they were lepers, she stood on the platform, trying to think what she had come here for, and what she meant to do. Everything that had seemed to her possible before was now so difficult to consider, especially in this noisy crowd of hideous people who would not leave her alone. One moment porters ran up to her proffering their services, then young men, clacking their heels on the planks of the platform and talking loudly, stared at her; people meeting her dodged past on the wrong side. Remembering that she had meant to go on further if there were no answer, she stopped a porter and asked if her coachman were not here with a note from Count Vronsky.

"Count Vronsky? They sent up here from the Vronskys just this minute, to meet Princess Sorokina and her daughter. And what is the coachman like?"

Just as she was talking to the porter, the coachman Mihail, red and cheerful in his smart blue coat and chain, evidently proud of having so successfully performed his commission, came up to her and gave her a letter. She broke it open, and her heart ached before she had read it.

"I am very sorry your note did not reach me. I will be home at ten," Vronsky had written carelessly....

"Yes, that's what I expected!" she said to herself with an evil smile.

"Very good, you can go home then," she said softly, addressing Mihail. She spoke softly because the rapidity of her heart's beating hindered her breathing. "No, I won't let you make me miserable," she thought menacingly, addressing not him, not herself, but the power that made her suffer, and she walked along the platform.

Two maidservants walking along the platform turned their heads, staring at her and making some remarks about her dress. "Real," they said of the lace she was wearing. The young men would not leave her in peace. Again they passed by, peering into her face, and with a laugh shouting something in an unnatural voice. The station-master coming up asked her whether she was going by train. A boy selling kvas never took his eyes off her. "My God! where am I to go?" she thought, going farther and farther along the platform. At the end she stopped. Some ladies and children, who had come to meet a gentleman in spectacles, paused in their loud laughter and talking, and stared at her as she reached them. She quickened her pace and walked away from them to the edge of the platform. A luggage train was coming in. The platform began to sway, and she fancied she was in the train again.

And all at once she thought of the man crushed by the train the day she had first met Vronsky, and she knew what she had to do. With a rapid, light step she went down the steps that led from the tank to the rails and stopped quite near the approaching train.

She looked at the lower part of the carriages, at the screws and chains and the tall cast-iron wheel of the first carriage slowly moving up, and trying to measure the middle between the front and back wheels, and the very minute when that middle point would be opposite her.

"There," she said to herself, looking into the shadow of the carriage, at the sand and coal dust which covered the sleepers— "there, in the very middle, and I will punish him and escape from everyone and from myself."

She tried to fling herself below the wheels of the first carriage as it reached her; but the red bag which she tried to drop out of her hand delayed her, and she was too late; she missed the moment. She had to wait for the next carriage. A feeling such as she had known when about to take the first plunge in bathing came upon her, and she crossed herself. That familiar gesture brought back into her soul a whole series of girlish and childish memories, and suddenly the darkness that had covered everything for her was torn apart, and life rose up before her for an instant with all its bright past joys. But she did not take her eyes from the wheels of the second carriage. And exactly at the moment when the space between the wheels came opposite her, she dropped the red bag, and drawing her head back into her shoulders, fell on her hands under the carriage, and lightly, as though she would rise again at once, dropped on to her knees. And at the same instant she was terror-stricken at what she was doing. "Where am I? What am I doing? What for?" She tried to get up, to drop backwards; but something huge and merciless struck her on the head and rolled her on her back. "Lord, forgive me all!" she said, feeling it impossible to struggle. A peasant muttering something was working at the iron above her. And the light by which she had read the book filled with troubles, falsehoods, sorrow, and evil, flared up more brightly than ever before, lighted up for her all that had been in darkness, flickered, began to grow dim, and was quenched forever.

***

Going out of the nursery and being again alone, Levin went back at once to the thought, in which there was something not clear.

Instead of going into the drawing room, where he heard voices, he stopped on the terrace, and leaning his elbows on the parapet, he gazed up at the sky.

It was quite dark now, and in the south, where he was looking, there were no clouds. The storm had drifted on to the opposite side of the sky, and there were flashes of lightning and distant thunder from that quarter. Levin listened to the monotonous drip from the lime trees in the garden, and looked at the triangle of stars he knew so well, and the Milky Way with its branches that ran through its midst. At each flash of lightning the Milky Way, and even the bright stars, vanished, but as soon as the lightning died away, they reappeared in their places as though some hand had flung them back with careful aim.

"Well, what is it perplexes me?" Levin said to himself, feeling beforehand that the solution of his difficulties was ready in his soul, though he did not know it yet. "Yes, the one unmistakable, incontestable manifestation of the Divinity is the law of right and wrong, which has come into the world by revelation, and which I feel in myself, and in the recognition of which—I don't make myself, but whether I will or not—I am made one with other men in one body of believers, which is called the church. Well, but the Jews, the Mohammedans, the Confucians, the Buddhists—what of them?" he put to himself the question he had feared to face. "Can these hundreds of millions of men be deprived of that highest blessing without which life has no meaning?" He pondered a moment, but immediately corrected himself. "But what am I questioning?" he said to himself. "I am questioning the relation to Divinity of all the different religions of all mankind. I am questioning the universal manifestation of God to all the world with all those misty blurs. What am I about? To me individually, to my heart has been revealed a knowledge beyond all doubt, and unattainable by reason, and here I am obstinately trying to express that knowledge in reason and words.

"Don't I know that the stars don't move?" he asked himself, gazing at the bright planet which had shifted its position up to the topmost twig of the birch-tree. "But looking at the movements of the stars, I can't picture to myself the rotation of the earth, and I'm right in saying that the stars move.

"And could the astronomers have understood and calculated anything, if they had taken into account all the complicated and varied motions of the earth? All the marvelous conclusions they have reached about the distances, weights, movements, and deflections of the heavenly bodies are only founded on the apparent motions of the heavenly bodies about a stationary earth, on that very motion I see before me now, which has been so for millions of men during long ages, and was and will be always alike, and can always be trusted. And just as the conclusions of the astronomers would have been vain and uncertain if not founded on observations of the seen heavens, in relation to a single meridian and a single horizon, so would my conclusions be vain and uncertain if not founded on that conception of right, which has been and will be always alike for all men, which has been revealed to me as a Christian, and which can always be trusted in my soul. The question of other religions and their relations to Divinity I have no right to decide, and no possibility of deciding."

"Oh, you haven't gone in then?" he heard Kitty's voice all at once, as she came by the same way to the drawing-room.

"What is it? you're not worried about anything?" she said, looking intently at his face in the starlight.

But she could not have seen his face if a flash of lightning had not hidden the stars and revealed it. In that flash she saw his face distinctly, and seeing him calm and happy, she smiled at him.

"She understands," he thought; "she knows what I'm thinking about. Shall I tell her or not? Yes, I'll tell her." But at the moment he was about to speak, she began speaking.

"Kostya! do something for me," she said; "go into the corner room and see if they've made it all right for Sergey Ivanovitch. I can't very well. See if they've put the new wash stand in it."

"Very well, I'll go directly," said Levin, standing up and kissing her.

"No, I'd better not speak of it," he thought, when she had gone in before him. "It is a secret for me alone, of vital importance for me, and not to be put into words.

"This new feeling has not changed me, has not made me happy and enlightened all of a sudden, as I had dreamed, just like the feeling for my child. There was no surprise in this either. Faith—or not faith—I don't know what it is—but this feeling has come just as imperceptibly through suffering, and has taken firm root in my soul.

"I shall go on in the same way, losing my temper with Ivan the coachman, falling into angry discussions, expressing my opinions tactlessly; there will be still the same wall between the holy of holies of my soul and other people, even my wife; I shall still go on scolding her for my own terror, and being remorseful for it; I shall still be as unable to understand with my reason why I pray, and I shall still go on praying; but my life now, my whole life apart from anything that can happen to me, every minute of it is no more meaningless, as it was before, but it has the positive meaning of goodness, which I have the power to put into it."

Made in United States
North Haven, CT
12 October 2022

25365063R00074